Heartstrings

By Inna Larsen

Heartstrings

All Rights Reserved

Published By
Port Town Publishing
601 Belknap Street
Superior, WI 54880

Web Address:
www.porttownpublishing.bigstep.com

ISBN 0-9716239-5-3

ACKNOWLEDGEMENTS

In chronological order: I would like to thank Karen Wiesner from Wisconsin Romance Writers Association for giving me positive feedback on the first chapter and encouraging me to seek publication; Jean Hackensmith of Port Town Publishing for reading through the manuscript and accepting it for publication; Linda Morelli for thorough editing and constructive advice to make the novel come alive; and Jean Hackensmith, again, for an excellent and comprehensive final edit and her meticulous attention to detail. Finally, I would like to thank my husband, Jeff, my daughter Karianna, and my cats, for putting up with being ignored while my fingers were glued to the keyboard and my eyes to the screen. I would also like to acknowledge the Minnesota and Ramsey County Historical Societies for assistance with my research.

AUTHOR'S NOTE

For more information about the *hardingfele* (English translation is hardanger fiddle), pictures and sound clips, please visit the Hardanger Fiddle Association of America web site at www.hfaa.org. Briefly, it is a violin with sympathetic understrings which resonate, giving the instrument a distinctive echoing sound. Please note that Kjersti is pronounced Shyersti. This is the closest approximation to the Norwegian kj combination. Being a cat person, I would describe the kj sound as a soft non-threatening hiss, mouth open in a smile and hissing from the back of the throat (not ssssss)! Few other notes on pronunciation: Bjørnsen is pronounced as Byornsen. The i in Nils is short, as in bills. Oddleif and Oskar are pronounced with an o as in orange. Solveig is Solvay without the "g." *Sølje* – solye, is traditional Norwegian silver jewelry. *Jeg elsker deg kjæresten min* – yai elsker die shyerestin min, I love you my dearest in Norwegian. Also note that until the beginning of the 20th century, Norwegian last names changed with each generation. So for example, Nils Bjørnsen's father was Bjørn. This man's last name, in turn, would be the first name of his father (e.g., Hansen from Hans).

FRONT COVER CREDITS

Front cover: Author's hardanger fiddle, made in 1913 by a K. Vang, Drammen Norway.

Back cover: Panoramic view of St. Paul, photograph reprinted with permission of Ramsey County Historical Society, St. Paul, MN

"Har du ikkje hoppet før, så hoppe du vel nå!"

"If you have not hopped before, you will certainly hop now!"

Norwegian hardanger fiddle tune.

Dedication:

To all the immigrants who have come to America seeking a new life, and enriching this country with their culture and traditions.

To Oddleif (King Plush): Our gray and white stray who came to us at a difficult time and made it easier and who gave us so much love and joy during the six years he graced our lives.

Heartstrings

By Inna Larsen

Chapter One

St. Paul, MN 1899

Anna Katz stood on the corner of Rice and Sherburne and glanced at the clock above Kaiser's Watch Repair shop every couple of minutes. It was already a half-hour past the time Fanny promised to meet her, and even on this sunny April afternoon the wind still had a touch of winter chill. Anna pulled the brown wool coat tighter around her and resolved to wait another fifteen minutes. *Maybe Fanny missed the streetcar, or slipped and fell.* Anna thought of the most unlikely reasons for her friend's delay, refusing to admit to herself that Fanny was simply uninterested in union organizing.

Fanny had stood Anna up twice before, giving trivial excuses. They worked at the St. Paul Garment Factory ten hours per day, bent over sewing machines. When Emil Kruse from Pigs Eye Foundry approached Anna about organizing the garment workers, she was excited to join the effort. Today would be her third meeting and plans for a citywide worker sign up were going to be discussed. Fanny or no Fanny, Anna had to be there and preferably on time.

She looked up at the clock again. Only five minutes had passed. Anna returned her gaze to street level and watched as a man crossed Rice with a meandering gait. His face was hidden in some sort of paper, and he headed directly toward her. She looked in the other direction, hoping that the drunk—or whoever this fellow was—would not bother her. A moment later, she heard a voice that spoke very broken English.

"Excuse me, I look for Minnesota and 4th Street, St. Paul Library. It is far?"

Anna's shoulders stiffened as she turned. The man next to her was about six feet tall, with clear blue eyes and a carefully trimmed mustache. His face was smooth, lacking the typical redness and puffiness of one who overused spirits. His brow wrinkled in confusion and the cool breeze ruffled his blond hair as he pointed to a spot on a greasy, torn map that marked the location of the library. Anna could see that a crease obliterated the intersection of Rice and Sherburne, and that he had at least two miles to go to reach his destination. She drew back her shoulders and began to explain as clearly as she could.

"Take Rice Street to University Avenue and turn left, then go right on Robert Street and left on 4th Street until you reach Minnesota Street. That's where the library is. But today is Sunday and it's closed." The obvious confusion that etched his features was enough to draw a sympathetic sigh from Anna. "By chance, do you speak Russian?"

Anna's family arrived in America eight years earlier, when she was fourteen, from a small Jewish settlement in Russia. The first couple of years in a foreign country were the most difficult for immigrants, especially those learning English. *Perhaps this man will turn out to be Russian. It would be a lot easier to explain things in his native language.*

"No, no Russia, Norway. My name is Nils Bjørnsen and I come from Voss, Norway to St. Paul, Minnesota. I been here six month. I am please to make your acquaintance, and I am very sorry for my poor English," he recited carefully, almost verbatim from what she was sure was an English-for-foreigners textbook. He took off his cap and extended a hand to Anna. She returned the handshake and surreptitiously studied the tall immigrant before her. He was dressed in the best and cleanest clothes he had, she surmised, and yet still the patches and spots on his coat and pants, and the scuff marks on his boots, were easily evident. Anna's father, a shoemaker, once told Anna that the state of a man's shoes was as good as an open book of his life and work. Nils Bjørnsen's boots looked like they had carried him all the way from Norway to St. Paul. He had a firm handshake and, even through the gloves, his hands felt rough to Anna's touch, like a farmer's or workingman's.

She smiled and lifted her gaze to the man's face. His cornflower blue eyes twinkled and looked directly into hers. She was captivated by them. "How you do you do, Mr. Bjørnsen. I am Miss Anna Katz, and I came from Russia in 1891. Welcome to America."

"Thank you. Every day I go work in stockyards, but I never see St. Paul. So now, weather is fine and this Sunday I want to find books in library and look at my new city. I am sorry, I talk so bad English."

"Not at all. You talk well for being here only six months."

Anna had her own reasons for keeping up a conversation with Nils Bjørnsen. Here stood a prime recruit for the union organizing efforts. She knew the stockyards were a brutal place to work and the bosses resisted all attempts by the workers to demand higher wages and better conditions. If she could convince him to go to the meeting, it would mean one more man for the union cause. Anna carefully broached the subject.

"I hear work in the stockyards is very hard. Is that true?"

"It is more hard on spirit than on body. All day I cut cows and pigs. I cannot talk about in front of lady. Their faces, I see every time I close my eyes. In Norway, I was farmer and I only kill animals for food for my family. But here, so many." Nils' face sobered with seriousness, and Anna's stomach turned at the image of millions of cattle being butchered so the people of St. Paul could have their pot roasts for Sunday dinner.

"You don't have to keep yourself to fine ladylike subjects in front of me. I had chickens in the old country. I know. I have not heard good things about the stockyards–miserable, filthy conditions, bosses that make men work twelve to sixteen hours days–and from what you are telling me, it's much worse for the animals." She straightened her shoulders and prepared to give her union recruitment speech. "In America, working men and women are forming unions. When many people belong to a union, they can demand fewer hours, safer conditions, more pay, and time off for sickness and holidays. It is hard for the factory owners to deny such things when all their employees are unified and refuse to work if their demands aren't met. I'm a seamstress at St. Paul Garments and am trying to organize the girls in our factory. It takes time, but in the end I know we will win. In fact, I am going to a union meeting right now. Would you like to come?"

Nils' eyes widened with surprise as he stared at the petite redhead. No Norwegian girl would ever be involved in such a venture. Those he knew in Voss were far more interested in finding a rich husband, following new fashions, or exchanging knitting patterns. This working girl though, barely twenty, already had a purpose in life. As she talked, strands of red hair came loose from under her hat, falling against her smooth cheek, and she brushed them aside. Behind the gold-rimmed spectacles, Nils saw green eyes filled with energy and fire.

How can I possibly say no?

"I like to see your meeting. Maybe I learn more things about America. Are there Norwegian people that join union?"

"There are all kinds of people—Russians, Norwegians, Swedes, Irish, Germans. You see, the bosses like immigrants. They come to America and don't know how much they should get paid, and they don't speak good enough English to ask, so their wages are a lot less than the native workers'. They are happy just to have a job to feed their families and the bosses know that."

"Ja, it is true. I come here first day and my cousin say to me, 'I find you job. They want strong men, ten cents for hour. You start tomorrow.' So, I never ask questions. I was glad to have job when I come to St. Paul. You hear true things about stockyards. Men work long hours for little money and place is not clean. Now, I know more, so I try to look for another job. But it is hard because other factories closed when I finish work."

Anna looked up at the clock above Kaiser's Watch Repair and realized that it was almost time for the meeting. She indicated the side door of the building and Nils followed. They ascended a flight of stairs to the second floor and entered a crowded, smoke-filled room. Nils strained to catch a word or two of Norwegian, but the loud din of conversation made it impossible to focus on a distinct language. He sat in the back of the room, while Anna made her way to the front to talk to Emil Kruse, the union president. She tapped the burly fellow on the shoulder.

"Emil, my girls are just too afraid to sign or do anything, but I think I've come up with an idea to get them involved. Also, I brought a greenhorn Norwegian to the meeting. He's sitting somewhere in the back and probably won't understand most of what we say, but it's a start. He's from the stockyards." Anna's voice bubbled with enthusiasm.

"Good work, Anna," he said as he stroked his handlebar mustache. "One more man for the union. I'll let you have the floor after Karl and Jimmy speak about the metalworkers and trainmen." Emil reached for the gavel and called the meeting to order.

Nils sat through the meeting understanding about half of what was said. Despite his lack of comprehension, the frequent bursts of applause and voices of affirmation told him that the men were passionate about the union cause. Finally, Anna stepped up to the podium.

"My fellow workers," she began. "I am Anna Katz from St. Paul Garments and I am leading the organizing efforts at my factory. It has been very difficult for me to convince the girls to join the union. They are scared to breathe, let alone sign up, because the bosses walk by every fifteen to thirty minutes. I think the best way to win them over is to talk to them outside of work." She glanced toward Emil. He gave her a nod of encouragement before she continued.

"I suggest we plan a picnic at some place like Como Park and invite the workers and their families. In between the sandwiches and fiddle music, we can add a couple of pro-union speeches and send around sign-up cards. I think we'll get a good number of people to come, because they are not going to pass up a free meal, considering they can barely afford to eat on the wages they make. What do you think?"

"I can play 'em a couple of jigs," yelled Joe Rogan from the back of the room.

"I got a harmonica," another added.

"Put me down for accordion."

"I can brew a barrel of good German beer."

Tom Trivisani, the foreman from Schmidt brewery, spoke up. "Good idea, Anna. I will spread the word among my men."

Hands rose as men eagerly offered their services for the picnic. Anna motioned for quiet. "I don't think having spirits at the picnic would be proper. We want the workers to pay attention to our message, instead of getting drunk and, besides, there will be families with children."

"Anna is right," Emil Kruse agreed. "The people are going to think of it as just a picnic, but for us it is a chance to speak about the cause and sign up fifty, or maybe even a hundred workers. We cannot let alcohol take it out of our hands. Let's pick a date and start planning."

Anna, Emil, and the other union members hammered out the details of the picnic and assigned tasks to volunteers for the next half hour. Nils stayed in the back, unsure if he should go home or wait for Anna. Obviously, she was smart and articulate. *What use would she have for me, a new immigrant who can barely speak English?* Nils thought to himself, then he decided to stay. *It would be proper to thank her for her help though, and offer to walk her home.* He was not in a hurry to get back to the house on Cayuga Street. An hour spent in the company of a pretty girl would be far more enjoyable than watching Oddleif and Oskar share the whiskey bottle on the front steps.

Anna walked toward the back of the room, and Emil followed. She introduced him to Nils. The men shook hands and exchanged greetings in a mixture of English, German, and Norwegian. Emil left soon after, and Nils had a chance to talk to Anna.

"I want to thank you for help with my map and ask me to come to the union meeting. I learn a lot from this. If I can ask you, maybe I walk you to your house? In Norway man do that. It is different in America, true?"

Anna felt warmth heat her cheeks at the offer. "No, it's not that different in America. I can perfectly well walk home myself, but I'll be happy to have your company. My only concern is that you find your way back with that map of yours."

Nils pulled out the map and a pencil stub. "You take pencil to write where we are now and where is your house. My house is big X on Cayuga Street."

Anna took the map and drew a line from Rice and Sherburne to her house on Pinehurst Avenue, and then another line from Pinehurst to Cayuga. Her hand paused in mid-movement though, when she realized it would be unwise to have a strange man escort her home, let alone give him directions from her house to his own. The newspapers warned of men who picked up naïve girls, and then raped and murdered them. *Tomorrow, my body could be found floating down the Mississippi River!* She stole a glance at Nils Bjørnsen's face. His blue eyes were full of trust and held no evil or indecent intentions.

She made a decision—and hoped it was the right one. "You know, if you accompany me and then go home, it will be about a seven mile walk, unless you take the streetcar. Perhaps a longer walk than you figured on for a Sunday afternoon."

He smiled at her concern. "It is no trouble. Norwegians like to walk. We go up mountains with goats and to forest for berries and mushrooms. Before I come to St. Paul, I never see streetcar and I take train only twice—from Voss to Christiania and New York to St. Paul. The rest of way, I come on ship and with my feet."

"I see that," Anna said as she glanced discreetly at Nils' shoes again. "My father is a shoemaker and I am sure he can fix up your boots so you could walk around the world several times over." Her smile prompted another from him, then she took a deep breath and buttoned up her coat. "Well, let's go."

Anna led Nils from the building and they headed south on Rice Street.

Nils tried to keep up a conversation during the long walk to her home. He knew of something he could do to participate in the union picnic, but due to his poor English he was too embarrassed to speak up during the meeting. "For your union picnic, maybe people like to hear Norwegian music?"

"I don't see why not. I would like to myself, since I have never heard it," Anna answered. "What do you play?"

"I play *hardingfele*. It is Norwegian violin with eight strings. In Voss, I play for dances and weddings. Here, not very often. It is hard to use same hands to play music God puts in my head, that I use to take life of so many animals He make."

To Anna, music was an outpouring of a man's soul and she sensed that her new friend was pained by what he did at the stockyards.

"Oh, please play your violin at the picnic," she implored. "You will give the people so much joy and happiness that perhaps you will start to feel better, too. Papa plays the violin, and I am sure that your Norwegian one will sound just as beautiful."

"You are very kind to ask me, so I play for your picnic. I try to think I am in Norway. I hear church bells ring, my mother call goats, water fall from the mountains—then music will come. Often I miss my farm, but maybe it take time and I like St. Paul better." Nils glanced at the pavement and stuffed his hands in his pockets. "Miss Katz, you are homesick for Russia after eight years in America?"

Anna thought about the question for several moments before she answered. "There are things that I miss and others that I am glad I do not have to live through again. It is not good to be born a Jew in Russia. Many times when I was little, bands of Russian men went through Jewish towns, burned houses, beat and sometimes killed people, even children, because they were Jewish. They said that it was their Christian duty to persecute the Jews, but, personally, I think they just liked to hurt people. We hid in the cellar, hearing their footsteps come closer and closer to our house, and wondered if we would be next. Mama tied rags around our mouths so we would not cry or make any noise. We were lucky, but our neighbors were not—the baby cried and they were found out. The bandits lined the whole family up against the wall of their own house and shot them one by one. Then they got on their horses and left. After that happened, Papa said, 'Never again. We are leaving now,' and so we came to St. Paul." Anna blinked away the moisture that misted her eyes, and then continued in a melancholy voice.

"What I do miss is having a house and a garden. When you were talking earlier about going to the forest to pick berries and mushrooms, I remembered doing such things with my family. We picked baskets of sweet blueberries and raspberries and, late in summer, many different kinds of mushrooms. We had to know which were good to eat; if we were not careful, we could get the entire family sick with just one mushroom. Mama fried the mushrooms with onions and potatoes and put sour cream on top. M-m-m-m, it was so delicious that I still remember how they smell even after all these years." Anna took a quick breath, half expecting the scent of fried mushrooms. "Since we came to St. Paul, I have never even been outside the city to see if there are woods here like in the old country, and we have no space for a garden by the apartment." A wry smile touched her lips as she looked up at him. "I guess this is a long answer to your question."

Nils gritted his teeth as he fought a flood of emotion—hatred for the men who perpetrated acts of unspeakable cruelty, and the urge to care for and protect the girl he had just met. He turned to face Anna and clasped his hands. "You tell me many things I think about seriously. I read Bible and Jesus Christ talk of love for all people. I cannot understand how men do so very bad things in His name. I can see why you leave." He paused for a moment. "Maybe when union make bosses give us holiday, we can go and see if there is forest with berries and mushrooms near St. Paul."

"That would be wonderful. I know the streetcar goes pretty far out, but if you want to go way out of the city, you have to take the train from the downtown station. I'll pack us a lunch and you can play your, how do you say it, herring fiddle for me." For a moment, Anna was caught up in fantasy, planning a trip out of town with a Norwegian fellow she just met. *What harm can come out of something that will never happen?*

"It is *har-ding-fe-le*." Nils pronounced the word carefully with a kind of a singsong Scandinavian accent.

"You will have to teach me some more Norwegian words. They sound funny, I don't mean in a bad way, but different. Oh, and here is my apartment block."

Anna paused before a three-story red brick building and glanced up to see her mother's face peering down from the second floor window. Her eyes narrowed as she tried to identify the tall blond stranger who accompanied her daughter. Her lips were pursed tightly in disapproval. "Thank you for walking me home, Nils. I enjoyed talking with you, and I hope you don't get lost on the way back."

Nils translated from Norwegian to English in his head as he frantically tried to find a way to arrange a second meeting with Anna. "It was very pleasant to talk with you, also. I practice my English. I think it is better. I would ask you if you like to talk again. Maybe next Sunday, three o'clock?"

Anna's mind whirled. She wanted to spend time with her new friend, but she knew her mother and neighbors would disapprove. Nils just could not walk up to #2601 Pinehurst Avenue, knock on apartment number two and ask to see Miss Katz. Not in this Jewish part of town, with Mama and her lady friends busy arranging a match between her and some upstanding Jewish fellow who, of course, had a good job, something in the bank, and came from a fine family. Nils would have to meet her several blocks away, on the border of the Irish and Jewish neighborhoods.

"Here, give me your map." Anna took the wrinkled paper and put an "X" on the intersection five blocks from her house. "Meet me here, three o'clock next Sunday. My family, they are not used to Norwegians."

Anna ran up the steps, turned at the door, waved, and then disappeared into the hallway. Nils tipped his cap, waved back, and started on the long walk home.

Chapter Two

Sarah Katz, a plump woman in her late forties met Anna at the door. "So, where have you been for four hours?"

Anna deliberated between telling the truth and a quick lie and chose the latter. She would soon be found out anyway, but she could at least try. "Out with Fanny, Mama."

"And since when does Fanny wear pants and looks like a dumb Swede? How dare you be seen with some *goy* in our neighborhood!"

Anna glanced toward the window. Her mother had seen her talking to Nils and holding the map, but maybe she could still talk her way out of it. Her mother's tight lips and narrowed brown eyes were proof she was upset, though. After all, a *goy* was the most insulting word a Jew could use to describe a gentile. She met her mother's stern gaze.

"Oh, he was just a fellow who got lost and I gave him directions."

Sarah Katz stood in the middle of the living room and wagged her finger at her daughter. "Anna, you are too old to lie to me. I know you go to those union meetings on Sundays, and that man was probably from there. You should be ashamed, a Jewish girl seen with a Scandinavian, and all the neighbors watching. Papa works day and night to put food on the table and what do you do—you spit dirt at him. He will lose half of his customers now that people know what his daughter brings home. You just put a large black X on our family. Instead of going with Benny Simkin, you have to find some dirty Norwegian to walk you home. Benny's mother stopped by today and asked about you. You mark my words. You continue with these union meetings, and your boss will find out and you will lose your job. And then how are we going to pay for your dowry—"

Sarah's eyes widened as she covered her mouth. She had just let the cat out of the bag.

Anna's face burned with anger. She moved to stand only a foot from her mother and screamed at the top of her voice. She did not care what the neighbors thought. "So this is what you have been doing with my hard-earned money. Putting it into a bank account to marry me off to Benny or some other *shlimazel* that you pick out for me? It is you who should be ashamed." Her fingers formed fists at her side. "All these years, I thought my money helped you and Papa take care of this family. Every day you complain that, between what Papa and I make, we cannot afford a new dress for Rivka, schoolbooks for Max, a baseball bat for Grisha, or night classes for me. But if we are so poor, why does our living room look all plush and pretty? I can tell you why. It has to look good, so that when Mrs. Simkin comes by, she knows the Katz's are a respectable family for her Benny to marry into. I bet you used my money to buy the sofa, that ugly table with claw legs, the leather-backed chairs, and the hundreds of lace doilies that Rivka and I wash and iron every week." Anna paused to catch her breath before she continued. "Well no more. I want all my money back, to the last penny since I started working four years ago. If Rivka, Grisha or Max want something, I will buy it for them myself. I don't break my back and squint my eyes over a sewing machine for you or Mrs. Simkin. It is finished. I am talking to Papa tonight."

She stomped toward the bedroom door, and then whirled to face her mother again. "And one more thing...that dumb, dirty Norwegian, as you called the man who walked me home, showed me more kindness and consideration in a few hours than any of those fellows you have been trying to match me up with, and if I want to meet him again, I will! I don't care what you or the neighbors think. I have nothing more to say." Anna stormed into her room and slammed the door.

Sarah Katz stared after her daughter, mouth agape. Never had Anna behaved so impertinently toward her. Sure, they had their share of disagreements, but for her daughter to raise her voice and scream the way she did—. Thank God the windows were closed! Hopefully no one heard the scene, except the children.

She sat down on the sofa to rest. *True, I can only blame myself for telling Anna where her money went. The girl is partially right. It is her money, but she is young and would spend it on foolish things. Children become so different in America. Back in the village, marriages were arranged, like mine and Moyshe's; the daughter's parents provided a good dowry, so the couple was set for at least several years.*

"Benny Simkin is such a good match—a smart, studious, Jewish boy," Sarah mumbled as she reclined on the sofa. "His father runs the Hebrew school. If Anna married into the family, Grisha and Max could attend the school and not pay tuition."

Why does she have to be involved in this union activity? All that talking and demonstrating is for men. As soon as she is married, she won't have to work. The children will come, so what union, shmunion. I am just trying to protect her. Now she thinks the Norwegian fellow treats her good. She will see for herself. He will get drunk and beat her. Worse yet, he is just meeting her so that he can drag her into one of those vacant lots by the river and rape her.

"Just like that bastard did to me." Sarah bit her lip and squelched a dark violent memory from the past. "Oh, my poor Anna, why do you stab your mother in the heart? Moyshe will have to settle all this tonight."

There was dinner to be made and, with the mood Anna was in, Sarah did not want to ask for help. She went into the kitchen and began to peel potatoes and cut chicken, taking out her frustrations on the food.

Anna shared a bedroom with her sixteen-year-old sister Rivka. Rivka was not as tall as Anna, and had a chubby figure that resembled her mother's. Her dark brown hair was done up in braids and she looked half-schoolgirl and half-grown woman. While mother and Anna had their confrontation in the living room, Rivka peered through the keyhole, her face pressed tightly against the door. She did not want to miss a word of what was said.

Anna is sure brave standing up like this to Mama, Rivka thought to herself. She would get into a lot of trouble if she did that. *Why does Anna not want to marry Benny Simkin,* she wondered. *He is not a bad boy and good-looking. too. Well, if Anna does not want him, I will take him, and then Mama will be happy.*

Rivka jumped back from the keyhole and her eavesdropping when Anna forced open the portal. The doorknob hit the younger sister squarely in the head. "Oy, Anna be careful! You nearly killed me."

"That's what you get for listening to other people's conversations."

"The way you were screaming," Rivka said, "I didn't need to be at the keyhole. I bet Mrs. Meier across the street heard it."

"I don't care if she did. I am so angry I could pound someone into meal, make *matzo balls* and throw them farther than that Saints pitcher that Grisha talks about all the time."

"Here, have a pillow." Rivka threw a lace-trimmed feather pillow at Anna. "So tell me, who is the Norwegian boy and what does he have that Benny does not? What is his name? Is he cute? Is he rich? Does he have a horse and a buggy? What did he wear and did he have good shoes on? You know how Papa feels about shoes." Rivka caught her breath and, gray eyes brilliant with curiosity, stared at her sister.

"So many questions. Let me see if I can remember." Anna fought a smile as she teased her younger sister. "His name is Nils Bjørnsen, he came from Norway six months ago, he is not a boy, probably about twenty eight or so, yes he is cute, no he is not rich and he most certainly does not have a horse and a buggy. He had patched up street clothes and boots in bad need of Papa's golden hands. What he has that Benny does not is independence, and that I value highly in a man." Anna paused before continuing. "Rivka, please don't misunderstand me. Benny is a nice fellow. I would even consider going with him if he asked me himself. But no, it is always Mrs. Simkin and Mama cooking up something. I have yet to hear out of his own mouth that he likes me. I just cannot marry someone under such circumstances."

"Would you marry this Bjørnsen fellow? Because if you do, I get Benny. You know he likes talking to me when I get Grisha from the Hebrew School class. This way Mama would get what she wants. Max and Grisha can study at the school for free, and you can have blond and blue-eyed children with Nils or Lars or whatever his name is, although you know if you do that, you will be on Mama and Papa's black list."

Anna felt her cheeks grow hot. Rivka's girlish fantasies, in a way, mirrored her own dreams. Even though she had only known Nils for a few hours, she felt comfortable with him and knew, given the chance, she could lose her head and heart very quickly. *That is what being in love is all about, at least according to the books. But how would I know? I never felt this way about anyone before.*

"Sis, don't be silly," Anna said finally. "How can I marry someone I just met? I barely know him. We will have to talk and do things together, and of course, he would have to pass your inspection, because he will never pass Mama and Papa's."

"I know what you mean about Mama and Papa. They would like all of us to marry into good Jewish families. That is how it was done in the old country. I guess it's hard for them to change and become American. I know you are mad at Mama about the money, but try to forgive her. She meant well and besides, I don't need a new dress." As always, Rivka tried to be the peacemaker in this latest family disagreement, but to Anna, her mother's actions were outright theft.

"What she did with my money was wrong, Rivka, and I will talk to Papa about it. He is more reasonable and willing to break with some of the old country traditions. I am even willing to give up some of the money that she took for the past four years, but from now on, I keep my own paycheck and decide how to spend it." Anna stamped her foot and threw the lace pillow back at Rivka. A pillow fight resulted and, for the next few minutes, the sisters giggled like little girls instead of young women.

Rivka straightened up her bed and went to help Mama with dinner, and Anna was left with her own thoughts. She could not get Nils' voice out of her head. Just hearing him say that strange word, *hardingfele*, in that funny Scandinavian accent, made her chuckle. Papa always told her that anyone who played the violin had a good heart, because it took something of a man's soul to make the instrument sing. No, Nils Bjørnsen was not dangerous or evil. Anna's first impression of him was that of a decent, hardworking man. Did it really matter that he did not make much money?

The word money made her think of Mama, her dowry account, and Mrs. Simkin. Anna pulled a comb out of her hair and threw it on the floor. She felt suffocated by tradition and rigidity and hoped that her father would be more understanding. Tomorrow she would ask Margit Sørensen to teach her a few Norwegian words, so she could surprise Nils on Sunday.

Anna picked up the comb from the floor and put it back in her hair. She took Sir Walter Scott's *Ivanhoe* from her nightstand and escaped into the world of medieval romance.

Moyshe Katz came back from playing at a *bar-mitzvah* and was in a jovial mood after a couple glasses of wine. He pecked Sarah on the cheek and slapped five dollars on the dining room table. "Here you go, my sweet wife, more money for Anna's and Rivka's weddings from their poor Papa."

Sarah's withering glance sobered him instantly. "*Oy vei*, Moyshe, we got trouble," she hissed. "I was not thinking and told Anna about the dowry money."

Moyshe shook his head. "Foolish woman. Why on earth did you do that?"

"Oh, I am foolish all right! You can sew my mouth shut with one of your shoe needles. But, Moyshe, I saw her hanging on some Swedish—oh she says *Norwegian* fellow, like there is a difference—right outside this house." Sarah waved toward the window. "The way they carried on, I could tell he was sweet on her and she was eating it up. What do you want me to do? Frieda Simkin is here daily. We are planning the wedding and Anna lets some *goy* walk her home. You should've seen his clothes—and his shoes. They aren't fit to be fixed. I don't know where she gets these tramps. Probably at the union meetings she goes to. Well, now she is all upset and says I stole her money without her permission and wants it all back. And of course, she could just spit at Benny. She was hysterical and screamed at me at the top of her lungs. I am sure all the neighbors heard it. Moyshe, what are we going to do? All the plans for Max and Grisha to go to Hebrew school... It's all gone."

Moyshe took his wife's hands in his and sat her down on the sofa. "Sarah, take a breath. Let's eat dinner and I will talk to her. We will figure something out. I tell you though, don't you and that Simkin woman plan any wedding. All you are doing is making Anna do the opposite of what you want her to do. That Swedish boy is an act of disobedience to your wishes and it will pass. You quit arranging the marriage and I am sure that, in time, she will find herself a good Jewish boy. Maybe even Benny." He paused as his shoulders rose and fell in a heavy sigh.

"This is not our little village in Russia. This is St. Paul, and times are different. Don't expect the children to act like we did twenty years ago. We are in America now and, as much as you want to hang on to tradition, the children will try just as hard to break with it. We do what we can. We raised them as good Jews, we give them advice, we take care of them. The rest will happen on its own and, have faith, it will all turn out okay, like they say in America."

"Oh, Moyshe, I wish I had your optimism. I just have a bad feeling about all this. No matter, tell the children dinner is ready." Sarah went into the kitchen and began bringing out the food.

Dinner at the Katz house was a silent affair. Everybody knew about the family disagreement, but no one dared to say anything, lest it provoke another outburst from either Sarah or Anna. Rivka tried to make small talk, so that the meal would be over with faster.

"So, how was the *bar-mitzvah*, Papa? Did they have a huge party and did Yaakov read the *Torah* without any mistakes?"

"Oh, a couple of little mistakes, but we gave him enough wine that he forgot about it!"

Sarah glared at Moyshe. "Oh for shame, Moyshe, getting a child drunk."

"Sarah, as a good Jew, you know that a *bar-mitzvah* celebrates a boy becoming a man. If that's the case, he has to learn how to drink like a man, and what better time to start than on his *bar-mitzvah*."

Anna and Rivka giggled nervously and glanced at their mother. Her face wore that pursed lips expression of disapproval again.

Sarah dished out the fried potatoes and glanced at the grandfather clock on the wall. *It is already past eight. What can be taking Max and Grisha so long*, she wondered. They were at a baseball game and that should have been over long ago. She looked at her husband.

"Max took Grisha to the baseball park. It's after dark, and I am worried about them."

"They did not go to the Saints baseball game, Mama," Rivka spoke up. "They cannot play on Sunday. This is the St. Paul Prophets and Minneapolis Messiahs, the Jewish league. Max said the game started at three o'clock, and usually they last about two to three hours. Then the streetcar ride home. They should be here any minute."

Sarah's chest rose and fell with a frustrated sigh. "Moyshe, you should really speak to the boys about this baseball. I don't approve of it. Instead of studying the *Talmud* or doing their schoolwork, they watch a bunch of men hitting a ball with a stick. I know these are Jewish fellows, but still, I think it is a waste of time. Mrs. Meier told me that her husband went to one of those games and there is tobacco chewing, spitting, and smoking—not appropriate behaviors for our children to see."

Moyshe finally tired of his wife's nagging and shook his head. *The woman finds fault with everything!* "Sarah, if they are outdoors, it will do them some good, and it is only once a week. They are good kids. They won't get into trouble. Besides, this is the Jewish league and families come to cheer on their players. I really don't think there is smoking and spitting going on."

At that moment, Max and Grisha walked in the door. "Sorry, we're late. We missed the cross-town streetcar and had to wait a half hour for another one," they spoke in unison. If one did not know the boys, they could be mistaken for twins—same short brown hair, ear curls, glasses, black overcoats and hats. Max was the taller one though, being fourteen, and Grisha ten.

"So, who won?" Moyshe asked.

Grisha was the first to answer. "The St. Paul Prophets, 10-5, of course. You should have seen the home run Mordechai Rappaport got off that Minneapolis pitcher. Over the fence and out of the ballpark, probably knocked some fellow in the *schnozz*."

"Grisha, it's not polite to use words like that, especially in front of ladies," Sarah reprimanded.

"Okay, knocked some fellow in the nose. Sorry, Mama."

The brothers recapped the game for their father and the girls, who were mildly interested. When the meal concluded, Rivka asked the boys to help Sarah with the dishes. They would be out of the way, so that Papa and Anna could have their talk. Rivka, of course, would be at the keyhole to hear what Papa had to say about Benny Simkin and Anna's money.

Once Sarah and the boys were in the kitchen, Anna walked up to Moyshe, who settled himself on the sofa to read the paper. She sat down next to him and whispered into his ear. "Papa, can I talk to you for a moment?"

Moyshe had a fairly good idea of what this conversation would be about, but he feigned ignorance. "And what is it that is troubling my Anna today?"

"Not so loud, Papa. I don't want Mama to hear."

Anna told her father everything that happened between Sarah and her that afternoon. She thought about omitting Nils all together, but decided that, at this point, truth would be the best course of action. Papa would not tolerate lies from his children.

Moyshe set aside the newspaper and listened attentively, all the while planning how best to resolve this latest Katz conflict. If he sided with his wife, he would upset Anna and she might do something foolish—like run away with the Swede. On the other hand, if he sided with Anna, he would be on Sarah's black list for weeks, if not months. The woman already nagged him to death and, as much as he loved her, he did not have the patience of Job to endure more complaints. Thus, he decided to take the safe middle ground, as he usually did when his wife was unhappy with something or someone and asked him to fix it.

"Anna," he began. "It hurts me very much to see you and Mama so upset. You are both good people, but when you yell and scream at each other, you accomplish nothing. You only get angrier. Even though you are all grown up, you should still respect your Mama. You know that she meant well by putting away that money, but that does not make it right. Mama thinks we are still in our little village in Russia, and that she has to arrange your marriage and pay out the dowry. We are in America now, and I understand very well that children here want to choose their life-long mates themselves." He gave her hand a reassuring pat. "I will let you make that decision on your own, but I would still advise you to choose someone who is of your heritage and religion. It will make it easier on your children and on all of us. What do we know about Englishmen, Irishmen or Norwegians? Next to nothing. I see them in my shop every day, but don't talk to them about much except what holes to fix in their shoes. They have their holy days, traditions, foods, even music. That is not bad, just different. America can accept all of us, but can your Mama? You don't have to hurry to get married. Take your time, go to a few *bar mitzvahs* with me, or to those intercity baseball games with the boys, and I am sure you will find yourself a nice Jewish fellow. It does not have to be Benny, and I told Mama that.

"Now about the money," Moyshe continued. "Mama saved you a pretty good amount, and I think the best thing to do is leave it in the bank to earn interest. When you truly need this money, you can take it out and use it for your wedding, night classes, a new hat or whatever. Just try to spend it wisely. Starting with your next paycheck, you can keep it. All I ask is that you give us a few dollars for room and board. You think I am fair?"

Anna nodded. "Yes, Papa, thank you. You are always fair." She felt a lot calmer after talking with her father. He was the great compromiser of the Katz family. Every time there was a family disagreement, Papa asked each person to "put on the shoes of the other" so they could see the situation from a different point of view. Usually both people realized that each of them was right on some things and wrong on others—something they could not do in the heat of anger. With peace restored, the Katz household could function for a week or two, until there was another crisis, usually manufactured by her mother. Anna kissed Papa good night and got up from the sofa.

"Papa, should I apologize to Mama?" she asked.

"I already talked to her. She understands, but she is still not very happy about this Simkin business. You both sleep on it. Tomorrow is a new day, and you can talk to her then. Good-night."

Anna went into the bedroom, relayed the conversation to Rivka, and prepared for bed. She turned off the light and lay in bed thinking about the day. Despite everything, it did not turn out so bad. She got the right to keep her paychecks and Benny Simkin was off her back. There was only one problem: Nils Bjørnsen. Her seeing a non-Jew was troublesome, even in her father's eyes. Sure, she could go to a couple of baseball games with Max and Grisha, see some *bar mitzvahs*, talk to a few Jewish boys her own age. But with every Jewish boy came a Jewish mother. Her mother was bad enough. Anna could not imagine having two Sarahs telling her how to keep her house, how to raise the children, what was unladylike and what was not, and how things were done in the old country compared to evil and immoral America. She wondered if Nils had a mother and what she was like.

Anna closed her eyes and drifted off to sleep, dreaming of Nils Bjørnsen playing his strange fiddle for her and picking mushrooms.

Chapter Three

Nils walked home with a light step. For the first time since he came to America, he had experienced a few hours of happiness. He thought it odd that a girl could make him feel that way, especially one that he had to struggle to talk to. *Perhaps God has some purpose in the meeting, even if it be only to practice and improve my English.* Nils rehearsed his conversations with Anna in his head, memorizing some of the new words he learned. He could not, however, get her face out of his mind, even as he forced himself to hum a folk song and think about applying for a job at one of the other factories in town.

Stars filled the dark sky by the time Nils reached home. His cousin Oddleif Pedersen and Oskar Nyborg, the Danish boarder, sat on the steps drinking whiskey. Oddleif was tall and thin and resembled Nils a bit, while Oskar was shorter and more muscular, with an unruly mop of coarse brown hair. Both men were quite drunk, laughing about some crude joke and poking each other in the ribs.

Oskar lurched forward. "So, Nils, did you find your library and read books until dark, instead of drinking here with us? Were they interesting, eh?"

Nils steadied the drunken man by holding him against the brick wall of the house.

"Oskar, if I drank beer with you and Oddleif all day, I would not be up and walking and, judging by your graceful step forward just now, neither are you! Anyway, I never made it to the library." Nils turned to his cousin. "Odd, your map was all off, so I asked a girl on the street corner to show me how to get there. She told me the library was closed, it being Sunday. We got to talking and she asked me to come to a union meeting. A lot of good speeches—even I with my bad English could understand that the workers have no patience; they want better conditions, more pay. Hope something comes out of it. So, then I walked her home. That seemed like the right thing to do with her being so helpful. She lives clear on the other side of town and it took me a couple hours just to get here and see your drunk faces."

Oddleif's eye closed in a brief wink and a lewd grin curved his lips. "Oh, so Nils found himself a girl on the street corner. Well, how is she?"

"What do you mean, 'how is she?'"

"Is she skinny or fat, Norwegian, pretty or ugly, bowlegged?

"Oddleif," Oskar interrupted with a snicker. "You forgot to ask him if she has big tits."

"She is just right and she is not Norwegian, which is good in one way. I got to practice my English for a couple of hours."

Oddleif slapped Nils on the shoulder. "Soon, you will be practicing more than English, Nils."

Nils shook his head in disgust. "It is no use having a conversation with you two. Your heads are full of whiskey. I am going inside to play my fiddle. The union is organizing a picnic and they wanted music, so I signed up for a few tunes. Anyway, so long. I will be pouring cold water on both of you tomorrow morning to fix up your hangovers."

"He hasn't played that fiddle in a month," Oskar whispered loudly to Oddleif as Nils walked into the house. "When he walked out the door today, he looked like a horse kicked him in the groin. Hard work and America will do that to a man. We escape by drinking, he reads books. He comes back humming a tune, almost skipping down the street. Oddleif, I tell you, whoever that girl is, she got Nils Bjørnsen's heart in her hands and he better watch it, because she will make putty out of it."

"You got that right, Oskar, but I hope she does not break it. A girl in Voss did that to him about ten years ago, and Nils doesn't deserve it a second time. His brother wrote me that one of the reasons Nils left Norway is to go as far as he could from the village, so he would not have to see that girl again. I guess he asked her to marry him. She said no and married a fellow with more money. That would drive me to drink, Oskar."

"Ja, it sure would. Hear it, Oddleif, there he goes, playing some waltz."

Strains of *hardingfele* music streamed down from the attic window. Oskar took the last gulp of the whiskey and threw the bottle into the front yard. Oddleif dug in his pockets for a match and the men shared a cheap cigarette before stumbling into the house.

Oddleif's wife Kjersti cradled a sleeping boy of about one in her arms. She lifted her blonde head and puffy gray eyes when they entered the room. "Shhh, you will wake up little Henrik," she scolded in a voice that was filled with fatigue. "He cried when I put him and Solveig to bed, did not want his bottle, threw off his blankets. I tried everything, rocking the cradle, singing a lullaby, then a hymn and still the baby would not sleep. Well, I tell you, as soon as Nils started playing that fiddle, Henrik quieted down and now look at him. He is like a kitten curled up after lapping a saucer of milk." Kjersti gazed lovingly at her son. "Nils should play more often. I can close my eyes and think I am in Norway again and there is a handsome young man named Odd asking me to dance. Nice dream, because as soon as I open my eyes I don't see a handsome fellow, but my no good drunk husband and his buddy Oskar, reeking of whiskey. Shame on both of you. You should take a lesson from your cousin and do something useful. He went to the library and what did you do the whole day—spent it drinking on the front steps."

"Now here is where you are wrong, dear." Oddleif dropped a slobbery kiss on Kjersti's lips. "Nils never got as far as the library. He told us he picked up some girl on a street corner and walked her home. And you know what else, she is not even a Norskie. So tell me, would you rather have me drinking on the front steps or out looking for a girl to pick up on a street corner?"

"I am sure she is a respectable girl. Nils is not the type to fall for some tramp. You know, now that you mention it, I did think he was acting a little strange when he came in. I asked him if he wanted something to eat and he said, 'No thank you, just want to get my fiddle out and play for a while,' and he practically ran upstairs. Girls will do that to a fellow's head. *Uff da*. Well, it's getting late and I am going to put Henrik to bed." Kjersti pointed to a cast-iron pot in the kitchen and headed toward the children's room. "There is fried cod and potatoes on the stove. Save some for Nils though. He might change his mind after he works up a sweat the way he's playing."

Nils took the *hardingfele* out of its case and tuned up the strings. A long time had passed since he last played, maybe a month. His father bought the fiddle over thirty years ago and it was still beautiful. The wood was *rosemaled* in exquisite black leaf and flower patterns, the peg box had a gold-painted dragon's head on top, and the fingerboard and tailpiece were inlaid with mother of pearl. As a boy, Nils often wondered how a poor farmer like his father could afford to buy such an expensive and fine-looking fiddle. Bjørn Hansen later told his son that he sold off a part of the farm and saved up money for five years, a secret he kept from his wife. The fiddle served father and son well. Since the age of six, Nils sat with his father almost every evening and learned folk tunes by ear. At that time, he had a child's small violin. Bjørn saw the boy had a natural talent for music and, on his twelfth birthday, bought him an inexpensive *hardingfele*. Five years later, Bjørn died, and Nils inherited his father's fiddle, which he brought with him to St. Paul.

Nils began playing, hesitantly at first, but then his fingers took on a life of their own, as though remembering the lively dance tunes, haunting goat calls and church bell melodies, and then the more modern polkas, waltzes, and *schottisches* young people asked for at dances. He preferred the old Norwegian tunes to their modern cousins, because he could put more of his soul into them. It was not difficult to play a waltz over and over, but to make the *hardingfele* sound like a gentle brook cascading into a waterfall, now that was an art. Hardly any young people knew the complicated dance steps that went with these old folk tunes, so at weddings he would spend hours playing the same tiresome waltzes and polkas for drunken guests, be it in Voss or St. Paul. Today, the fiddle sang under his fingers and he could dream of playing through the night, never waking up to go to work tomorrow. Maybe he really was in Norway, and the stockyards were a just a bad nightmare.

He paused for a moment and rubbed his eyes. No, this was his attic room in St. Paul and from below came a crash of glass, probably Oskar smashing the whiskey bottle. If America was a bad dream, then the girl he met today brought him out of it for a few hours. He played, if not for himself, then for Anna, for being sweet, kind, and helpful to him, a lost and homesick Norwegian immigrant. "She probably does not even realize how she lifted my spirits," he said to himself.

It was well past midnight when Nils finally put his fiddle away and went to sleep. He dreamed of dancing on the corner of Rice and Sherburne with a girl who had red hair and green eyes.

Chapter Four

Anna was out the door to catch the streetcar to St. Paul Garments at seven o'clock Monday morning. Thankfully, her mother said nothing during breakfast and Anna had reason to believe that the events of the previous day were settled.

Fanny Feldman waved to her from a block up Snelling, then yelled. "Anna, hurry up. We are going to miss the streetcar."

Anna quickened her pace and met her girlfriend at the stop.

Fanny dressed according to the latest fashions, in clothes not necessarily new, but sewn and altered to look like they came out of the Sears Catalog. She was a diminutive girl with curly black hair, sparkling brown eyes and pert red lips. Her hat, a silk flower garden of pink roses, fuchsia carnations, and yellow daffodils, made her stand out among the non-descript gray kerchiefs of Jewish women and black top hats of the men waiting for the streetcar.

"Fanny, were you too busy weeding your hat to come to the meeting yesterday?" Anna joked as she reached Fanny's side.

"Very funny, Anna. No, actually, I was at a concert with Jacob Hirsch. You know, the jeweler's son. It was Brahms' 4th..." Fanny said *Brahms* in a voice several times louder than normal, revealing that she wanted the people around her to be impressed by her attendance at a concert and her knowledge of classical composers. Anna suspected though, that Fanny's recent interest in classical music was feigned and the real reason she went to concerts was to be with Jacob Hirsch. A couple months ago, Fanny was an expert on medicine for the sake of Isaac Lechter, the medical student, and Anna could not help but wonder what field Fanny would choose to study once she got tired of Jacob.

"It was a good meeting and we are planning a citywide union picnic. I will tell you about that later." Anna added the next in a whisper. "And there is something else. I met a really nice Norwegian fellow who walked me home."

"You met a *what*?" Fanny stared incredulously at Anna. She knew her friend associated with union organizers and other radical elements, but thought she was wise enough not to get involved with them. No drunk Swede was going to earn enough money at the mill to keep Fanny happy.

The streetcar came and Anna waited until they sat down next to each other on the wooden bench to continue.

"A Norwegian fellow named Nils Bjørnsen. He even plays the fiddle, like Papa. Fanny, if you meet him, I think you will like him. He's not a Mama's boy, like Benny Simkin or whomever Mama will try next to pawn off on me."

Fanny brushed a stray curl off her forehead to mask her disapproval. "And so where does this Nils work?"

"At the stockyards. Fanny, I know what you are thinking, but he has been here for only six months. What else could he do, not knowing English?"

Fanny rolled her eyes. "Anna, you are mad. You pick out a greenhorn who barely knows how to say a word of English and works with blood and guts. I don't even want to ask how much he makes. Besides, he is not even Jewish."

Anna sighed in exasperation at having her best friend question her judgment. "I never asked him how much he makes. I know it is not a lot. That is why we are fighting for union representation. His English is pretty good for having been here only a few months. Mama saw him walk me home and she boiled over like a teakettle. I guess I ruined all her matchmaking plans, but who's even talking about marriage. I hardly know the fellow."

Fanny grabbed Anna's black wool coat. "Do you ever think of getting out of St. Paul Garments, of living in a nice house, of going to fancy restaurants and concerts, of buying clothes without looking at the price tag? Despite your union preaching, I am sure you do sometimes. There is no way a fellow who works at the stockyards is going to buy the two of you tickets to the Minneapolis Symphony and, besides, what does a Swede know about Brahms?" Fanny continued with a determined look and released her grip on the coat. "I am just biding my time in the sweatshop until I meet the right man with the right amount of money. I have paid my dues working for the past five years. No more bending over a sewing machine for me. Fanny Feldman is cut out for more than a working girl's life, and I intend to prove it to you. Just watch me."

"I don't want to spend the rest of my life at St. Paul Garments, Fanny, and who would not like to live in a nice house? But at what price? Money cannot buy you happiness. I would rather be happy with a man who made less, than miserable with one who had so much that all he did was count it day and night." She turned from the spark of resolve that flashed in Fanny's eyes and glanced out the window. "Well, speaking of the dreaded factory, here it is. We can dream of getting out all we want, but we still have to go in."

Anna and Fanny entered a redbrick building and trudged up to the fourth floor. In an area no larger than a classroom, fifty women were crammed behind small tables with sewing machines and piles of fabric. Only one small window let in air for the entire room, making the noise and heat unbearable. Anna and Fanny sighed and took their places, prepared to spend the next ten hours working on men's shirts and pants.

At one o'clock, the bell rang for break. Anna took out her lunch pail and spread the contents on her table. "What did you bring today?" Fanny asked her.

"A hard-boiled egg and leftover fried potatoes. Why, want to trade?"

"No, not today. Golda Hirsch sent some *knishes* home with me and, mmmm, are they good. Two Mamas are better than one. I will never have to cook." Fanny bit into a pastry stuffed with potatoes and carrots.

"Two Mamas like mine, Fanny, and your head will be corseted so tight you won't be able to open your mouth to eat those *knishes*!"

"Oh, Anna, your Mama is not so bad. All she wants is to find you a good match and, from what you bring home, I can understand why."

"You are some friend, Fanny!" Anna got up from her chair and left Fanny to her lunch. She walked over to a table several rows behind where the blonde Norweigan girl, Margit Sørensen, sat.

"Margit, can you teach me a couple of words of Norwegian?"

"And why would a Jewish girl like Anna Katz want to learn Norwegian?"

Anna thought of a reasonable excuse. "Oh, I need to be able to talk to several recent immigrants who come to union meetings."

Margit giggled, as she did whenever anyone mentioned boys. "And those *people* wouldn't happen to be some cute Norskie fellow that you are sweet on, would they? Otherwise, you could always take me to help you out."

Anna was not going to allow a fifteen-year-old kid to back her into a corner, and she certainly did not want Margit's translation services. "Margit, you are always welcome at union meetings, however I don't think I need that much help. He does speak some English. I just thought it would be kind of nice to learn a few words."

"Oh, so I was right. It is a he. What's his name? I know most of the Norwegians in St. Paul and even some in Minneapolis." Margit's face betrayed a young girl's insatiable curiosity. Anna decided not to satisfy it just yet.

"Oh, he just came over several months ago. You probably don't know him. Besides, all your names sound alike. There are Larsons, Olsons, Svensons, Petersons—I don't even know how you can figure out who's who. Just teach me how to say hello, how are you, goodbye. You know, things like that."

"All right, but you owe me a look at this fellow sometime. Here is what you say." Margit taught Anna several words and phrases and added in closing, "If he says '*Jeg elsker deg*,' come to me then, and I will tell you what it means."

"Why not now?" Anna asked. Margit winked and her lips curved in a devilish grin. "Ask me later."

The bell rang again, signaling that break was over. Anna walked back to her desk and started work. Whispers flew around the room through the clang of sewing machines. By the end of the day, all fifty women knew that Anna Katz was seeing a Norwegian fellow.

Anna picked up a handful of Norwegian words and phrases from Margit during the next couple of days. She did not think it would be that difficult to learn a fourth language, considering that she was already proficient in three. However, the fact that many words were similar to English and Yiddish, and several were almost identical in Russian, surprised her.

At home, life returned to normal. Sarah did not mention the Simkin's, but grumbled under her breath about Anna passing up fine Jewish fellows for a no- good Swede. Rivka, Max, and Grisha were busy with school and asked

Anna to help with homework. Sarah always had a cleaning project, and this week it was Anna's turn to polish the furniture and do the ironing.

Shabbos, the day of rest, began at sundown on Friday. The girls lit the candles and the family sat down to dinner. Rivka made delicious braided *challah* bread that was still steaming when it was cut and passed around the table. Papa said the *Shabbos* blessing over the candles, wine and bread and, for a brief moment, Anna felt comforted. The bickering and disagreements were forgotten.

Saturday morning the Katz's put on their best clothes and walked to synagogue on Highland Avenue. Moyshe and Max stood in the front, prayer shawls draped over their shoulders, intently reading from the opened prayer books. Sarah, Anna, Rivka and Grisha sat in the balcony, designated for women and children. Grisha focused his intent gaze on the activities below. He could not wait until his own *bar-mitzvah*, when he would join Papa and his brother in the men's section; being kissed, hugged, and pinched on the cheeks by Mama, his sisters, and well-meaning *babushkas* was just too much for a ten-year-old boy.

All the women wore scarves to cover their heads in the synagogue. Married women went a step further and wore wigs to cover their shaved heads. Anna and Rivka shuddered at that last Jewish tradition, fearing the day their waist-length hair would be cut by Shmuel, the barber. He made wigs out of the tresses and sold them back to their original owners.

The highlight of the service for Anna was the reading of the *Torah*, the first five books of the Bible. A man from the congregation would go behind the curtain, take out an ornate silver case and unroll the *Torah* scroll. The reading was conducted first in Hebrew, and then was translated to Yiddish for the congregation. Anna was amazed that the same book, almost three thousand years old, survived through time and was the foundation of Judaism and Christianity. She longed to read it on her own, but that was forbidden for women.

Anna frowned. *And where in the* Torah *does it say that it is forbidden? Where does it say that women have to shave their heads, or that marrying a non-Jew is the ultimate act of betrayal? Did God command all these rules to Moses?* To her, God had become like her mother, more concerned with the trivial than the One who commanded Moses to part the Red Sea. When Anna asked

Moyshe one of her many questions, he would answer by referring to obscure verses in one of the Books, and even more obscure commentaries of ancient rabbis on those verses. Anna usually ended up more confused after Moyshe's explanation than she was before she asked.

The *Shabbos* service lasted until noon and, after the families went back to their homes, the long wait until sundown began. The Katz's ate leftovers from Friday night, washed them down with cold tea, and took prolonged afternoon naps, since all work and household activities were prohibited during this time. Anna and Rivka pulled books from under their pillows and read. Anna welcomed a time of rest from work and family, but she would have rather spent the time outside enjoying the spring weather. Como Park had a beautiful flower conservatory, and visiting a garden was an acceptable *Shabbos* activity. Taking the streetcar to get there was not.

Perhaps she could ask Nils to go to the park with her tomorrow. Anna thought of her Norwegian friend and began to silently rehearse the phrases that Margit taught her. She imagined them taking a walk and talking together, she in broken Norwegian and Nils in broken English. Perhaps, he would hold her hand... Anna felt her face grow hot and forced herself to stop daydreaming. She did not want Rivka to notice.

Grisha and Max lay on their beds and whispered about batting averages and pitching styles of the St. Paul Saints, wishing they were at Saturday's game. Even Sarah could not stand a long-period of inactivity and, after lying on the sofa for an hour or so, she paced back and forth from the kitchen to the living room, all the while telling Moyshe what was happening on the street and who was violating *Shabbos* rules.

Moyshe sat in the easy chair with his eyes closed and a *St. Paul Jewish Weekly* in front of him. He stole a glance at the paper whenever his wife headed toward the window and turned the pages as soon as she headed for the kitchen. After several minutes, he set the paper aside and closed his eyes. He had a long night ahead of him. The Shapiro's youngest was eight days old and Moyshe was asked to play for the dinner and dancing after the circumcision ceremony. The boy was supposedly named after the President, but somehow William McKinley Shapiro sounded neither entirely American nor entirely Jewish to Moyshe.

Finally, dusk arrived and the Katz's house stirred to life. Grisha and Max went to play outside with the neighborhood boys, Moyshe left for the

Shapiro's, the girls were sent to the grocery store, and Sarah busied herself in the kitchen until Mrs. Meier came over to gossip and play cards.

Anna prepared for bed later that evening, gnawed by doubts about tomorrow. *Am I doing the right thing by meeting Nils again, considering Mama's opposition? Maybe I should not show up, or tell him that I can't see him for some reason or other?* The minute these thoughts crossed Anna's mind, she pictured Nils' face, heard his Norwegian accent, and shook her head. He was too nice and sweet to her to be brushed off. She picked out a gray dress and stockings to wear the next day and braided her hair.

Rivka watched her sister going through the dresses and, waiting until Anna crawled under the covers, made a guess of her own. "Anna, are you doing something special tomorrow?"

"No, why do you ask?"

"Because that gray dress is too nice to wear, unless you are going somewhere with a fellow." She gave Anna the *'I am your sister and you cannot fool me'* look.

"I might be doing something in the afternoon. I'll have to see." Anna knew all attempts at deceiving her sister were futile, but she did not want to directly admit to meeting Nils.

"I think I can guess, and you just better hope Mama does not find out."

"She won't if you don't tell her." No one besides Rivka knew that she was seeing Nils on Sunday so, to preserve the peace of the Katz household, Anna had to come up with a good excuse to be out in the afternoon.

On Sunday morning, Anna made an extra effort to be helpful around the house. Sarah appreciated the help, but wondered if her daughter had a hidden motive in being so nice. Moyshe told her not to meddle and, as difficult as it was to do, she obeyed her husband. When Anna mumbled something about going to the park with a group of friends and hurried out the door, Sarah shouted after her. "It better be your Jewish friends and not that Scandiwegian!"

One of these days, Moyshe will come to his senses, and it will be too late, she thought as she closed the front door.

Chapter Five

Nils walked across St. Paul whistling a hymn from that morning's church service. The past week had been good to him. Perhaps, with meeting Anna, his luck in America had finally begun to change. Monday, he bought a Norwegian newspaper and a *MEN WANTED* notice caught his interest. The flourmill in Minneapolis was looking for strong men to work the grain elevators and load flour onto the barges on the Mississippi River. After six months at the stockyards, Nils was ready to take any job, as long as he did not have to butcher animals. The only problem was that the flourmill was open the same hours as the stockyards, and he could not be in at two places at once.

Oskar offered to tell the stockyard foreman that Nils was sick with consumption, got trampled by the streetcar, or drank too much whiskey to come in. As much as Nils despised lying, it was unavoidable in order for him to take time off to apply at the mill. He cautioned Oskar against spinning an elaborate web of lies, which could lead to more questions and ultimately catch the unsuspecting fly. Nils went to the mill on Tuesday morning and spoke to the foreman in the best English he could manage. The man answered in Swedish and asked Nils to start the following week. Nils left with a smile on his face and a sense of accomplishment that lightened his long stride. The wages were no better than the stockyards and he would have to take the streetcar to Minneapolis, but his conscience would at last be clean and he would not come home smelling of blood and entrails.

Nils spent the rest of the week counting the final hours at the stockyard and studying English at night. He did not want to embarrass himself in front of Anna or misunderstand something that she might say to him. When he was tired of English grammar, he played his fiddle—more for Kjersti and little Henrik than for himself. The music calmed the boy and, exhausted from housework, two young children, and Oddleif's and Oskar's drinking, Kjersti asked Nils to lull the baby to sleep so she could rest from a long day.

Sunday morning he went to church with Kjersti, Solveig, and Henrik. Oddleif was too hung over to get out of bed and Oskar lay in a pool of vomit on the porch. Kjersti gave Oskar a sharp kick to insure that he was still breathing. When he merely groaned and rolled over, she addressed Nils.

"So, this is how a man claiming he played tennis with King Christian of Denmark ends up."

The church service was conducted in Norwegian. Nils followed along in his Bible as Pastor Grundseth read the scripture text for this Sunday. The sermon was directed toward recent immigrants, comparing them to the Jews who left Egypt, wandered in the desert, and finally settled in Israel. The message was not to give up hope; to look toward the river Jordan and the Promised Land—America. Nils listened, but was not entirely certain that America was the land of milk and honey. In some ways, conditions were worse than in Norway, but as long as he was there, he would make the best of it. To Nils, God was present as much in St. Paul as He was in Norway. Nils prayed for his brother Per, somewhere at sea; for his sister Ingrid in Norway; for Oskar and Oddleif to give up the whiskey; for Kjersti to have an easy day with the children; for the start of his new job; for nimble fingers on the fiddle; and for pure thoughts about the Russian girl whom he could hardly get out of his mind. When the service was over, he walked Kjersti and the children home and started on trek across the city to Anna's neighborhood.

At three o'clock, Nils was on the corner of Pinehurst and Cleveland. Having never owned a watch, he told time by the sun and was rarely wrong.

Cleveland Avenue was a study in contrasts. On one side, serious men in black hats stood in bunches on the steps of the houses and talked with their hands. On the other side, sounds of a fiddle and stomping feet could be heard a few houses down. The Irish were celebrating something. Nils squinted at the sun and felt something soft brush his legs. A skinny gray and white cat twined about his ankles and looked up at him with big green eyes.

"Little gray cat, I don't have anything for you," Nils said in Norwegian as he petted the cat's bony back and scratched behind its mangy ears. The cat purred loudly, arched its back and rubbed its muzzle against Nils' hand. He thought about taking it home for Solveig and Henrik, but despite being skinny, the animal was very friendly and probably had an owner.

Anna walked the five blocks from Pinehurst Avenue to Cleveland. Fear and anticipation battled within her with each step she took. *What if he doesn't show up and, by now, forgot all about me? No,* her gentler side argued. *Nils Bjørnsen is not the type of fellow to forget. He will be there, and I can't wait to see him again. He has such beautiful sky blue eyes...* " Anna's breath caught in her throat and her heart pounded as she approached the designated intersection, then her chest rose as she breathed a heavy sigh of relief.

Nils was indeed there, as promised. She smiled as she watched him, sitting on the balls of his feet and petting a gray and white cat. *A man who is kind to animals has a good heart.* Anna took out the paper that Margit gave her and quietly tiptoed toward man and cat. She reached his side, hesitated as she squinted at the words Margit had written, then uttered a Norwegian greeting.

Nils heard a woman's voice address him in what sounded like bad Norwegian. He turned around and saw Anna in a gray dress, red hair in a bun, staring intently at a sheet of paper. He stood immediately, the cat forgotten. She looked beautiful, even with her forehead wrinkled as she struggled with an unknown language.

She smiled and repeated her phrase very carefully. *"God dag, Nils, hvordan stor de til?"*

Nils was not sure in which language to answer her simple question, but chose to practice his English. "Good day to you, too, Miss Katz, and thank you for asking. I am very good, and you?

Anna stared at the paper again and spoke the Norweigan words for 'Very well, thank you.' *"Bare bra, takk."*

Nils returned her smile with a broad one of his own, flattered that the girl liked him enough to take the time to learn his language. "You speak so well in one week. How you learn so fast?"

"Oh, a girl at work taught me some simple words and phrases."

Anna showed Nils the paper. He looked it over and saw that Margit could barely write Norwegian herself and made glaring mistakes in spelling and grammar. "I trade with you. I teach you Norwegian if you teach me English."

"That's a deal. Say, I think that cat likes you."

Nils glanced down at the cat, who resented the sudden inattentiveness of his newfound friend. It rubbed against Nils' boots and meowed plaintively.

"Ja, little cat, all bones. I talk to him in Norwegian and I think he understand. He look like he forgot to wash soap after shaving."

"You're right. What an odd-colored face." One half of the animal's muzzle was gray and the other white. Anna sighed. "I wish I could take it home, but my mother would kill me."

"Why, she not like cats?"

"Not just cats, any animals. They are too dirty, too much hair, ruin the furniture. When I have my own house, I will get a cat. They are so silky and soft."

"I like cats. We had them on the farm in Norway, good for us, bad for mice. If he is still here when I walk you home, I ask the children." Nils pointed to the rag-tag bunch of Irish kids running up and down Cleveland. "How do you say when a cat has no home?"

"Stray."

"If cat is stray, I take it. My cousin have two kids and they will be very happy. I talk to children later. Well, I ask you what you want to do today?"

Anna ran several possibilities for an outing through her head. It would be nice to go to Como Park and see the flowers, but it was a little too far, and a walk around her neighborhood was out of the question. Suddenly, her face lit up with an idea.

"Nils, how would you like to see downtown St. Paul? Last time we met, you said you have never been in the main part of the city. And what did I do? I dragged you to a union meeting. So, I owe you a tour and we can even see the library, so you know where it is next time you decide to go. It's about two miles and we can take the streetcar back. What do you say?"

"I say that is okay. I will be very glad to go with you. Much better than map and getting lost like last Sunday."

"You won't get lost with me, I promise. Let's go."

Nils and Anna walked along St. Paul's west side toward downtown. It was the end of April and spring had at last come to Minnesota. The trees were covered with green fuzz and the lawns around them exploded with the bright colors of tulips, irises, and daffodils. Even the air had that peculiar spring fragrance of sticky fresh buds and lilac blossoms. The squirrels knew that winter was finally over and chased e ach other through grassy yards and up and down the tree trunks. Nils pointed up and Anna saw one of the small creatures running along the electric light wire, like a nimble tightrope walker.

"How does it not get killed by the current," she wondered aloud.

"It run fast!" Nils offered.

Soon they were on Minnesota Street and Anna showed Nils the library building.

"You will have to get a card to check out books. If you don't return them on time, you will have to pay a penny a day. There is a big cabinet with files called the card catalog. You can look up any book you like in there."

"Any book, even in Norwegian?"

"I think so. I checked out a couple Russian ones several months ago. I prefer to read the Russian writers in their own language. They sound strange in translation."

"I know what you mean, because I think I sound strange in translation. Everything I say to you, first I think Norwegian, then how it is in English, and then I try to speak. Sometimes, I have trouble to understand myself."

Anna laughed. "I used to do that too, but as I got better at English, I didn't need to translate in my head. Give yourself two or three years, and by then you will speak like a native. Look, there is the Capitol. It should be finished in a couple of years." Nils followed her glance toward the end of Minnesota Street and saw the grandiose marble building, encased in scaffolding. He wondered if it was a church, or if some rich railroad baron was having a mansion built.

"Anna, this Capitol, they build it for person with a lot of money?"

"No, it's a building where the Governor of Minnesota, and all the other people who make laws for the state, work." Anna patiently explained the basic functions of the State legislature and the governor. "You see, Nils, the unions ask senators to pass laws about working hours, better wages, child labor. But, unfortunately, the people who are elected get money from the bosses, so they don't vote on anything the workers want. Why? Because then the bosses won't give them money. Sometimes, bosses even fix the elections, so that their favorite candidates win."

"So, what you tell me before about people voting for these senators to do what we ask, it is really not true?"

"I am afraid so. But maybe by the time you become a citizen and can vote in 1904, there will be changes, hopefully for the better. We are organizing more working people to join unions, like that picnic we are planning in May, so in a few years we will have more votes and influence with the senators." Anna and Nils walked up the granite steps to get a closer look at the Capitol complex in progress. "I hope the new Capitol will have men in government who will do the right thing," she concluded.

"Ja, I hope so too. I read paper in Norway and in many countries women ask if they can choose people for government. I think that is good thing to do. Here in America, can woman do that?"

"No, not yet, but there are women called suffragettes who are fighting for our right to vote. Just think, if women could vote, we would have twice as many voices. For that matter, I would not stop there. Maybe some day women will be elected to serve in the legislature, right here in St. Paul."

Nils smiled and cast an admiring glance at Anna. "You speak so good for your union, I vote for you, Anna. But you are right. Women know more about taking care of children and family, and they can tell men what is better."

"Well, if more men thought like you, we would not be having all these problems with the factory bosses." Anna pointed to a street heading toward the waterfront. "I was going to show you the Mississippi River. That's the biggest river in America."

"I read about it. But after ocean, no river is so big. You know that Norwegians cross big ocean one thousand years ago and come to America first?"

"No, they didn't. Our history teacher said that Columbus discovered America in 1492," Anna retorted with the self-assurance of facts.

"Well, that is true too, but there was man, Leif Erikson, he had red hair like you, and he come here and back and another man write down, so we know that Norwegians was in America."

"I guess if it was written down, it must be at least somewhat true. Did they write down that he had red hair?" she asked.

"Ja, that they did, and many, many other things. The men, we call them Vikings. They come from Norway to Iceland to America, but they call it Vineland. Take many days to travel to America. Their ship, it was not big like now, made of wood and on the front Vikings put animals, like lion and dragon. I have that also on my *hardingfele*. I show that to you some time."

The story was interesting, but it almost made Anna seasick. "I would love to see your fiddle, but I don't have fond memories of the two weeks spent crossing the Atlantic. We were packed like sardines, two hundred immigrants in the bottom of the ship and coming on deck only to throw up. How was your trip?"

"I never get sick, because in Norway I take boat for fishing in good and bad weather. But I remember babies crying, many people sick. I stay on deck most of the time. It was beautiful at night to see stars. They are the same as in Norway. I look up and think, I am just a little man in a big world and what I am doing on this ship."

"Didn't you get cold?"

"No, I did not think about cold, but I feel sad and hopeful and afraid all at once. Sad because I look back to Norway and everything that I love I leave behind. Hopeful, because I look forward to new life in America, but afraid what will it be like here."

"I think all immigrants have the same feelings. The worst part for me was landing at Ellis Island and being examined by the doctors and customs officials. They were not nice at all, got upset at us for not speaking English, and sent some people back home because they were so sick. Mama was so afraid that my brother Grisha would cough that she kept feeding him sugar cubes. We passed the inspection, but it was not a good welcome to a new country."

"Ja, they look at me too and ask what I can do. I told them, I am strong and can do all kind of work, so they give me directions to the train station. I buy ticket to St. Paul and next day I was here. I never think that in six month, I meet a pretty girl who will show me my new city."

Anna felt her cheeks burn and her breath catch. She glanced at her shoes so Nils would not see her face.

As they continued walking, Nils wondered if it would be appropriate or too forward to take Anna's hand, but could not think of the perfect moment to ask. Luckily, the opportunity presented itself on 4th and Cedar. Warm temperatures melted a huge pile of snow shoveled all winter by the street crews onto a vacant lot. As the snow melted, it sent a sizable stream of muddy water and garbage across Cedar.

Anna stopped, not wanting to get her shoes or the hem of her dress wet and dirty. "We can go another way, just a couple blocks around."

"Just a little water. That is no trouble. Here, take my hand." Anna did not expect her daydreams to become real so quickly. Her hand shook until Nils clasped it within the warmth of his own, then he bent down, scooped her legs with his left hand, and headed across Cedar Avenue. Anna, unprepared for this act of gentlemanly gallantry, grew light-headed and her heartbeat quickened. She felt like the snow pile being melted by the spring sun—the warm water trickling to the tips of her toes. No one had ever held her so intimately, and she could not imagine Benny Simkin wading in ankle deep water for her sake. Nils' arms were strong, yet gentle, and she felt cared for and protected.

As Nils carried Anna across the street, he looked into her green eyes, *almost like a kitten's*, he noticed. They showed complete trust, and Nils knew then that he could never betray it. She was light, almost fragile, in her soft wool dress and her hair gave off the scent of rosewater. Nils lowered her until her feet touched the sidewalk, and then exercised the utmost self-control. He dared not kiss her right in the middle of downtown St. Paul. Even so, she kept her right hand in his as they walked the few blocks to the Mississippi River.

Nils pointed toward the barges swaying on the river as he told Anna about his new job. "Just think, that flour will make bread in China or Africa, or maybe even Norway. It will be hard work, but I feel better about it than in the stockyards."

"I'm glad you got out of there," Anna said. "What a miserable place for both humans and animals. Do you find it hard to eat meat now?"

He nodded and blinked to dispel the disturbing images of his old job. "Yes, I think too much when my cousin's wife make dinner. What is the difference between a cow and that little gray cat we saw?"

"Nils, you think deeply about a lot of things most fellows don't concern themselves about. That's what I like about you." Anna looked into his blue eyes and smiled.

"Thank you." Nils gave her hand a gentle squeeze. " I like the same about you. Many girls, they think about money, clothes, not making world a better place." Nils noticed how the setting sun reflected the red highlights in Anna's hair. "Anna, be careful you do not make fire with your hair."

Embarrassed by his flattery, Anna retrieved her hand from his and brushed at the loose strands that fell on her forehead. "Oh, I honestly don't know who I got this hair from. Papa said that grandma Hannah, for whom I was named, might have had the same color. People always mistake me for an Irish girl. Mama's opinion is that red hair gives you a hot head, which means that I don't do what she tells me."

"But you are not little child. You can do things on your own." Nils was glad he was a man. Women were always under the thumb of their mothers, even those as spirited and independent as Anna.

"You don't know my Mama, Nils. She is a very nice woman and loves her family, but she has my sister's and my life planned: Whom we should marry, what we cook, how we arrange our houses, and what to name our children. In fact, last Sunday she saw you walk me home and I won't even begin to describe to you the little 'talk' that we had afterwards."

"Oh, Anna, I am so sorry that I cause you so much trouble. Maybe I can meet her and tell her I work hard, I don't drink or smoke, I try to make a new life here in America. She is from Russia, she will understand."

Anna shook her head. "No, Nils, she will never understand. Her whole life is tradition and the fear of punishment for breaking it. According to Jewish law, God commanded that Jews are not to associate with non-Jews. It says that somewhere in the book of Moses, but since the law does not permit women to read it, I cannot tell you where."

"Is that true, you cannot read your Bible?" Nils stared at her, dumbfounded; the Lutheran church encouraged Bible study and reading on a daily basis. "I read the second, third, fourth, and fifth Moses books. They have a lot of laws, but it is very hard to follow them all and some are very old and I do not understand what they mean." Nils thought for a moment and continued. "Anna, I hope I do not say anything wrong about your religion. See, I think God wants us to be good people to each other, not steal, not kill… What do you call in English the ten big laws he give Moses on the mountain?"

"The Ten Commandments."

"Ja well. So we try to live by these Ten Commandments and even that is hard. The small laws, almost not possible. If I want to do something, I ask God, 'Is this right?' I think about it, and then decide. I can ask God again, but I think that Norwegian man and Jewish woman can be friends."

"You did not say anything wrong and I am not offended, Nils. In fact, I think the same way you do, but it is hard to change older people like my parents. I guess I will keep trying." The sun sank into the Mississippi and Anna felt a spring chill in the air. "I better be getting home. It's almost six."

"I walk you home. Here, take my coat. You look cold."

"You don't have to. Besides, then *you* will be cold."

"Anna, I am from Norway. We have winter for half year, a lot of snow. For me, this is summer." Nils wrapped his Sunday coat around Anna's dress and put his hand in hers. "You feel warm now?"

"Yes, thank you."

Nils noticed that Anna's eyes were misty behind the glasses. "Anna, I say or do something wrong?"

"No, not at all." Her voice was shaky and thin and she squeezed Nils' hand tighter. "It's just no fellow has ever been so nice to me like you. I met you only twice, but I feel I have known you for many years, and that we can talk about anything. I want to be your friend, but every time I see you, I must lie to my family, and it is painful for me to do that. I wish they could understand."

"Anna, maybe I try to talk to your father. You said he play violin. We can play some music together. I have good ear for that. So he know I am not a bad person."

Anna turned the suggestion in her head. Moyshe Katz was more accepting of people, and Nils did need to get his boots fixed. "Papa owns a shoe repair shop and takes his violin to work. He hangs it on the wall. Ask him to play it and tell him that you play yourself. He likes that. The Irish fellows always play a couple of jigs anytime they stop by. Just don't say anything about me. Not yet. Besides, Papa tells me that his best customers are Swedes and Norwegians, because they pay on time."

Nils glanced down at his boots, which needed serious repairs. Perhaps with his first paycheck from the flourmill, he could get them fixed. "Anna, tell me where is his shop and I go next week. I promise I say nothing about you. Just want to have my shoes look better."

Anna described the location of Katz's shoe repair on Snelling and Highland. Moyshe Katz was always pleasant to his customers, and she had no reason to doubt he would treat Nils like any other person that came into the shop.

Anna and Nils approached the corner of Cleveland and Pinehurst. It was past seven and the streetlights gave a warm glow to a spring evening. The gray and white cat was nowhere to be seen. Anna gave Nils his coat and started to say good-bye.

"I had a wonderful time, Nils. Thank you. I have to run home now. It would be best that you don't come with me, like last time."

"No, Anna, it is too dark for a girl to walk by herself. I walk with you until your block and see that you get in your door. I stay on street corner, so your mother will not see me. If something happen to you, I will never forgive myself."

"All right, but just up to my block. There is an alley behind the houses, and I can manage from there." Nils escorted Anna to the place she designated, trying to stay out of the street lamp beams and away from open windows. The alley was dark and tree branches obscured the second floor windows of the Katz's apartment.

"Well, see you next week? *Ha det.* That is good-bye in Norwegian." Nils still had Anna's hand in his. He was not sure if it was appropriate to kiss her just yet. Perhaps next time. He drew her close against his chest and gently stroked her hair.

Anna did not resist and wrapped her arms around him. The coarse linen shirt that smelled of lye soap tickled her face. She could hear his heart beating. For a brief moment she closed her eyes and felt as if she was melting. *Is this what being in love is like?* she wondered. She felt as if she could stay in his arms forever. Nils whispered something in Norwegian. Anna would ask him next time.

The sound of footsteps coming from the street toward the alley jerked her abruptly back to reality. "Same place, same time next Sunday."

Nils watched as Anna ran through the backyard into the rear door of the apartment building, and then he disappeared into the blackness of the alley.

Chapter Six

Nils stood on the barge at the Ceresota Flour Mill and hefted the 100-pound bag, then stacked it on top of the ever-growing pile of flour. He was a farm boy and the work was easy at first, but after ten grueling hours of lifting, his back knotted up. Nils was glad to be outside, and not the man loading the bags in front of the flour chute. He would be covered with flour from head to toe, and would have difficulty breathing in the thick grain dust. Still, Nils preferred the mill to the stockyards and even met a couple of Norwegians to talk to during lunch break.

By Thursday of his first week, he decided to pay Katz's Shoe Repair a visit. Nils rushed out of the mill at six and took a streetcar from Minneapolis to St. Paul. Anna told him that Moyshe closed the shop promptly at seven, so when Nils got off the streetcar, he ran the remaining few blocks. He arrived with ten minutes to spare. The scent of old leather, glue, and shoe polish greeted him as he stepped inside.

Katz's Shoe Repair resembled a large closet with shelves of old shoes. Sheets of different-colored leather hung on the walls, and a sign in Yiddish and English described prices for services. Moyshe Katz, a short, balding man who Nils decided was about fifty, sat behind the counter, his side toward the door as he played what Nils believed was a folk tune on his violin. *So this is Anna's father.* Nils could not detect any resemblance between the skinny red head and this pudgy fellow.

Moyshe heard the bell and set the violin aside. *My bad luck, to have another customer ten minutes to closing,* he thought as he stood and faced his new customer. *He better be fast. Looks Scandinavian.* "What can I do for you, sir?"

Nils walked over to the older man and placed his boots on the counter. "I need my shoes fixed, but first, please finish your song. You play so well. I never hear this music. What country it is from?"

"Well, thank you for the compliment. Just playing a little gypsy tune, but I am really in the business of fixing shoes. Let me see these." He opened the paper sack before him, took one look at Nils' boots and shook his head. The soles and heels of the boots had worn completely through. "Young man, what did you do to these shoes? They will need some major work."

Nils smiled and nodded in agreement. "I come from Norway to St. Paul and work in the stockyards and now at the flour mill. I do not take the streetcar often, so I walk many miles, all in these boots. Now, I have my good shoes on. Those are for Sunday, not for work."

"A Norwegian, eh. My daughter is seeing some Norwegian fellow, or was it Swedish? Hope he treats her well, but it would be better that she marry one of her own kind. It's nothing against you Scandinavians, but you know, I am her father."

Nils wished for a black hole to open in the floor and swallow him. He forced a smile and hoped that Moyshe Katz did not see him turn beet red. "Ja, most Norwegian men treat women good, but if they drink whiskey, then that is big trouble for the girl." Nils switched the subject back to shoes. "Mr. Katz, I pay you now. Just tell me how much it cost to fix."

"There is no need to pay me now. I'll get them ready next week, and it will be two dollars." His lips curved into an amused grin. "I take it you don't approve of drinking whiskey?"

"I play a Norwegian violin for dances and weddings, and I see what whiskey can do. Very bad."

"You don't say." Moyshe's eyes widened in surprise that he had something in common with the Norwegian fellow. "If there is a Jewish celebration and they need a musician, they ask for Moyshe Katz. So, I fix their shoes during the day, fiddle for them at night. I know you don't drink, but a few glasses of wine at a wedding, that doesn't hurt no one. Tell me, what's the difference between my violin here and your Norwegian one?"

"Well, we call it a *hardingfele*. It has the same four strings like your violin, but there is four more under these ones and they make fiddle ring. I show to you when I get my shoes, if you like."

"Please do, I am always interested in different countries' music. Here, try this one," Moyshe handed Nils the violin. Nils raised it up to the pitch of the *hardingfele* and played several lively dance tunes from Voss.

Moyshe clapped Nils on the shoulder. "You are a heck of a good fiddle player and that's only on four strings. I want to hear it on all eight next week. What's your name?" Again, Nils wished for that black hole. On one hand, he did not want to lie, but on the other hand, the truth might prove embarrassing to both him and Anna. In a split second, he opted for the half-truth. "Bjørnsen, from Voss, Norway." Nils extended his hand to Moyshe Katz and hoped that all the 'sen's would sound alike to the Jewish ear. He was right.

Moyshe rolled his eyes and shook his head. "Another 'son'! How do you Scandinavians tell each other apart? I swear, every other fellow that comes in here is either an Olson, Larson, Peterson, or Hanson and now, Bjørnson." He handed Nils the receipt. "Well, I better close up. The wife is waiting and, trust me, you don't want to get on her bad side. Bring your fiddle next week and your shoes will be as good as new." Moyshe let Nils out the front door, locked up, and the men separated, each heading in different directions on Snelling.

"Moyshe, why are you always late? You know perfectly well that I have dinner ready at seven thirty, so what do you do? You make us all wait for you and the food is getting cold." Sarah's hands left her hips and she banged a serving spoon against the kitchen counter.

Sarah is at it again. Two weeks of relative peace and quiet and now something else is eating her. Moyshe answered as calmly as possible. "Sarah, I run a business and I cannot just tell the customer, 'Sorry, the store is closed now. You will have to come back tomorrow, because my wife has dinner waiting'. A fellow came at ten of and I needed to take care of his shoes. They were pretty bad."

"You tell me, Moyshe, how long does it take for you to look at the shoes and write the man's name on the slip? Not more than five minutes. I still say, you should have been done by seven. But no, you got to talk to him, ask about his family, where he came from, and so on and so on. Pretty soon, a half an hour passes by and you slap your head and say '*Oy*, I forgot, the store is closed. It's time to go home'." Sarah released a disgruntled sigh and folded her hands on her chest.

"You are right. Taking down the repair order takes one or two minutes, but if I did only that, I would not have a business. What's the difference between that and a streetcar conductor? I talk to the customer, ask him a couple of questions, make him feel at home. Next time, he will come back and tell his friends to get their shoes repaired at Katz's. So I get more business, meaning more money for you to buy food for that cold dinner you are complaining about."

"And to whom did you extend the courtesy tonight?"

"Oh, some Norwegian fellow I forget the name, ends in 'son', like every other Scandinavian who brings his shoes to be fixed. He even offered to pay in advance. Must have walked from Norway across the ocean the way his boots looked. He saw my violin and said that in Norway he played a fiddle— what did he call it, herring something—with eight strings. I gave him mine to try and I tell you, that fellow plays so good, he would make us Jews tap our feet at a *bar-mitzvah*."

Anna's spoon froze in midair. She was certain that Nils was Papa's customer. She forced herself to swallow, regained her composure and hoped that her mother did not notice.

"What is it with you and Anna and those Scandinavians? Your Jewish customers aren't good enough for you, so you fiddle with the *goyim*. *Feh*." Sarah wagged her finger at Anna. "Young lady, if you went to the park with some friends last Sunday, it was not any of the ones I know. I asked. I'll bet your Papa a hundred dollars you were with that Swede. You take him for walks, Papa fixes his shoes, and he is so happy he fiddles all day. Moyshe, is this what you brought us to America for?"

Moyshe's sigh betrayed his exasperation. "Sarah, how many Scandinavians are in St. Paul? Maybe ten thousand? So, out of these many people, I cannot fix one pair of shoes? At least they pay. You should have seen Abram Feldman today. 'Dear Moyshe,' he says to me sweet as honey, 'since we are old friends, how about a fifty percent discount for me.' He says it so loud that, Shulman the butcher, hears it. Well, then Shulman starts in on what a good friend he is of mine, and you know I cannot stand the sight of him. It's a miracle I make money on all these friends."

Moyshe finished his meal and started on the newspaper. Anna helped Rivka and Max with their homework and stayed out of Sarah's way. No amount of lying on Anna's part could get past her mother and she honestly did not know how long her deception could continue.

Meanwhile, Sarah thought of a plan that would expose Anna's weekly lies once and for all and, that Sunday morning, she called Max into the kitchen. "Max, how would you like to have a whole dollar to spend on a baseball game, soda, and candy for you and Grisha?"

Max stared at his mother open-mouthed. Mama did not approve of baseball, soda, or candy, and the boys had to ask Moyshe for a quarter to cover the game and the streetcar ride.

"Um, well, thank you Mama. That is very kind of you. Can we go this afternoon?"

"Not so fast, young man. The dollar is for next Sunday, because today I am going to ask you to help me."

Now comes the catch to getting the money. Max braced himself for some drudgery like scrubbing the floor or hauling coal for the boiler. Still, a whole dollar! The possibilities of buying the most expensive soda and stuffing Grisha with candy swirled in his head. He would even have enough left over for a program and scorecard. Max imagined himself biting on a pencil while writing down the balls, strikes and outs. He would be the envy of all his friends, who would have no idea what Ks, FOs, 2Bs meant.

"Max, stop daydreaming about what you will do with the dollar and start listening to me on how you can earn it."

"Okay."

She lowered her voice to a whisper. "Your sister Anna tells me every Sunday that she is at a union meeting, or at the park, or with Fanny—you name it—but I know she is lying. She is seeing that dirty Norwegian fellow. What I want you to do is find out where she goes and what she does with him. Stay about a block behind so you won't be noticed and tell me everything."

"But Mama, she is my sister. And what if she sees me?" Max rubbed the palms of his hands against his pants. The baseball scorecard was not worth it.

"Max, you are not a boy any more. You are the oldest son and it is your duty to protect your sister. Even though she is much older than you, she is high-strung and foolish. You don't want that evil man to hurt her, do you?"

Max's brown eyes narrowed and his brow furrowed with concern. "No, of course not. I guess I can do it."

Sarah smiled in triumph and held a coin toward him. "That's my Max. Here's a quarter for today, if you need to take the streetcar or buy yourself something to eat. When you come back, I will give you the dollar."

"All right." Max took the money and shuffled out of the kitchen. He was not looking forward to this afternoon at all. *Unless...* Max paused as a thought occurred to him. *If I can convince Anna to take this fellow to a baseball game, I can watch the game and Anna at the same time.* Max decided to give his plan a try. He found Anna and Rivka outside weeding the tulips in front of the apartment building. "So, what are you girls doing today?" he asked casually.

Rivka tossed him a dejected glance. "I have to stay home and write a composition for Monday. So, to answer your question, nothing fun."

Anna shrugged. "I have a union meeting—"

"Anna," Rivka interrupted. "You just had one Thursday night where you made signs for the picnic. Why do they need to have another one two days later?" Her eyes bored into her sister. "They don't, because there isn't one today. How do I know? Because your face is red and you don't want us to know that you are going to take a little walk with the Norskie fellow."

Max mentally thanked his sister for an excellent introduction for his plan.

Anna glanced away. Rivka was too smart and now Max would know about Nils, as well. "I have my own plans," she said as she resumed weeding, hoping to end a touchy conversation.

"Anna," Max said, his voice earnest. "I don't really care if you go to the union meeting or with the Swede, but if you do go with him, why don't you take him to a baseball game? I bet he has never seen one before. I can sit way on the other side of the park, but if you want me to, I can explain the rules. I mean, if my sister is seeing some fellow, I want to make sure he's okay. Don't worry, though. I'm not like Mama. He can be green with hairy ears and six fingers, and I won't say anything. So, what do you say? The game starts at three."

Anna quickly considered Max's proposal for the afternoon and decided to take him up on it. Nils had never seen a baseball game, and it would be interesting to learn what her brother thought of him. Max was a smart boy, made friends easily, and would not be judgmental, like Mama and Papa. There was only one sticky point—Grisha.   Her little brother followed Max everywhere, especially to baseball games. She was certain that everything that happened at the game—scores, statistics, what Nils said to her and vice versa—would be relayed at the dinner table. The last thing she wanted was another scene.

"Max, you think of the best ideas. I have one request though. Don't take Grisha along, because he will tell everything to Mama. We will leave the house separately and meet at the game. It would be better if we sit on the Minneapolis side, because I don't want Mr. Goldstein to tell his wife who he saw and with whom, and have Mrs. Goldstein run over here and report to Mama."

Max nodded as he smiled. "Okay, Anna, see you at the game." He turned to the younger girl. "Rivka, why don't you come to the game and write a composition on baseball?"

"Very funny, Max," she answered. "This is for history, and I have to choose a topic from ancient Rome or Greece. I don't think Julius Caesar hit a home run."

"Then how do you explain those old statues with broken noses?" he replied, his eyes twinkling with humor. "I bet they were hit by a wild pitch!"

Rivka shook her head. "Max, do you think of anything else besides baseball?   When you grow up, you won't have time to go to games and memorize those numbers."

"Oh yes, I will. I am going to be one of those newspapermen who gets paid to watch the game and write about it. I read that, in New York, they are showing moving pictures. So, when I grow up and attend the games, I will talk into one of those big bullhorns. A man will make a wax disk out of that, and then play it along with the picture for the people who cannot be at the ballpark."

Rivka laughed. "Moving pictures. How silly! Who would want to watch them anyway? Keep dreaming, little brother." Rivka rose and went inside.

Anna saw Max shrug as he, too, left the yard, then continued her gardening chores until it was time to meet Nils.

Chapter Seven

Anna and Nils met on the same corner as always, unaware that a half block away a boy in an oversized black coat and knickers watched them, his body pressed against the side of a building. Max held a notebook and pencil in his hands as he pretended to be Sherlock Holmes, lacking only the pipe. He glanced ahead furtively, took a couple steps forward and ducked behind a hedge. He spied nothing exciting or criminal, but rather what he, at fourteen, considered to be a normal meeting between a man and a woman. His pencil moved furiously as he scribbled into his notebook.

"Commenced following Anna Katz from 2601 Pinehurst, her place of residence. Miss Katz headed north on Pinehurst up to Cleveland Avenue at an even pace. Subject wearing a brown skirt and white shirt with lace collar. Man standing at corner of Cleveland and Pinehurst. Black pants and vest, white shirt, blond hair. Has red and yellow flowers in his hand. Probably the fellow Mama suspects. Miss Katz greets the man, who gives her flowers. She smiles at him. Man sees a gray and white cat on street corner. Bends down and gives something to cat, who eats it. Cat twines around his legs and is petted by him. Man takes Miss Katz's left hand in his right hand and they head south on Cleveland to the Highland Baseball Park. As Mr. Holmes was always a half block behind, he could not make out their conversation, except a few words here and there. The man has a thick Scandinavian accent. He cannot pronounce his j's and w's and rolls his r's like a Russian."

Several minutes later, Max paused to make another note. *"Both people hold hands until the Baseball Park, where they join a line to buy tickets. Mr. Holmes chose another line in order not to be seen and buys his ticket for the game between the Minneapolis Messiahs and the St. Paul Prophets. Miss Katz sees Mr. Holmes and motions him to join her. She is blushing and holding the flowers, which are red tulips and yellow daffodils."*

Max tucked away his notebook and pencil, then waited until he was seated in the stadium to continue his 'observations.' *"Man introduces himself as Nils Byornson from Vos (not sure of the spelling of his name or location), Norway. He gives Mr. Holmes a firm handshake and says he is glad to meet him. He is tall, about six feet, has blue eyes, mustache, and a chipped front tooth. Mr. Holmes accompanies the couple to the seats in the upper deck. He is slightly behind so he can write down the observations just made. Due to the circumstances, Mr. Holmes is forced to put the notebook away during the game, as not to arouse suspicion of the couple being observed. To be continued, my dear Dr. Watson..."*

Max pulled out his notebook as the game started and, on a clean sheet of paper, drew a diagram of a baseball diamond. He spent a good half hour explaining the game to Nils, alternating between pointing at the field and the paper diagram. Nils understood the basics of baseball—how a man scored by hitting the ball and running around the bases—but the concepts of sacrifice flies, force outs, and the batter's strike zone were harder to grasp.

Nils squinted at the pitcher, watched the ball speed toward the catcher, and shook his head. He could not tell if the ball thrown was a strike or not, while Max had to only casually glance at the ball to figure that out. Nils turned around to address the young boy seated behind him. "Max, that pitcher, he throws too fast. How you can tell which is ball or strike?"

"I've been to many games," Max replied. "After a while, you just know. Some of those pitches are so fast, you cannot even blink or you'll miss them." He leaned forward, closer to the older man. "I read that Hippo Vaughn threw a ball eighty miles per hour. They had to have a special instrument to measure it."

Nils raised a brow in surprise. "Does pitcher hit batter often? That man will have a big hole in his head then."

"It happens, but I never heard of anyone dying from it. They just look a little off." Max glanced at Anna, noticed her intently scanning the St. Paul audience on the opposite side of the ballpark, and shook his head. "Anna, did you get a ticket to look at the field or the bleachers? You have nothing to worry about. Mr. Goldstein's vision is not that good. And besides, this place is full of

Americans, Germans, and Irishmen who just want to see a game on Sunday when the Saints and the Millers can't play."

Anna shrugged and tossed her brother a smile. "You're right, Max. I did not pay to see Mr. Goldstein's bald spot." She turned to the handsome man beside her. "What do you think of the game, Nils?"

He grinned. "Well, we do not have baseball in Norway. Max is a good teacher, and I think I understand this game a little, but I would like to go to two or three more games. Then I know it better."

Max beamed with delight. He had found a new friend. "You just tell me when you want to go and I will come with you. I'll bet that, in a month, you will know the difference between a fastball, a curveball, and a spitball. And, if you want to try it out, us neighborhood kids play in the empty lot on Snelling. Except the Irish boys always win."

"You let an old Norwegian like me play?"

"Sure, because you're big and strong and you will hit a lot farther than the little Jewish kids." He paused as Nils laughed, then continued. "I will pitch to you before the game so you can take a few practice swings."

"I try. It is like cutting hay at the farm. I do that every summer in Voss. I go and get ice cream for you and Anna for taking me to the game, okay?" Nils dug in his pockets for change.

"You don't have to get any for me," Max said, his pleasure evident in the happiness that tinged his voice. "But I know Anna likes the one with berries in it."

"Max." Anna's lips curved as she shook her head. "You have ice cream written all over your face, so just say thank you. Nils, don't get it for me. My little brother earned his, and I will pay for it. I insist."

"I buy for both of you. You are worse than two Norwegians. They meet on little path high in mountains, they cannot go both, because is only room for one man. One says 'if it is no trouble I go now, but you can go first,' and other one says 'no, I wait, you go first.' So they go around and around, and soon the sun is down, they still talking. It start raining, then winter comes and they are still in the same place. You go there now and you will see them, I promise. Max, you come with me and we pick ice cream with berries and what you like."

"Thank you Mr. Bjørnsen."

"You call me Nils and I call you Max. Mr. Bjørnsen, that is an old man with two teeth and goat feet who steals the milk from the farmers. You heard of trolls?"

The boy's forehead wrinkled in confusion. "No."

Nils stood and, motioning with his hand for Max to join him, said, "I tell you about them."

As Max and Nils left for the ice-cream stand, Anna looked after them and smiled contently. They were becoming fast friends. Her brother enjoyed the role of teacher and baseball mentor to a man twice his age. Max was used to taking direction and advice from his elders, so to have the tables turned gave him a feeling of importance and responsibility. Anna hoped that, as Max grew up, he would not lose his friendly and outgoing personality and be crushed by the demands of taking over Papa's business. He had no interest in shoe repair whatsoever, so why shouldn't he follow his dream of being a baseball newspaperman? *This is America after all, where anyone can be someone.*

Max came back several minutes later, licking a big scoop of vanilla ice cream as it melted into a waffle cone. Nils handed Anna a cone of vanilla with cherries, then sat beside her. She struggled to remember the word for thank you in Norwegian.

"*Tusen takk.* Is that how you say thank you?"

"Yes, you remember your Norwegian well. *Tusen takk* to you and Max for the game. So, St. Paul team is the best this time?" The game was in the 9th inning and the St. Paul Prophets were leading 6-2.

Max answered. "The St. Paul Prophets win almost all the time. Those Minneapolis players don't know how to pitch, or field, or hit. Come on, let's go to the lot and I will show you the Rappaport pitch. I just have to run home and get the ball and bat."

"You go on, Max," Anna said as they all stood and headed for the tiered aisle. "We'll meet you at the lot. The last thing I want Mama to see is all three of us walking home together. I guarantee our supper will be stuck in our throats if that happens."

Anna grasped Nils' hand as Max raced down the stairs. She had another reason to send her little brother ahead. She wanted to spend some time alone with Nils.

* * *

Max ran home and never once thought of recording his ball game conversations into his notebook. As far as he was concerned, Nils Bjørnsen was a nice fellow and treated his sister very well. *Mama, as usual, is getting worried over nothing.*

Grisha was sitting on the front steps sulking. "Rivka kicked me out 'cause I'm bothering her. She is writing a com...composition. Where were you?"

"Oh, places." Max kicked his shoe against the bottom step and glanced down the street as he evaded the question. He knew Grisha would be heartbroken if he found out about the game.

"Places. Like the ballpark?"

"Who told you?" Max cringed inwardly, aware he just gave himself away.

"Nobody. Why didn't you take me?"

"Because little kids were not allowed today."

"You're lying!" Grisha's eyes welled with tears. "I hate you!" The younger brother rose to run upstairs to the apartment, and Max's mind whirled. Grisha's tears, he knew, would bring pointed questions from his mother about the "spying adventure." He had no choice but to let his little brother in on the secret and hope that fear would force him to keep it.

"Grisha, wait," Max said, following his brother to the top of the stairs. "I have to tell you something."

"What? That it was a good game and that you had an ice cream cone." Grisha noticed crumbs of waffle cone around Max's mouth, sniffled, then rubbed his sleeve against his nose. "Who won?"

"St. Paul, of course. Grisha, you have to keep a secret, because if you tell anything to Mama, I will kill you. I will sit on your face, break your legs, twist your neck, and I mean it. You promise."

"Promise."

"Let me get the ball and bat and I will tell you more on the way to the lot." Max ran upstairs and breathed a sigh of relief when he found Rivka alone in the house, poring over books for her school report. Their mother was at Mrs. Simkin's, 'scheming over Anna's future,' as Rivka put it.

"Tell her me and Grisha are playing ball at the lot, okay?" Max rushed out the door and joined his brother, who waited on the front steps.

"Grisha." Max lowered his voice to a conspiratorial tone as they started walking down the street. "Here's what happened. Mama is all worried about Anna and that Norwegian fellow, and she asked me to find out what they do every Sunday. The good thing is that I will get a dollar from her for this job and, next week, you and I are going to the ballpark and you can buy all the candy, peanuts, ice cream and soda you want. I am getting a score card, myself."

Grisha wiped the tears on his sleeve again and, stopping, stared wide-eyed at his brother. "A whole dollar? You're not making this up?"

"Yes, a whole dollar," Max said as they continued walking. "So, you know how I earned it? Very simple. I really did not want to spend the whole afternoon following my sister, so I asked her if she was interested in taking Nils, that's his name, to a baseball game. That way I could sit with them, watch the game, *and* get paid for it."

Grisha's brown eyes widened even more with admiration. "Max, you are really smart to think up a plan like that."

Max raised his chin a notch. "So, she and Nils went to the game and I explained how to play baseball, and you know what, he bought me and Anna ice cream."

"So why couldn't I come along, especially if someone was buying ice cream?"

"Because Anna was afraid you would tell Mama that we all went to the game, and then I won't be getting the dollar. Now that you know, don't you dare squeal."

"I promise. I did not hear anything. Just get the dollar for next week, okay?"

"I can almost feel it in my pocket, Grisha. Can you just picture Isaac, Sammy, Boris, and the other boys turning green from watching us with our candy, ice cream, program, and scorecards? I can't wait until next Sunday."

The boys were almost to the vacant lot when Max noticed his sister sitting on the grass, with Nils' arm around her shoulder.

Grisha saw them as well. His brow wrinkled with curiosity as he turned to his older brother. "Hey, Max, what's Anna doing at the lot? Is that the fellow who bought you ice cream?"

Max nodded. "I promised to let him take a few swings with the bat. I think he understands the game and, if he's good, we'll put him on our team and whip the Irish kids."

"But that won't be fair, because he's a grown-up."

"It is to fair, because he has never played baseball and we're just trying him out."

"Jimmy Finnegan will tell you that's a bunch of horse shit." Grisha smacked the palm of his hand over his mouth and attempted to swallow the swear word.

Max seized the opportunity to exploit his brother's mistake. "Now we're even. You don't know nothing about today's game, and I never heard what you just said. Deal?"

"Deal." The brothers slapped each other's hands and walked towards Anna and Nils.

Max paused beside the tall man. "Nils, are you ready to hit some balls? This is my brother Grisha, and he is a big baseball fan."

Grisha squinted and looked Nils over. "So, you're the Norwegian that Mama does not want Anna to see? You gonna marry her instead of Benny Simkin?"

Instantly, Anna's cheeks warmed with embarrassment. She rushed to upbraid her brother before Nils could answer the boy's prying inquiry. "Grisha! Didn't you learn any manners? When you first meet a new person, you don't start asking dumb questions. You introduce yourself as Gershon Katz and extend your right hand. Then you say, 'I am pleased to meet you.'"

Grisha parroted Anna's words and shook hands with Nils.

Anna turned to Nils. "You have to excuse my brother. He repeats what he hears at home." Anna paused a moment as she considered how to tactfully diffuse the comment about Benny Simkin. "That Benny fellow he mentioned, there's nothing to it. For the past four years, Mama and Mrs. Simkin have been working on arranging a marriage, like in the old country. Even Papa thinks it's a big joke, but it keeps Mama busy. Benny is actually sweet on my sister, which is just fine with me. I would rather be bitten by a snake than go with him."

Nils frowned, unsure of what to make of Anna's arranged marriage "joke" in the Katz family. "Why is that?"

"Because Benny does not exist," she replied. "He is not a person. He is a shadow behind Mr. and Mrs. Simkin. He won't say a word without looking around to make sure that they approve. I have my doubts that they even allow him to breathe on his own." Anna paused as Max motioned for Nils to play ball, and changed the subject. "Nils, why don't you try to hit some baseballs? I know Max was anxious to teach you. I brought a book along, so I'm fine right here on the grass on a beautiful spring evening."

Nils rose and nodded. "You are right. I play little game with your brothers. Sometimes, it is good to forget that tomorrow I work a long day, and be ten years old again."

Anna watched as Nils ran off to join Max and Grisha and smiled as the two boys put him through an intense practice of pitching and hitting. At first Nils swung wildly, not connecting the bat with the ball, and the boys delighted in yelling "strike!" With Max's consistent pitching, however, Nils finally got the knack of knowing exactly when to swing the bat. Soon, the balls flew a hundred feet out.

Grisha chased a ball, then returned and tossed it to his older brother. "Max, now that we know he can hit a home run, teach him how to pitch."

Max nodded. He noticed how his younger brother ran slower and slower each time he chased the balls to retrieve them. "Okay," he replied.

As the boys switched places, Nils glanced toward Anna who, true to her words, sat quietly reading her book. He studied her for several moments, enjoying the way the sunlight reddened her long hair, and the gentle curves of her face. He returned his attention to the boys and began to throw the ball, but soon realized that he needed to adjust the speed and force of the throw, depending on whether Max or Grisha was at bat. Max turned most of Nils' wild pitches into salvageable hits, while Grisha swung and missed.

"Throw it underhand to Grisha," Max yelled. "It will be easier for him to hit."

Soon, Grisha's ability to strike the ball improved substantially. Slowly, a small group of boys started to gather around them, and Nils found himself pitching to redheaded Irish twins of about eight with missing front teeth, three Jewish kids near Max and Grisha's age, and a chubby blond Russian boy. The kids were eager to get a chance to practice hitting without taking a turn to pitch, and Nils did not mind.

Anna lowered her book and watched Nils. *He would make a good father—someone who is patient and would spend time with the children.* She loved Papa dearly, but he would never take the time to play baseball with Max and Grisha. The business, *bar-mitzvahs*, and reading the newspaper took precedence. Those were a man's adult affairs, once he left his childhood behind. *Perhaps children were raised differently in Norway, or maybe Nils treats everyone he meets with kindness and consideration.*

She got up from the grass and walked toward the baseball players.

"Max, Grisha, it's almost dinner time and you are tiring out Nils' arm. He has to work a long day tomorrow, and we better be getting home."

"All right." Max yelled to his brother. "Grisha, you're done after this at bat."

"Maxth, doeth your thither like the pitcher?" lisped the twins simultaneously.

Max ignored the question and shrugged his shoulders as Nils approached. He handed Max the ball. "Thank you, Max, for a fun afternoon."

Max smiled as another idea struck him. *Since the cat requested me to spy on the mouse, I might as well bring the mouse right to the cat. Mama can ask Nils whatever she wants herself and leave me out of it from now on.*

"Nils, why don't you come to dinner with us. Mama is a good cook, and I know she was interested in meeting you."

Nils hesitated at the offer. He was anxious to meet Anna's parents and make a good impression on them. Her father seemed friendly enough at the shoe repair shop, but the older man did not know that he was seeing Anna. *Maybe Anna's mother would change her mind once she realized that a Norwegian man is not so different from a Russian or a Jewish one.* "Well, thank you, Max." He glanced at Anna, waiting for her response.

Anna lowered her head. Max's sudden invitation surprised her, and she was not sure what to make of it. The more she got to know Nils, the more she wanted a serious friendship. She knew that, at some point, he would have to meet her parents. Despite her mother's animosity toward non-Jews, she would at least have the civility to feed Nils.

"I think Max has an excellent idea," she said, raising her head to meet Nils' expectant eyes. "Come to dinner with us."

Grisha piped in. "Mama is making a honey cake. She told me so, and it is very good."

"Okay," Nils answered, then smiled broadly. "I come with you. I try Russian food."

The other boys left as Max led the way across the five short blocks from the lot to the Katz apartment. Max opened the door and ushered in his brother, sister, and Nils. The table was already set, no doubt by Rivka. He found his father reading the newspaper in his chair.

His mother appeared in the kitchen door. "It's about time. Who is this?" Her eyes narrowed with disdain as she glanced at Nils, then wiped her hands on her apron.

Max decided to make the introduction. "Mama, Papa, Rivka. This is Nils Bjørnsen. We went to the baseball game and he was very kind to buy us ice cream and throw pitches at the lot. So, I thought we could have him over for dinner."

Moyshe, immediately recognizing Nils as the fellow who played the fiddle at the shop, set his paper aside. Rivka just looked on with curiosity.

Sarah's face remained impassive, although anger made her blood boil. She swallowed hard and squeezed out a, "Pleased to meet you." Sarah turned to face her family. "As we have a guest, you all take care of him, and I will serve dinner." With that, she disappeared into the kitchen.

Sarah's hands shook with fury as she set out Nils' plate, filled it with soup and then poured in a large handful of salt. His potatoes received more salt, and then some onions, pepper and mustard for good measure. She left a measly amount of meat on the chicken and put the salted bones on the plate, then she peered out into the parlor and addressed the guest. "Do you drink wine with your dinner?"

"No," Nils answered. " I do not drink wine or whiskey. Not good for my head."

"See how your head feels after this," Sarah said through gritted teeth as she dumped another handful of salt into Nils' water glass.

She glanced into the parlor. Moyshe was showing Nils his violin. Anna sat at the table and moved her head away as Rivka leaned forward to whisper in her ear. She heard Max recapping a baseball game for Grisha and knew then, that the uninvited guest had somehow swayed Max in his favor. *Well, we'll see about that!* she thought as she called them to dinner.

Nils took several swallows of the soup and fought the urge to gag. *Maybe, it's a special Russian dish,* he thought and took a sip of water to kill the salty taste. To his surprise, his water glass contained a liquid more suitable for herring swimming in the fjord. Nils looked around. Everyone else was eating their food with no trouble. He forced himself to eat the full bowl of soup.

Sarah served the chicken and potatoes next. Nils said a silent prayer of thanks. As far as he knew, potatoes were cooked the same all over the world and, although these were in some kind of sauce, they looked safe. He took a forkful and swallowed a mixture of salt, pepper, mustard and onion. Tears filled his eyes and he started coughing. Again, he reached for his water glass and took a large gulp of the salty water, which brought on another coughing spell.

Sarah leaned forward, her face creased with concern. "Do you want more salt on your potatoes?"

Nils' eyes widened in horror as she pushed the salt shaker toward him. Any pretensions he had of making a decent impression on Anna's family vanished as he forced himself to finish the dinner. He knew it was proper to leave a clean plate, but the price he paid for civility grew unbearable. *Either I am not used to Russian food or I am getting seriously ill.*

Nils glanced at Anna, whose eyes were filled with concern. Just then, her mother began to ask him questions about where he worked, how much money he made, who his parents were, and how he spent his free time. He answered in gasping monosyllables between coughing, blowing his nose, and wiping tears from his eyes.

Moyshe had enough of his wife's meddling and spoke up. "Sarah, will you leave the man in peace. Don't you see he is not feeling well?"

"I am not feeling so well," Sarah replied, "considering the consumptive character Anna is seeing. Young man, how long have you had this cough? It could be very contagious." A smile played around the corners of her mouth before she added, "Would you like some dessert?"

Nils realized he had an avenue for escape—one he needed desperately. He stood and spoke in a rush. "I go now. I do not want you to get sick. I am very sorry. Thank you for dinner."

The Katz's living room became a blur as he stumbled out door and down the stairs. He managed to walk about half a block before he collapsed in someone's hedge and vomited the remains of the most distasteful dinner he ever had in his life.

I am no better than Oskar, he thought as he rose, holding onto the hedge for support. He felt slightly better, but was extremely thirsty. The salt had coated his mouth and he swore that, if he could find a dirty puddle of water, he would lap it up like a stray dog. As he started on the long walk home, he searched for signs of water, but it was Sunday night and the pubs and stores had already closed. He walked about a mile before he sat down on the sidewalk to rest. *I can't walk another four miles. Not in this miserable condition.*

Nils heard the distant rumble of thunder and decided to wait for the storm. He said a silent prayer of thanks as the heavy downpour from the late spring thunderstorm rolled through St. Paul. Within seconds, his clothes were soaked clear through, but Nils did not complain. Instead, he bent back his head, cupped his hands around his mouth and began to gulp the precious water.

Grisha stood off to the side after Nils' sudden departure, watching as his family silently busied themselves in newspapers, homework, books, and washing the dishes. He thought it funny that no one discussed what happened at dinner, especially since that nice man had played baseball with him and Max.

Grisha gave a shrug of his shoulders and glanced toward the kitchen, then the table, where Nils' piece of honey cake lay temptingly on a dessert plate. The boy wanted a second piece and even the word 'consumption' did not deter him. Grisha passed by the plate, quickly stuffed the piece of cake in his pocket, and slipped into his and Max's bedroom. He took a big bite, anticipating a sweet honey taste, and gagged. Grisha spit the piece of cake out and ran to the bathroom. It was locked and Mama told him from the inside that she would be a minute.

Nils might be a good pitcher, but why would he put salt and pepper on dessert? Norwegians must have strange customs. He wanted a drink of water desperately. He ran into the living room and noticed a half-full glass that was left on the table. Grisha reached for it, took a big gulp, then promptly spit it out. The contents ended up on the tablecloth. Grisha replaced the glass and yelled, his voice filled with complete frustration. "What is with all the salt?"

Moyshe was so startled by the boy's scream that he put aside his paper. "Salt? What do you mean?"

"Well, I saw during dinner that Nils never ate his dessert, so I took it just now, Grisha admitted with a sheepish grin. "I don't think he even touched it, if you're afraid he has con...consumption. I ate a piece of the cake and it was saltier than peanuts at a ballgame, and it even had pepper inside it, so I ran in here to get some water. It tasted like pickle juice. I didn't know whose glass this was. Will I get sick now? Do Norwegians like salt a lot?"

Moyshe exchanged glances with Anna. He knew instantly who was responsible for the ruined food and Nils' sudden illness. Judging from Anna's tight lips, she knew as well. Moyshe smiled down at Grisha and patted his shoulder reassuringly. "You have nothing to worry about. Some people like to put salt on different foods." Grisha went into the kitchen and drank himself full from the faucet.

Just then, Sarah entered the living room and headed for the table to clear away the remaining dinner dishes. She turned her gaze to Moyshe's stony look, to Anna's angry glare, and then to the table again. The cake was gone, and she knew precisely who had taken it. Grisha! *He just had to ruin everything,* she thought. *I'll box his ears for swiping that cake!*

"Sarah," Moyshe said in a voice that was tight with rancor. "I would not treat a mangy, stray dog the way you treated our guest tonight."

Sarah glanced at him through wide eyes that feigned ignorance. "What do you mean?"

"Don't play innocent with me! You put so much salt on that Norwegian's plate, I am surprised he did not turn into a pickled herring right here at the table."

"That will teach him to stay away from our daughter."

"He will stay away from the shop as well," Moyshe replied, "and tell his Norskie friends to do the same. You just lost me a customer, and then some."

"Why would you want to fix his dirty shoes? I don't consider it a loss at all."

"Because he asked me to and, unlike many of my Jewish customers, the Scandinavians always pay on time. I seem to remember having the same conversation with you a week ago about whose money puts food on this table."

Sarah's face flushed in anger as she untied her apron and threw it on a nearby chair. "Why is it that you are so kind and concerned about your *goy* friends and customers? You know what the *Torah* says about mixing with the gentiles. I am ashamed of you, Moyshe Katz! Compromising the faith of your fathers to make an easy dollar on a Swede and leading your daughter by example."

Moyshe moved to stand before her. "Don't you quote the *Torah* to me, woman! You know perfectly well that I have been an observant Jew all the years we have been married. Name me a *Shabbos when* I wasn't at synagogue? Have I ever forgotten to say the dinner blessing? But there is more to being a Jew than following all the rules in the *Torah* and *Talmud*. You remember that God gave Moses the Ten Commandments, and that the last of them was to love your neighbor as yourself. If I treat this Bjørnsen fellow like some kind of *no-goodnik*, what is he going to think? 'Aha, just as I thought, a crooked, dirty Jew.' But, if I show him that I respect him and treat him well, he will walk away with an impression that I am decent man. You see, Sarah, the gentiles have persecuted us Jews for so long that we have to work twice as hard to look good. That's what I try to do in my business and with anyone that comes to my house."

"Moyshe, it's no use talking to you. You're putting your business ahead of your daughter's future. I am going to bed and, Anna, I don't want to see that miserable creature set foot in my house ever again. The diseases he could pass to the children, feh." Sarah spat into her hand and disappeared into the bedroom.

Anna's eyes welled with tears of frustration and resentment. Her mother's reaction made it obvious that she would never accept Nils. Worse, she would make every attempt to destroy their friendship. Why, her mother's actions bordered on deliberate harm, if not outright poisoning. *Why can't Mama be as reasonable and calm as Papa?* she thought as she sank to the sofa and covered her face.

Moyshe released a heavy sigh as he moved to sit next to his daughter. "I am sorry your friend had such an awful meal, but I think we can do something tomorrow to make up for it."

"What can we possibly do?" Anna wiped at the tears that rolled down her face. "Nils will probably never want to see any of us again, and I wouldn't blame him one bit."

"Well, I still have his boots and they are all done, good as new. I told him to pick them up this Thursday, but the least I can do is to not charge him for the repair." Moshe paused to grin at Anna. "In fact, I have his address in my book and I thought we could drop them off tomorrow after work and apologize for my wife's bad cooking."

Anna sniffled, then returned his smile. "I think I would throw in a couple of bottles of water with the boots. He might need it."

Her father laughed. "Come to the shop at seven and we'll take the streetcar. I wanted to see that Norwegian fiddle of his anyhow. I know the boys think the world of this fellow, but it would be best if just you and I paid him a visit. Now, Anna," he said, giving her hand a gentle squeeze, "try to get some sleep. Tomorrow will be a better day."

"Thank you, Papa. I am sure tomorrow will be better." Anna gave her father a kiss on the cheek, and then rose to prepare for bed. She stumbled into Grisha in the dark hallway.

Before she could say anything, he tugged on her arm and motioned for her to lean down, then whispered into her ear. "Me and Max think Nils is the best fellow, lots better than Benny. We really like him, even if he does put salt on his cake. I think Papa likes him too, but is afraid to say it. I don't care if he is not Jewish, like Mama does. He can sure pitch." Grisha paused then, and handed a worn baseball to Anna. "I heard you and Papa are going to his house tomorrow. Here, this is from me and Max, okay?"

Moisture again tinged her eyes as Anna gave her little brother a hug, comforted that at least most of her family actually likes Nils.

She smiled as her little brother ran to his bedroom, then walked into her own and faced Rivka. "Well, what do you think?"

Her sister's shoulders rose and fell in a non-committal shrug. "What am I supposed to think? That he is wonderful or something? Sorry, Anna, he does not pass my inspection. You bring some coughing Norwegian here, upset Mama, and expect me to like him. He doesn't even know how to eat with a knife and fork. I watched him. You saw him blow his nose into a napkin. No manners." She paused to catch her breath, then added, " I honestly don't know what you see in him."

Anna's eyes widened with surprise at her sister's criticism. Rivka, the peacemaker and compromiser, suddenly exposed her harsher side.

"Rivka, didn't you hear Grisha gag on the cake just now? You know perfectly well that Mama over salted Nils' food. I don't think I would remember my manners if I was being poisoned. He had enough manners to clean up his plate. He is probably throwing it up as we speak."

Rivka shook her head in disbelief. "I won't be so sure he didn't salt the food himself, and then blame us. You know, it's always the Jews' fault." She paused a moment, then her voice grew soft. "Anna, you probably hate me right now, but I am not trying to be mean. It's just that you are breaking Mama's heart, and that will break our family. He might be a nice fellow, but think about it. If you marry him, you will never see any of us again; or if you do, it would have to be on some street corner. Just think about the future. Good night." Rivka turned off the light.

Anna remained silent as she considered her sister's words, then began to undress. "All right, little sister. I will think about it."

Chapter Eight

Anna walked into Katz's Shoe Repair promptly at seven carrying a small package that contained two bottles of fruit-flavored water, a poppy seed cake from the bakery next to her home, Grisha's baseball, and a note for Nils. Moyshe grabbed Nils' boots and locked the shop.

They boarded the streetcar and, within a half hour, arrived in the northeast side of the city. They walked only a short distance on Cayuga Street before they heard the sound of Nils' Norwegian fiddle. The melody flowed toward them, alternating between a sound similar to a trilling bird song and a bubbling brook. Anna stopped on the sidewalk to listen, then closed her eyes as Nils' music resonated within her.

Moyshe's voice broke through her dreamy trance. "I never imagined that a violin could sound so beautiful. I can't wait to take a look at its construction." He took her arm. "It will sound even better once we actually see him play."

Anna and Moyshe neared the house and noticed two men sitting on the front steps drinking beer. Anna's brow creased in a frown as she paused beside the front gate. She remembered Nils telling her that he lived with a cousin and a Danish boarder, who were far too friendly with the bottle. She could not recall their names, but believed one was named Odd something or other.

Both men turned their way as Anna and Moyshe walked up the sidewalk toward the porch. Oddleif eyed the pretty redheaded girl and older gentleman who entered their yard, then scratched his head as he searched for the correct English words. When he finally spoke, his slurred voice reflected his drunken state. "You here to see Kjersti about the baby bed and clothes?"

Moyshe shook his head as both he and Anna stopped before them. "No. Does Nils Bjørnsen live here? We are here to see him."

Oskar pointed to the attic with an upraised thumb. "You hear the fiddle. That mean he is here." His gaze lowered again to skim Anna's body. "You the Russian girl and that's your father?"

"Yes." Anna nodded. *So, Nils mentioned me, but what did he tell them?*

"You come here with more salt, eh?" Oskar grinned and continued. "He never had Russian food before. Was in the kitchen for an hour drinking glass after glass of water."

Moyshe glanced at Anna and noticed the deep red tinge that crept into her checks. He cleared his throat as he faced the two men. "My wife got a little happy with the salt, so Anna and I decided to make up for last night's dinner. We came to deliver some good food and Mr. Bjørnsen's shoes. You are...?"

"Oddleif Pedersen," he replied as he stared at the shiny black boots. They bore no resemblance to the scuffed-up, worn-through things that Nils owned. "You mean these are his old boots?" he asked incredulously.

"That they are. Moyshe Katz of Katz's Shoe Repair." He extended his hand to Oddleif. "I am on the corner of Snelling and Highland. You bring shoes to my shop, I give you a 25% Norwegian discount. Tell your friends, I do good work at a good price."

"Ja, we will. You give Danish discount too?" He waited until Moyshe shook Oskar's hand, then added, "Oskar is not Norwegian."

Moyshe's face broke in a broad grin. "All right, for Oskar, I will make it a Scandinavian discount."

Anna watched the exchange and smiled inwardly. Her father probably just gained himself two new customers, if not more.

Oskar turned to Oddleif and said something in Danish. Oddleif nodded and motioned Oskar to speak. "You know, you come here with new shoes and a nice gift for Nils, like you want to marry off your daughter, not because of salty dinner. That's good, because she marry the best Norwegian in St. Paul. Me and Oddleif, we work, we come home, we drink, we sleep and next day we do the same thing." Oskar took a swig out of the beer bottle to underscore his point. "Nils, he don't drink or smoke, never miss a Sunday at church, reads books, can fix anything—has hands of gold. See the fence, swing for Solveig, picnic table," he said, nodding his head toward each item. "Made it all himself. He play his fiddle for dances, but never dance. Anna, she marry him, he treat her very good, no bad words. She is a lucky girl to meet a fellow like him, isn't she Oddleif?"

Oddleif slapped Oskar on the shoulder and took over the praises of his cousin. "Oskar is right. I know my cousin from Norway. Bjørn Hansen, that's Nils' father, died when he was seventeen. Nils was the oldest and took over the farm. Like Oskar said, golden hands for work. I know Nils all my life—he don't talk much, but think a lot and always does what is right. You get married, you be very happy. I bet you a hundred dollars."

Anna lowered her gaze to the ground as her cheeks flamed with the heat of embarrassment. If anything, Oddleif and Oskar reinforced what she already knew about Nils *and* gave her father an opinion not tainted by her mother's prejudice.

Oskar and Oddleif rose simultaneously. "We go tell Nils you are here."

Nils heard the heavy clomping coming up the steps and, when Oskar and Oddleif entered his room, stopped playing. Their news that he had guests sparked his curiosity and he rushed downstairs. His lips curved in a wide grin when he saw Anna and her father standing on the front stoop of his house. Nils stepped forward and shook hands with Moyshe. He wondered all through the workday how he would explain to Anna about last night's dinner without offending her mother's cooking. He was certain that the rest of the family's impression of him was dismal.

Moyshe broke the awkward silence. "I want to apologize for my wife's cooking. She is not used to new people and, well, this time she went a little heavy on the salt. Since the dinner caused you a lot of trouble, I thought the least I could do is deliver your boots. Here, try them on."

Nils eyes widened in disbelief as he took the boots from Moyshe's outstretched hands. *These can't be mine. I can barely recognize them.* "Thank you. They are like new. How much I owe you? I pay for delivery, too."

Moyshe shrugged his shoulders and dismissed Nils' offer with a wave of his hand. "You don't owe me anything. All I ask is to see your fiddle. I heard you play and I just want to see how you do it on eight strings. Beautiful music."

"Ja," Nils replied, unable to keep the pleasure from creeping into his voice. "I show you my *hardingfele*. It is very kind of Anna and you to come, and thank you again for fixing my shoes."

Anna waited until Nils' eyes locked with hers before she stepped forward and handed him her package. "This is something from the rest of us. Hopefully, you will think better about Russian food. I am sorry about dinner last night."

Nils stared at the package for a few moments, embarrassed by the gifts and attention, before he again met Anna's gaze. "Please, do not apologize. Thank you so much for everything. I go and bring the fiddle."

He turned on his heel and bounded up the stairs two steps at a time, elated that Anna still wanted his friendship. He placed the gift on his bed, grabbed the fiddle, and returned to Anna and her father.

Moyshe's eyes were bright with curiosity as he accepted the instrument Nils handed him. "Fascinating," he said as his fingers traced the mother-of-pearl inlay on the fingerboard and around the edges of the violin. He brought the fiddle closer to his face to examine the intricate flower and leaf designs inked on the wood. "It is so exquisitely decorated and looks more like a work of art than a violin. Quite a fearsome dragon on the scroll. I better hand it back to you, before it breathes fire on me." Moyshe returned the fiddle to Nils.

Anna looked at the gaping wooden mouth, pointed ivory teeth and protruding tongue and recalled Nils' story of the Vikings. "Papa, Nils told me that in the old days, Norwegians put these dragons on their ships. I suppose I would be scared if I saw a ship with a big dragon head coming right for me."

Nils chuckled. "Now, there is no Vikings and only little dragons on fiddles, so you do not be afraid." He turned toward Moyshe and showed the four understrings that gave the *hardingfele* its distinct sound. "I play you two dance tunes from Voss, Norway."

Nils drew the bow over the strings and, once again, Anna was mesmerized by the beautiful music that flowed toward her. She found herself in a trance, but now she could fix her gaze on the handsome man playing the fiddle, savoring the music and wishing the moment would never end. An involuntary sigh of disappointment escaped her as the last note echoed through the air and Nils handed the fiddle to Moyshe.

"Here, try it. It is like your violin."

"Thank you," Moyshe said as he ran his fingers over the strings. With every bow stroke, the violin resonated in unexpected overtones, grating on Moyshe's ear. He shook his head after a few minutes. "I tried a gypsy tune, but it sounds odd. I better let the master have it. If you got time, come to the shoe shop and teach me to play one of your Norwegian tunes. I'll trade you for a Russian one."

Nils grasped the fiddle and bow the older man held toward him, then inclined his head in a nod. "I do that, and I tell people that you fix shoes good. Thank you again for them."

Moyshe turned to Anna. "Well, it's getting late, so we better be going."

Her father headed toward the gate, and Anna took a step closer to Nils. "Thank you for the music. It is so beautiful. Can I ask you to play just for me sometime?"

She extended her hand in a farewell gesture. Nils grasped it within his own and ran his thumb across her palm. He looked staight into her emerald-green eyes. "If you ask, I play for you. I can say more with music than with my bad English. Thank you that you come here."

Anna withdrew her hand and whispered for his ears alone. "See you next week."

Nils stared after them until father and daughter disappeared from sight, then raced up the stairs. He closed the door to his room before Oddleif and Oskar could begin their drunken inquisition. His brow wrinkled in curiosity as he reached for the little lumpy package that Anna gave him. Nils untied the twine and opened it. A worn baseball rolled to the floor, accompanied by a note scrawled in a child's handwriting. It was from Grisha. *"Nils, thanks for pitching for us. You can practice with this ball. I have another one. Me and Max think you are great, even if you put a lot of salt on your food. You can come to the game with us any time. Grisha."*

He smiled as he retrieved the ball and placed it on a nearby table, then viewed the contents that remained in the package: a poppy seed cake, two bottles of soda water, and a folded note with his name. He reached immediately for the note and, as he opened it, the faint scent of rosewater drifted his way. He knew then that it was from Anna.

"Dear Nils," he read. *"I am so sorry about my mother's cooking making you sick. Here is some water, because you might still be thirsty after last night! No matter what she does, I very much would like to see you again. Your friendship means a lot to me, and now to my brothers. Thank you so much for spending time with them.*

"This Sunday, I have to be at a union meeting, preparing for the picnic next week. We could use help with the signs, so if you have time you can meet me at Pinehurst and Cleveland at two o'clock. Otherwise, I will be done at four and I will see you then.

"The cake is a traditional desert from the old country. I hope it is as sweet as you have been to me. Your friend, Anna."

Nils' heart tightened as he lowered her note, rubbed the mist out of his eyes, and then released a heavy sigh. Next Sunday was so far off, and all he wanted was to hold Anna in his arms.

Chapter Nine

Anna turned the corner a block from her apartment building, then paused when Mrs. Meier pulled her aside. "Anna, how could you. Think of your poor Mama. Bringing disease to your family." Mrs. Meier's eyes widened as she covered her mouth and took several steps backward. "Come to think of it, you probably have it yourself. Good day."

Anna stared after the older woman. Mrs. Meier's comments made it clear that her mother was determined to have her way and had even resorted to spreading the word that Nils was her daughter's "hacking, consumptive" Norwegian acquaintance.

Fanny, her best friend, was even less kind as they headed for work the following morning. "Jacob gave me a gold necklace with earrings. Isn't that romantic? And what did your Norwegian give you? A mouthful of spit!" The other girl crinkled her nose in disgust.

Anna's eyes stung with hurt and humiliation. "I thought you were my friend, Fanny. Mama put so much salt and pepper on the food, the poor fellow almost died. He is perfectly healthy, strong as a horse." Her friend's brow dipped with doubt. "Don't you believe me?"

"No, Anna, I don't," Fanny retorted. "All the neighbors are talking about it. Mrs. Shapiro swears her husband saw a drunken Norskie throwing up in the hedge half a block from your house Sunday night."

Anna changed the subject, since the "Norskie" might well have been Nils. "The union picnic is in two weeks. Do you think you have any time to help me post signs? If not, bring Jacob. There is going to be food and dancing."

"Actually," Fanny replied in a stiff voice. "I am busy and, to tell you the truth, I don't really want to go to a union *anything*. Once I get married, no more factory, no more streetcar. I get myself a maid and a carriage. What will I care about a union? The Hirsches are too wealthy to mingle with the workers at a picnic. Think about it. Could a ring be far behind the necklace and earrings?"

Anna glared at Fanny. "Fine, do nothing. As far as I can see, you don't have the ring yet. You're not married, and you're on the streetcar going to work in a sweatshop for the next ten hours. Personally, I would like to work eight hours and get paid a decent wage. I will fight for my, and your right, to do so. I would not be so sure about being Mrs. Jacob Hirsch."

Fanny's eyes narrowed with anger. "I can be more sure of being Mrs. Jacob Hirsch than you can of becoming Mrs. what's his name, Olsen or Larsen." Fanny paused, then lowered her voice and put her face to Anna's ear. "Anna, listen to me, you don't want to get sick. What about your family? You let Max and Grisha play baseball with him. They probably already caught it. How can you be so selfish?"

"I have been your friend for eight years, and I told you why Nils was sick. But no, you would rather believe all the Mrs. Simkins and Meiers, gossips that they are, than me! I have nothing else to say to you." Anna turned and blinked away tears of frustration as she stared through the streetcar window.

Her life was becoming a nightmare and, in fact, her father warned her of that possibility the past Monday evening as they headed home from Nils'.

"Be careful, Anna," he said. "Your mother has the ability to spread the most damaging and noxious gossip. She will not stop, especially when it concerns her own daughter." Moyshe paused a moment before he added, "Nils is a fine fellow and would be a good son-in-law if you married him, but— " there was always a 'but' "—he is not Jewish and that would be a problem for your Mama, for the family, for my business, for the neighbors and, ultimately, for you."

Anna's shoulders rose and fell in a heavy sigh as she continued staring through the window. She was already beginning to feel how big of a problem it was.

Anna avoided Fanny and the neighbors for the rest of the week, and hardly spoke to her family. Rivka's rejection of Nils stung her. She could not believe her own sister would side with their mother.

Grisha asked her if Nils was going to the baseball game on Sunday, but Anna did not know. When she told Grisha to go with his older brother, she learned that her mother never paid Max for his spying efforts and also withheld his allowance for bringing the "consumptive Norwegian" into the house. As a result, the boys did not even have a quarter for the game.

Anna stood at the usual street corner at two o'clock on Sunday. Nils, who was always early, did not appear. She waited for fifteen minutes before she walked to the union meeting with a heavy step and her head hung low. Troubling thoughts ran through her mind. *Maybe he no longer wants to see me. Maybe I forgot to put the note in the package. Or worse, maybe he really is sick, like Mama said.*

She plunged into making picnic signs in Russian and Yiddish at the meeting, but her heart was not in it. She kept looking at the clock and asked Emil Kruse several times to repeat something that she either did not hear or forgot.

Emil's brow furrowed with concern. "Anna, you don't look well. Go on home and rest. We will manage without you. You work enough already."

Anna's thoughts rested on Nils and she stared at Emil for a second until his words registered. She shook her head. "No, I'm fine. Just a headache."

"Then I insist you rest." Emil walked her out of the room. "I can see if any of the fellows drove a wagon to the meeting. We'll get you home."

"That's okay, Emil. By tomorrow, I will be myself again. I am spreading the word at the Garment Works, so hopefully we will have a big turnout."

Anna waved good-bye to Emil and headed home. Nils stood on the corner of Pinehurst and Cleveland, and she stopped dead in her tracks. *Who is the little girl in a blue calico dress, hiding behind his pant legs? Why didn't he tell me he had a child?"*

Nils smiled when he saw Anna walking toward them, and then spoke to the girl in Norwegian. "Solveig, don't be so shy and give Anna the flowers we picked."

The girl poked her blonde, pig-tail adorned head from behind Nils to look at the young woman who stopped before them, then hid herself again.

"I bring children this time. My cousin's wife take care of Henrik. He is sick with bad cold, and Oddleif and Oskar have, how you say it? Overdrinking? So, I take Solveig today. She speaks only Norwegian, but we try to learn English together. I am sorry I cannot be here at two o'clock. I think Solveig like zoo better than union meeting."

Anna bent down to the little girl's level and asked her about the animals at the zoo while Nils translated.

Solveig gave her a timid smile, then handed her a crumpled bunch of pansies and lilies of the valley. Surprised by the gesture, Anna found herself stumbling with the language.

"*Tusen takk*," is all she managed to say. "Nils, what are 'flowers' in Norwegian?"

"*Blomster.*"

"Solveig, *tusen takk for blomster*. Blomster is 'flowers' in English. Can you say flowers?"

The little girl mouthed the word, then her face beamed with sudden curiosity and delight as she pointed to the gray and white cat coming toward them. "*Katt.*"

"That's right, cat." Anna petted the animal and named the English words for eyes, ears, nose, paws, whiskers and tail.

Solveig turned pleading eyes toward Nils and spoke in Norwegian. "Can we take it home for Henrik?"

"No, we cannot take it without knowing who the owner is. What if there is a little girl just like you who lives here and it is her cat. Tomorrow she wakes up and cannot find it anywhere. She will be very sad."

"But can you ask, Uncle Nils. Please?"

"I will try. We'll find you a cat, maybe as big as the one you saw at the zoo. Would you like that?"

"No, just little cat. The zoo cat will eat me and Henrik." Solveig picked up the cat and busied herself with pretending it was a baby.

"Anna, I am sorry we talk Norwegian. I translate for you."

Anna stood and tossed Nils a warm smile. "There is no need to apologize. You speak slowly enough to Solveig so that I can try to learn a few words here and there. It almost reminds me of your fiddle music."

Nils nodded and smiled back. "Ja, Scandinavians do that. We talk high and low and up and down and the Americans think it is because we are stupid. You are the first one to say that it is like the *hardingfele*."

Anna looked at Nils, her green eyes twinkling with admiration. "Because I heard you play and felt like I was dancing in a dream through the forest. I can't describe it. It's magical and I cannot wait to hear more next week at the picnic."

"You say too good things. I just play, but I am glad it make you happy." Nils took Anna's hand in his. "Well, we have a little girl here. She is never tired. I try to think what we can do."

Anna ran some ideas through her head. "Have you been to Minneapolis? I mean, outside of work?"

"No. Too far to walk."

"Would you and Solveig like to take the streetcar to Lake Harriet? There is a place where they play music, and I can buy Solveig an ice cream cone." Solveig heard the word ice cream, whirled, and released the long-suffering cat from her arms.

"That is one English word she knows very well. I buy her one at the zoo. Maybe not good that many in one day. But she never ride on streetcar. She will like that."

Anna and Nils walked to the streetcar stop, while Solveig held their hands and skipped gaily on the cobblestones. Her excitement was obvious, in any language, and when the car came, Solveig dropped the coins into the fare box, tore off the tickets and handed them to the conductor to be punched.

The little girl pressed her nose to the window during the ride, pointed at the people outside and asked Nils question after question, which he was obliged to translate for Anna's sake. Anna's head filled with new Norwegian words. *If they could only stay in there and not go into one ear and out the other!*

The streetcar stopped at the Lake Harriet Bandshell, a gray wooden structure with a stage protected from the rain and a building to the side, which housed concession stands and restrooms. Twenty rows of benches stood in front of the stage to allow people to sit and enjoy the music and ice cream. Anna, Nils and Solveig searched for a seat, but nearly every place was filled, mostly with an upper class audience listening to a medley of Strauss waltzes. The men wore suit coats and ladies boasted hats with varied arrangements of flowers and plumes.

Solveig pointed to the feathers and asked Nils if they were at the zoo again. Nils chuckled and picked out a spot on the grass from which they could still hear the musicians. He read in newspapers about orchestras of many musicians playing different instruments, but had never seen one. A couple of fiddlers and an accordion was the most required for a dance in Voss or here in America, and Nils wondered how fifty people could play, read written music, and look at the man directing, all at the same time. He tried to pick out individual parts, but had difficulty separating them from the entire melody. He gave up finally, and surrendered himself to the music.

Anna glanced at Nils, his blue eyes riveted to the stage, and smiled. *Perhaps listening to the symphony orchestra play has the same magical effect on him as his hardingfele playing has on me.* She listened to the music and kept her eye on Solveig as the little girl ran about. She pretended to dance to the music for several moments before she stopped to talk to a little boy, dressed in a sailor suit. Anna doubted he knew how to speak Norwegian, yet oddly enough, he seemed to understand what Solveig was telling him.

When the music stopped, Nils craned his head to look for his niece. Anna pointed to the group of kids a few feet away. "See, she does not need any English. Children can understand each other in any language."

"You are right," Nils agreed. "They do not care if their friend is Russian, Norwegian, Irish. They play now, but in ten years they learn from their parents about other people. Then they stop to be friends and start saying bad things to each other. That is how war happen." Nils paused for a moment. "Thank you for watching her. I am sorry, I listen to music. I never see so many people play at one time. In Bergen, a big city in Norway, they have a music hall. I wanted to go there and hear Edvard Grieg. He is a Norwegian who writes music for big orchestra, like I play on the *hardingfele*. With farm work, I never have time. He comes to America, so maybe he come to St. Paul and we can go."

Anna hesitated as she thought of Fanny and the Brahms episode. "I have, or maybe I should say *had*, a friend that goes to the symphony. I can ask her about the schedule and prices."

"Why you say you *had* a friend?"

"For the same reasons you mentioned a few minutes ago. When we came to America, Fanny and I became best friends as two immigrant girls from Russia would. We live a few blocks from each other, went to the same school and work at the Garment Factory. But now, the only thing Fanny is interested in is finding a rich husband. She has some fellow who takes her to concerts, but I suspect she is not interested in the music. What hurts me the most is that she believes everything Mama says about you, even though I tell her it's not true. My own sister won't even trust me, Nils."

Anna glanced away so Nils would not see the tears that welled in her eyes. He noticed them anyway and, cupping her chin in the palm of his hand, gently turned her head until their gazes met.

"Anna, you do not have to hide tears from me. I am very sorry I cause you so much trouble. Sometimes I wish I had the farm like in Norway and we go and live there. You have a garden and your chickens. I do the work and play my fiddle. You teach me English and Russian, and I teach you Norwegian. No people to tell us we are doing the wrong thing. But why I talk? We are here. You have family. Forgive me." He released her chin and glanced around to check on Solveig.

"I think about these things too, Nils. I love my family, but there are days I just want to run away from all of them. What if one day I was go to work and not get off at the right stop, but ride as far as the end of the line, and then take the train and another train, and then another train. Then I will be far away. But I am too scared to do it, unless . . ." Anna paused. She knew it was all a whimsical fantasy, so she added, "unless you come with me."

Nils clasped Anna's hands in his. "Anna, I come with you, but I do not want you to leave your family. We take train for a picnic, maybe in summer."

"That's a better idea." Her green eyes lit up with the thought. "We'll look for some mushrooms and berries."

The orchestra began another waltz. Anna glanced down to see Nils beating time with his foot. "You know how to dance a waltz?"

"Ja, I play it so many times and see people do it, but never try. Fiddle player has no break. In Norway, a wedding is three nights, so I work on the farm in the day and play at night. I drink many cups of coffee, otherwise I go to sleep."

"Papa plays for the *bar-mitzvah* and they give him wine. He comes home happy enough from it."

"I try that when I was young—beer, Norwegian whiskey. But it is no good. I cannot play with heavy head, and not for three nights. In Voss, the fellows getting married ask for me, because they can dance and drink so long. Do you know how to dance?"

Anna's shoulders rose and fell in a shrug. "Not really. It is not something a good Jewish girl does. My sister and I pretended when we were about Solveig's age, like little girls always do. You know, a couple fellows offered to show me how, but I want to wait until I find the right person." Anna smiled and looked into Nils' eyes. "We can try next week at the picnic. You are not the only fiddler, so you will get your break, and we can see about making our four feet try something they have never done before."

"I try, but I think I play fiddle better than I dance." Nils faced the orchestra, hiding the joy that filled his chest. He was certain that he was the right person for Anna, and there was no doubt in his mind that this was the girl he was going to marry. *God arranged a chance meeting on a street corner a month ago for a purpose. Perhaps, I should ask her next week at the picnic.* The only problem he foresaw was her mother, but he did not want to think about Sarah Katz. Not now, when his heart was so full of happiness.

A loud crash pierced his reverie, followed by several sharp slaps, and then Solveig's tears. Nils rushed toward the little girl, who cried a few feet away, fully aware that Anna followed in his footsteps. A matronly woman alternated between wagging her finger at a cowering Solveig and pointing toward an overturned picnic basket. Solveig whimpered, "I am sorry," in Norwegian, but the woman only grew more irate. She saw Anna and Nils heading her way and turned her anger on them.

"What kind of parents are you, letting your child run all over the place? Look what she did! She ruined my food, the little devil!"

Nils bent to pick up Solveig and, holding her close, wiped her tears with his handkerchief. "What happened, sweetie?"

Solveig answered in between sobs. "I...I was dancing around and around and did not see her basket. I tell her I am sorry. She hit me right here and it hurts."

Nils clenched his teeth in anger. He took out several coins from his pocket and gave it to the flustered woman. "Here, this is for your basket. Little girl did not see it. We are sorry, we watch her better next time. But now I talk to you myself, because I am very upset with you."

"How are you upset with me, if I am the one who suffered the damage," the woman said, her voice mocking Nils' Scandinavian accent.

"You hit her! She is only four years old and she speak no English, only Norwegian. She tell you she is sorry. You cannot hit other people's children. I pay you for basket, but I hope you never do this again." He pressed several coins into her hand. "Now, you tell Solveig you are sorry for hitting her and we all forgive each other."

The woman's mouth gaped open for several seconds before her eyes narrowed with rage. "I will do no such thing. You already ruined my dinner, now leave me alone."

Anna had heard enough. She stepped forward and, hands on hips, glared at the woman through her glasses. "I think you better apologize," she said, her voice tight with fury, "because I am about to look for a policeman. Hitting a minor child is a punishable offense! Your food is fine. Look," she said, reaching down to grasp an apple. She held on before the woman's face. "This isn't even bruised. Solveig's face, however, is another matter. You're making a fuss over nothing. Shame on you!" She tossed the apple back to the ground, then turned to Nils. "Don't give her a penny of your money. I am going to get Solveig an ice cream cone and see if a policeman is around." She pointed a finger at the accused. "You better make a fast decision of where you want to spend the night, at home or in a cold dark cell with rats." Anna squared her shoulders and turning on her heel, marched away.

The older woman stared after the retreating red head, and then faced Nils. "Your wife sure has a temper. Must be Irish with that head of fire," she added. Her voice took on a pleading note. "This was a simple misunderstanding. Tell the little girl that I was upset, but not any more. Here is your money." She returned the coins to Nils', then hesitated a moment before she bent to retrieve the apple. "Here's a little something for the child." She handed the ripe red fruit to Solveig, whose face wrinkled in confusion, as though she did not know what to make of this sudden act of kindness.

Nils was not about to explain that Anna was not Irish, let alone his wife, or that Solveig was not their daughter. He thanked the woman for the apple, apologized yet again for Solveig accidentally kicking over the basket, then grasped his niece's hand and headed back to his spot on the grass.

Anna returned several minutes later carrying an ice cream cone and joined Nils and Solveig on the lawn. The little girl licked at the frozen dessert, promptly forgetting the mean old woman and her basket. Nils told Anna what happened after she left.

Anna nodded. "I'm relieved that the woman at least apologized. I think she got scared when I mentioned the policeman. I don't like to scream at people like that, but sometimes you have to. I never looked for one anyhow, but I did find something that Solveig would like: a carousel with pretty wooden horses and music."

Nils translated for Solveig, who jumped up and tugged on her uncle's sleeve to hurry him along. Nils noticed the twinkle in Anna's eyes and, reaching down, hoisted Solveig into his arms. He decided to carry her through the throngs of picnickers to avoid any more accidents. They neared the carousel's out-of-tune calliope and Nils saw immediately that the horses were too big for Solveig to ride alone, and far too small for his big frame.

"Anna, can you go with Solveig? I am afraid, she is so little, she fall off horse."

"I'll ride with her, but what if she asks me something. How can I answer without my translator?" Anna laughed mischievously and lightly touched Nils' hand.

"I talk to her now. No questions until carousel stops." Nils picked up the little girl and whispered into her ear.

He purchased two tickets and a wizened old man led Anna and Solveig onto the carousel. The little girl picked a white horse with a golden mane. Anna sat on the horse beside her. Off they went, round and round to the sounds of the calliope, played one-handed by the old man as he turned the crank for the carousel with the other. Solveig and Anna waved to Nils as they passed him. Toward the end of the ride, the little girl closed her eyes and, when the carousel ground to a halt, Anna carried her off.

Nils retrieved his niece from Anna's arms and spun her in an opposite direction from the ride. "You feel less dizzy now. Say thank you to Anna for taking you on the carousel." Solveig mumbled something in Norwegian before she rested her head on Nils' shoulder. "She is tired. Long day for her, so many new things—streetcar, zoo, ice cream, concert, carousel, angry woman with basket." He paused for a moment and smiled broadly. "Thank you, Anna, for taking us here."

Nils and Anna boarded the streetcar back to St. Paul several minutes later. Solveig remained fast asleep in Nils' arms, even when he shifted her so he and Anna could sit beside each other. Anna glanced at the sleeping child, then the man who held her so tenderly, and her lips curved into a dreamy smile. *Will Nils one day hold one of their children within his arms?*

Just a few weeks ago, I did not dare think about marriage and family. Warmth spread through her chest and settled within her heart, filling it until she swore it would burst. *Is this what being in love feels like?*

She closed her eyes and allowed herself to fantasize, if only for a few moments. *Our children would be half Russian and half Norwegian. What would they look like? What would we name them?* "You tired, too, like Solveig?" Nils asked, his voice soft so as not to awaken his niece.

Anna opened her eyes and her shoulders raised in a light shrug. "No, just thinking about something."

"What?"

Anna cheeks blushed with the heat of embarrassment. "Nothing, just silly things."

Nils whispered in her ear. "If it is important for you to think about it, that is not silly. You tell me next time, if you want to."

"I will, Nils. I just want to wait for the right time, like for the dancing." Just then the conductor announced Anna's stop. She stood and turned to him. "I am getting off here. See you at the picnic."

"I walk you home."

"Absolutely not." She placed a hand on his shoulder as he began to rise. "Solveig is very tired and the next streetcar is in an hour. I live only one block from here. Trust me, nothing will happen." She leaned forward and added, "Tell Oddleif and Oskar to come to the picnic. We need more people to join the union."

Nils nodded his understanding. "I talk to them, if they remember with the whiskey and beer. See you next week. Thank you for today."

Solveig stirred and opened her eyes. "*Ha det*, Anna."

"She say good-bye in Norwegian," Nils translated.

"Goodbye," Anna said as she caressed the little girl's cheek. She noticed the tenderness in Nils' eyes. *I wish I could stay with him just a little longer.*

She turned quickly then, and rushed from the streetcar.

Solveig woke up a couple of stops later and peppered Nils with questions.

"Uncle Nils, did you like the carousel, the animals at the zoo, the ice cream? Wasn't the lady with the basket mean? Can you ask about the gray and white cat for me and Henrik? Do you think Henrik is feeling better?"

Nils patiently answered the little girl's questions until she changed the subject to Anna. "She is really nice. She bought me ice cream. Is Anna your sweetheart?"

"Oh, you can say that." Nils did not know what Solveig would repeat to Oddleif and Oskar. It did not matter, however, for they would find out soon enough.

"Are you going to marry her, because I want you to play your *hardingfele* so I can dance at your wedding. Pa and Uncle Oskar will come, too, and they'll drink a lot and break the bottle."

Truth comes out of the mouths of babes. "Solveig, I play my *hardingfele* for you any time, just ask. I will tell Oskar not to break bottles. It's not good for little girls to hear such things."

Solveig possessed the persistent curiosity of a child and would not let her question go unanswered. "But will you and Anna get married, since she is your sweetheart?"

Nils smiled down at his little niece. "I will ask her very soon. If she says yes, then we have a wedding and I will play a song just for you. Now, close your eyes and pretend that you are on a white horse and you are going around, around, and around on the carousel. Solveig is getting very dizzy and sleepy, because it's past her bedtime."

The little girl fell asleep again and did not awake until Nils handed her over to Kjersti.

Chapter Ten

Anna spent every spare moment during the week before the picnic either in her room preparing her speech, or with the union organizing committee working out the last minute details. Food, music, posters, program order and union cards needed to be planned and, for Anna, the work was almost overwhelming. The hardest part was convincing the girls at St. Paul Garments to come. While they were not averse to free food and music, they knew that Anna belonged to a union, and most likely the picnic would involve some kind of an organizing activity. Anna knew the fear of losing their jobs kept many of them from accepting her invitation, although about twenty promised to come.

Margit Sørensen had a special reason to go: She wanted to see Anna's Norwegian fellow play his *hardingfele*. During a break at work, Anna again asked about the phrase she previously refused to translate. "Margit, what does that *elsker*, or whatever it was, mean?"

Margit batted her eyelashes and played coy. "Why would you want to know? Did he say it?"

"I don't think so, but he may." Anna felt the heat of embarrassment flush her cheeks. "You know, us girls can just feel these things coming. He's teaching me some Norwegian words, though."

"Well, if he is really sweet on you, he will say '*jeg elsker deg kjæresten min*,' which is 'I love you my dearest' in English." Margit paused and wrinkled her nose. "I can now see why he would say this sooner rather than later."

Anna's brow knit in a frown of confusion. "Why?"

"Fanny tells me the poor fellow got consumption, so he wants to marry you as fast as he can before he dies."

Anna let out an exasperated sigh. "Margit, Fanny is repeating the gossip my mother is spreading around the whole neighborhood. None of it is true. He is just fine. You'll see for yourself Sunday."

"Okay. I believe you. I can't figure out that Fanny anyhow." The younger girl patted her hand. "I'll bring some *rømmegrøt* to the picnic. It's a special Norwegian porridge. If you are going to marry the fellow, you better get used to Norwegian food. I can teach you how to cook. All you need is fish, potatoes, milk, flour, butter, sugar, salt, and a big pot of coffee. You can make just about any dish from that."

"I won't mind a lesson sometime." Anna glanced at the clock. "Break is over, I better get back to my sewing table."

Anna used up an entire ink bottle and well over half a notebook working on her speech at home during the week. The pile of crumpled sheets of paper that littered the floor grew as Anna worked alone in the bedroom. Rivka did her homework on the kitchen table. Since the disastrous dinner over a week ago, the sisters barely spoke.

Anna made an attempt to invite everyone to the picnic during dinner Thursday night. Grisha's eyes lit up. "Will they really have baseball and games?"

"As long as I am alive and mother to these children," Sarah said through gritted teeth, "no one, and I repeat, no one is going to any kind of picnic! You know that if Anna is there, that worthless, diseased, ugly Norwegian will be there too. Do you want to catch consumption and die? I forbid all of you to associate with him, and Moyshe, you can do whatever you want with his shoes. That is your business, but this is my home and my children, and as their mother, I have to protect them."

Anna, not surprised by her mother's response, glanced at her father, but Moyshe said nothing. A disappointed Max stared at his plate. Grisha, however, rubbed his temples and scrunched his face, as if trying to figure out a problem. "Are you forbidding Anna to see Nils too? Because if she goes and she does not get sick, that means we won't catch anything."

Sarah glared at Anna as she answered her son. "Grisha, your sister is a grown woman who will not listen to her mother or father. She is so selfish to put this entire family in danger and betray her faith for that no-good, sick bum. Don't you ever call him by his name. As far as I am concerned, he has none."

She addressed Anna. "As long as you are going out, you might consider taking a look at some rooming houses. I will not have you defiling our family under my own roof."

Moyshe banged his glass on the table, startling everyone. "Sarah, she will do no such thing. You are not turning our daughter out on the street. I live here too, and I forbid it!"

Anna stood so fast the chair nearly toppled behind her. She glanced at the faces of her family, one by one, and fought to keep her voice steady. "I am going to a meeting. Mama, Papa, please don't have an argument over this. I will find myself a room, so I won't trouble you any longer. It's the middle of the month, so it might be several weeks, if you can bear it."

Anna marched out of the room and slammed the front door behind her as she left the house.

Nils bent down to open the heavy wooden emigrant chest in his attic room. He took out a gray vest embroidered with flowers much like on the *hardingfele*, woolen gray pants, a clean white shirt, and shoes with silver buckles. This was the traditional fiddler's outfit in Voss—passed from father to son. Nils tried the clothes on. They still fit, but hung loosely on him. His father, Bjørn Hansen, was a shorter and stockier man to begin with, plus the large amount of walking and the hard work Nils did in America took off a few pounds. He removed the clothes, laid them out on the bed, then picked up his fiddle and played through several tunes.

Nils put the fiddle down, took a book from the shelf, looked up an English word and headed for the small table covered with half-written sheets of paper, some in Norwegian and others in English. He wrote down the word, then rehearsed his most recent attempt at asking Anna to marry him, first in Norwegian, and then translating into English, paying careful attention to correct pronunciation. Nils took up the fiddle again, then put it away after one tune. He felt too restless to play, and decided to work on the garden.

Kjersti noticed him hoeing with more force than needed, throwing big clumps of earth in the air, and knew something was bothering him. The fellow had hardly eaten a bite for the last five days, played his fiddle in spurts, paced in the attic, and overworked the garden. *It must be the Russian girl.* After all, Solveig told her that *'Uncle Nils was going to ask Anna to be his sweetheart and play his fiddle at the wedding.'* Kjersti usually dismissed such foolish talk as the child's imagination, but in this case, Solveig might be right.

Kjersti slowly shook her head. The whole idea of marriage to this girl was problematic. *Heavens, she is not Norwegian or Lutheran, and even Nils will be unable to convince the pastor to marry them. The attic room barely fits one person, let alone two. If they move, I will lose not only a boarder, but a handyman, fiddler, gardener, babysitter, and friend. Oddleif and Oskar look up to Nils. If he leaves, the two will be at the bottle day and night, pouring hard earned money down the drain.*

"*Uff da,*" Kjersti said, then wiped her forehead and went back into the house to put the children to bed.

Nils approached Oddleif and Oskar, where they sat on the front steps in the growing darkness drinking up the dregs of a whiskey bottle. "I will be playing the *hardingfele* at a union picnic next Sunday. They will have food, music, and well, if you want to sign the union cards, Anna asked that I tell you about that, too."

"As long as we can take the bottle along, we'll go anywhere. Right Odd." Oskar slapped Oddleif on the shoulder.

"The union men said specifically no spirits," Nils replied. "Oddleif, I play you a *vossarull*. Give Kjersti a twirl or two."

Odd waved Nils off with his hand. "I have been in America for six years. I think I forgot how to dance the old country way."

"You didn't forget, Odd. Just lay off the bottle and you'll remember how to walk straight. Then you can dance!"

Oskar interrupted the two men. "You play a lively polka, and I'll see if I can get Sigrid Dahl to dance with me. Every day when I go to work, she waves at me. The other day, I stopped by and we talked. You know, that tennis story always impresses the girls."

Oddleif poked Oskar in the ribs. "Oskar, my friend, who *did* play tennis with the King of Denmark?"

"Oh, some third cousin. But they don't need to know that here in America. How will they find out if it wasn't me?"

"Suppose they ask you to play a game of tennis," Nils said. "What are you going to do then?"

Oskar guffawed. "I have yet to see a Norskie with a tennis racket and a ball, so I have nothing to worry about. Oddleif, fetch us another beer."

Nils shook his head, then went upstairs and did a final read through on his English text. It was not perfectly memorized, but understandable. He read a bit from the Bible, needing the comfort that it alone could bring, and blew out the candle. As he lay back against the pillow, he prayed for God's guidance on what he planned to do tomorrow.

Anna looked out the window on Sunday morning and moaned when she saw the ominous gray clouds that hovered over St. Paul. The picnic would still be held even if it rained, but no doubt only the organizers themselves would attend. Who else would want to spread out a blanket on wet grass and eat soggy food? By late morning, however, the sun peeked through the clouds and Anna's hopes for nice weather finally materialized. She changed into a gray skirt and white blouse, put her hair up in a bun, and dabbed some rosewater on her neck. Anna walked from empty room to empty room as she read through her speech, enunciating the words for maximum effect. Her mother was with Max and Grisha, who were at the Simkin's for Hebrew school; Rivka went to a friend's house to look at the Sears catalog; and her father was at the shop.

Before the boys left, however, Max stopped Anna in the hallway and whispered in her ear. "Tell Nils me and Grisha say hello. Even if Mama does not like him, he can come to the lot and play a game with us."

"I'll make sure I tell him," she said with a smile. "You're both good kids. Give it time. Maybe Mama will come around." Anna tried to sound hopeful for her brothers' sake. Inside, she knew that Sarah Katz was immovable.

Anna took the streetcar to Como Park and felt utterly alone. All the members of her family refused—or had been forbidden—to go the picnic. Except for the union organizing committee and a handful of girls from the Garment factory, she would know only one person—Nils. Her chest warmed at the thought of him. Today, after all the speeches were given, she would dance with him. *How will it feel to be held by those strong arms? Will he kiss me if we go for a walk?* Anna surrendered to dreams and fancy for a few moments before she stepped from the streetcar and faced the hustle and bustle of final meeting preparations.

As she approached Como Park, she noticed the transformation immediately. The grassy area now held a makeshift stage, tables with an assortment of food, drink and union leaflets, and several musicians tuning up their instruments. Anna made her way toward the stage, her eyes on the papers before her, intent on rehearsing her speech. Suddenly, the ground beneath her right foot sank and, a split second later, she lost her balance and fell. Her glasses flew in one direction and her speech in another.

What a way to start the day! She began to rise, then bit back a cry at the twinge of pain that raced up her leg from her right ankle. She was lifted by strong arms a moment later.

Nils' blue eyes were warm with concern as he carried her across the grassy lawn. "Anna, you hurt your foot? I wish I catch you before you fall."

"I should've watched my step," she admitted as he lowered her onto a blanket. She glanced at his embroidered vest and the shoes with silver buckles. *Nils Bjørnsen looks so handsome in his Norwegian attire.* "It does not work to read and walk at the same time," she said as she tossed Nils a grateful smile. " Thank you for catching me. Fine sight I'll make, limping onto the stage to give my speech."

"They think you hurt your foot at the factory, maybe they sign more union cards."

Anna laughed. "That might just work. So tell me, do Norwegians always dress this fine for a picnic?"

Nils glanced at his outfit, then returned her smile. "Ja, if it is important day. This was my father's and in Voss we wear different clothes than people from another part of Norway. Women have very beautiful dress and a lot of silver jewelry. It is called *sølje* in Norwegian. Sometime I show you my mother's. I go get cold water for your foot."

"Nils, I'm all right," Anna protested. "It's not necessary to fuss over me."

Despite her protests, Nils headed for the food area and asked the lady in charge to chop off a small block of ice. He returned a minute later and placed the ice on the ground next to her black, laced-up ankle boot. "Here, take off your shoe and put ice on your foot. It feel better so fast you can dance."

Anna unlaced her boot and put the ice on her ankle. "This must be a Norwegian cure. Mama always put hot tea compresses on the area if us kids fell and hurt ourselves."

Nils glanced at the small delicate foot and wished he could see it bare, without the black stocking. "I learn this from old fisherman. He said that when a person falls, the foot grow big. How you say that?"

"Swelling."

"So, cold stop swelling and pain. Keep ice on your foot until it is water. Then I help you walk for your speech." He paused to glance around, then returned his attention to her. "Your family did not come today?"

Anna released a disappointed sigh. "No, they are too afraid of you. *'Those Norwegians are a very bad influence on the children,'*" she said, mimicking the comments she heard more than once. "My brothers wanted to come, but Mama said no, so I am alone."

"Oddleif and Oskar promise me to come, so you sit with us. Kjersti cook good Norwegian food and she bring it today."

Anna glanced around as the ice began to ease away the pain in her ankle. People started to arrive for the picnic, and a multitude of languages soon echoed over the field. The aroma of Italian pizza, Irish corned beef hash, German sausage, Russian cabbage rolls, and Norwegian fish balls blended into a true ethnic melting pot. Peddlers roamed around the blankets, selling cold drinks and treats.

Anna recognized Mendel Berkowitz, holding his basket of *piroshki* and *kvas,* and motioned with her hand. He approached Nils' blanket. "Mendel, two *piroshki* and two bottles of *kvas*. What's the filling today?"

"Cabbage and eggs." The old man bent down and whispered into Anna's ear. "So, this is the Norskie? I heard from Goldstein, who heard from Simkin, who probably heard from Mrs. Simkin that Anna Katz had some Norwegian fellow. You picked a handsome one, Anna. Give him a bottle of *kvas*, it's on me, although if he's going to put up with your Mama, he will need more than *kvas*!"

Anna fought a smile as she turned to Nils. "Nils, this is Mendel Berkowitz from our neighborhood. He sells real Russian food and he would like to give you a bottle of *kvas*."

"What is *kvas*? Russian whiskey?"

Mendel laughed. "No whiskey or beer. Russian drink. Won't go to your head. Try it."

Nils tasted the sweet, malted concoction, then the cabbage-filled pastry, which was delicious and without a hint of salt. "Very good, thank you. Come back later. My cousin bring Norwegian food."

Mendel nodded, and then shouted as he walked away with his basket. "Cold *kvas*, warm cabbage *piroshki*."

Anna breathed a small sigh of relief. *At least one person from my neighborhood is on my side.* She glanced over Nils' shoulder and saw Emil Kruse walk onto the stage.

"Attention everyone," he said. "Thank you for coming, and welcome on the behalf of St. Paul Unions." His speech was brief and stressed the solidarity of workers to win concessions from the bosses. The next two speakers outlined the union demands for an eight-hour day, breaks, sick and holiday pay. In the meantime, other members walked through the crowd and passed out sign-up cards.

Nils filled out his name and address and handed the card back to Anna. "Now, I belong to your union, and I try to tell men at the mill about it."

"Thank you, Nils. From this moment on, you are a union brother and if, God forbid, you lose your job or get sick, we will help you. Anna smiled warmly, put the card in her purse, and then ran her eyes over her speech one more time. "I'm due to speak next."

She wiggled her toes and turned her ankle. It did not feel painful. *The ice must have worked.* Nils, however, insisted on accompanying her as far as the stage. She approached Emil and apologized. "Sorry, I should have helped you up front here, but I fell and sprained my ankle and I was under orders not to walk."

Emil's eyes narrowed with concern. "Anna, you have done enough already. That fellow," he added. "I remember him from the meeting a month ago. He is the Norwegian fiddler?"

"Yes. I think he is up after the Schmidt Brewery Brass Band." Anna reached into her purse and handed a small piece of paper to Emil. "And here is his membership card."

"The first sign-up out of hopefully many for the day." Emil waved to Nils and gave Anna an encouraging nod. "Well, get those girls organized."

Anna walked toward the podium and smiled at the crowd. "My name is Anna Katz and I am from St. Paul Garments. I want to thank all of you for coming today. My message is to the women and girls of this city. You are the seamstresses, cooks, mill workers, maids, clerks. Without you, this city would stop. But think for a moment—do your bosses appreciate your efforts enough to pay you a decent wage? When your child is sick or you feel an oncoming cold, do you lie awake all night figuring out what to say to the foreman about a missed day? If you do such good work, don't you think that in a ten hour day, you deserve more than a thirty minute break for lunch, safe working conditions, paid holiday and sick time?" She paused for a few moments, glancing at a few of the female attendees while her questions sank in.

"It's only fair, considering that we spend more than one third of our lives at our jobs, the other third sleeping, and have a precious few hours to be with our families. I am part of the union because I want change. The more of you that join our cause, the more we can do. When we are together, we become strong, and the bosses will have no choice but to listen to our demands or risk a strike." She inclined her head in a nod. "I know your fears about unions. 'The boss will find out and fire me.' That is always a risk. But, for every good worker they fire, they have to replace her with a new person that has to be trained. They cannot replace and replace forever. Soon it will start affecting their business and, to the boss, profits are everything. Less profit means that their wives won't be in Paris for the summer and their daughters won't go to charm school. As a union, we sit down and talk to the bosses. We tell them that 'the way you treat your workers is bad business. Put just a little money into higher wages, pay for holiday and sick time, reduce the day to eight hours and provide breaks—then you will have happy workers whom you don't have to replace over and over. They will be loyal to your company and will do good work, because they know that you are concerned about them.'"

She paused once more and spotted Nils standing beside the stage, waiting to escort her back to their spot on the grass. She faced the crowd again. "That is why I would encourage you to sign your union cards today. I cannot go up to the head of St. Paul Garments and make these demands by myself. But if all the women at our factory walked into his office, that would make a big difference. Think also of your children. Do you want them to toil at a sweatshop? If we do not organize, they will follow in our footsteps—coughing from the lack of fresh air and mill dust, having fingers cut off by machinery accidents, and exhausted from the long hours. If you don't want to fight for yourself, do it for the sake of your children." She leaned forward. "We are entering a new century. Let's hope that we, the workers of the 19th century, can better the lives of the workers in the 20th century. Thank you."

Anna stepped back, surprised and pleased by the rousing applause. She scanned the audience and picked out several faces from St. Paul Garments, then Emil and the other organizers gathered around her on stage to complement her on her speech.

Nils felt suddenly uneasy with all the union fellows crowding around Anna. *Why would she want to marry me when she can choose from ten of them. They're smart, can speak English, share her passion for the cause. What am I, but a poor Norwegian farmer? Maybe I better not ask her.*

Chapter Eleven

Anna managed, after several minutes of handshaking and hearty congratulations, to finally disengage herself from the group. She walked towards Nils.

"That was a very good speech," he said as he held out his hand and helped her down the steps from the stage. "I try to understand with my poor English. You have it on paper so I can read it?"

"I don't know if it was that good. I cut out a lot of things I wanted to say. Not much time and too serious for a picnic. But I do have it written down."

Anna and Nils made their way toward the picnickers. Nils saw Kjersti on a gray wool blanket, dishing out fishballs and potatoes to Oskar and the children.

Solveig was the first to glance up and spot them. She tugged on Kjersti's sleeve. "Mother, see, there's Uncle Nils and Anna. I think he is going to marry her. Can you ask him if he asked her? She is really nice and she bought me ice cream and told the mean lady off."

Kjersti glanced toward Nils and Anna, then returned her attention to her daughter. "Solveig, eat your dinner and don't ask me silly questions. Don't you see I have my hands full with Henrik." The little boy was fussing in Kjersti's arms and spitting up what was fed to him.

Oskar turned to the little, curious girl. "Uncle Oskar will ask for you, Solveig." He waved to Nils. "Nils, bring the Russian girl and we'll feed her good Norwegian food. No salt, we promise!"

Nils and Anna sat down at the edge of the blanket and Kjersti filled two more dishes. She handed one to Anna and the other to Nils.

He spoke to her in Norwegian. "Not so much for me, Kjersti. I have to be playing soon."

Kjersti put half of the food back into the pot. "The way you have been eating this week would make a fasting pilgrim look fat. What a full stomach has to do with playing the fiddle I don't know, and I won't ask."

"Solveig knows," Oskar said, also in his native tongue. "And she wanted Uncle Oskar to ask." He winked at Nils. "You're not hungry, you hardly say a word, I hear you pacing back and forth in the attic. Something tells me you're working up to asking the girl a very important question. Solveig, what's Uncle Nils going to ask?"

The little girl was quick to answer. "When the wedding will be and will we have lots of ice cream?"

Nils refused to answer the inquisitive child. Instead, he spoke in English. "Oskar, Anna does not speak a word of Norwegian, so it is only polite of all of us to speak English from now on."

Oskar's brow knit into a frown of concentration. "Ja, how you like Norsk food?" he asked Anna finally.

Anna glanced at Nils as she finished eating the fish ball and saw a curious redness flush his cheeks. It happened after Oskar mentioned her name, and she could only assume whatever he said had embarrassed Nils. *If only I could speak Norwegian....* "It's very good, similar to Russian food—fish, potatoes, cabbage."

Oddleif chose that moment to stumble onto the blanket beside his wife. He smelled of beer, and Anna could not help but wonder if he had more than one as he handed a tin cup of frothy liquid to Oskar. Anna's eyes widened with surprise as Oskar emptied it in one gulp.

"The Irishmen were generous today," Oddleif said. He grabbed his wife's arm. "Come on Kjersti, let's polka like we did in the old country."

Kjersti yanked her arm away and irritation laced her voice. "Don't you see I have two children to mind. Make it four with you and Oskar."

Anna hid a smile as she reached out her arms toward the baby. "Kjersti, I will sit with the children. Go on and dance."

"Only if it's no trouble," Kjersti said. Her warm gray eyes spoke *thank you* as she handed Anna the baby. "We dance so little, only when Nils plays."

Anna placed the child in her lap, then hid a smile when she noticed Nils' watching her. He glanced away. "I play soon, Kjersti. Oddleif, you are in

Karlsen's barn, you see a pretty girl, and you ask her to dance. Remember that and your feet will know what to do."

Kjersti ran a hand over her face. "Heavens, Nils, that was so long ago I hardly remember it myself. And now look at him—drunk, lazy fool!"

Nils took his fiddle out of the case and began to tune the eight strings. He was due up to play in only a few minutes. He headed for the stage, and Kjersti and Oddleif followed him.

Anna was left with Oskar, a fussy baby and a very nosy little girl whose questions never seemed to end. Oskar translated her curiosity about the wedding as best as he could, although his slow English could not keep up with the bubbly enthusiasm of a four-year-old. Anna felt warmth flush her cheeks as she tried to explain that Nils had not asked her to marry him, and no one was even thinking about a wedding, but that did not seem to phase Solveig. She, apparently, insisted on arranging a day filled with cake and several flavors of ice cream; a white dress with a long train; a carriage with six horses, each a different color; and Uncle Nils playing the fiddle.

Henrik squirmed in Anna's arms, and then started wailing, despite her attempts to quiet him. Oskar merely shrugged. "He will stop crying when Nils plays his fiddle. You'll see. That's how Kjersti makes him sleep."

Oskar was right. As soon as the little boy heard the familiar sound of Nils' *hardingfele*, he settled down. Anna listened to the music for several moments until a thought occurred to her. *Maybe Oskar has a dancing partner and stayed behind so that I would not need a translator for Solveig.* "Oskar, I can manage the children myself if you have a girl to dance with. I learned a little Norwegian, so Solveig and I will be able to understand each other. And, besides," she smiled, "we talk a lot with our hands and point. It was fine last week."

"Oh so many girls, but no one so special as little Solveig. Come and waltz with Uncle Oskar." Oskar grinned and bowed to the little girl.

Solveig's eyes brightened and, rising, she curtsied, took Oskar's hand in hers, and skipped toward the stage.

Anna watched after them for a moment, then glanced down at the baby. Henrik was most definitely asleep in her arms. Anna gently stroked the blond wisps of hair around the baby's face and then turned toward the stage, intent on enjoying the music.

Nils played waltzes, polkas, *schottisches*—tunes easy to dance to and well-known by immigrants and Americans alike. They had a sort of Norwegian lilt to them though—trills and twirls, and the haunting drone of the *hardingfele* strings. *Papa would love to own one of these, she thought, but the Sears catalog does not sell Norwegian fiddles and who has the money to order one from across the ocean?*

Anna saw Kjersti and Oddleif waltz by a few moments later, domestic troubles temporarily forgotten. Oskar spun Solveig around and around, making the little girl laugh and, no doubt, grow dizzy.

Her gaze drifted toward Nils then. She realized he was giving them all a gift—a happy tune for the children, fond reminiscences of the old country for the adults. Listening to the music deepened Anna's feelings for Nils, but she did not know what to make of them. One moment she wanted to close her eyes and imagine herself in his arms, dancing; but then who would play the fiddle? The next moment she wanted to sit beside him and drink in every note, watch the rhythmic tapping of his foot, and his nimble fingers as he moved them across the strings.

The time passed far too quickly. Nils played for half an hour, but the minute two old men replaced his uncle, Henrik awoke, started fussing and covered his ears with chubby hands. One coughed out a bawdy song while the other accompanied him on a wheezing, out-of-tune accordion. Nils returned to the blanket, followed by a panting Oddleif and Kjersti. Oskar and Solveig joined them also, the little girl still chattering away.

"Thank you, Anna, for watching Henrik," Kjersti said. The little boy calmed when Kjersti gently rocked him in her arms.

Nils sat beside Anna. "How is your foot? You think you can walk or dance?"

"Let me try walking on it first, and then I'll see."

Oddleif's brow furrowed in a puzzled frown as he looked at Nils. "Who is going to play the fiddle if you dance?"

"The Swedish fiddlers are coming up in an hour." Nils extended his hand toward Anna and helped her stand. "We go for a little walk."

Oddleif winked and switched to Norwegian. "Ja, little walk, big plans. I have a bottle ready under the blanket for whatever she says."

Oddleif is right, Nils decided. *Why shouldn't I ask Anna? If she would rather marry one of these union men, well, what can I do? I can only ask and pray that she says 'yes.' I have known her for a month, and I think I know her heart.*" Nils gave his cousin a noncommittal shrug and carefully guided Anna through the maze of blankets and picnickers toward a park path.

A myriad of people strolled along the path: couples holding hands, mothers with baby carriages, old men relying on canes.

"Does your foot hurt?" Nils asked.

"No," she replied. "There's no soreness at all. The ice worked."

He remained unusually quiet as they walked and, when he grasped her hand, his felt clammy, although the weather was pleasantly dry. Anna could not help but wonder why. *What can be bothering him so? Is he going to tell me that he can't see me anymore? No, that can't be it. What were those exchanges in Norwegian with his cousin and Oskar that caused him to turn color? It had something to do with me, I'm sure of it. Even little Solveig figured that out. Was he going to ask?*

"Anna, I am sorry. I walk too fast for you."

Anna was, indeed, out of breath, but not from walking. She felt as though her nerves had settled in her throat, choking her, and her mouth was filled with cotton. "No, not at all. My foot is fine, really."

"I want to walk a little far so we do not have so many people. Please do not think I try what men do. I just want to talk to you."

"Nils, I trust you wouldn't do anything. I know what you mean, though. It would be nice to sit in a sunny spot all by ourselves."

Nils led her along the path until it was almost overtaken by the grass and shrubs that edged Lake Como. Anna looked around and noticed there were no people in close proximity. "Would this be okay? The grass is pretty dry."

"Ja, we can sit here." Nils picked out a grassy area by a group of lilac bushes, where they could catch the warmth of the late afternoon sun.

For a few minutes, neither one of them spoke. Finally, Nils took a deep breath and, grasping Anna's hands in his, began the speech he prepared for during the past week.

"Anna, I know you only for one month, and you make me happy since I come to America. I think about you every day and cannot wait to see you on Sundays. You are very kind to show me St. Paul and Minneapolis, and when I talk to you more and more, I feel that God made us meet for a reason.

"Last week, you said you want to dance, but only with the right person. For me, you are the right person to dance and I hope to do everything else with in my life. So, I think hard, I ask God, I ask myself, and now I will ask you if you want to marry me. Forgive me if I am a poor Norwegian immigrant asking for too much. I will work very hard so you have a good house for you and our children. I try to be friend to your family. Maybe with time, they think better of me. I want to buy a little farm so you do not have to work in the factory any more. I will play my fiddle for you every day."

Anna's eyes filled with tears of happiness. She threw her arms around him and let the tears flow. "Yes, Nils, I will marry you. I knew the first day we met that you were the right fellow," she whispered between sobs. "I'm sorry I'm crying, but these are tears of joy.

"Anna, my dearest, I am a man, but now it is hard for me to have dry eyes." Nils stroked Anna's hair and planted tiny kisses on her forehead. *How beautiful she looks with strands of red hair around her face. The tears turn her eyes into the brightest green.* Nils half expected to see tiny black slits in the middle. "My little cat with green eyes." He could not think of the right English words, so he caressed her with Norwegian endearments.

Anna needed no translation; with Nils' every touch, the words he whispered, he transported her into a magical fairy tale—one that she only read about in books. *Is this what being in love is like?* It reminded her of the flowing tunes Nils played on his *hardingfele.*

Nils cupped her face with his hands and stared lovingly into her eyes. "Can I ask to kiss you?"

Anna nodded and closed her eyes. *This is what heroines in novels do,* she thought, *but I am not curled up on my bed reading a book. This is real.*

Nils' mustache tickled her lips as his mouth gently brushed hers. He lingered for a moment, savoring the sweet taste of her, the soft feel of her, before he buried his face in her hair. *"Jeg elsker deg kjæresten min,"* he whispered as he held her tight against him, afraid to let her go.

Anna returned his embrace. Even if she wanted to, she could not let go, because Nils' kiss turned her bones into putty. He had finally used the words Margit told her and she wanted the moment to last forever. Slowly, Anna opened her eyes and smiled at Nils. *"Jeg elsker deg.* Is that how you say it in Norwegian?"

Nils kissed her lightly on the cheek and repeated the phrase slowly for her. He stopped and looked away for a moment; the feelings that stirred inside him during the kiss were not only the noblest ones of true love, but also the passionate energy of desire. Not even Kari Hagen ever made him feel this way. He swallowed the bitter memory of his youth and now, holding Anna, knew that at last he had found the woman he would love for the rest of his life.

He released her slowly, then reached for his fiddle case. Anna watched, her damp eyes curious, as he withdrew a package wrapped in brown paper. "I am sorry, I do not have a ring for you. I save up for our wedding. But here is little thing you ask for." Nils placed the package in Anna's hands.

Anna understood all too well that Nils could not afford an engagement ring. "It's just a symbol anyway," she assured him, "and I wouldn't want you to spend your hard-earned money on such trifles. Besides, I honestly don't remember asking for something." Anna felt the package. "I think it's a book. Hmm, I wonder what it could be." She opened it and took out a small bound leather volume entitled *Holy Bible* in gilded letters.

Nils saw the puzzled expression on her face and explained. "Three weeks ago, when you show me Capitol and St. Paul, you said that you wanted to read the Moses books for yourself. So, now you can. It has the Christian books there too, but you do not have to read that part. I hope I do not make any trouble with your religion."

Anna placed the book on her lap, then took his hands in hers. "Thank you. Nils, you are so thoughtful. I do want to read the Bible and all of it, Jewish and Christian books, but you're right, I just have to be careful at home. I will have a lot of trouble if my family finds out and, God forbid, the Rabbi, although I don't understand why. He reads it himself every day, so why can't I? They think a woman does not need to know what men know, since she will only be in the house cooking, cleaning and taking care of children." Anna corrected herself. "Don't worry. When we get married, I will cook you good food and I will scrub the floor until I see my own reflection. And I love children very much. I took care of Rivka, Max, and Grisha since they were babies. It's just that, once in a while, I would like to read a book and have an intelligent conversation outside the kitchen."

"It is too bad people think like that. Times change and religion should change with it. We cannot live like Moses in the dry land. In the Bible during Moses' time, a man can sell women and own people. What do you call them in English? America had a big war about this thirty years ago."

"Slaves. Yes, the Civil War."

"Ja, now, we cannot do that anymore. It is sin that we cannot have slaves and Bible says we can? No, people change and how they think about God change, too."

"Yes, you're right, but tradition is what binds Jews together and, to many, change is a bad word."

"Not only Jews. I see that in Norwegian church, also. In Voss, pastor come to me and say that I play the fiddle and do devil's work. Only good music is what we sing in church. Other is sin. I ask myself many times if playing *hardingfele* is a sin, but I cannot believe that God thinks so."

"Nils, the music you play on your *hardingfele* is the most beautiful I have ever heard, and don't let anyone tell you otherwise. If there is a heaven, that's what the angels play—little Norwegian fiddles to make the weary people forget their troubled lives. And think of it; very soon, I get my own piece of heaven every day just by sitting and listening to you play. Nils, I am the happiest girl in St. Paul. No America—the world—since you asked me." Anna rested her head against Nils' shoulder.

He bent down to give her a quick kiss. "Anna you are very sweet to say this. I try to play better for you. Well, would you like to go and dance—more devil's work to do? The devil must be very busy with all the fiddle players and dancers, he has no time for the really bad people."

Anna squeezed Nils' hand. "I would love to dance with you, Nils Bjørnsen."

They walked back to the picnic area to drop off the fiddle and Anna's handbag. Solveig ran up to meet them, and she practically bubbled over with excitement. "Uncle Nils, Uncle Oskar and me we want to know if there's going to be ice cream. I mean, if there's going to be a wedding and cake and ice cream."

Nils lifted her into his strong arms. "Solveig, just for you and Uncle Oskar, we will have a wedding, the biggest cake—as tall as a house—and an ice cream with berries in it."

"Will you play your *hardingfele* like you promised?"

"More than that, I will write a tune just for you. What should we call it? *Solveig's waltz.*"

"Let me down. I go tell mother, father, and Uncle Oskar." Solveig skipped toward the blanket while Nils translated for Anna. Oskar, Oddleif, and Kjersti heard the good news and rose to offer the couple their congratulations.

Oskar magically produced a bottle of whiskey from under the blanket. "Toast to the happy couple. Nils, this is a special occasion. Just a tiny drop."

"No, Oskar. How am I going to dance with Anna if I am drunk? The Swedish fiddlers are playing now, so we will give it a try."

Oddleif and Kjersti exchanged glances as the young couple headed toward the stage. "I hope," the latter worried, "that this girl doesn't turn out to be like Kari Hagen, from Voss."

"So do I," Oddleif said. "He deserves better."

Nils and Anna neared the stage filled with twenty fiddlers, ranging from ten-year-old boys to seventy-year-old men, arrayed in colorful regional costumes. They played a polka, drawing their bows across the strings almost in perfect unison.

"How do they do it so well without reading music?" Anna asked.

Nils explained the secret. "The boys, they just learn how to play violin. The old men, they have sick fingers and miss notes. The others some play good and some not so good, but when all of them play, we hear nice music. That is how I start playing and I make many mistakes at first, but no one hear them. We wait for a waltz, it is not so fast." Nils held Anna's hand as they stood just outside the dancing area. After another polka, the fiddlers started on a slow waltz. Nils led Anna to a patch of grass away from the other dancers and showed her the basic steps that he remembered from nights fiddling at barn dances. For Nils, it was an odd feeling to actually be dancing with a pretty girl, instead of being glued to the *hardingfele* and a pot of coffee.

Anna watched Nils, then observed the other dancers and caught on to the steps quickly. His arms, encircling her gently around the waist and shoulder, felt just right, as though she belonged there. Soon she would, forever. She studied his face, the lock of blond hair falling over his forehead, the chip on his front tooth, the blue eyes speckled with gray. The eyes were truly the windows to the soul, for they reflected the love and respect he had for Anna. If his kiss was the main course, dancing was the sweetest dessert.

The musicians paused for a moment and curiosity got the best of Anna. "How did you break your tooth?"

"Oh, that was long ago. In Norway, we have grass on roof for goats. I was six years old and my mother ask me to bring goat down. I try and try, but goat is bigger than me. So, he kick me and I fall on the ground where rocks are.

I eat some and break many tooth and this one was not a baby tooth, so I still have it."

"Did you cry?"

"Ja, I was mad at the goat, myself and mother. My father, he see me and say 'Thank God you do not break your hand. How you play fiddle then?' Next time, I give the goat hay, so he think I am his friend. We have him for maybe five years more and he was like a dog, ask me for food all the time."

Anna was amazed that, even as a child, Nils showed compassion and concern---the qualities she admired most in him as a man. "Why Nils, any other kid would have gotten so upset that the next chance he got, he would have kicked the animal back."

"I think about it too, but I had a job to bring him from the roof, so it is better that we like each other. Well, the Swedes are done. I think Norwegian man and Russian lady dance good for the first time. Your foot, you have no pain?"

"Maybe a little. I never thought dancing would be that easy. I would like to try something a bit faster next time, after the foot gets better."

"We have many years to try, sweetheart."

Margit Sørensen appeared out of nowhere as Nils and Anna walked back to the picnic area.

"Anna, I told you I would come. So, this is the fellow. I hope my lessons were handy." She winked.

"They were, Margit. We have some good news. Nils asked me to marry him. You're one of the first people to know, but by tomorrow it will be all over the factory."

Margit gave Anna a quick hug. "Congratulations, I am so happy for you." She turned to Nils and switched to Norwegian. "I work with Anna and taught her a little Norwegian. So, where in Norway are you from?"

"Voss."

"A *Vossing*, eh. Fine *hardingfele* you play. I grew up here and don't know how to do the old country dances."

Out of courtesy to Anna, Nils answered in English. "St. Paul have Norwegian club where you can learn the old dances. I play there several times."

"I have no one to go with. You know a good Norskie fellow for me?" Margit lowered her lashes and her lower lip protruded in a pout.

Nils thought of Oskar, but he would be twice as old and a drunkard—no one a young girl should get mixed up with. "Maybe you go to club and find a Norwegian man there."

Anna touched Nils' arm, then nodded toward Kjersti's blanket. "I think Oddleif and Kjersti are packing up to go. See you tomorrow, Margit."

Margit walked toward a boy of about seventeen, who took her hand and escorted her toward the stage where the Irish fiddler was warming up for a jig.

"Funny girl," mused Anna as they approached his family. "In one breath she complains that she has no one to dance with and, in another, she is off dancing with a boy she probably just met."

"Ja, she is more American than Norwegian now."

Oddleif handed Nils his fiddle "Congratulations, Nils and Anna, on your good news. It is time we go home."

Henrik was asleep in Kjersti's arms and Solveig hung on Oddleif's neck like a wet rag. Oskar was nowhere in sight.

Nils turned to Anna. "I walk you home."

"Nils, how silly," she objected as the family started walking away. "You live close to here. It makes no sense for you to go clear to the south side of town. Besides, my foot is bothering me a little, so I will take the streetcar, just like I did to get here."

"If it was not St. Paul, I take you in my arms, and then you do not have to walk. I take streetcar with you."

"You are a sweetheart, but really, I am fine. Sometime, when we are married, we can take the train out of St. Paul and..." Anna's voice trailed off. They both had dreams of how to spend their time out in the country.

Nils insisted, however, and while they waited for the streetcar, Anna asked him why he left Norway. He brushed away several strands of hair from his face and thought for a moment. *No, this is not the time to talk about Kari and all that happened. Perhaps later I will tell Anna, but not now.*

"Well, it is a long story. It was not like your family. You were not safe and you must leave. No, I leave because a man with money try very hard for two years to buy our farm, our land. We are poor, he is rich, so in the end, he get what he ask for."

"What happened, Nils? You can tell me."

Nils helped Anna onto the streetcar. He waited until they were seated before he answered her question. "It was spring of 1896. A man, Jens Ulvang, come to our house and he want to cut trees on our land. He want to give money. I say, 'No, I cut my own trees.' He leaves. This Jens, he has a lot of money and is boss of two or three places. Maybe six month later he come back with a map and show me that my trees are not mine. We live on mountain, so farm is low and trees is high. He say where trees are is not my land. I show him my map from 1889 when my father died and there they write, 'Nils Bjørnsen owns this land,' trees and all. He tell me to go to town and check. I do that and ask man in map office to show me Bjørnsen farm. He show me the same map as Jens. I tell him that seven years ago, he gave me my map, which is right. He look for a long time, scratch his head and he cannot find it. I think Jens pay him to not find it. So, I write several letters, talk to town president and no answer. Now I have no trees and Jens start cutting and I cannot do anything. My brother Per and I grow up with these trees. Hard to watch that.

"But now it get worse. Jens comes back in 1897 and say he will buy farm from me. I say, 'No, you already have trees, no more.' So, he show me letter they want to put Oslo-Bergen railroad go through my farm, so they offer money. I write letter to the railroad. No answer. I think it is not true, because we live too high for trains. Now I know, because I have new map of Voss and the train go fifty kilometers from the farm. We leave in summer of 1897 and move to town. So, it is mother, Per and me. She is old and stay home. My brother and me, we try to find work, but it is hard. Help at factory one week, cut trees other week, little fishing.

"After six months, mother is sick and we cannot leave her at home. We want to send her to my sister Ingrid in Tromsø, north Norway, but doctor say she must not travel and is very sick. So, one week Per works, I stay home, next week I work, he stay home with her." Nils sighed and looked away, his face clouded by sadness. "I remember it was April 10, 1898. I was home and she ask me to play *hardingfele*. She like that because she remember my father. I play for her for one hour, maybe more. After I say something to her, but she does not answer. So, I ask again and think maybe she is sleeping. She was, Anna, but she will never wake up. Doctor come and he call her sickness with a long word, I forgot. It is not important, because I know she die of a broken heart. She live her life on the farm, many memories for her; her husband, children and she like to work. We move to town and she sit alone, no friends, no work, only think about life before. We bury her in the church with my father and two brothers. They die when they was children.

"After, I go to our farm. No one live here, no train, no more trees. Windows in house are broken. Anna, I am a man, but I see it and I have tears because what happen to our home. I sit for a minute and close my eyes and see it like it was. Only my old cat is there. Many mice now. He meow like he ask me why I leave. What I can tell cat? So, I take a little earth with me as memory. I bring it to St. Paul. I go away and I know that I never come back, so next day I write Oddleif and ask him about America. My brother, Per, he always want to be on a ship, so once mother die, he go away. Oddleif write and say to come, so I am here. Forgive me if this is so long story."

Anna clasped Nils' hand tighter and looked into his eyes, her own brimming with tears. "Oh, Nils, it must have been so awful to lose your home and your mother like that. Having left our village, I know what it feels like to go away from a place you lived all your life. Why did that man want to take your land? Did he have something against you?"

"That is another long story. I tell you later." Nils did not want to reveal Jens Ulvang's reasons for forcing him off the farm. Kari Hagen had married well, but after six years she still exacted her revenge, through her husband.

Nils realized the streetcar was approaching Anna's stop on Snelling and could not imagine that he would not see his sweetheart for another week. Perhaps he could meet her after work during the week. They got off on Snelling and walked several blocks to their usual meeting place. The gray and white cat greeted them as old friends, purring and twining between their legs.

Nils bent down to stroke it behind the ears. "Anna, when we get married, can we take this cat? I think he needs a home."

Anna tossed Nils a warm smile. "Of course, we will take him. If I had more money I would build a special place for stray dogs and cats. They would have food, warm rugs to sleep on and people to love them. But then, there aren't enough homes like that for children and old people. If only bosses didn't pocket all the money they squeeze from us, but gave just a little away to help the less fortunate, this world would be a lot better place to live."

"Money make people blind. Anna, I am so glad you are not like other girls. You think about what is important. I want to thank you for the best day of my life. Is it trouble to see you after work?"

"No, I was going to ask you the same thing. How can I live without my Norwegian sweetheart? Thursday, seven o'clock, same place, unless it rains. Okay?"

"Okay. Today I walk you home."

Anna paused in mid-step, then took Nils' hand and crossed the street. "I would like that." *Considering what Mama will hear from me shortly, what harm is there in Nils walking me home?*

Though the sun would soon set, it was a warm, pleasant May evening. Nils glanced around, noticed several open windows, and more than one face peering their way. He did not feel right kissing Anna good-bye in full view of her neighbors, so he bent down and whispered in her ear. "I love you." In one swift motion, his lips brushed Anna's cheek, then he rose to his full height and squeezed her hand gently.

"*Jeg elsker deg.*" Anna replied in Norwegian and let her hand linger in his. "I can't wait to see you Thursday."

Nils waited until Anna closed the door behind her. *This is truly the happiest day of my life*, he thought as he began to walk home.

Finally, after years of hard work, fighting for the land, losing it, and coming to America, there was at last a ray of sunshine: Anna. The only cloud he could foresee was her mother, but he did not want to think about it and spoil the moment.

His footsteps grew faster as he thought about the coming weekend. *Tomorrow night, I will talk to the pastor about the wedding. Eivind Grundseth probably won't agree to marry a Norwegian fellow and a Jewish girl in a Lutheran church, but at least I can give it a try.*

A smile curved his lips as he walked through the streets of St. Paul, lost in dreams of married life: buying a farm, teaching his little boy to play the *hardingfele*, wondering what it would be like to make love to Anna. His dreams would soon become a reality, and Nils could not wait to begin his new life.

Chapter Twelve

The implications of Nils' proposal struck Anna the moment she walked through the front door and saw her family sitting at the dinner table. She was late and Sarah frowned her disapproval. "I don't know where you were and I don't really want to know, but do us all a favor and wash your hands."

Anna stiffened at her mother's implication. "Of course, Mama. You know all the germs a person could get on the streetcar."

"I wasn't talking about the streetcar, Anna."

"Mama was thinking of those Norwegian germs," Grisha interjected with a wink.

"Grisha," Sarah scolded, "don't talk about that thing at the dinner table. You will give me an upset stomach."

The young boy lowered his head. "Sorry, Mama."

Anna, rather than leaving, stood her ground. *Here's my chance, so long as we are already discussing Nils. I'll just tell them the truth now, have the obligatory scene and get it done and over with.* Anna took a deep breath, released it in a heavy sigh, and then dove in.

"Mama, Papa, everyone, may I add one small comment on our Norwegian friend?" Anna did not wait for a response and continued. "Nils asked me to marry him, and I was very happy to say yes."

Sarah nearly choked on her chicken. Rivka's eyes widened with disbelief as she swallowed a large mouthful of potato. Moyshe looked down at his plate, and the two boys exchanged glances and giggled.

"What's so funny?" Sarah pointed a finger at Max and Grisha. "That my own daughter is trying to kill me?" She shot an exasperated look at her husband. "Moyshe, aren't you going to do something? She is not only ruining herself, she has brought shame and disgrace on our family." When he did not answer, Sarah faced her daughter. "Anna, I want you out of the house this instant and I never want to see you again."

Moyshe sighed. "Sarah, let's try to finish dinner without a scene and afterwards we can talk about it. I am not happy with Anna either, but I am not going to argue and get heartburn."

Sarah grumbled under her breath. "Try to have dinner when this is happening. What kind of a father are you? You're just content to drink your tea and read the paper, while your daughter drags our family through the dirt. Feh." Sarah shoved a teacup toward Moyshe. "Here's your tea. I have a headache and chest pains. I think my heart is bad, and you have Anna to thank for it." She put her hand on her chest and returned her attention to Anna. "How could you betray us like this? For whom? For a worthless, dirty, consumptive, no-good, ugly *goy*. How can I face my friends? Did you ever think of Papa's business? No, Papa will be fine; he is as friendly with them as you are. It's me that will have to suffer." Sarah wiped the tears from her face, rose from her chair, and then marched toward the hallway. "I will be in the bedroom, and I don't want to be disturbed. Who knows, I may be dead in the morning."

Anna ran after Sarah, her voice a plea. "Mama, please understand. I'll always love all of you, but I love Nils, too. Just today he mentioned that he wanted to get to know all of you better, and this after what you did to him at dinner several weeks ago. This is how he is, Mama. He does not hold grudges. He treats everybody with consideration and respect, be it Jew or Norwegian. I couldn't have found a better fellow, I am certain of it."

Sarah slammed the bedroom door in Anna's face. Soon the sounds of wailing and moaning filtered from behind the closed door. *Is it a put on,* Anna wondered, *or is Mama genuinely distraught over the impending marriage?*

Anna returned to the living room, where Max, Grisha, and Rivka were clearing the table.

Moyshe stared at her a moment, then addressed his other children. "Your mother is upset. You three do the dishes while I speak to Anna." He had to restore some sense of order and calm to the house. He did not think Anna's involvement with Nils would deepen so soon and, in truth, he actually liked the Norskie fellow. *But this*, he thought as he plugged his ears with his fingers to drown out Sarah's moans, *I cannot live with.* He knew that if Anna's news sent Sarah to hell, his wife would drag him behind her to the fiery pit.

He motioned Anna to the couch. "Sit down. You and I need to talk. This is a very serious matter."

Anna heard the uncertainty in her father's voice, one that usually held the normal self-assurance of the peacemaker and compromiser. She obeyed him immediately. The news devastated even him, and she was certain he was struggling to figure out how to handle it in the best possible way for all involved.

"My child," her father said as he sat beside her. "Let me say from the start that I have nothing against Nils Bjørnsen. He is a nice fellow, has a good heart, plays the fiddle, and I can see that he would treat you very well." Moyshe lifted his finger. "But, and I know you are going to say to me, 'Papa, there's always a but.'" He lowered his hand. "Anna, you marry him and you two will be happy, but there will be five others miserable, maybe six, because you know that you will never be welcome here so long as Mama is alive. I know that Jewish law says that I should cut off my child if she marries a gentile, but, as a father, I could never do that. Yes," he added as he took Anna's hand in his. "Me, a devout Jew, I will break the law, but then where would we meet and how? You cannot come here. It would not be a good idea for you to be seen with me at the shop, because of malicious tongues wagging. So, we would have to arrange a meeting in secret on some street corner in St. Paul. You will certainly never see your sister, because Mama will be sure to guard her like a hawk after what happened to you. You will never take Max and Grisha to a baseball game and, if you meet them there, you would have to look around and make sure that no one saw you. What will our lives be like? I don't even want to think about it.

"You hear the moaning? It will continue day and night, and I am almost afraid to go into that room tonight. Mrs. Simkin and the rest of them will be here cursing poor Sarah's ungrateful daughter. They already do to some extent now. I might lose some customers, because how could Moyshe Katz, a pillar of the synagogue and a businessman, allow his daughter to marry a Swede?" Moyshe put his hand over his wrinkled forehead. "Anna, I am fifty-five years old and I don't know how much longer I have to live. But whatever is left, I want to spend it in peace and quiet. When I am too old and tired to work, I will be happy to sit at home, play my violin and read the paper. If you marry Nils, your mother will be so bitter and hurt that she will do everything possible to make my life as miserable as hers. I also think of your children. Their own grandfather will never see them; they won't have cousins, aunts, or uncles. And

I would very much like to be a grandfather. Who will I teach to play the fiddle? Does Nils have any other relatives besides those two drunks?"

"No." Anna clutched her hands and rested them in her lap. "His father died when Nils was seventeen and his mother about a year ago. He told me that his brother is somewhere out at sea on a Norwegian ship, and his sister is in old country. Oddleif is his cousin, and the other fellow is a Danish boarder."

"That's what I mean. The only kin your children would have are a drunk Norskie and a drunk Dane. The other point I want to bring up is religion. I know young people these days don't pay attention much to God and the old traditions. But have you both sat down and talked about who is going to marry you, which one of you will take the other's faith, and in which faith you would raise your children? I am assuming Nils is Lutheran, like all the Scandinavians, and will not particularly want to convert to Judaism. Nor would Rabbi Geller and the synagogue elders look too kindly on having this blond fellow on *Shabbos* with them. I suspect he would ask you to get married in the church. Do you know what that means, Anna?"

She stared at her father for a moment, then lowered her head. "No, Papa, we have not talked about these things yet. I know he respects our religion. He has told me so several times."

"I figured as much. Two young people in love, why should they worry about these matters? Well, if he marries you in the church, you would have to undergo the most shameful experience of your life—getting baptized and renouncing your Jewish faith. Think about it," he added as she looked up at him. "You have spent the last twenty years learning about being Jewish and, in a matter of minutes, you will wash it all away with a handful of water. I don't doubt these pious Lutherans will rejoice at saving a Jewish soul from eternal hell, as they put it, but the rest of us here will mourn, for we have lost one of our own. I just cannot bear the thought of my own daughter taking on the faith of the ones who have mercilessly persecuted us."

Anna's chest rose, then fell as she released a deep, worried sigh. She had not thought at all about the church and what role it played in Nils' life. "Papa, Nils is not the kind of fellow that would force a girl to his religion. Aren't there people in the city that can marry us?"

"Yes, there are. You go and fill out a piece of paper and a man signs it. Then you are married. You call that a wedding?" He held his hands palm up, then lowered them. "No. You can be sure we won't be there, and I am not so certain his Norwegian Lutheran friends will come. Their priests probably think that him marrying you is as much of a sin as we do. So then, it's you and him, no friends, no traditions. What would you teach the children? From what book? How would they know God or tell right from wrong? Will you still love each other then, if both of you are separated from everything and everyone that you know? These are very hard and serious questions to think about, Anna." Moyshe covered his daughter's hand with his own and his gray eyes were sharp with concern.

Anna glanced down at her lap and bit her lip nervously. If her mother shattered Anna's happiness, her father threw a dark cloud over it. But he had a point. She and Nils never discussed plans for the long-term, such as religion; or for that matter, short-term details of the wedding. *Will I be able to live with the pain of never seeing my family ever again? Am I doing the right thing?*

"Anna," her father said as he placed his hand on her arm. "Here's what I think you should do and again, I would like you to take my advice, but what can I do if you don't? When do you see him again?"

"Thursday after work, if it does not rain."

"Well then, Thursday, you tell him about what you and I spoke of tonight. I think he will understand my concerns and the pain that separation from your family will cause you. If he loves you as much as you say that he does, he should think about the questions I raised." He gave her arm a gentle squeeze. "You can still be his friend, Anna. Unlike your mother, I don't see anything wrong with that. It will even help my business. And you know, as you see each other more often, perhaps you both will realize there are things you don't like about one another and say to yourselves 'if I ever marry this girl or fellow, I'll go crazy.' After a month, what do you really know about each other?"

Moyshe released her arm and lowered his voice. "Anna, Mama's and my marriage was arranged, and I never saw her until the wedding day. Although I love your mother and I am thankful for all of you children, I wish I had time to know her beforehand. I am not so sure I would have made my own decision to marry her then. But getting back to you and Nils now, I also think that you both should take a rest from seeing each other. Say a couple of weeks or a month."

Anna's breath caught in her throat. "Papa, that's so long."

"Yes, but I think you will need time to cool your heads, look around you, think about your lives. He might find a Norwegian girl that would be a lot less troublesome to marry than you. You, on the other hand, can see some nice Jewish fellows, and I don't mean Benny. There are a couple that come to my shop and have asked if I have a daughter. I just smile, and say 'I might.' One is studying to be a doctor, is from a good family and I mean brains, not money. The other one has his own business, I forget what, but he's always been polite and has given me tips. I am asked to play at a *bar-mitzvah* almost every Sunday and you can get a pick of fellows at a place like that. I look them all over." His brows rose in a mischievous arch. "They might think I am playing the fiddle, but I can see everything and everyone, and I know who would be good and who's a *schlimazel*. Anna, this is the first fellow you met and it's normal to have strong feelings for him, but it's good to see other ones before you make a final decision to marry. You might find, to your surprise, that you enjoy their company as well as Nils'. Let me ask you a question and you don't have to answer it if you think your old Papa is prying. Does it look like you are the first girl he's asked to marry? Has he ever mentioned anyone else?"

"I don't know Papa," she said, fighting the small ball of jealousy that formed in her stomach at the thought that she was not his first sweetheart. "He has never said anything about any other girl, and I never asked. I know he's had a hard life working on the farm, and then some man with money forced them off the land, his mother was very sick and died, and then he came here. I am not sure if he had time for girls."

"He looks like an honest man, so I think he's telling you the truth, Anna. But I watch him and I am twice as old as both of you, and life has taught me a few things. The way he looks at you, he's like a lovesick puppy. You're all he's got since he came to St. Paul. And you know what his eyes say to me?"

"What Papa?"

"They say, 'A long while back a girl broke my heart very badly, and I will hang on to the one that I got now the best I can.' To me, that's the wrong reason to marry. You want to love a fellow, not feel sorry for him."

Anna's brow wrinkled as she recalled Nils' telling her about Jens Ulvang. It sounded a bit odd when he related it to her earlier. She asked Nils why this man spent so much effort getting the Bjørnsen farm, but he shrugged it off as another long story. Perhaps there was more to it than that. *Why would one man exact such revenge on another, unless...unless there was a woman involved!*

Anna's voice echoed her determination. "I will have to ask him the next time we meet."

"No," Moyshe replied with a shake of his head. "Let those old wounds alone. I don't think he wants to talk about it. It's just something to think about and, who knows, maybe I'm just making things up in my head. Now, go to sleep and tomorrow your head will be clearer."

Anna and her father stood at the same time. She kissed him on the cheek. "Good night, Papa."

Anna walked into the bedroom and began to undress for bed. From behind her, Rivka muttered under her breath, "Traitor."

Anna ignored the remark. She knew little good would come from responding. Instead, she turned off the light, but sleep evaded her. A myriad of thoughts ran through her head and, besides, her mother's fitful moans kept her awake.

Papa is right. I didn't think this marriage through. Perhaps it was too rash and unplanned, based more on feelings than on reality. But how can I tell Nils that? He cares for me so much. It would be the ultimate betrayal of his love and trust. Yes, I could give it two weeks off, think about it in the most logical and rational way, and please Papa.

Deep in her heart, however, Anna knew that no amount of careful planning and foresight would diminish her love for Nils. Not seeing him would only make her want him more. She thought of his tender kiss and could almost feel his lips pressed against hers.

So many changes in one day! If only she could close her eyes and dream of her sweetheart, but instead her mother's screams and curses resonated throughout the house.

Anna pulled the covers tighter around her head. "I wish she would stop! I think by now she has made her point," she said with a note of exasperation in her voice.

"You're a fine one to talk," her sister hissed in the darkness, "considering you're the one driving her to an early grave. How could you and for whom?"

"Rivka, don't you see that she is putting on a spectacle for all of us and the neighbors to hear? You just wait; tomorrow very early she will put on black, cover her head up with two scarves and have Mrs. Simkin over. The conversation will go something like this. 'Sarah you look awful.' 'Oy that you should notice, Frieda. I did not sleep a wink last night and my head feels like a load of bricks. My oldest Anna is marrying that Swede *goy*. Can you believe it. What a disgrace, after all we have tried to do with Benny. She is taking a knife and stabbing me in the heart. I had chest pains last night.'

"Need I say more, because by the time I will be coming back from work, people that I hardly know will stop me and ask how could I cause so much grief and misfortune to my mother."

"You are, Anna. We had a nice family until you met that man. Look what's happening. Mama is sick, Papa is grumpy, and we, sisters and best friends, are not getting along. Are you willing to trade one fellow for the love of your family?"

"No, a thousand times no. I just don't understand why you cannot accept him. He has never done anything to earn the hatred that has been poured out on him. The boys think he is the greatest and even Papa does not think he is all that bad."

Rivka leaned over the edge of her bed and whispered. "Anna, he might be a nice fellow, but he is not Jewish and that will tear this family apart. I heard what Papa was talking to you about. Don't you think I want to see your children and for mine to have cousins to play with? Of course, but not if they are wild little things who don't respect *Shabbos* and eat pork."

"Rivka, do you really doubt that Nils and I can raise well-behaved children, just because he is not Jewish? Well, I am Jewish and I will make sure they will get instruction in the faith." Anna sighed and her voice revealed a note of anger and frustration. "And if you all were not so closed minded, you would see them and add to what I do at home. But no, your Judaism only allows you to forbid. Mama has been an excellent teacher to you, little sister. I cannot wait to see the fellow she will pick out for you."

"I can assure you he will be a lot better and have more money than that Scandihoovian of yours. I have school tomorrow. Good night." Rivka fluffed up her pillow and went to sleep.

The next day, rumors flew at St. Paul Garment Works. Margit spread the good news, which grew into a tangled web of lies as it was passed from one seamstress to another. By the time it reached Anna, she was supposedly running away to Mexico with Nils to get away from her mother.

Fanny Feldman pursed her lips in jealousy, clenching the needles between her teeth. Jacob Hirsch had not given her a ring and it did not look like one was forthcoming. Her best friend would be the first to get married, but to whom? The thought of marrying a penniless, sweaty mill worker revolted Fanny. *Anna was always a little odd, but this time she's gone too far. She will realize her mistake when she is popping out babies and cleaning up the vomit from last night's poker game.* At the end of the workday, Fanny hurried home to design a new hat and perhaps catch the attention of David Gantman, the dentist. A man who put in gold fillings is worth going after.

Anna's evening predictions came true as she walked the few short blocks from the streetcar to home. First Mrs. Simkin, and then Mrs. Meier passed by her, shook their heads solemnly and whispered insults under their breath. Mrs. Meier even had the audacity to speak. "Ungrateful girl! Stabbing your mother in the heart. God will surely punish you." Anna put her hands over her ears, then ran home, tears stinging her eyes. By the time she reached the front door, she realized there would be no escape from the pain.

Sarah's day was busy. She put on the blackest dress and scarf and went door-to-door telling of the awful news. Tears spilled into teacups in parlors, while the ladies offered their support and advice. With visiting done by mid-afternoon, Sarah turned to one small but important matter and walked a half-mile up Snelling to the Minsk Tavern, the only Jewish pub in St. Paul. The tavern was patronized by mostly scruffy, unemployed men of dubious reputation. Sarah knew they hung around the outside and were always in need of a good bath and money. She drew back her shoulders as she approached five men engaged in semi-drunken conversation. Her eyes narrowed as she examined them. Two of them glanced her way, then spit on the sidewalk. *They're filthy, disgusting creatures,* she thought. *Four of them will do.*

"How would you fellows like to earn some money this Thursday?" she asked.

"What do you have in mind? We don't beat rugs or wash windows," answered a short burly man in a torn jacket. He gave the dowdy housewife a once-over with his glance. "Or is your husband not doing a good job?"

Lewd titters from the others almost made Sarah lose her temper, but she pursed her lips tighter and continued. "No, nothing as hard as housework. That I would not trust to a man. No, my daughter is seeing a Norskie fellow and they want to marry. Imagine that, a nice Jewish girl marrying some Swede. He is a worthless mangy dog and I don't want him anywhere near her. I am sure he has taken liberties with her already, the way she looks when she comes home. So, all I ask is that the four of you to show him out of the neighborhood Thursday evening. For that, I will pay five dollars and you can split it amongst yourselves however you wish."

"That's a good sum for fifteen minutes worth of work. What's he like?"

"Nothing to speak of. Blond, pale-faced, looks like he wouldn't know how to fight. Plays the fiddle. You know the type—afraid to get his fingers hurt. Don't kill the fellow, I wouldn't want you to get in trouble, but break a couple of bones. That should teach him."

"Oh, we'll break more than that, won't we boys?" The burly man spat to underscore his point "We'll fix him up so good he won't play the fiddle again, and he will never dream of girls so long as he's alive. When on Thursday?"

"About seven. They meet on the corner of Pinehurst and Cleveland. My daughter has red hair, so she will be hard to miss. But don't be obvious. Wait until she goes home, and then get him. Nils Bjørnsen is his name. It's settled then?" Sarah handed the man a five-dollar bill.

"You got our word, Mrs…?"

"My name is not important. My husband is a prominent businessman here and this is not to be breathed to a soul outside of you and me," Sarah hissed and quickly walked in the other direction. She hoped that no one she knew saw her.

From Monday to Thursday, Sarah's eldest daughter ceased to exist for her. It was little things—the dinner plate deliberately not set, the family photo turned around on the shelf, curtains that Anna sewed for the kitchen replaced by new ones. Sarah avoided all conversation with Anna and forbid Max and Grisha to ask their sister for help with their homework.

Moyshe observed but said nothing, hoping that by Thursday Anna would resolve the situation with Nils herself. Perhaps then, life would return to normal.

For Anna, the week was a trial, and one that bore a heavy influence on her decision. The fact that her family shunned her, treated her as though she did not live there, devastated her. If she married Nils, would this be the extent of the contact between them—an exchange of sharp, disapproving glances? No, it could not be. Anna hated what her mother was doing, but could not bring herself to disown her entire family because of it. Part of her wanted to marry Nils now, run away with him and forget the Katz's, while the other part prepared for the painful decision of breaking off the engagement. She realized, with fearful clarity, that either option would cause anguish for her and the others involved.

Chapter Thirteen

The Norwegian Evangelical Lutheran Church Ladies Aid met for Bible study Wednesday night, with Pastor Eivind Grundseth leading. Nils entered the church and waited while the ladies finished the lesson. To his surprise, Mrs. Olsen and Mrs. Fossheim, his neighbors, walked right past him, their faces turned away. *Odd, perhaps they just did not recognize me in the dim hallway.*

Pastor Grundseth was a gaunt man with thinning hair and his face exuded piety. He wore a black robe with a fluffed up Elizabethan collar, which made him look at least three centuries out of date. He noticed Nils in the hallway and approached. "Nils Bjørnsen, God moves in mysterious ways for I want to have a word with you. Come into my office."

The two men stepped into a small room filled with books and a desk cluttered with paper. "My sermon for next week, as you can see." The pastor pointed to the papers. "What can I do for you?"

"Well...Pastor. I found a girl that I am going to marry and I am, if I could ask you...if the Lutheran Church or you would marry us?" he spoke haltingly, looking down at the floor.

"Is she a member of our congregation?"

"No. She is not Lutheran."

"Catholic, then. Nils, you know it's best to marry within your own faith. She would have to be baptized in the church."

"Actually, she is not Catholic."

The pastor's tone held a hint of annoyance. "Frankly, I am surprised by you, Nils Bjørnsen. I wanted to talk to you, because I am very concerned about your spiritual life. Today during Bible study, one of the ladies who takes care of Solveig for Kjersti mentioned that the little girl spun a whole tale of Uncle Nils dancing with a red haired girl who did not speak Norwegian. Solveig also told her that Uncle Nils asked the girl to marry him and there would be a big wedding. It could be childish fantasies, but as a pastor I wanted to be certain. Children are usually very honest." He paused and studied the younger man, then added, "I can see little Solveig was telling the truth."

Nils felt the heat of embarrassment to the roots of his hair. *So, the pastor already knows and from what an unlikely source. Truly, there is not much difference between Anna's mother and Mrs. Fossheim. No wonder she did not greet me tonight. Well, he might as well hear the rest.*

He straightened his shoulders in determination as he began to speak. "She is from Russia and her family is Jewish, although I am not sure how seriously she practices her religion. She told me that by Jewish tradition only men can read the Bible, so I do not know what women do."

The pastor's face darkened, betraying his contempt and horror. "Nils, you are meaning to tell me that, for your life mate, you chose a girl from the tribe that crucified our Lord Jesus Christ? Don't you see, the devil is very powerful and is tempting you with her? I am sure she was all too happy to dance with you, and yet you know perfectly well that our church does not allow dancing. How easy it is to backslide into the abyss of temptation, especially if Satan looks like a pretty girl!" He shook his head and his voice took on a solemn note. "I never liked the fact that you play the *hardingfele*; that's the devil's instrument. Still, I knew you as a decent fellow, hardworking, in church every Sunday with Kjersti and the children, an example to those two drunkards, Oddleif and Oskar. But this—wanting to marry that girl—that's a sin worse than any dance tune you might have played. Have you thought about where she will spend eternity and that you will surely follow her there?"

Nils could not believe the vitriol of the pastor's speech. *My Anna, a sinner destined for hell? Surely, a merciful God will not punish a person simply for being born in a family with a different religion. The pastor is a representative of this God, or is he?*

Nils measured his words carefully as he spoke. "Pastor Grundseth, this girl should not be punished for what her ancestors did almost two thousand years ago. She has never showed any sinful behavior and has been kind, truthful, and considerate to her family and me. She has worked tirelessly on the behalf of the girls at the garment factory. I just don't see your point."

The pastor's eyes narrowed. "No, Nils, you wouldn't. The devil has made you blind. I trust that you still read your Bible and you know what the destiny of the unsaved is."

Nils stiffened as he fought back his rising anger. "Yes, I read my Bible. But do you really think that millions of good, hardworking Chinese and Negroes in Africa will be sent to hell simply because they are not Christian? I seem to remember a passage in Romans about the heathens being less sinful, because they did not know the law."

"That's why we have missionaries, Nils, to bring as many as possible into Jesus' flock, before the time comes. You are right, if they have not heard of Christ, they are forgiven their ignorance. Once the missionaries tell the Gospel story, the natives make a decision on where they want to spend eternity. But the Jews, they deliberately rejected and murdered our Lord. They are the worst of all sinners."

"Even if they do good works and try to live a decent and upright life?"

"Yes, even if they do good works. 'It is by grace that you are saved through faith, not of works lest any man should boast,'" Pastor Grundseth quoted from Ephesians.

Nils stood up, towering over the sitting cleric. "So, whom would you consider a Christian? A lazy selfish man who attends church every Sunday or a heathen who spends his entire life ministering to the sick and poor?' His voice raised a notch. "Who in your estimation would deserve to go to hell?"

Eivind Grundseth's face was inscrutable, but inside he was uncomfortable with the turn of the conversation. *None of my parishioners tread on theological thin ice, but tacitly accept the Lutheran dogma fed to them every Sunday. This Bjørnsen fellow is different. He just has to question everything!*

"What kind of question is this?" he said finally. "You know that a good Christian life is a balance between faith and works, but works alone do not decide your place for eternity."

"I think Jesus put it differently," Nils countered, walked over to the bookcase and took out a Bible. "You know the story in Matthew when He accepts the righteous into the Kingdom of God," he said, his hand tightening on the closed Bible. "He tells them that, 'when I was hungry and you gave me food, thirsty and you gave me water, a stranger and you took me in, naked and you clothed me, sick and you visited me, in prison and you came to me.' The people ask the Lord when they have done all these things for Him. And He replied 'As much as you have done these things to the least of my brothers, you have done it to Me.'" Nils paused when he noticed Eivind Grundseth's pinched face. His voice deepened with determination as he stared into the pastor's eyes. He wanted the man's full attention as he made his point. "These verses to me, pastor, are the crux of the gospel. And if Jesus took the time to say them, I think he meant for many to be called righteous. And if a so-called heathen or Jew does good works that please our Lord, I would dare say it would make him a Christian in Jesus eyes." Nils placed the Bible on the pastor's desk and headed toward the door.

Eivind Grundseth stood and, his lower lip trembling with fury, pointed a finger at Nils.

"Nils Bjørnsen, I have had enough heresy from you tonight. You are twisting the Bible and the words of Jesus Christ beyond recognition. If you think Jews and Negroes are Christians, when they do not know an iota of the gospel, then you no longer belong in this church of God-fearing people! Go home and think about what we talked about, read the Bible, and save your soul while you still can. The devil has taken hold of it and I will pray for you, but I do not want to see you here again until you have repented."

Nils stormed out of the church. *What is it about religion that made people so closed-minded? The Ten Commandments and the truths that Jesus spoke about were so simple; yet the pastor added layers upon layers of complexity, laws, and catechism. If Hell is reserved for people like Anna, I would sooner go there than spend eternity with stodgy Lutheran priests and gossipy old ladies.*

He marched toward home, his determination mounting with every step. *I am going to marry Anna and I don't care what Grundseth thinks.* He heard that, in America, there was a special official in each town who married people. He would ask the men at work if there was such a person in St. Paul.

Nils bounded the front steps of his home two at a time, then closed the door to his room and reread the Bible passages that he discussed with the pastor. *Can two people read the same text and come to completely different conclusions? To which one does God speak the truth,* Nils wondered.

He turned off the light and prayed for wisdom and understanding of God's word, for Anna and himself to be ready for this marriage, and for strength in dealing with relatives and people who did not approve of it. God never answered in words, but Nils felt a sense of peace and calm as he drifted off to sleep.

Tomorrow he would see his sweetheart. Thursday night could not come soon enough.

Chapter Fourteen

Nils arrived at the corner of Pinehurst and Cleveland promptly at seven. Since it was already late, the best he could hope for would be a little walk around the neighborhood with Anna. He would have to tell her about what transpired at his church and ask if she would mind being married by some kind of civil authority. Nils saw Anna from several blocks away, but she was walking slowly, huddled into a brown shawl. *She must be cold.* The air was chilly for late May and the clouds threatened rain.

Nils glanced at Anna's face as they greeted each other and noticed dark circles under her puffy, reddened eyes. Her hand lay limp in his, and she avoided looking at him as they walked. *What could be troubling her so.* "You do not sleep good?"

Anna gave a slight nod of her head. She did not even know how to begin the conversation. Her heart pounded with every step she took. Her stomach tightened with a wave of nausea and tears choked her throat. "I am very tired. Too much work at the factory."

"I try very hard to save money and soon you do not need to work." Nils reassured Anna, but suspected that it was not the workload at the factory that was eating at her. *Perhaps talking about our future plans will cheer her up.* "Well, I think after we get married, I look for a little land. I grow up on a farm and do not like big city. Too many people, too busy. You think you want to try live on farm?"

"I don't know, Nils." Anna paused and sighed. "I have not thought that far ahead yet. I am not even sure who would marry us, come to think of it. The rabbi is out of the question, and I doubt that a priest in your church would let a Jew inside, let alone allow you to marry one."

"Ja, you are right. I talk with him last night. Not much difference, priest or rabbi. One afraid of Norwegian, one afraid of Jew, and both think they are right before God. He do not like that I ask many questions, so he does not want me to go to church. But St. Paul is big and they have man who marry people, not priest or rabbi, it is true?"

"Yes, I think there is one, called the Justice of the Peace or something like that." *So, Nils is being shunned by his pastor. What has this marriage proposal done? Brought two people together, at the cost of severing them from everything they grew up with. Papa is right. If I can only convince Nils that this marriage is impossible under the circumstances. How difficult it is to start, but I must.*

Anna took a deep breath and swallowed a lump in her throat. "Nils, perhaps this is not such a good idea."

"What?" Nils was not sure what Anna meant.

"Us getting married. All that seems to be happening is that our friends and family hate us for what we are doing. Your pastor, being one. I won't even tell you what went on at home during the past four days. No one talks to me, not my family or the neighbors. It's as if I no longer exist for them." Anna looked up at Nils through the tears brimming in her eyes. "I love you, Nils, but I am afraid if I marry you, the only friends we'll have are Oddleif and Oskar. It's wrong how my parents treat me, but they are just following Jewish law. Marrying a non-Jew is the ultimate act of betrayal to our faith, and the person is completely excluded from the community for life." She grasped Nils' hand and lowered her gaze to the ground. "Nils, I just don't know if I can bear never seeing my parents, Max, Grisha and Rivka again. If we have children, they will not have any grandparents or cousins. I gain one person, but lose five."

Nils' throat went dry as he struggled for words. *So, that's what's been keeping Anna awake and anxious. This independent and spirited girl cannot withstand the pressure from her family. Is it over just in four days?*

Nils gently cupped Anna's chin in his hands. "Anna, sweetheart, I am sorry about your family and I cause you trouble with them. But you and I decide to marry, not them, not pastor. If we do like they tell us, they think they are right, but they are not. It is not wrong for you to marry me. God made man and woman so they leave parents and have children. That is in the beginning of the Bible. Then man write more books, more laws and they forbid one thing or another because man like to forbid. It gives him power, like the bosses you fight against with the union. You know what happen if no one signs union cards because they scared of boss. Same here. We have to be strong and not listen to them. Maybe they think different when they see we are happy and when we have children, because I want you to see them and not think that you lose them forever."

"And, they will never think differently, Nils. It's mostly Mama, but as long as she is alive, she will make sure that I will never be known as her daughter. Once I marry you, the door to my previous life will be slammed shut and I'm not sure I'm ready for that. Papa and I talked last Sunday. The first thing he said to me is that he thinks you are a fine fellow, but.... He raised a lot of buts, such as violating Jewish tradition, the questions of who would marry us, what religion will we raise our children, our happiness if we have no friends or relatives." Anna's green eyes pleaded for understanding. "He is an old man, Nils, and he wants to spend his last years in peace, to be a grandfather, teach the children violin. If I marry you, Mama will not only make his life miserable, but watch the boys and Rivka, forbidding everything—baseball games, friends. That's no life for them. Papa told me that he would want to see me if we marry and he would break Jewish law do it. But how awful! I cannot come home, he cannot see me at the shop because of the gossip, so he is reduced to meeting me in secret on a street corner in St. Paul, with both of us looking around to make sure no one sees us. The only way I would see my brothers will be at a rare baseball game and again, we would have to keep track of the people around us. I just cannot imagine a future like that, Nils." Anna sobbed and buried her face in her hands.

Nils offered Anna his handkerchief and wrapped his arm around her. *What can I do to help Anna? She is in such despair.*

"Your father is a very wise man and I understand what he say, but I cannot help how I feel for you, Anna. I love you since the first time we meet, and I never think if you are Russian or Irish or Jewish. It makes no difference to me. Your family, they ask you for a difficult decision, me or them, and on a scale they are much heavier then one Norwegian man."

Anna tilted her head and looked at Nils with a tear-stained face, her eyes a bright glazed green. "I am not going to put you or them on a scale and see who tips it, Nils. I have to make the decision myself. Can I ask you for two weeks time to give my answer?"

Nils' voice strained with hurt and anger. "I do not know, Anna. Today you tell me you have to think about it. I go home and feel bad, because just last Sunday you say 'yes.' So two weeks later you say 'no,' and I feel worse. So, why do it twice? Just say it now so I can forget about May 1899, forget St. Paul, forget America, forget the girl that I ask. I buy a ticket and go back to Norway, because there is nothing for me here." He wiped his face with his shirtsleeve and looked straight ahead. If he turned toward Anna, she would see the tears that formed in his eyes.

"Nils, please don't forget me. I only ask for two weeks and I want the answer to be yes, just as much as you do. And no matter what happens, we will still be friends." She half-smiled through the tears in her eyes.

"So, if you say 'no' for me to marry you, it is okay for us to take walk like this, go to Minneapolis, eat ice cream? Anna, I cannot do that. It break my heart. I can eat ice cream with Solveig." Nils grasped Anna's hand tighter and brought it against his chest. "But I want you for my wife."

Anna jerked her arm from Nils' touch. Her face twisted with pain and anger as she lashed out at the man she loved. "You are as selfish as Mama, Nils Bjørnsen! With both of you, it's either all or nothing. You all want me. Too bad. You can't have me. Maybe I'm the one who should buy a ticket out of town. Remember when I told you about taking the streetcar to the end of the line, and then getting on a train and then another train? I might just do that and leave you both empty handed!"

Anna whirled and ran across the street. Nils caught up with her and tried to take her hand. "Leave me alone." She tried to yank it away. "Let me go, Nils. Please," Anna sobbed.

"Can I walk you home? You are very upset."

"I know my way home. The sooner you go, the less upset I'll feel. I'll keep my promise and tell you in two weeks." Anna quickened her pace and headed down Pinehurst Street.

"Anna, I still love you," Nils whispered after her, his voice choking with his own tears.

Nils watched Anna disappear from sight, then shoved his hands into his pants pockets. Head lowered, he headed toward home, each step causing the pain in his heart to deepen. *It is over. How quickly happiness passes—a fleeting month! And I thought God had me meet Anna for a reason. Now I know—it was to test me, give me everything I longed for, and then snatch it away. Will I come out better than last time with Kari Hagen? Is God so interested in human failings that He will test at the price of misery and despair of the very beings He created? This merciful and loving God whom just yesterday I defended—He is no better than the devil. Maybe He is the devil. Is there really a difference? What now? Back to the mill and Oddleif and Oskar and their whiskey bottle. Tonight, I will join them. It is better to drown in the bottle than in painful memories. Maybe I will take that same train that Anna was thinking of and go far away.* Nils blinked and blew his nose so no one would suspect that a grown man cried.

He walked a few blocks before he became aware of the heavy footsteps behind him. He glanced over his shoulder and spotted several men. He stopped and so did they. The hairs on the back of his neck stood on end as he quickened his pace. He approached a vacant lot and the back of some warehouse, then cast a furtive glance around him. Not another passerby was in sight.

The footsteps behind him hastened. Suddenly, a man bumped him in the side. Nils turned and stared at a stocky fellow's grim face. He and his three buddies were small, scruffy-looking men. Under normal circumstances, he would have no trouble fending them off. But not with four against one. It would be better to hand them what they wanted and hope that they leave.

"You want money?" Nils took the dollar he had in his pocket and handed it to the shorter man. "Here, take it, buy whiskey for your friends."

The thug snatched the dollar and smirked. "Thanks for paying us to beat you up. That makes six, boys. Not bad."

A skinny man flanked Nils on the right.

"What you want?" Nils asked as the other men surrounded him. "I give you money, I have no more."

The stocky fellow's mouth twisted into a sneer. "You don't ask the questions, you stupid Norskie. We saw what you did to that girl, running after her across the street. I bet you wanted to get under her skirts, didn't you?"

Nils felt the blood drain from his face. *How did they know? Were they following me since I met Anna?* The very notion of such a likelihood disturbed him. "No, we just talk."

"Oh, 'vi yust tak.' You can't even speak proper English and expect to catch a redheaded prize like that?"

The skinny fellow who stood behind Nils voiced his opinion next. "You think you're the only fellow she sees? Ha, little do you know that she sucks off the whole gang here. She's good—even better when she spreads her legs. Mmmm, redhead pussy." The man made a smacking sound with his lips and his friends responded with lewd guffaws.

Nils did not understand the slang, but knew instinctively that the men had said something despicable about Anna. "You do not talk bad about Anna. She never do this. I go home and you go drink whiskey. I gave you money."

Nils made to move, but the burly man blocked his path. "So, you wanna fight us for the girl? Or you are too much of a chicken to hurt your pretty fiddler's fingers? Come on, Norskie, show us what you got." The man jabbed Nils hard in the ribs, almost taking his breath away.

So, they know about the fiddle, too. An awful thought crossed Nils' mind—one he struggled to bury, but could not. *Was Anna so upset by my insistence that we marry that she hired these fellows to beat me up right after she broke off the engagement?*

That would certainly ensure that he would never see her again, especially the way they talked about her. *To go from the depth of despair to fighting off four men.* Nils just wanted to be left alone. Fighting was something left to animals and ignorant men. Unfortunately, Nils faced four of them now. If they had knives, they would kill him for sure. *Now that Anna is gone, does it really matter? I'll show them all.*

"*Fanden ta deg!*" Nils sent the stocky fellow to hell in Norwegian just before he punched him in the face.

The man lost his balance and pitched backward to the ground. Blood seeped from his mouth as he stared with disbelieving eyes at Nils. He did not anticipate such force from a fiddle player—nor did he know that Nils' arms were as strong as steel after twenty years of farm work. He spit out a bloody, broken tooth and yelled. "Let's get him, boys."

In a split second, the four men surrounded Nils. He struggled to fight them off, but as soon as he hit one, the other three took his place. Nils knew he was fighting a losing battle as the men continued to kick and punch him. The coppery taste of blood filled his mouth as he struggled, then two of the men grabbed his left hand. One twisted the wrist in an awkward direction while the other pulled back the fingers. A sickening crack preceded Nils' scream of agony.

"No more fiddling pal," one of the men smirked.

Two of the men grabbed his arms, and they dragged him toward the warehouse wall. The leader clenched Nils' hair within his tight fists and, his eyes wild with anger, pounded the Norwegian's head against the brick.

Unbearable pain exploded in Nils' skull. Again, and yet again, his head connected with the unforgiving stone behind him. His life flashed before his eyes and his knees weakened.

Is this truly the end, to die on a dirty street in St. Paul? Tomorrow they will find my bloody corpse. With no papers, they'll throw it into the potters' field. Oddleif won't even know to write Per and Ingrid.

"You'll never think of a girl for the rest of your life after this." A fiery pain ignited in his groin and the words echoed in his brain before blackness enshrouded him.

Redheaded twin boys crept out of the bushes a few moments later and ran to the warehouse wall.

"Jimmy, them fellath wath yellow. It'th no fair to have four againtht one. Look at him. He'th dead."

"No, he ain't." Jimmy poked Nils with the end of his shoe. "He'th thtill breathing. Tommy, ain't he Maxth' and Grisha'th thithter'th fella?"

"The pitcher?"

"Yeah, him."

"Thure lookth like 'im."

"We better tell Dad."

"No, we'll get in trouble if he knowth where we wath. Don't worry, he'll wake up like Mr. Finnegan alwayth doth after too much whithkey."

"Let'th go home. It'th too creepy here. What if them bad fellath come back?"

The twins ran home and, on the way, made up a story about why they were late. Tomorrow they would go to the sandlot and, if Grisha was there, they would tell him about the bloodied, beaten Norskie fellow.

Chapter Fifteen

Nils opened his eyes to complete silence. His groan echoed in the darkness that surrounded him. *I have died and gone to hell.*

Nils rubbed his eyes with his right hand until they adjusted to the dark. He was lying against the brick wall of the warehouse. Memories of the fight returned, and he knew then why his whole body throbbed with pain. There was no feeling in his left hand, and it was swollen. He remembered the horrible cracking sound and knew the bones in his wrist were broken. He reached up to gingerly touch the combination of sticky blood and pieces of brick in his hair. His groin, too, was indescribably sore. Nils tried to get up, but paused when a wave of dizziness and nausea assaulted him. *No matter. I have to walk home somehow, even if it takes me all night. If I can just go to sleep in a warm bed*, he reasoned, *the pain will go away.*

Another kind of pain gnawed him as, with his good right hand, he pushed against the ground, then the wall, and managed to stand— a pain that lay deep in his heart. He forced it aside. Anna was a fuzzy dream now; his mangled body demanded all of Nils' concentration. He trudged to the northeast side of St. Paul, more by feel than by sight, pausing to rest every few blocks. A cold drizzle began to fall during his ordeal and, by the time he finally reached home, his body shook from chills and exhaustion. He headed for the kitchen and his foot struck the bucket by the door. It clattered down to the basement.

In the next room, Kjersti eyes flew open, then she shook Oddleif. She clutched his arm. "Odd, did you hear that?" she whispered. "Someone's breaking in!"

"It's only Oskar," he mumbled, "coming in from his drinking binge."

"Oskar knows about the slop bucket, and Nils wouldn't kick anything. Go check."

Oddleif heaved himself out of the bed with a groan, lit the kerosene lantern and opened the bedroom door. The man covered in blood and standing in the kitchen barely resembled Nils. "What the...! Kjersti, Oskar, come here, now! It's Nils," he yelled.

Kjersti followed her husband and her eyes widened in horror. "Nils, God in Heaven, what happened to you?"

"Well, the devil," Nils replied in a defeated, hoarse voice. "Or maybe it was God played a dirty trick on me today. I lost the girl I was going to marry and four thugs nearly killed me on the way home. Why say nearly? They did. My left hand is broken and what good is a fiddler with a broken hand? They did not fight fair, so even if I was to marry the girl, there wouldn't be much I could do with her. My head has brains coming out of it, and I can hardly breathe." He pointed a trembling right hand at Oskar. "Oskar, you've been waiting for a long time, and now you got your wish. I am going to ask you for the bottle of whiskey. I want to forget what my life was and not be reminded of what it has now become. You now have yourself another drinking buddy, fellows, at least until I save up money to go back to Norway. America—the land of opportunity they tell the immigrants. More like the land of misery." Nils collapsed into a nearby chair.

Oskar moved to stand before him. "What happened with the girl, Nils? Who were the bastards who beat you?"

Nils looked at him through glazed eyes, but said nothing. He did not have the strength to speak.

Kjersti put a kettle of hot water on the stove. *I have to get some hot liquid into him. The broken head is bad enough, and I don't like the rattling sound in his lungs.* "Oskar, leave him alone with your questions. Can't you see he is in a bad way? Get the whiskey bottle. For once, he will need it."

Nils faded in and out of consciousness as Kjersti opened a kitchen drawer, pulled out some bandages, then cleaned and dressed his wounds. The whiskey felt good as it trickled down his throat, and then flooded his chest with warmth.

Oddleif knelt beside him and carefully felt Nils' left wrist. Realizing that he would be unable to set the bones himself, he shook his head. "He better go and see a doctor about the wrist. The bones are all off."

Kjersti set the bandages aside. "Odd, what do you know about the bones being off?"

"On a trip to *Lofoten*, a fellow slipped on deck and I fixed up his hand."

"You and your *Lofoten* fishing stories," Kjersti said, dismissing her husband's remark. "Nils better see a doctor about everything. Have you taken a look at his head? It's all smashed in. It's a miracle that he made it home and can still talk." She paused when Nils' eyes sagged shut. "Help me get him to bed and tomorrow we'll figure out what to do. He might be better in the morning."

Oskar and Oddleif carried Nils up the stairs and, as they removed his clothes, they uncovered more bruises on his chest, arms and legs. Oddleif pulled a blanket over his cousin and followed Oskar down back down to the kitchen. Kjersti and the two men sat for an hour and speculated on what could have happened to Nils. The more they talked, the more certain they were that the Russian girl was involved. Nils told them that he lost her, and whatever she said to him was serious enough to turn a churchgoing teetotaler into a blaspheming, whiskey-drinking bum. Perhaps tomorrow Nils would be better and could tell them the full story.

Morning came, and Nils' condition had worsened. His left hand had swollen considerably, and the head injuries appeared to cloud his mind. He was not sure where he was and kept asking Kjersti about the farm in Voss, people no longer living or the ones remaining in Norway. It was like the last seven months in St. Paul were now completely erased from his memory. *Perhaps it's better that way. He will never remember the Russian girl or the beating.*

Solveig ventured up to the sick room early that morning and could not understand why her uncle Nils did not recognize her. Kjersti sent both of the children to Mrs. Fossheim's for the day, so she could care for her patient. She prepared a hearty bowl of porridge, but the sick man would not touch it. By afternoon, he had developed a fever and a raspy cough—a cough which now produced blood. Kjersti's brow furrowed with worry. She would send for the doctor as soon as either Oddleif or Oskar came home. She did not dare leave Nils alone.

Oskar returned soon thereafter, carrying several bottles of patent medicines that another fellow at the stockyards recommended. "If Nils does not like them, I will drink them myself." The liquid base of the medicines was his favorite—alcohol.

Kjersti snatched the bottles from Oskar and attempted to spoon-feed the greenish-tinged syrup to the sick man. Nils gagged and vomited up the horrid brew, and she faced Oskar. "These bottles are mixed by that Italian crook who skims off stupid men like you, who believe everything you read. Go fetch Doctor Schultz and beg him to come now." Kjersti lowered her voice. "Otherwise, you may be running for the undertaker by morning."

"Is he really that bad, Kjersti?"

She wiped the sweat from her forehead with her apron. "I don't know, Oskar. I just have a bad feeling about it."

"Did he tell you who did this to him?" His chest protruded with a rare pride and anger. "As soon as I get the doctor, me and Oddleif will hunt these bastards down and beat the living crap of out them. Better yet, we'll kill them and throw them in the river. Sons of bitches that they are, cowards—four of them taking on one man." Oskar kicked the wall, and Nils twitched in pain.

"Shhh. Don't disturb him. People who are this ill need peace and quiet. No, he did not tell me anything. I tried asking." Kjersti went down to a whisper. "They hit him in the head so bad, his mind is gone. He thinks he's in Norway, talks as if his mother and father are still alive. It's so sad to watch. Only time will tell if he gets better. But the cough, that's more troublesome. I suspect he was bruised on the ribs, bled inside, and then got chilled from the rain coming home."

"What are we going tell the foreman at the mill?" Oskar asked.

"Not to worry. Oddleif promised to go there today. The foreman is Swedish, and Nils is a hard worker. What can they do if a man is sick? I just hope they hold his job until he comes back. *If* he comes back…" Kjersti's voice trailed off.

Oskar returned within an hour, accompanied by Dr. Schultz, a graying man with gold-rimmed glasses and a black medical bag. He spoke with a trace of a German accent as he examined Nils and asked questions of Kjersti and Oskar. Nils was delirious with fever and revealed no details of his injuries. Dr. Schultz motioned for his relatives to step outside the sick man's room.

"I'm afraid the news is not good," the doctor informed them. "He has a fever and his lungs are filled with fluid. The internal bleeding complicates matters somewhat, and I felt a couple of broken ribs. I would like to put a cast on his left arm and set the wrist properly. He also has a bad injury to the groin and chances are that he will not be able to perform any functions of a husband in the future."

Dr. Shultz' brow knitted in concern. "What worries me the most is the state of his mind. After such a severe beating on the head, it is very likely that he would lose his memory, as you have stated he did, and may never recover fully. In the best case, he would forget the beating and whatever happened a couple of days beforehand. In the worst case, he will remain as he is, if not get worse. In that case, you would have to take care of him and watch him as you would a two-year-old child." The doctor glanced toward Nils, then returned his attention to Kjersti. "He looks like a strong fellow, so I think he will live through the pneumonia, but I would like you to take him to the hospital first thing tomorrow morning. He needs to be observed and treated at least for the next couple of weeks. Once his lungs are clear, we will start to work on his head injuries. It is absolutely imperative that his room be totally quiet. Any noise can be a setback to his recovery. We will insure that at the hospital, but when he comes back home, keep your little ones out of this room. Try to talk to him about familiar people and things, so that he will begin to remember. I am on rounds at St. Paul City Hospital, so when you take him tomorrow, tell the admitting nurse that I referred you."

Oskar showed him the two bottles that he bought for Nils. "Doctor, what you think about these medicines? Do they work?"

The doctor took the bottle with the green liquid, opened it and sniffed the contents. "No, it's whiskey, sugar, and some coloring. Nothing more. The whiskey will warm up the insides and dull the pain, but nothing more. Basically, you just spent your hard-earned money on some pretty colored bottles."

"What did I tell you, Oskar?" Kjersti turned to the doctor. "Nils has a little money saved up, and I'll pay for your visit today. About the hospital, will that be very expensive if he stays long?"

The doctor gave her a reassuring smile. "Let's get him well, and then we'll talk about the bill. If he recovers, he can pay the hospital once a month. If he does not, there are asylums where he can be put up as a charity case. Let's hope for the best, though."

"Thank you, doctor," Kjersti said with a relieved sigh. "Can we do anything for him tonight?"

"Try to get him to drink water or tea. A body can live without food for several days, but needs liquids every couple of hours. Run a wet cloth over him to break the fever, but don't let him get chilled. If his breathing gets worse, don't wait until morning. Bring him to the hospital during the night. We have a doctor on duty. I must be going. I have another patient to attend to. Good evening."

Dr. Schultz left the house and was replaced a moment later by Oddleif. "Talked to the foreman. He sends Nils a speedy recovery. Says he's a hard worker, strong as an ox, and wants him back as soon as he gets well. Of course, I did not tell him exactly what happened. Just said a broken wrist and left it at that."

Kjersti threw herself in Oddleif's arms. "Oh, Odd, I wish it was just a broken wrist. Last night, at least he knew where he was. Now, he thinks he is in Norway and that Bjørn and Marta are still alive. Odd, he did not even recognize Solveig, and he has a rattle in his lungs and spits up blood. The doctor said that even if he makes it through the pneumonia, his mind may never get well. It will be like taking care of Henrik, feeding, changing, watching over him. God forbid that should happen. The doctor wants him at the hospital tomorrow morning."

Kjersti broke down into sobs as Oddleif drew her into his arms. "I think he will pull through. He is strong from all the farm work. Give him a little time and his head will be better. I'll go and get the children from Fossheim's. You rest now. Me and Oskar will cook something."

Kjersti headed for the bedroom. She would need the rest as she spent another sleepless night at Nils' side.

Despite all of Kjersti's attempts to break his fever, later that night Nils' forehead remained hot and he was barely conscious. His breathing became more labored and several times, after a particularly nasty coughing spell, she was afraid she would lose him. She could barely understand the sick man's delirious ravings, but Kjersti could have sworn that she heard him mention Anna's name more than once.

Kjersti was sure the following morning that if they did not take Nils to the hospital, he would not survive another night at home. Oddleif borrowed a cart and horse from Helge Dahl and set off to the hospital with his cousin.

Kjersti wrapped him in several blankets, but Nils' teeth still chattered from the chills that wracked his body. "Where are you taking me, Oddleif. Let me die at home on the farm. I know the end is near," the delirious man pleaded.

"To the hospital. The doctor said he'd fix you up as good as new. They got medicines in there. What do we got, but whiskey?"

"It's too late, Odd, too late." Nils' voice faded into unconsciousness.

The St. Paul City Hospital was an imposing red brick structure. It was immaculately clean inside, and only the rustle of nurses' starched uniforms broke the quiet. The admitting nurse asked Oddleif several questions, explained the visiting policy, and then told him to leave.

"Nurse," Oddleif said, "he don't speak no English, only Norwegian. We come this evening so you can ask us what he told you."

The woman nodded her understanding. "There is a Norwegian nurse here. It will not be necessary. This man should not be disturbed. Mr. Bjørnsen, come this way please."

Nils stared blankly at the nurse as she took him by the hand. The woman spoke in a language he could not understand. *What does she want of me?* He turned to his cousin with a look of utter despair in his clouded blue eyes. "Oddleif, don't leave me here. The medicines won't help. When I die, promise that you will bury me in the churchyard by mother and father."

Nils' body was attacked by another coughing fit, and the nurse held him up as he struggled for breath. Oddleif patted Nils on the back. "I won't make any promises, because you are not dying. Kjersti and I won't allow it. We'll see you tonight. I got to be at work now, and Kjersti has to take care of the children. Your job for the day, Nils, is to get better and that's an order."

"We will take care of him," the nurse added. "You are free to leave. Remember visiting hours end at eight in the evening." She dismissed Oddleif and returned her attention to Nils. "Now, you come with me and don't cause any trouble."

Nils forced his feet to move. *If only this lady would take me somewhere to lie down.* But before being given a bed, Nils had to undergo the mandatory bath and delousing, and it took a strong male orderly to keep him from falling as he slipped into unconsciousness.

At last, Nils felt the warmth of a blanket covering him. He closed his eyes and drifted into sleep, uncertain—and not caring—if he would ever wake up again.

Chapter Sixteen

Anna walked home, tasting the salt of her tears. *I just drove away the man I love, never to see him again. How can I face him in two weeks after how I treated him tonight?*

Anna closed her eyes for a moment as she tried to shut out the memories: her first kiss, Nils' funny way of speaking English, how he carried her across Cedar Avenue in downtown St. Paul. All that remained was the look of utter despair that appeared on his face when she broke off the engagement.

Nils, I wish I could be in your arms now. Let's take the train, run away, and leave St. Paul behind. I can turn around now and catch up to him. She paused and wiped away the fresh tears that stung her eyes. *But what would Papa say?*

Anna opened the apartment door several minutes later. Moyshe looked up from the paper, saw his daughter's tear-stained face and shook his head. *She did as I asked. In time, she will get over the boy.*

Sarah nodded at Moyshe, her lips pursed in a thin line of satisfaction. Rivka paused from dusting the figurines and photographs on the shelf, and the boys exchanged curious glances with each other. Moyshe heard the bedroom door slam, and then his daughter's muffled sobs reached his ears.

Sarah rolled her eyes and turned to Moyshe. "Do we all have to listen to this sniveling? You are her father, do something."

"Sarah, the best way to fix this is to do nothing. Let her cry it out and she will get over him faster." Moyshe shrugged his shoulders and resumed reading the paper.

Anna could not concentrate on her work the following day. She tried to undo her poor stitching on several pieces of material and, as the thread became more entangled, she tore at the fabric in frustration. The girls around Anna noticed her mishaps and whispered among themselves. "It must be that Norwegian fellow. She is not one to get out of sorts."

Anna made it through the day, but she did not look forward to going home. Neither did she want to eat with her family, so she got off the streetcar several blocks early and bought bread and cheese at an Irish store. At least there, the girl behind the counter did not ask her any questions or chide her for driving her mother to an early grave.

Anna brought the food home and, slamming the front door behind her, headed straight for the bedroom. Rivka said nothing as she gave Anna a cursory glance, then left to finish her homework in the kitchen.

Max and Grisha caught the few hours of daylight before the beginning of *Shabbos* by playing a few pickup games of baseball with the neighborhood boys. The games were split—one for the Irish and one for the Jewish boys, with Max hitting a two run double for the team. As the Katz boys walked home after the game, they discussed the disturbing story they heard from the Murphy twins.

"Grisha, I wouldn't trust two lisping eight-year-olds with anything." Max sliced the air with his index finger, trying to prove his point. "You know what Sherlock Holmes relies on.... Facts, evidence. They could have seen some drunk Irishman who resembled Nils and drew the wrong conclusion. Besides, it was dark. It could have been anyone."

"I know they're probably wrong but...but what if there is the tiniest chance they're right? I think we should go over there and take a look for ourselves."

"We do that, and we get in so much trouble for coming home late, Mama will never let us out. Maybe Sunday."

"Should we tell Anna?"

"No, she's already upset as it is. She and Nils want to get married, but with Mama the way she is, Papa talked Anna out of it."

Grisha tugged at his brother's sleeve. "If it was my friend, I would want to know if he was dead or beat up. I think Anna should know."

Max shrugged. "Well then you can tell her, Grisha. But if the twins are wrong, which I am sure they are, you can take the blame for all the screaming and crying that will happen. Besides, Nils didn't seem like he would fight with anyone."

The boys arrived home just on time for dinner. Anna did not come out for the meal, but stayed in the bedroom reading. After dinner, Grisha knocked on the door under the pretext of asking help on his homework.

"They gave you homework for the summer?" Anna's voice lifted with surprise.

"No." Grisha paused, unsure how to begin. "Well, you know me and Max were playing ball with the Murphy twins?"

Anna forced a smile. "Yeth, the lithping twinth with the mithing teeth," she mimicked. "How can I forget?"

Grisha stepped from one foot to the other and nervously bit his right thumbnail. "Anna, I hope you don't get upset at me, but I need to tell you something."

"Grisha, you know that I don't get upset. Especially not at my little brother. What is it?"

The boy lowered his voice and moved closer to his sister. "Well, I am not sure if it's true. The twins were out playing last night and they watched four men beat up another one and they said the fellow that got beat up looked like Nils."

Anna felt the blood drain from her face. "What did they see and where?"

"It was by that brick warehouse in the Irish neighborhood. Jimmy and Tommy were not supposed to be there anyway. They said he tried to fight them off, but there was four of them and they got him in the head. When the bad men left, the twins came out of the bushes. Jimmy thought the man was dead, but Tommy poked him with his shoe and said he was breathing. He was all covered with blood, but they both said that he looked like Nils." Grisha rubbed his eyes and sniffed. "Anna, I hope it's not true. They *are* little kids. Maybe it was a fight between some drunk Irishmen."

"Grisha, did they tell you what the four men looked like?"

"Sort of. One was short and fat and the other three were skinny. Tommy thought it was funny that they all wore hats and tried to keep them on while fighting."

Anna's voice hardened and the boy noticed sparks of fire in his sister's green eyes, even behind her glasses. "The Irish are not so fastidious about fashion when they fight. Grisha, I think I have a pretty good idea who these men were and who sent them and, in less than thirty minutes, I will find out if I am right."

"What's fastidious?" Grisha asked.

"Since you came to ask for help with homework, I'm giving you an assignment. Look it up in the dictionary and write it in a notebook. Learn one new word a day and by the time the school year starts, you can impress all your friends in fifth grade with how much you know. Thanks for telling me about the twins. I promise double scoops of ice cream for all of you. But first, I need to make a little trip." Anna gave her brother a hug and left the apartment. When Moyshe asked where she was going, Grisha pleaded ignorance and busied himself with the dictionary.

Anna marched toward the Minsk tavern, located a few blocks up on Snelling. She had no doubt that the short fat man was Leon Weissberg and the two skinny ones were the Rabinowitz brothers. She was not sure about the fourth fellow; probably another drunk who was looking for excitement. Those men had a reputation for violating every letter of Jewish law. They fought, never held down decent jobs, but their hats? Those they kept on as a pathetic concession to their Jewishness.

Would Mama stoop so low as to ask them to beat up Nils?

Anna shuddered in horror at the thought. Nils could be dead or gravely injured. He was a strong fellow, but certainly no match for four men. *After how I treated him yesterday, he probably figured that I sent the thugs after him to make a point.*

Anna resolved that, first thing in the morning, she would check on Nils. That is, if he was still alive.

The sidewalk in front of the tavern was empty, but she heard the raucous laugher and clinking of glasses from inside. Anna walked into the smoky, foul smelling hall and ignored the lewd guffaws directed her way. Sure enough, Weissberg and the Rabinowitz brothers sat at the bar drinking beer and playing cards.

Weissberg spotted her first. "Does the little girl want a drink?" he asked as his gaze raked her, finally settling on her chest.

Anna clenched her teeth, then took two dollar bills from her purse and waved them in front of the men. "No, I'll pass on the drink, but I am giving money away."

"Whaddaya know, a girl paying us," Simon Rabinowitz tittered.

"Yes, I want four or five strong men for a little job. There's a Norskie fellow who just won't leave me alone. What's a Jewish girl to do? Don't kill him or anything. Just break a few bones, if you know what I mean. I'll pay you two dollars today."

Before Leon Weissberg even had the chance to agree and pocket the extra money, Chaim Rabinowitz threw his hands in the air. "What's the deal with you women?" he exclaimed. "First the mother, then the daughter! We fixed him up pretty good yesterday. I don't think he'll bother you again."

Leon spat. "Chaim, you idiot, you just pissed away two dollars."

"No, I'll add a couple of dollars to the pot," Anna countered. "You didn't kill the fellow, and I certainly wouldn't want you to get into trouble with the law."

"No, nothing so evil," Chaim replied. "Just broke his wrist, cracked his head in a couple of places and....well, we can't say the rest in front of such a fine lady. Let's just put it this way. He won't have much in his head left to remember you by, so he can go home and cry on his fiddle. Except his hand is too broke to play it. So, he wants to take up with a girl sometime. The spirit may be willing...but the flesh will be weak, if you get my drift. Trust me, that Norskie will never think of you again."

Anna's hands balled into fists at her sides as she struggled to retain her composure. "I think the last part was unnecessary, but here's the money for your hard work." She slid the money across the dirty oilcloth. "Buy yourselves another beer. There is no need to do anything more."

Anna's worst fears now confirmed, she ran from the tavern and plunged into the June evening. *Papa talked me out of the marriage based on reason and common sense, but Mama's tactics were downright murderous. How could she hire those men?*

Tears blinded her as she headed home in the growing darkness. *The bastards! My Nils, left beaten and broken. No use going to the warehouse tonight. The workmen probably found him this morning. God only knows where he is now. First thing tomorrow, I will go over to Odd and Kjersti's and find out what happened.*

Anna longed to hold Nils in her arms and heal his broken body with her kisses. She blamed herself for lashing out at him yesterday. His last memory before he died would be of her rejection. *Nils, I love you. I'll be with you soon.*

Please, God, keep him alive. For the first time in her life, the prayer came from the bottom of her heart.

The front door slammed with such force that it sent the family portrait crashing from the book shelf to the floor. Broken glass shattered all over the living room.

"How appropriate that the picture fell." Anna squeezed out the words between clenched teeth. She stared directly into her mother's eyes as she continued. "My trust in this family is shattered into more pieces than the glass here."

Sarah frowned as she put her knitting aside and stood. "How dare you talk about trust, the way you've been carrying on—coming and going at all hours, and with whom? Max, Grisha," she said, voice stern, "off to your room, now!"

Anna bridged the distance to her mother, then raised her hand until her index finger almost jabbed Sarah in the chest. "It is *you*, Mama, who has to look in the mirror and ask yourself about trust. How quickly did you forget why we left Russia, to come here and participate in the same brutalities as the people who persecuted us!"

Sarah was, for once, speechless. Moyshe stood, his face flushed with anger. "Anna, you must be sick in your head. You and Mama have disagreements, but to accuse her of something so vile. Stop this instant!"

Anna faced her father and her voice cracked as she continued. "Papa, you can form your opinion after you hear me out. You remember that the governor paid thugs, soldiers, and all kinds of down and out men a good sum of money to have a *pogrom* on our village? While we picked up the pieces of our lives, the villagers and soldiers were having a feast. Ours was a river of tears and theirs of vodka." She paused to let her words sink in, then continued.

"Someone here has forgotten the pain, because that person gave money to four men to beat up Nils Bjørnsen last night. Those men were drunk enough to brag about who hired them and how they did it. I don't even know if Nils is alive, but I will find out tomorrow." Anna's body shook with her anger as she paused to glance toward her mother. "The first thing I will do, however, is pack my things and take a room at a boarding house. I refuse to stay another day with a person who sanctioned a vicious beating of an innocent man."

Moyshe tried to inject reason into a crime he could not comprehend, let alone believe was associated with anyone in his family. Yet, as he glanced at his wife, Sarah turned white and sat down on the sofa. *Sarah wouldn't stoop so low—or would she?* "If they were drunk, Anna, how do you know they were telling the truth to begin with? Besides, there are plenty of troublemakers who would beat up an immigrant for money."

"There were witnesses to the crime," Anna replied, "and the thugs confirmed what the witnesses saw. I intend to have a talk with the police because, unlike Russia, in America, justice will be served."

Sarah's lips tightened as her world fell apart. *The bums just had to wag their tongues! And who were the witnesses? Stupid, worthless drunks! I was just trying to protect my daughter, but no more. It is high time to tell her who she really is.*

Sarah rose and faced her daughter. "Anna, look at me." A ball of emotion stuck in her throat, making her voice sound raspy to her ears. She swallowed hard before she continued. "You...you dare to say that I have forgotten the pain of a *pogrom*? Never! I have looked that pain in the face for the past twenty-three years. And that face is you."

Anna knitted her brow in confusion. "What do you mean, Mama?"

"Moyshe," she said, turning to her husband, "you might as well know." She paused for several moments to rub her shaking hands, then faced her oldest daughter. "In 1876, a band of soldiers and riff-raff came through our village. I was about your age, Anna, engaged by the *yentl* to Moyshe. My family, we hid in the cellar and feared the approaching hoof beats. Within a few moments, we were discovered, our possessions were broken, Mama, Papa, my brothers and sisters were beaten. I thought I was lucky that I was spared, but no, they left me for last. A big brute with a crop of dirty orange hair picked me up, took me upstairs, and threw me on my parents' bed. He always wanted to 'do a yid girl,' as he put it. He violated me and, as he laid on me, I smelled his foul onion breath and looked into his savage green eyes. It was over in less than five minutes." Sarah's brown eyes bored into her daughter's green ones. "You were the result of this hideous act. No one knew except my Mama and Grandma Katz. They married me off right away, so, when the baby came, everyone assumed it was Moyshe's. We made up stories about Grandma Hannah's red hair, Great-grandpa Leizer's green eyes, so that your father and the neighbors would not suspect anything. I think they did anyway. So, I spent my whole life trying to make you Jewish. If I did anything, it was to protect you, so no man would do to you what he did to me. But I only made half of you. The other half is that hot-headed beast who rules your soul."

Sarah wiped her forehead with her hands and sat down again. "I can do no more. You were never my daughter. Go away to your Swede and never, ever set foot in this house again."

Anna sucked in a breath and swallowed convulsively as her mind reeled from the news. Conflicting emotions raced through her simultaneously: Hate for the woman who hired men to beat up Nils, outrage and disbelief that she had been conceived through such a brutal act, pity for her pale-faced father, and an urge to comfort her mother. Love won out.

"Mama, I am so sorry—"

Anna approached the sofa, but her mother drew away. "Get away from me. I wish you were never born. You and your Norskie *goy*, it's all the same. My chest!" Sarah clutched at her bosom, above her heart, and started to collapse on the sofa. Moyshe caught her. He began to stroke her hair in gentle, calming motions, and she burst into tears. "Moyshe, now that you know, I am not worthy to be your wife and to live in the same house with you. I betrayed you and the children. I just want to die."

"Sarah," he said, his voice soft with tenderness. "I knew the day Anna was born that she was not my daughter. What could I do? I raised her and loved her, as I would my own child."

"How did you know, Moyshe?" Sarah gasped.

"They married us very quickly. Besides, there were too many whispers around the house. I suspected something was the matter." He lifted his shoulders in a small shrug. "When this little redhead with green eyes came into the world, what I suspected was confirmed. Don't blame Anna or yourself for what happened. There is not much we can do about it now. As far as I am concerned," he paused and tossed Anna a smile of reassurance before he continued, "I am her father. That man contributed a very small part to her, but we spent over twenty years taking care of her. She is as much a Jew as you or I, Sarah."

"And how does she repay us for it?" Sarah retorted. "What's the difference, Moyshe? A *goy* is a *goy*."

"I would say it makes a big difference, Sarah. I met the Bjørnsen fellow, and so did you. He is a decent man." His eyes hardened. "I certainly hope you were not mixed up with the men who beat him up. It's not right and bad for my business."

"I don't want to talk about that, Moyshe. Who knows who beat him up? I am tired."

"We are all tired, Mama," Anna cut in. "And after everything that happened, I think it would be best if I lived somewhere else. We cause each other too much pain." She turned to Moyshe. "Papa, thank you for raising me as your own. As far as I am concerned, you are the only father I have. That man who…took Mama by force, he means nothing to me."

Moyshe nodded. "It's about time we get to bed, being *Shabbos* and all. Tomorrow is a new day and let's hope it's better." Moyshe helped Sarah stand and led her into their bedroom.

Anna walked into hers, knocking Rivka off balance. "Listening by the keyhole again, sis?"

"How could I not? You think it's true?"

"What?"

Rivka stared at her as though Anna was daft. "The savage with the dirty orange hair, of course."

"Why wouldn't it be? Mama has never liked me, even since I was a little girl. Now I know why. Besides," she added, heading for the closet, "if I am half-Russian, it wouldn't matter who I marry. But then Nils might already be dead, thanks to her."

"Anna, you don't really think that Mama would pay someone to do that?" Rivka always defended her mother and could not accept her being involved in something so evil.

"It does not matter now." She began to undress. "What's done is done. I just hope that Nils is all right. I told Mama and Papa I am leaving, so you can have a room to yourself. I think it would be best for all of us."

"I'll miss you."

Anna heard the tremor in Rivka's voice. "I'll miss you too, and no matter what Mama says, I *will* see you. We'll figure something out." She slipped into bed and turned out the light. "I have a long day tomorrow, so I better get some sleep. Good night."

"Good night."

* * *

Anna tossed and turned all night. After everything that happened sleep would not come to her. *What am I? Russian, Jew, bastard daughter? How is Nils and where is he?*

She blamed Sarah, then herself, then the thugs for his situation. She dozed off toward dawn, but woke up early enough to pack the most necessary items in a large wicker basket. As she tiptoed through the living room, trying hard not to make the floor creak, a bedroom door opened and Moyshe came out.

"Anna, I won't stop you from leaving. Perhaps now it's the right thing to do. But I wanted to say good-bye." He put an arm around his daughter. "What Mama told us yesterday did not change anything. I love you now as much as I did before."

"Papa." Anna's eyes misted with tears as she threw herself in Moyshe's arms.

"Come to the shop after closing Monday and we'll talk more. There's also the matter of your savings. I want you to have it. It's your money, after all. I hope Nils is not in a bad way. Wish him well for me."

"Thank you, Papa. I will see you soon."

Anna gave her father a hug and slipped out the front door.

Chapter Seventeen

A few hours later, Anna had booked a small room at Mary Pinkham's Boarding House for Young Women. She tossed her basket of belongings on the bed and rushed for the streetcar that would take her to Cayuga Street. Her heart pounded with fear as she approached Nils' house. No one was in the front yard, so Anna knocked on the door. Kjersti opened the entrance a minute later and Anna released a surprised gasp. She barely recognized the woman with dark circles under her eyes and her pale face. She looked haggard and so worn out that Anna was certain she barely had the strength to stand up. Solveig and Henrik, at last free from the confines of the house, slipped by Kjersti and dashed outside to play in the yard.

Kjersti stepped forward and, grasping the door's edge, leaned against the frame to bar the entrance to her home. "What do you want from us? You caused Nils enough trouble, and it's too late now."

"What do you mean?" Anna's throat constricted in pain. "Is he...?" She could not make herself say the word.

"No, not yet, but he is very sick. His mind is gone and his lungs are bleeding. It's awful to watch. Why did you do it?"

"Do what? If you mean about the men who beat him up," Anna said in her defense, "I had nothing to do with it. The only reason I know is two Irish kids told my ten-year-old brother that they saw four men beating up a fellow who looked like Nils. He played baseball with these children a couple of weeks ago, so that's why they remembered him. I found out yesterday evening, and by that time it was too late to come here. You must believe me."

"I mean, why did you say 'no' to him? You broke his heart. I think that's why he cannot get well. A girl in Norway did the same thing to him and it was hard for him the first time. I don't think he can survive this time. You killed him, Anna. Now go home." Kjersti retreated a step and began to close the front door, but Anna stuck her foot in the opening.

"Kjersti, no! You have to listen to me!" she pleaded. "We met Thursday and he told me that his pastor is very angry at him and won't marry us because I am *not* Lutheran. My family is upset that Nils *is* Lutheran and my father told me to think about the marriage, what religion will we raise our children, whom will we have for friends if our family and church do not accept us. All I told Nils was that I wanted to think about it for two weeks. Kjersti, I love him so much that I know I would have said 'yes' in any case. He did not take it so well at all, though. Perhaps if he's been hurt before..."

Kjersti's gray eyes softened with sudden understanding. "You were wise. I am sorry about what I said. Men just fall in love and don't think things through." She stepped aside and, drawing the door open, waved her hand for Anna to enter.

She stepped into the house and followed the other woman. "What happened in Norway?"

Kjersti motioned for her to take a seat at the kitchen table and poured two cups of coffee. She set a cup before Anna, and then sat opposite her. "Well, it was about ten years ago. Nils was eighteen or so, and he played for weddings. One day this pretty girl took a fancy to him. I think she was not very pretty on the inside, but Nils noticed too late. Kari Hagen was her name. He fell in love with her, they spend the summer together, and we think soon there will be a wedding. So, he asked her to marry him and she looked at him and said something like, 'Why should I marry a poor farmer like you, Nils? You were fun for the summer and I always wanted to say that I knew a fiddler. But marry you? Never.' She walks away. Nils' heart is broken. He quit playing and, for about a year, stayed at home and worked the farm horses too hard. This girl married a rich man and took a special pleasure in passing by his farm in her fancy carriage. It was like putting salt on an old wound. The girl was not finished yet, because she whispered a lot of mean things to her husband, and that man spent two years forcing Nils off his farm. That's why he's here in St. Paul."

So Kari Hagen was the missing link to Jens Ulvang's schemes, Anna thought as the truth hit her. *My suspicions were right. There was a woman involved.* "Nils told me about the land and his mother. How sad. Is Nils at home? Can I see him?" Anna rose and, determined, left the kitchen and headed for the steps that lead to the attic.

"No." Kjersti followed her. She waited until Anna faced her before she spoke again. "He's at St. Paul City Hospital. But prepare yourself. He does not seem to remember his life in St. Paul at all, and I am pretty sure he forgot his English. His cough is awful. The doctors really don't think he will last more than a few days. Once Odd comes home, we will be there." Kjersti rubbed her eyes. "You have to excuse me. I have not slept for two nights."

Anna's heart went out to the other woman. "I can watch the children if you want to take a nap."

Kjersti's eyes widened for a moment, then she shook her head. "No, you go. I heard him asking for you last night. Maybe just hearing your voice will make him better."

Anna took both of Kjersti's hands in hers. "Thank you for taking care of him. I'll do everything I can from now on. Well, I better catch the streetcar to the hospital. I'll come by and see you tonight."

Kjersti opened the front door to let Anna outside. "God bless and keep him until then."

Anna heard her call for Solveig and Henrik as she ran to the streetcar stop.

The almost overpowering odor of antiseptic struck Anna as soon as she walked into St. Paul City Hospital. She checked with the nurse, who led her through several corridors toward Nils' room. She glanced through open doors on the way and cringed at the beds full of moaning, sick people. Several other patients, who were on the road to recovery, wandered about the halls. The nurse approached a door with a sign that said "Quiet - Neurological Ward" and reinforced the warning by placing a finger on her lips.

"Try not to overexcite the patient," she cautioned. "He needs peace and quiet to recover his memory. Talk about familiar things, but nothing traumatic. Ring the bell if you need us."

"Thank you." Anna tiptoed through the room, which held five beds, looking for Nils. Human lumps concealed under blankets occupied two of the beds. The third held an emaciated man with greasy dark hair, who sat and stared at the wall. *Is that what Nils will be like now?*

Anna looked away from the man and walked on, toward the fourth bed. Nils had tossed off his covers, and she could hear the rattle in his lungs as he breathed in his sleep. His head was wrapped with gauze bandages and bruises marred his fever-flushed face. His left arm hug limply from the side of the bed, encased in a cast.

Anna pulled a chair up to the bed, then took a seat and waited for him to wake up.

Nils heard the sound of wood scraping wood and opened his eyes. A woman sat beside the bed, and she took his hand in hers and whispered softly. "Nils, my sweetheart. It's me, Anna. I promise you will get better soon. We'll be married in no time, and you'll buy that little farm you always wanted. I just know it."

He stared at the red-haired girl, and his brow knitted in confusion. She looked familiar. In fact, there was something about her that was very important, but what was it? Nils struggled to remember, but could not. The girl spoke in a language he did not quite understand. For that matter, the doctor and the nurse did, too. *If I am not in Norway, then where am I? Maybe she will at least understand a few words of Norwegian.*

"Can you please help me?" He swallowed as the urge to cough tickled his throat. His voice sounded hoarse and his throat was drier than a desert. *"Where am I? Who are you?"*

"Nils, it's all right. I understand only some of what you're saying, and I'll do my best to answer. You just listen and things will come back to you." The woman bent over to kiss him on the cheek, then switched to Norwegian. "It's me, Nils. It's Anna, and you're in St. Paul, Minnesota."

Nils was sure he was dreaming. This girl was like an angel, and she even spoke his language. Not well, but she spoke it nonetheless. *Anna. Where have I heard that name before? And St. Paul—that's where my cousin Oddleif lives, in America. But how did I get to St. Paul? If this is indeed a dream or some kind of heaven, I do not want it to end. Perhaps she is an angel sent to take me from this earth.* His grasp on her hand tightened as sharp pain sent daggers through his body. *It is time. The pain is unbearable.*

Nils closed his eyes until the agony slowly eased. "Don't leave me, my beautiful angel," he whispered. "I am ready to go home. I am so tired."

Anna stroked Nils' hand as he dropped off to sleep and his breathing grew steady. She longed desperately for a Norwegian dictionary or a translator as she remained by his side, but knew she could do nothing but hold his hand until Kjersti came.

Nils awoke several times during the next hour, and Anna used those brief periods of consciousness to recount how they first met, the outing to Minneapolis with Solveig, the union picnic, his proposal and their first dance. Each time, Nils held onto her hand and said something in Norwegian, and then dropped off to sleep again. If he could learn English once, she reasoned, the second time should be much easier.

A nurse came in after two hours and asked Anna to leave. "You need to let the patient rest. You can come back in the evening for another hour."

Anna stood and gently squeezed Nils' hand. "*Jeg elsker deg*, Nils," she whispered.

Nils opened his clear blue eyes and looked directly into hers. "*Anna, jeg elsker deg.*"

She rose and left the room with a small smile curving her lips. His last words were all the proof she needed. Nils' memory was coming back.

Nils lay in the bed after she left and pieced together the returning fragments of his life in St. Paul. Anna's face and her voice had finally brought it all back. *Of course. I asked her to marry me, and she said, 'Yes.' That's my last memory. Am I really dying, never to marry my sweetheart? Why, God, why?*

Nils buried his face in the pillow. He had to get well, if not for himself, then for Anna.

Anna returned to the hospital that evening. Kjersti and Oddleif were already standing beside Nils' bed with a strangely dressed man, who looked several centuries out of date with his starched ruffed collar and black robe.

Kjersti noticed Anna's arrival, but remained silent, uncertain how to go about introducing the woman to the pastor. The meeting, she knew, would be uncomfortable for both of them. Anna remained just inside the door and her eyes squinted with puzzlement. Kjersti inclined her head in a nod—a silent signal for Anna to stay where she was for the moment. She returned her attention to the pastor, who sat on the corner of Nils' bed and spoke in a low monotone, almost as if preaching a sermon.

Nils stared at Pastor Grundseth and his lips tightened. *"Are God and the devil really battling for my soul? What did I do that would make the pastor so upset?* "I know I am dying and I confess to all my sins, but why do you say God is punishing me with a sickness for a great sin? Did I do something so awful that I don't remember?"

Eivind Grundseth's eyes darkened at the question. "You wanted to marry the most despicable of heathens—a Jew, the temptress of the devil. God in his mercy gave you this sickness, for he would rather take your soul home than have it plunge into the depths of hell. Do you now renounce the works of the devil, Nils?"

Anna noticed Kjersti and Oddleif exchange glances, then returned her attention to the stranger.

Why is the ruff-collared man getting agitated and pointing a finger at Nils? That much excitement cannot be good for him.

Suddenly, Nils covered his face with his hands, as if to block a blow. "Go away from here! You are tormenting me! I don't know why I am sick, but it is not for the reason you speak of. I told you, I confess my sins. Now please, leave."

Nils broke into a nasty fit of coughing and Anna could watch his torture no longer. She ran to the bedside and, bracing Nils with her left arm, gave him a handkerchief. He felt even hotter than in the morning, but she knew fevers always climbed toward night.

She faced the oddly-dressed man and hoped that he understood English. "Sir, I do not speak Norwegian, but whatever you said to Mr. Bjørnsen seems to have upset him. He is very fragile and cannot be overexcited. His recovery depends on it."

"I apologize, nurse," he replied in a heavily accented English. "I am just very concerned about his soul."

"I am not the nurse, but these instructions were given by her and the doctor. Perhaps you could see him another time? His soul is fine, but his body is very broken."

Eivind Grundseth opened his mouth to speak, but Kjersti rattled off an explanation in Norwegian, and then translated to Anna. "I told Pastor Grundseth that you help the nurses with the patients."

Anna caught onto the lie and held her tongue.

Nils regained his breath enough to speak again. "Kjersti, don't lie to the pastor. This is the girl I am going to marry, and she is doing a lot more for a sick man now than the priest, with his pompous words about saving my soul. I think he wants me to die, so he can check off my name as one of the saved. He may get his wish very soon, but I will fight to the last breath to live, because now I have someone to live for."

"Nils, I think you have done enough talking." Anna placed her hands on his shoulders and gently pushed him back against the pillow. She tucked the blanket in around him. "You better rest." His eyes closed, and Anna turned. She pressed a finger to her lips and whispered to Kjersti, Oddleif, and the pastor. "I think he ought to get some sleep. He really should not talk so much. Perhaps you can come back when he is better."

Eivind Grundseth walked a few steps from the bed, then turned to Anna, eyes narrowed and lips pinched in barely disguised hatred. "I know who you are, the killer of our Lord, Jew daughter of the devil. You're going to rot in hell for taking the soul of this Christian man."

Anna cringed as memories of the Russian Cossacks shouting the very same words whirled through her mind. Visions of being in the cellar with Mama, Papa, and the babies flooded her mind; knowing that at any second the door could be flung open by a sword-wielding soldier. But she was in America now, and there was no one to be afraid of.

She drew back her shoulders and met the cleric's fierce gaze. "The sick room is no place for such behavior. You will leave immediately, or I will call the doctor on duty to escort you out."

Eivind Grundseth stiffened, turned on his heel and left the room.

"I better get the doctor." Oddleif headed toward the door, and Kjersti followed.

Anna ignored the curious stares of the other patients as she returned to Nils' bedside. His eyes were half closed and drops of sweat glistened on his face. The confrontation with the pastor and the coughing fit had cost him a lot of strength. She reached for the damp cloth that lay on the bedside table and sponged his brow.

"Sweetheart," she said as she tossed the cloth onto the chair and reached for Nils' hand. "That man is gone, and I'll make sure he never comes back here again. I could not understand the Norwegian, but I did not need a translator to figure out what he was trying to do to you. Now, you close your eyes and go to sleep. Tomorrow is a new day, and I am sure you will feel a lot better in the morning."

Anna pressed a kiss to Nils' flushed forehead and prepared to leave. At that moment, however, Kjersti and Oddleif returned with Dr. Schultz. He asked them some questions and listened to Nils' lungs, then motioned for them to step outside the room.

"From what you are telling me, his memory seems to be partially recovered. That's a step forward, however, the pneumonia has taken a turn for the worse. I do not like the high fever and the rattle in his lungs. He'll be lucky to make it through the night. As much as you want to stay with him, the best medicine for him now is rest. We will do everything we can to keep down the fever and quiet the cough. Come tomorrow morning. Perhaps then I'll have better news—if he is still alive."

Kjersti went into Oddleif's arms and sobbed at the grim prognosis. Anna, too, hid tears behind her glasses. Oddleif stared at them both, then grabbed Kjersti's shoulders and held her at arm's length. "Kjersti and Anna, you go back in there to say goodnight to him looking like this and he'll think you're coming to his funeral. Now, wipe the tears off your faces and tell him he has to make it until morning. Besides, those doctors—what do they know? He's no better here than at home. At least the whiskey kept the fever down."

Kjersti wiped her face with a handkerchief. "You're right Odd. He cannot see us like this."

The three of them tiptoed quietly into the room again, only to find Nils sitting up in the bed. His eyes were glazed and his voice was a hoarse, gasping whisper. "So, what did he tell you? That it's... all over? He does not need to tell me. I can feel it... in my chest—the death rattle. Odd, keep my... *hardingfele*. Maybe... Henrik can learn someday. Kjersti, give my mother's... silver brooch to Anna. The rest is... for you and Solveig. Odd, you can add my years... to the Bible." He paused, coughed, and then added, "for whatever that's worth. That's all. I have no more... things to give away."

The tears came back to Kjersti's eyes. She knelt by Nils' bedside, grabbed the cast on his left arm and sobbed.

Anna struggled to understand the Norwegian. "Oddleif, what did he say?"

"He's giving his things away. Not good."

Anna fought down the fear that tightened her chest and knelt beside Kjersti. She reached for Nils' other hand and gave it a gentle squeeze. *Maybe he can understand some English, even though he could not speak it.* "Nils, don't talk this way. You say to yourself 'I'll make it until morning.' And tomorrow morning you say, 'I'll make it until the next morning.' You are not going to die on me, because I can't live without you. Never to hear your *hardingfele* sing, or dance a waltz in your arms? No, I forbid death to come for you! You have to get well!"

Nils glanced beyond the sobbing women and noticed Oddleif nervously biting his lip. The room swam before his eyes as a wave of dizziness assaulted him, then his throat tightened. Certain he would eventually choke to death, he had one request to make before he died. He spoke haltingly as he struggled for air.

"Odd, in my room... in the desk drawer, there is a little bag... with soil from Voss. Can you bring it here tonight? I cannot... be buried in Norway, but I want to die with... a little piece of my homeland in... my hands." Nils thought of the farm and tears sprang to his eyes. "I'll see... mother and father very soon. Oddleif, take care of ...Kjersti and the children. Tell Oskar I'll... miss him." Nils feebly grasped Anna's hand. "Anna, my sweetheart, I'll... keep you in my heart to the last... moment. You have so... much to give, and you have to forget about... me. Find yourself a fellow who... will be very lucky to have you. I love you all and we'll... meet again on the other side. Good-bye."

Nils broke down in a paroxysm of coughing and tears, then suddenly he began ranting. His words were incoherent and, alarmed, Anna and Kjersti held tighter to him. A streak of crimson dripped from his mouth and stained his nightshirt, and Oddleif's eyes widened in sudden horror.

"I better get the nurse." He ran from the room in search of anyone who could help, and returned only seconds later.

The nurse took one look at Nils and her lips tightened. She grabbed the two women by the arms and, motioning to Oddleif, ushered them to the door. "He has to rest and visiting hours are over. You must leave now."

Kjersti, Oddleif, and Anna stared at the door that closed behind them, and then walked from the hospital in silence. Nils was going to die.

Anna's shoulders sagged as she trudged beside Nils' relatives. On the way home, Kjersti translated Nils' last words to Anna. *I will never find another man like Nils. Why, God? Why does he have to die?* Her fingers formed fists at her side, her eyes stung with tears. *Papa's God is mean. He created men only to punish them. I hate Him.*

"Kjersti," she said, "when Nils was rambling there at the end, did you catch anything that he said?"

She nodded. "He talked about people in Norway, about us, but there *was* something strange. He mentioned a gray and white cat and said he was sorry he did not take it home. He was worried about who would take care of it now. He was probably hearing and seeing things that were not there."

Anna swallowed a lump in her throat. "No, he was not seeing things. I know about the little cat. It's a stray from my neighborhood that he befriended. I'll take care of it for him. He was always so kind to all, people and animals."

Oddleif, remembering Nils' last request, spoke up. "Kjersti, he asked for the soil. I walk you home and come back. It's the least I can do."

"No, Odd," she replied. "They won't let you back in until morning and, besides, it's a hospital. They will just throw it away. Go back tomorrow and, if we find the worst, then we'll put it in his hands." Kjersti clutched Oddleif's arm. "I just cannot think of him there, dying alone. Please God, don't take him away from us." She turned to the now sobbing Anna and took her in her arms. "I am a Christian and every Sunday I go to church to listen to that pastor. I always respected him, but what he did tonight, I just cannot agree with that. You have made Nils so happy in the last month. At least if he must die, it will be with good memories."

They reached the house on Cayuga and saw Oskar on the porch, cradling two sleeping children in his arms. "How is he?" he asked.

"Not good." The looks on the faces the other three people told Oskar all he needed to know.

Kjersti invited Anna to stay. She put on some coffee and the four of them spent the night in the small living room, alternating between crying and reminiscing, and even managed to catch a few snatches of fitful sleep. During the time Anna was asleep, Kjersti told Oddleif and Oskar that Anna found about Nils from her younger brother.

"We must find out if she's telling the truth," Oddleif said.

Oskar nodded his agreement. "And exactly what these boys know about the men."

"We will make those bandits pay for hurting Nils."

Anna awoke, tossed the covers over the back of the couch, stretched her arms and yawned.

"Good morning, Anna."

She turned to see Oddleif walking her way. Oscar followed a few steps behind.

"Good morning." She reached for the blanket, folded it, and returned it to the couch.

The two men exchange glances. Oddleif spoke first. "When Nils came home Thursday, he told us four men beat him up. The boys who saw this, do they know who these men are?"

She hesitated, and Oskar prodded her on. "Don't be afraid to tell us. We won't go to the police, but we will take care of them, if you know what I mean."

Anna lowered her head. *Yes, it would be just revenge to see Leon Weissberg and the Rabinowitz brothers get their due, but... Why is there always a 'but' in my life?* A heavy sigh left her lips. *I can't let Oddleif and Oskar settle this score. If they do, the men who beat Nils will surely tell why they did it and who paid them. The matter might go as far as the police, and then Mama would be implicated. As much harm as she caused, I cannot allow her to be sent to prison. That would destroy our family.* Another voice nagged at her heart. She was certain Nils would not approve of Oddleif and Oskar hurting anyone on his behalf.

Anna raised her head and addressed the two men. "The boys who saw this were eight years old. I am not sure how much they are to be trusted, but usually children have a grain of truth to their stories. They told my little brother, who passed it to me. I am glad I took their word for it. Apparently, it happened in the Irish neighborhood by some warehouse. Who knows, perhaps they were looking for money to buy whiskey. My brother told me where these twins live, so I can take you over there and you can question them yourselves. I have not had time to even think about the thugs today. If Nils gets better, maybe his memory will come back and he can tell us more about what happened."

Oskar and Oddleif nodded. "Ja, we ask the boys and Nils. Maybe they remember. But we find these men and they will be very sorry they met us, right Oddleif?"

Oddleif sighed. "Oskar, I have a family and I don't want to get in trouble. If we find them, we don't do to them what they did to Nils, but just scare them. They're not worth going to prison for, those cowards."

Just then, Kjersti entered from the kitchen. "Why are you two bothering Anna? Don't you see she is tired? We all have a long day ahead of us."

Anna was grateful for the interruption, since it changed the unpleasant topic of conversation.

No one really felt like eating and, after a cup of coffee, Kjersti, Oddleif and Anna set out for the hospital, hoping for the best—and dreading the worst.

Chapter Eighteen

Nils shielded his eyes against the beams of sunlight that bathed his face. He felt warm, but the throbbing ache in his head had lessened to a dull thud and he could take a breath without coughing profusely. *I must have died and this is heaven. Too bad for pastor Grundseth. He was hoping not to see me here.*

He lowered the blanket and, turning away from the window, realized that heaven looked very much like a hospital room. A nurse entered and placed a tray of food, a glass of water and several white pills beside his bed. "I see you are awake." She stuffed a thermometer in his mouth, then wrote some notes in his chart.

Nils eyed the steaming bowl of cereal hungrily. *It must have been days since I had a square meal.* A low rumble started in the pit of his stomach at the thought.

The nurse's mouth curved into a smile. "I can hear that you're hungry, but you can't eat yet, you big Norskie. You made it through the night, but you're not fully recovered by any means. Take these first, and then you can have your oatmeal." The nurse grabbed two white pills from the tray and handed them to Nils with the glass of water.

Nils propped himself on the pillows, popped the medicine into his mouth, grimaced at the bitter taste, then gulped down the water. *I will swallow anything that will get me out of here*, he thought as he handed the glass back to the nurse.

"All right, you've earned your breakfast," the nurse said as she placed the tray on his lap. "Don't eat too fast now." Nils ignored her admonition as the nurse left his side to check on a fellow patient. He swallowed the large spoonful of oatmeal, closed his eyes in pleasure for a moment, and then downed the bowl's contents. The toast and tea soon followed. He finished in no time and yearned for a second bowl, but set the tray on the nightstand instead and looked around him.

Only two other beds held occupants. One was a motionless form huddled under the blankets and, directly across from him, the nurse was spoon-feeding a very skinny dark man the same oatmeal he had just eaten. This man, though, kept spitting up the food like a little baby and rocking back and forth. Nils shook his head. *I am lucky. This fellow is much worse off than me.*

Dr. Schultz and another nurse came in soon after and examined the two other patients, saving Nils for last. He pulled up a chair beside Nils' bed and glanced at the empty food tray. "Looks like you are feeling better today. I see you finished your breakfast. Good, let me take a listen to your lungs." The doctor adjusted the earpieces of the stethoscope and pressed the bell-shaped end against Nils' chest, while the nurse translated his words into Norwegian.

Nils understood some of the doctor's words, but when he responded, Norwegian came out instead of English. Dr. Schultz did not seem phased by the language barrier and kept talking, as if he could understand.

"Your lungs are much better, but we have to watch you so you don't relapse. That fourteen-hour rest helped. Your head wounds are healing, which is a good sign. If you would excuse me." Dr. Schultz pulled back the blanket and examined the groin area. "The swelling is down. That is also a good sign." He covered Nils up again. "Now, I heard about your visitors yesterday and what state they put you in. No more of that. I will tell the nurse only to let one person in for thirty minutes, and visits must be two hours apart. If you are tired, just close your eyes and go to sleep, visitors or not. Let's see your hand."

Nils extended his left hand, encased in a cast. "This stays on for another 4-5 weeks. Move your fingers for me." The doctor wiggled his own fingers, communicating what he wanted Nils to do.

Nils made a motion as if playing the fiddle, and then pointed to the cast. The doctor nodded in understanding.

"You are asking if you can play violin after the cast comes off? Probably, but time will tell for sure. This does not look like a very bad break, just a couple of little wrist bones. They might get stiff when the weather is bad."

Dr. Schultz reached into the breast pocket of his white jacket and handed Nils a piece of paper and a pencil. "You got hit in the head pretty bad, so I want to ask you some questions. Write the answers down in whatever language you can."

Nils understood what was needed of him, straining to comprehend the doctor's English, but relying more on the nurse's translation. He wrote his name, what city and country he was in now, what country he came from, and his date of birth. He was not sure of what hospital he was in or what day of the week it was.

Dr. Schultz took the paper Nils held toward him, glanced at it briefly, then nodded and stood. "The orderly will take you to the washroom. After sweating through all those fevers, you need a good bath and clean sheets. Don't try to walk on your own, though. You are still weak. The last thing we need is to have you fall and hit your head again."

"*Tusen takk*, doctor." Nils extended his right hand in the firmest handshake he could muster. The doctor grasped it, returned his smile, and went off to continue his rounds.

Kjersti, Oddleif, and Anna were at the hospital at eleven that morning. Anna's stomach knotted with fear as she approached the admissions desk. "We are here to visit Nils Bjørnsen in the Neurological Ward. That is if he is still..." Anna swallowed hard to stifle a sob.

Kjersti took Anna's hand and wiped her own eyes with the other.

The admitting nurse frowned as she looked over the visitors. "Yes, he is alive and much better, and lucky to be so, considering what your visit did to him last night. Per the doctor's orders, visits are two hours apart. Only one person can see him, and then only for thirty minutes."

"You go, Anna," Oddleif offered.

"No, you ought to," she said. "You are his cousin. I will come back in the afternoon."

"Thank you. We'll tell you how he is."

"I'll come to your house around two." Anna walked out of the St. Paul City Hospital, disappointed that she could not see Nils, but with a much lighter load on her shoulders than when she came in.

Oddleif put his arm around Kjersti and cast a pleading look at the nurse. "She is my wife and she took care of Nils before he came to the hospital. Sat up two nights with him. Can we go together?"

The nurse let out a sigh and wrote two names in the visitors' log. "All right. Go, but make it fifteen minutes and don't talk much to the patient." Kjersti and Oddleif followed the nurse through the antiseptic corridors toward Nils' room.

Kjersti tapped Oddleif on the hand and whispered. "Odd, don't show him the packet of soil you have in your pocket. He probably doesn't even remember last night. We've got to tell him about all the good things happening here and not let him dwell on the memories of the old country."

"So far he hasn't had that many good things happen to him here, Kjersti."

"Voss wasn't much better."

"Ja, you're right."

The nurse opened the door to the ward and, grasping the chain that hung around her neck, looked at the suspended watch. "I will be back in exactly fifteen minutes. Be very quiet and do not excite the patient. He is better, but he still could take a turn for the worse if you are not careful."

Kjersti and Oddleif entered the room and Nils waved to them from his bed. Kjersti eyes widened with surprise as a smile curved her lips. *What a difference! Our Nils with clear eyes, sitting up and smiling. Thank God.*

"Hello Odd and Kjersti. I am still here. I think you came yesterday, but I don't remember much of it. How are Solveig and Henrik?"

Oddleif stood between the bed and the window, allowing Kjersti to claim the bedside chair. She sat and reached up to touch Nils' forehead. For the first time in three days, it was not hot. "They're with Oskar. Nils, I am so glad you're better," she replied as she lowered her hand, then glanced at the empty food tray on the table beside her. "Are they feeding you good here?"

"Well, I had some oatmeal and tea for breakfast, but if they gave me a second bowl, that wouldn't be so bad. I don't know when the last time was I had a meal." Nils paused and his brow knitted with confusion. "To tell you the truth, my last memory is waltzing with Anna at the union picnic. After that, I don't remember much. What did happen? I mean, why am I here?"

Kjersti tossed Oddleif a warning glance. He nodded his acknowledgement before she addressed Nils. "All we know is that you came home after work Thursday like this. It was raining and I suspect you got a chill walking home. I washed out your head wounds and Odd wanted to set wrist your bones. Lucky for you, he let the doctor do that. Oskar plied you with whiskey and you actually drank it. We asked you what happened, but you couldn't tell us because you were hurt so bad and were faint. I looked through your pockets and did not find any money there. So, we suspect some thugs took your money and you put up a fight, but were outnumbered. Minneapolis and St. Paul are big cities and all kinds of bums are out there trying to take advantage of hard working immigrants. Take the streetcar from now on."

Nils' forehead wrinkled with concentration, then he shrugged. "That's odd. I think I would remember something like that."

Oddleif shook his head. "No, the doctor said that people who get hit in the head often lose several days of memories before the incident. At least you're doing better than that fellow over there." He nodded toward the skinny man who still rocked back and forth on his bed.

"Ja, poor man, his mind seems to be gone. Once I get strong enough to walk, I'll try to talk to him." Nils stopped in mid-sentence. "Talk to him. No, I can't. There's something very troublesome that I have been trying to figure out. I cannot talk English. I can understand a bit of what people say to me, but when I answer, Norwegian comes out."

Odd winked at him. "Don't worry, it will come back soon. At least you have Anna to practice with."

"Does she know? I think I heard her voice last night, but I don't quite remember."

Kjersti smiled and nodded. "Yes, she was here yesterday and she is coming this afternoon. The doctor said visitors only for a half-hour and one at a time, because you need to rest." She heard the foot steps in the hallway. "Odd, it's almost time. Perhaps we better let Nils get some sleep."

"I don't feel that tired. Did the doctor tell you how long I have to stay here?"

"A couple of weeks."

"That long!" Nils gasped and worry creased his face. "What will happen to my job at the mill? Dr. Schultz said the cast won't come off until a month from now. I have some money in the trunk. Just take it for rent and food for this month. I promise to make it up as soon as I can."

Oddleif patted his cousin on the back. "Nils, I talked to Arne, the foreman. He said he will take you back because you are a hard worker. Everything is all right. Don't worry about the money. Oskar owes me so much back rent, but he pays in whiskey bottles."

"Ja, how like Oskar." Nils returned his cousin's smile, then rubbed his eyes. *Why do I feel so weak and tired all of a sudden?*

Kjersti took one look at Nils' pale face and stood. "Odd, we have done enough talking. Nils, get some rest. We'll be back tomorrow and we all will be praying for you to get better." Kjersti headed toward the door.

"Can you bring my English book next time?" Nils said as Odd followed her. "It's on the table in my room. I will start from page one again."

Odd nodded. "We'll bring it. See you tomorrow."

Nils watched until they disappeared from sight, and then closed his eyes. He struggled to remember fighting someone who took his money, but his mind was blank. *Perhaps it is better this way to erase all memories of unpleasant events. Soon I will see my sweetheart.*

The thought of Anna brought a warm feeling to his heart and he fell asleep, effortlessly gliding into a dream—first playing his *hardingfele,* and then dancing with Anna. The dance went on, seemingly forever, but when it finally ended, he gave her one final turn. Her hand still lingered in his and he asked her for another dance. She put her other hand on his shoulder and stroked it several times. Suddenly the music stopped and Nils opened his eyes.

Anna sat on his bed, holding one of his hands and gently rubbing his back with the other. She looked as beautiful as ever with her red hair, but Nils noticed that her face was drawn and, behind her glasses, dark circles marred her eyes. *She probably stayed up all night with me and I am too sick to remember it. How am I going to talk to her in English? I can only speak Norwegian and hope she understands a word here and there.*

Nils squeezed Anna's hand. "Anna, my sweetheart. Thank you for coming today."

"*God dag, Nils. Jeg er glad....* Anna paused a moment, and then struggled for words she did not know. Finally, she switched to English. "I am glad you're feeling better. Can you understand me?" Nils nodded. "Good, you just shake your head for yes or no and I'll do the talking. Save your strength for getting well. We'll have plenty of time to practice English once we are married."

Nils smiled at her mention of their future life together. *All I have to do now is get out of the hospital, get my old job back and start saving money for the ring, the wedding, and the farm.* A myriad of doubts ran through his head. *Did the head injuries and pneumonia sap my strength so that I won't be able to do a man's work and provide for Anna? Can I even have children or even fulfill the role of a husband? What if I can never play the hardingfele again? Right now, I cannot even express my thoughts to her. Surely she does not deserve such a broken man.*

Anna noticed the lines of worry that etched Nils' face and, reading his mind, she edged closer to him on the bed and looked straight into his blue eyes. "Sweetheart, I cannot wait to marry you, but I have a feeling that you are thinking about money for the wedding, your job at the mill, or whatever else that may trouble you. Please don't. We will manage. I have a little saved up that Papa will take out of the bank for me tomorrow. I don't want a ring or a big wedding. The best present you can give me is yourself, up and well again. After that, we can dream of anything we want to do. Maybe we will take a train out of St. Paul and look for berries. In a month or so, the raspberries should be sweet and ripe. Do you know how to tell good mushrooms from bad ones?"

Nils nodded and gently stroked Anna's hand as she continued. "Good, then we can pick the mushrooms, dry some for the winter and fry the rest with potatoes."

Anna thought of the upcoming winter and searched for a topic that would be familiar to Nils. "You know in the winter, St. Paul has a Carnival, but I have never been there. They have ice rinks, toboggan rides, and they even build an ice castle that we can walk through. I don't know how to ice skate, but maybe I can learn. You'll have to hold my hand though, because I'm afraid I'll fall. During the Carnival, the papers write of these fearless Norwegians who jump off the biggest hills. They have these long sticks on their feet that they use to slide on the snow. Maybe you can tell me."

Nils' face lit up with recognition as he explained to Anna in his native language. "You mean the Norwegian ski jumpers. Here I can show you." He reached over to the bed stand, took out a piece of paper and a pencil and drew a figure on skis jumping off a cliff. Nils wrote the word *ski* with an arrow pointing to sticks on the man's feet. Below, he drew two people gliding on level ground with trees in the background and wrote Nils and Anna under the figures. Then he pointed to the first picture and drew a big X through it. "Not so dangerous," and pointed back to the second picture.

Anna's brow wrinkled as she intently studied the pictures. "So, these sticks are called skis. I seem to recall the word from the newspaper. But what you're saying is that there are two ways of using them: One for jumping, which looks very scary, and another to glide through the snow to just about anywhere. I would love to learn how. It would be better than sitting at home during the cold winter days looking for things to do. But where do we buy skis? I have never seen them sold anywhere, even in the Sears catalog and they claim to have everything."

Nils had made skis in Voss. It was not hard. All he needed was four long thin boards, four poles, and some straps of leather for the binding. It would take several weeks of filing down the wood, and then bending it at the tips. Then it would be time to apply the kick wax. A paraffin and pine tar mixture seemed to work the best, as long as the weather was not bitterly cold. Perhaps in the winter he could take Anna to the park and show her how to ski. *The word for å lage, what was it in English? Make? Yes, that was it, make.* "Anna, *jeg* make *ski for deg.*"

Anna tossed Nils a warm smile. "You'll make skis for me? Nils, is there anything you cannot do with your hands? I know one is broken now, but it will heal in no time. I can't wait to hear you play your *hardingfele.* See, I told you your English will come back." Anna glanced toward the clock on the wall, then stifled a disappointed sigh. "It's almost time for me to go. The nurse said only a half hour. I am going to a union meeting and we will count all the cards from the picnic. I will see you tomorrow after work, and I am certain you'll feel even better then." Anna bent down and kissed Nils' hand.

He drew her closer to him and lightly kissed her on the cheek. *"Jeg elsker deg."*

Anna ran her fingers over Nils' hair, careful not to disturb the bandages. "Nils, I love you so much. I know you will get better with every day." Anna heard the door creak open. She hurriedly sat up on the bed, brushed away stray hairs, and tried to look prim and proper. "I'll see you soon."

Anna followed the nurse out of the room, and Nils spent the rest of the afternoon trying hard to remember a few English words before sleep finally overtook him.

Anna got off the streetcar and ran to Kaiser's Watch and Repair. She was already fifteen minutes late for the meeting. She bounded up the stairs to the meeting hall and waited several seconds until her breathing returned to normal before she walked through the door. She saw Emil Kruse sitting with five other men at a table piled high with white union cards.

Emil glanced up a she entered, then stood to meet her halfway. "Just about ready to count the cards." He stared for a moment at Anna's careworn face and his voice took on a worried tone. "Are you all right? If I may say, you look a bit tired."

Anna shrugged. "After the last three days, I cannot even imagine what it feels like not to be tired. Remember Nils Bjørnsen, the Norwegian fiddler?"

Emil nodded.

"Well, he was beat up and robbed on Thursday. They broke his left wrist and cracked his head in several places. Somehow, he made it home, but he must have caught a chill in the rain. By Saturday morning he was delirious and his cousin took him to St. Paul City Hospital. We did not think he would make it through the night but, thankfully, he is doing better today. In fact, the doctor said that if he continues to improve, he could go home in two weeks. I just came back from visiting him, so that is why I am late. Sorry."

Emil clasped his hands together and his brow furrowed with concern. "How terrible. No wonder you look like you haven't slept for two nights. I am glad he is better. Do the police have any clues about the robbers?"

"No, Nils doesn't remember anything. In fact, his last memory is the picnic. We assumed he was robbed, because he had no money on him." Anna's lips curved into a radiant smile. "Emil, Nils asked me to marry him last Sunday. I guess with the bustle of the picnic, I never had the chance to tell you. When he gets well, we will have a wedding and you are invited."

"Congratulations and thank you. I will certainly come." Emil paused. "What about his job at the mill? Will they hold it for him?"

"Yes, his cousin talked to the foreman, and Nils will have it back. Although, I don't know how much the hospital bill will be, and there is no sick pay while he's out."

Emil lowered his voice. "Anna, after we're done counting the cards, I'm going to pass the hat around. Nils is a union member and we take care of our own. We'll see if we can help with the doctor bill."

"Emil, that's very kind of you, but you don't have to. I mean, we'll manage. I have a little saved up."

The older man waved her comment aside. "Anna, I am not listening to you. What you got saved up is for the wedding and for your children. Just accept this from us, okay?"

"Thank you." Anna grasped both of Emil's hands for a brief moment, then followed him as he joined the men waiting at the table.

Emil Kruse banged the gavel against the table for order. "All right, each person grab a pile of cards and we'll sort them by work place locations." Emil pointed at each person as he spoke. "I am Pig's Eye Foundry, Anna is Garment Works, John is Harvester Works, Bill is Schmidt Brewery, Henry is the mills, Patrick is the railroad, Tom is stockyards, and Joe put the rest in a separate pile."

The union members busied themselves with the cards and the messy pile in the middle of the table was quickly transformed into neat stacks.

Emil, took a pencil from behind his ear. "So, what are our totals? I got thirty men."

"Fifteen for Harvester," John answered.

"Ten for Scmidt," offered Bill.

"Forty from Pillsbury and Ceresota," added Henry.

"Got you fifty trainmen." Patrick smiled as the other members clapped and cheered.

Tom waited until the noise lowered before he added, "Twenty meat cutters."

All eyes focused on Anna as Emil turned to her. "How many girls you got for us, Anna?"

"I'm sorry," Anna's voice broke and she blinked away tears of disappointment. "Only... five. I walked around the factory, talked to them on breaks, visited their homes, and only a handful came to the picnic. I think they have more fear of losing their jobs than the men, so they don't want to cause trouble. I'll try harder next time."

Emil's gray eyes met Anna's. "Don't feel bad. I think you're right about them being afraid. We'll get more next time," he added with a reassuring smile, "and you will have five others to help you do so." Emil turned his gaze to a thin young man across the table. "Joe, how many cards we got in the odd fellows pile?"

"Eighty, from all over the place, factories, shops, and even a couple from housewives."

Emil chuckled. "You men treat your wives good, otherwise they'll go on strike." He scribbled on the paper in front of him and added up all the numbers. "We come out with two hundred and fifty new members. Great job, and a big thanks to all of you for help with the picnic, and especially to Anna who came up with the idea!" Emil faced the young woman, who blushed with being the center of attention. "Don't think that you gave us only five girls, Anna. You gave us all two hundred and fifty cards."

The men cheered and clapped as Emil announced the number and thanked everyone. He put a hand up for silence.

"Now comes the hard part. In the next month or so, we have to talk to every one of these people and invite them to a meeting. For those not working with us, we have cards with their addresses, and we'll have to make home visits. Joe," he said, facing the younger man, "I'm sorry I didn't tell you this beforehand. Split that pile into Minneapolis and St. Paul, so we can look at the addresses and take the ones closest to ours."

Emil dug his cap out of his pants pocket. "There is one more thing, and then we're done. You might remember Nils Bjørnsen, the Norwegian fellow. He came here for one meeting and played fiddle for the picnic. Anna just told me that he got badly beaten up and is in St. Paul City Hospital. Looks like he will be out of work for a good two months. I am going to pass the hat around and take up a collection to help him pay his hospital bills. We're fighting for sick pay, but for now, we take care of our own."

Emil slid his cap to Tom Trivisani, and then it made its way around the table. One by one, each man placed bills and coins into it, then passed it on. Emil took out his wallet and added his contribution, then gave the hat to Anna.

"Hope this helps."

"Thank you, on behalf of Nils, as well." Anna acknowledged the generous union men as she transferred the contents of the hat to her purse.

The men crowded around her with questions. "Did the police catch those thugs?"

"How badly is Nils hurt?"

"What did the doctor say?"

"Can we visit him?"

The barrage of questions made Anna's head feel as though a vise clamped down on it and tightened. She patiently answered each question in turn, until she could take it no longer. She rubbed her temples to dispel the growing pain.

Emil noticed the movement and raised his hand for silence. "The poor girl has not slept in two nights, so don't badger her with questions." Anna's tired eyes tossed Emil a thank you as the men grabbed a handful of cards and left the room.

Emil walked Anna out. "I got the wagon today, so I could take you home," he offered.

"Thank you, but I'm fine. I'll wait for the streetcar and try not to nap during the ride. Don't want that precious money stolen." Her comment brought a chuckle from Emil. "Once I get home, I'm going straight to bed." Anna clasped her purse to her chest. "Thank you so much for this, Emil. We'll pay you back next time a collection is taken for someone else."

They both turned as the sound of metal wheels neared. Her streetcar drew to a stop a few feet away. "Good-bye, and I'll try to come next Sunday."

Emil waved as Anna boarded the car. "Now, you take care of Nils and don't worry about next Sunday."

Anna nodded and, finding a seat, held onto the purse and stared out the window as the city passed her by. She blinked to keep awake and sighed.

The money is all well and good, as long as Nils gets better.

Please God, make him better each day.

Chapter Nineteen

Anna visited Nils daily for the two weeks that he remained in the hospital. He improved a little each day and, by the end of the first week, was allowed to take short walks outside. The view of sky, trees, and flowers, and the sounds of birds lifted his spirits considerably and he was eager to rejoin life again. His English came back by leaps and bounds. If he forgot a word or a phrase, Anna was right there to remind him. The doctors and nurses also made a special effort to speak slowly and correct his pronunciation and grammar, at his request.

Anna tried to live as normal a life as possible under the circumstances. She stopped by the shop to talk to Moyshe. He transferred her savings to a separate account, and she was surprised that a sizable sum had accrued over the past four years. He asked about Nils and was relieved that the young Norwegian fiddler was on the mend. When Anna inquired about her mother and siblings, Moyshe simply said, "They are doing well. The neighbors know only that you took a room at a respectable boarding house for young women. No one mentions Nils."

Anna longed to see the rest of her family, but was not sure when her mother would be ready to talk to her. As rain drops hammered on the windowpanes of her room, she stared at an old family photo on the dresser. *Perhaps never, and I wouldn't blame her. Every time she looks at me, she sees that awful man. Sometimes, I wish I was never born. All I did was bring misery to Mama, and if Nils never met me he wouldn't be in the hospital. If he knew who I was...he might not marry me. I love him, but I feel so dirty and ashamed.* Anna bit off a hangnail and watched a trail of blood trickle across her left index finger. *His blood.* She poured the pitcher of water over her hands. *I can pretend to be clean on the outside, but I will never be clean inside.*

At work, rumors flew about why Anna no longer took the Snelling streetcar. Was she already married to that Norwegian fellow or, God forbid, was she living with him in sin?

Anna did not say much, except that she had a room at Mary Pinkham's Boarding House and that Nils was very ill from an unfortunate accident. She and Fanny talked, and she learned that Fanny was through with Jacob Hirsch. Now, the girl talked incessantly about David Gantman, the dentist, and how he put a gold crown on Mrs. Feldman's tooth. Apparently, Brahms was a fleeting interest, being surpassed by glittering teeth. "One of these days," Fanny insisted, "I will find the man that will give me everything I desire, and then you won't see me anywhere near St. Paul Garments."

Anna did not plan to stay long herself. Now that she possessed a savings account, she considered several options. *Perhaps I can buy a sewing machine and open up a small shop? Or maybe I could take some night classes and become more active in the union and the Socialist Party.* Then again, Nils' idea of buying a farm sounded appealing, and she could pitch in for the down payment. For now, however, any plans would have to wait until Nils recovered.

Nils learned early Friday morning, much to his relief, that he would be released from the hospital the next day. His broken wrist was on the mend and the rest of his body had made considerable progress toward total recovery. He still tired easily and suffered an occasional memory lapse, but the doctor pronounced him healthy enough to finally go home. He swore he would not touch another bowl of oatmeal for months.

That evening, Anna came to visit and they took a walk outside. The perfume of the flowers planted on the hospital grounds wafted on the gentle breeze as Nils drew the warm June air into his lungs. "Anna, it is good to take deep breath again. I cannot do it two weeks before. So many flowers and so beautiful, like you, sweetheart."

Anna shrugged. "Oh, Nils, I am just a regular person. Nothing special about me." *If he only knew who made a part of me, he would never consider me as beautiful.* She shuddered as she tried to push away the mental image of her mother's rape.

"Anna, you are cold? We can sit here in the sun." He led her toward a wooden bench, golden in the last rays of the evening sun.

They sat side by side, and Nils took Anna's hand. "Anna, I want to say something to you."

Her hand lay limp in his, and her voice quavered. "And I would like to talk to you. I hope you will still marry me."

"Well, that is why I want to talk to you."

Anna's breath caught in her throat and she felt like she was hurtling toward a yawing black abyss. *So now, after he is better, he is going to change his mind. Maybe he found out who I really am.*

Nils noticed tears well in her eyes, and he took her hands in his. "Anna, I love you and I want to marry you. But you need to know one thing. These bad men hit me in one place where it is not good to hit a man. So, I do not know if I can be husband or father." Nils paused and spoke haltingly. "Maybe...maybe, you marry another fellow, not broken like me."

Anna's lips curved into a half-smile, and her cheeks blushed with the topic of conversation. "Nils, my sweetheart, that makes no difference to me. I don't even know what men and women do together, except what I've heard from other girls. If I have lived without it for twenty-two years, it must not be that important. And about children, do you know how many poor starving orphans are in St. Paul waiting for a decent meal and a warm home? It would almost be a travesty to bring a child of our own into the world where there are already so many in need. So, if one part of you does not work that well, fine. I am marrying all of you, and the rest of you is just fine."

Anna snuggled close, and Nils drew her into his arms. "Anna, you are very kind and sweet girl. Thank you. The wedding is next month and, by that time, maybe I will be better." Nils surmised that Anna spoke the truth. She did not know what truly happened between a man and a woman. *But then what do I know myself, except drunken bragging and talk. We will both have to figure things out once we get married.*

Anna pulled away from his embrace and lowered her gaze to the ground. "Nils— her voice sounded tremulous to his ears "—I have something to tell you, too. I am not who you think I am. In fact, *I* don't even know who I truly am. That nice man who plays the violin and fixes your boots, he is not my Papa. Remember I told you about the men on horseback, who would go through Jewish villages burning and killing?"

Nils grasped Anna's hand and gave it a gentle, but tight, squeeze. "Yes, I remember that."

"Well, one of them did the most unspeakable evil to my mother. He...was with her for only five minutes, but I...I was the result of that." Anna threw off her glasses and wiped the hot tears that suddenly gushed from her eyes. "All she remembers is that he had red hair and green eyes, so every time she looks at me she sees him. In English, such children are called 'bastards' and they are a shame to the family. Now that you know my origins, I wouldn't blame you if you did not want to marry me."

Anna whirled and began to rise, but Nils held onto her wrist. "Anna, sit here next to me. I answer you, but first I ask you question. Your father, he know this?"

"Yes, he has known since I was born that I was not his. But he raised me as his own child."

"He is right, and I marry you as his daughter. That man, he is nothing. He is bad memory for your mother." Nils retrieved Anna's glasses from the ground and, carefully, put them on her face. He wiped away the tears that cascaded down her cheeks with his thumbs, then cupped her chin and forced her to look at him. "So, he give you orange hair and green eyes, but they look very nice on you. Five minutes, twenty years ago." He shook his head. "We forget about it."

Anna stared at him and her lips trembled for several moments before her chest rose and fell as she released a heavy, relieved sigh. "These are almost the exact words Papa said to me. I have nothing to forget. It's Mama that has to deal with the pain, but now I understand why she has been so adamant about me being Jewish. She retreated into tradition, so that what happened to her would not happen to me, but she went about it in the wrong way. You know though," Anna paused and bit her lip. "If my real father was not Jewish, I am only one half, so it should make no difference to my family who I marry. At least now that I have my own room, they don't have to look at their bastard daughter."

Nils eyes darkened for a moment, until he realized that it was her lingering anger—and not her heart—that spoke. "Anna, do not talk like that. I am Lutheran. You are Jewish or half-Jewish. God is big for all of us, and we tell that to my pastor and your mother. It is hard for them to understand. We get married, we talk to your family more and more and maybe they think Norwegian man is not bad. Your father and brothers, we talk already, so we try with your mother and sister."

Anna shivered at the slight chill that permeated the air and noticed the shadows growing longer in the setting sun. She rose from the bench and faced Nils. "Well, we better be getting inside or the nurse might come looking for us."

He nodded and grasped her hand as they headed back to the hospital. Anna knew his words were meant to reassure her, but wondered if he was right. *Will Mama ever forget her shame, or does she relive it every time she sees me? Will that incident so many years ago always be a barrier between us?*

"Nils, you are too nice. My mother has treated you so poorly." *Poorly enough to nearly kill you,* she added silently. "And you still want to get on her good side. Perhaps for now, the less we see of her, the better it will be for all of us. It's like those two people in Norway, Kari and her husband. Now that you don't see them tormenting you every day, don't you feel a lot better?"

Nils kicked a small rock down the garden path. "So, Kjersti told you?"

"Yes. I was wondering why that man wanted your farm so much and suspected that there was something more to your story, but did not want to ask. Kjersti filled in the missing piece. Don't worry, I won't hold it against you that you had a girl ten years ago."

"Ja, it was long time. I was not wise, did not think. When she marry Jens, for whole year I work on the farm very hard, do not play fiddle, do not sleep. I hate him, her, myself. My mother worry that I get sick. So, I ask myself, 'Why I do this?' Hate in your heart, it eats you from inside. Not good. Better to forgive and forget about it. I feel better because I find you, not because I do not see them." Nils paused in mid-stride and stared straight into Anna's green eyes. "Anna, please do not think....I never do things with her, like married man and woman. I never do those things with any girl."

"Nils, that didn't even cross my mind," Anna lied. *Our wedding night will be the first time for both of us.* "So, when you go home, will Oskar try to have you take his medicine?"

"No, he say he do not drink much. Him and Oddleif, they spend time and try to find the four man that hit me. They ask me, but I do not remember. They talk to little Irish boys, but each boy see different things. I tell Oskar and Oddleif, it is good I forgot. Yes, men did bad thing, but if Odd and Oskar do same thing to them, that is bad, too. I do not want to cause any more trouble. These men, they know in their heart what they do was wrong. Maybe they think about it and decide to be better people."

"You are right. It will forever be in their memory and, at some poi
they will have to come to terms with what they did." Anna sighed her relief th
Nils did not want to investigate his beating any further. At this point, she w
not ready to tell him who masterminded the entire operation. If he h
forgotten, there was no reason to dredge up the details.

Anna left the hospital and went over to the Pedersen's to plan
homecoming celebration for Nils. For several hours, she and Kjersti busi
themselves in the kitchen, baking. Solveig made a special cat-shaped cookie 1
her uncle, but for the most part, she and Henrik were content to lick out 1
bowls.

The next day, Oddleif brought Nils home. Nils noticed the table lad
with food as soon as the two men walked into the yard--a smorgasbord
Russian and Norwegian dishes. Kjersti rushed over, carrying a plate piled w
so much food that any passerby would wonder if the poor fellow had a meal
the last month. Nils ate as much as he could handle, and still Kjersti encourag
him to have more.

He waved her off. "It was all very good, thank you, but really,
more."

"Look how skinny you are. They did not feed you at the hospital.
saw that watery oatmeal the nurse passed as breakfast," Kjersti fussed.

"Ja, but I think today I made up for the two weeks I was there." N
switched to English. "Anna, what you call Russian things here. They are v
good."

"*Piroshki*. Remember, you tried them at the union picnic."

"Yes, and that sweet drink." Nils frowned as he struggled to recall
name.

"*Kvas*," Anna filled in for him.

"Right. So much good food, you and Kjersti was busy. How is
garden?"

Kjersti pointed to Oddleif and Oskar. "Ask them. I weeded it here a
there, but those two were supposed to take care of it. Knowing them, they
probably growing whiskey bottles in there, hoping to get a whiskey tree."

Nils chuckled. "They have whiskey tree and I think I plant a mor
tree now. The doctor show me what it cost and I think I go to hospital again."

Kjersti scolded Nils. "Stop worrying about money. In a month, you will be back at the mill, and then you can start paying off the bill. Dr. Schultz is not going to knock on your door every week demanding payment."

Anna continued when Kjersti paused. "There's something more. Since you are a union member, I talked to Emil Kruse and we took up a collection to help pay your wages for the time you'll be off work." Anna reached for the purse she placed on the front steps, opened it and handed Nils an envelope. "Here it is."

"Anna, I cannot take money. It is not mine. Emil and the union people, they do not know me well. Why they want to pay me?"

Anna looked directly into his blue eyes and grasped his good hand. "We take care of our own, Nils. Accept it. Next time one of them gets sick, you can give a little money to help out."

"I promise that I give more than little. I come to next meeting and say thank you."

Just then, the sound of a scratchy fiddle pierced the air. Oddleif opened the gate and ushered in Helge Dahl, an old man of seventy who sawed at the strings of a cracked violin.

"Look, Nils," Odd said as he stepped aside. "I got a little music for you."

Nils knew Oddleif wanted to cheer him up with the music, but the effect of seeing Helge Dahl tightened Nils' stomach into a knot of dread. He stared at Helge's twisted arthritic fingers as they clutched the violin's neck, the bow hand as it jerked across the strings from the tremors of age, and the mouth—a thin line of grim determination as the old man tried to produce a recognizable melody from the instrument.

Nils listened, out of politeness, to a mangled version of a polka, but inside, the reminder of his broken wrist and the possibility of never being able to play the *hardingfele* again tormented him.

What does it really mean to play a musical instrument? Yes, Helge Dahl plays the fiddle, but there is a vast difference between a dance and wedding fiddler, and someone who merely scratches out a tune. When the cast comes off, Nils wondered, *will my fingers be as stiff as Helge's? What anguish would it be to hear every twirl and turn of a tune in my mind and not be able to reproduce it on the hardingfele?*

Nils could accept the ravages that old age would eventually have on his playing, but the thought of being struck down before thirty was like a heavy rock crushing his chest. It took his breath away. He broke out in a cough as Helge squeaked out the last dying notes of a waltz."

"You get better now." The old man wished Nils well and left.

Kjersti ran toward the children, who fought over the swing on the big silver maple in the corner of the yard. Anna, alone with Nils, noticed that his mood changed as soon as the old fiddler arrived, but could not understand why the old man's scratching bothered Nils, who was by far the more accomplished musician. Anna rolled her eyes and threw Nils a mischievous grin. "Nils, as my Papa would say, that man played as if he stepped on cats' tails."

"Ja, well, he is old and has a bad fiddle." He looked down at the cast on his left hand and sighed. "When that thing on my hand come off, maybe I will be like him, maybe more worse."

Anna's eyes widened as she suddenly realized why Helge Dahl's visit upset Nils so. "You said yourself that the doctor did not think the break was serious enough to affect your playing."

Nils' voice held an edge of frustration. "What he know about it, Anna? If he mean I can take fiddle in hands and put fingers on strings, that I know I can do. But to give my fingers everything I hear in my head and feel in my heart…" Nils' voice trailed off as he stared blankly toward the street.

Anna put her hand on his forehead. It felt warm, as though he had a touch of fever. "Perhaps you better rest. There have been too many people and too much talking."

"I am not tired."

"Well…" She hesitated a moment, then decided to address Nils' worries directly. "I have no doubt you will play just as well as you did before and, if you make a mistake, most of us won't even notice. Papa said that one wrong note sticks in his head for days afterwards, but to the listener it does not last even a second. You know how it is. They are too busy drinking and dancing so long as the music is there. I'll bet they wouldn't mind old Helge's playing!"

"I try, for you, Anna. I try to be best fiddle player. Your father, he is right. I know, because we both play for dancing." Nils got up and walked with Anna toward the house. "I feel little tired, but tomorrow I feel better. I want to clean garden, too much grass. I need fix fence and make Henrik little swing.

"Don't forget to make those skis for us, too," Anna added in a teasing voice.

"I make them soon. I promise. Thank you, you tell me about them."

"With one hand of course. Two would just be too easy."

"It take more time with one, but I try."

Anna could not keep up the act any longer. She rested her hands on Nils' shoulders and looked straight into his worried, sad eyes. "Nils Bjørnsen, did you *really* think that I would ask you to make skis only with one hand?"

"Girl want things from man. Many want new hat and you, skis. You ask. I do it."

Anna's lips curved into a smile. "Don't be silly. We still have six months to winter. But I am willing to help you, so together we have three good hands. I have weeded a lot of gardens in my life and if you want something hammered or sawed, I'll give it a try, or at least hold the piece of wood for you."

Nils reached up and clasped Anna's hands and covered them with his large rough fingers. "Anna, that is man's work. You have little hands. I am afraid you hurt them."

Anna pulled from Nils' grasp and spread her hands, palms upward, in front of his face. "They're big enough to run a sewing machine all day, get pricked by needles, scrub the floor, cook, do the washing, and help a stubborn Norwegian. I'll be here tomorrow morning," she added as she lowered her arms to her side, "and we'll start weeding around those whiskey trees. Now, go get some rest, okay?"

"Okay, Anna." Nils led her inside the house and into a small hallway between the kitchen and the bedrooms. He glanced around to insure they were alone, then drew her to him. He lowered his head and his lips softly brushed against hers. "My little cat with green eyes. I feel better already."

Anna savored Nils' tender caress and the tingles that raced down her spine. "Nils, I love you so much. Thank God you are well now. Two weeks ago, I never dreamed a day like this would ever come to pass." She heard Oddleif's voice calling them and, instantly, stepped away from Nils. "I'll...see you tomorrow."

Nils followed Anna to the front door and said "Good-bye." He waited on the steps as she retrieved her purse, walked over to the gate, and then waved. He returned the motion, stared after her until she disappeared from sight, then headed upstairs. He lay in bed for a long time thinking how lucky he was to find a girl like Anna. In a month they would be married, and he could hardly wait until that day.

Chapter Twenty

Anna spent most of her spare time during the next month at Nils' home while he recovered. They worked on household projects, tended the garden and took care of the children when Kjersti and Oddleif needed to go out. Nils' English improved even more as he learned words for different tools and garden plants. Anna, in turn, picked up some Norwegian words, including the ones uttered when a hammer lands on a finger instead of a nail. They decided to hold off on the Russian, until Nils had a good grasp of English.

They grew more comfortable with each other as they worked side-by-side, learning how to compromise when each thought their way of doing things was the right one. Kjersti, now relieved of a good share of responsibility by Nils and Anna, hinted that they were welcome to stay in the attic room after the wedding, and even offered to reduce the rent. The young couple said little about their plans for after the wedding, although it was agreed that the ceremony would take place the Saturday before Nils was due back at the mill. Anna decided to at least let her father know about the wedding date. It would be the evening after *Shabbos,* and he would have no restrictions in coming.

Anna stopped at the shop the following day. Max and Grisha were; helping Moyshe cut leather. Grisha looked up from the work table when his sister stepped into the store. He grinned—the same pleased smile reflected on Moyshe's face.

"Papa," Grisha implored, "now that Anna is here, can we please go to the sandlot. She knows how to cut. She's helped you a thousand times."

Max, being older and wiser, kicked his little brother on the shin. "Like Anna wants to work some more after a ten-hour day at the factory, you idiot. We'll play baseball tomorrow. If you weren't so lazy, we wouldn't be here this long." Max turned to Anna. "How is Nils?"

"A lot better. In a month or two, he will be ready to play baseball, so long as no one hits him in the head with a ball."

"Tell him to come to the lot and we'll be careful," Max said.

"Yeah, if he's on our team, we'll win more games. Hope he gets better soon," Grisha added.

"I'll tell him all your wishes, and he says hello to you as well." Anna turned to Moyshe. "Papa, can the boys go? It's too nice out for them to be cooped up in the store."

Moyshe slapped his hands on the cutting table. "Yes, go. You've caused enough trouble for today."

Max and Grisha threw down their scissors and rushed out the door. "Thanks, Papa, bye Anna." The former paused to turn back to his sister. "Say, can you and Nils come to the game Sunday? We'll sit on the Minneapolis side as before, and no one will see us. Is that okay, Papa?"

Moyshe inclined his head in a nod. Surely an innocent baseball outing would not get back to Sarah. "Fine with me. Just make sure that Mama doesn't know about it."

Anna reached into her purse. "We'll be there at three o'clock. Here is a dollar. Buy us the tickets, and we'll meet you by the ice cream stand."

Grisha's eyes widened with surprise. "Thanks, Anna! Bye."

Alone in the small shop now, Moyshe noticed the hesitation in Anna's eyes. He pulled a chair from behind the counter, relieved that, apparently, his daughter was not distressed or upset. *Hopefully, some good news for a change.* "Anna, sit down. I have a hunch you want to talk to me about something."

Anna stood by the chair and balanced her right foot on one of the crossbeams. *I might as well just say it and get it over and done with.*

"Papa, Nils and I will be getting married by the Justice of the Peace, and then having a little celebration on Saturday, July 16th." Anna gasped to catch her breath after blurting out the invitation. She continued. "Nils is afraid that he won't be that good on his fiddle only two weeks after the cast is off, so if you can come bring your violin. Can you be there after *Shabbos* is over?" She held her breath as she awaited his answer.

"Let me think here." Moyshe scratched his head. "Suppose I tell your Mama that I am going to a *bar-mitzvah* in Minneapolis and will be back late, because of the streetcars. It's the same house on Cayuga, right?"

"Yes." Anna threw her arms around her father. "Oh, Papa, thank you. I am not even your child and marrying a Norwegian, and you will still come!"

Moyshe grasped her wrists, then her hands before he locked his gaze on her green eyes. "I am going to my daughter's wedding, and that's all there is to it." He released Anna and went behind the counter. "Now, I have to think of a gift for the both of you. What do you need the most?"

"Papa, you don't have to get us anything. The best gift is that you will be coming to the wedding." Anna sighed. "I just wish the rest of the family would be with you. Can you take Max and Grisha?"

"No." His voice reflected his unhappiness. "I better not. Mama has a way of fishing, and the boys are not smart enough to stretch the truth. It's sad, Anna. The neighbors, they ask her about you and she says, 'I have no daughter. I don't know.' Then they ask me, and I tell the truth—that you decided you were old enough to live on your own and I leave it at that. Of course, their next question is about your Nils. My answer is, 'Ask her yourself. I don't get mixed up in my daughter's affairs.'" Moyshe took the store key out of his pants pocket. "I better be getting home. You want the rest of your things? I will bring them to the shop so you and Nils can pick them up. I am not sure about the dresser and the desk. Mama won't let it go and I don't want a scene, but I'll see what I can do."

"Don't worry. Nils has a desk and he makes his own furniture. He's even going to make me skis for the winter. You know," she added when Moyshe's brow knit in a frown, "these long thin boards to glide on the snow. One thing I can say about him is that he is not lazy with his hands."

"That's a good trait for a man." Moyshe untied his apron and started to close up. "If he was Jewish, I would take him into the business, because I have a feeling neither of the boys wants to learn. Somehow Katz and Bjørnsen Shoe Repair just doesn't sound right. I'd hate to sell this place when I get old. It would be nice to keep it in the family."

"We'll see. Who knows, maybe in twenty years or so, Jews and Scandinavians can work side by side. I'll see you next week, Papa."

Moyshe walked Anna to the streetcar stop, and then headed home. He was happy for her, but his heart was heavy for the separation of his family. *God has given me this lot in life, and it is my duty as a Jew to bear it.*

* * *

Nils located a Justice of the Peace and planned a one-day honeymoon trip to Wildwood Amusement Park in White Bear Lake. He spent some of his savings money to buy a plain metal band for himself, a silver one for Anna, and then polished his mother's silver brooch in preparation for the wedding.

Nils went to the hospital on a Thursday, two weeks before the wedding, to have the cast removed. Dr. Schultz listened to his chest first. "You are as good as new. No sign of pneumonia."

He then took a formidable pair of scissors and cut away the plaster. "Move your fingers for me." Nils moved the fingers of his left hand and did not feel any pain in his wrist. "Now, bend your hand."

Dr. Schultz asked him to perform a series of exercises. His hand was a little stiff, but the doctor reassured Nils that was normal.

"I try play violin," Nils told the physician. "It is okay with the hand now?"

"You can start playing the violin today. I am pretty certain you have not lost any function. Just don't catch heavy flour bags at the mill, and be sure to take it easy the first couple of weeks. I will write you a note to give to your boss. If you feel feverish or dizzy at any time, take a rest. You have recovered well from a very serious beating. I would advise you to avoid areas of the city where you might be robbed again. Next time, you may not be so lucky. How is your memory?"

"I think all right. I forget one week when I was sick." Nils paused, unsure how to phrase his delicate question, then plunged on. " Doctor, I get married in two weeks. You think I have...trouble?"

The corners of the doctor's mouth twitched upward. "How do you feel when you're with her?"

Nils felt heat flush his face. "Like I want to marry her."

"All I can say then, is see what happens. If it does not work, give it a little time. I want to see you again in three months, so we can talk about it then."

"Thank you doctor. I pay you when I go to work. I promise."

"I trust that you will." Dr. Schultz wrote a note on the chart before him, then his eyes grew stern. "One more thing. No swimming this summer, not with the pneumonia that you had. Try your best not to get chilled."

"I do like you ask me," Nils said as he stood. "Thank you again."

His pace quickened as he walked down the halls, then through the front doors. Once outside, Nils ran home. He would barely wait to play his fiddle.

Nils opened the case and took out the *hardingfele*. He had not been played it in a month, and the strings were all out of tune. He spent several minutes tightening the pegs to pitch, then inhaled and released a heavy breath. He was ready to take the big step. His hands shook, partly with the excitement of playing the instrument again, and partly with fear that he would not measure up to his own expectations. His left hand was stiff at first, but after half an hour, he could play most of the tunes with almost no trouble. It would take time to get his fingers used to the twirls and trills again, but at least Solveig would get her own song at the wedding, as he promised her. Nils stopped playing after forty-five minutes. He did not want to take a chance that he might strain the newly healed bones and muscles. He would practice each day and increase the time and the difficulty of the tunes so that, by their wedding day, he was at least able to play a couple of hours worth of dance music.

Anna stopped later that evening to take a look at Nils' hand—minus the cast. The pair sat on the front steps in the waning summer sun.

"How does your hand feel?" She carefully stroked the pale skin around his left wrist.

"Fine. No trouble. I play *hardingfele* for you," Nils added as he rose, then bounded up the stairs to retrieve the instrument. He returned, opened the case and took out his fiddle. Beautiful tones once again burst forth from Nils' hands.

Anna smiled and tried to tap her foot to the beat, but could not figure out the rhythm. It seemed to be different every couple of notes. She gazed lovingly at Nils, drinking in the music.

"I knew you'd pick up that fiddle and play right away. I am so glad to hear my Norwegian angel is making heavenly music again. What kind of a tune did you just play? I could not figure out the time with my foot."

"It's Norwegian waltz. We call it *springar*...means to hop in Norwegian. Here, I show you." Nils took Anna's hand and walked a small circle in the front yard, counting the beats, "One, two, three." On the second beat, he made a slight hop and Anna repeated his movement. Once she mastered the footwork, Nils turned her several times, while he hummed the tune. Anna finally figured out why the beats in this tune were off. It was a lot harder to fit the walk, the hop, and the turns into a neat 'one-two-three' waltz figure, so the fiddler had to adjust to the dancers.

Nils, noticing the unspoken question in Anna's eyes, set his fiddle aside. "I ask Kjersti and Oddleif to show you. I cannot dance and play together." He went inside and came out with the Pedersen's a moment later.

Kjersti wiped her hands on her apron and laughed. "Odd's got two left feet and I will look like a cow trying to dance, Nils."

"I see you do it in Norway. You were very good. You need to learn again for wedding, so try it now." Nils put the fiddle up to his chin and began playing.

"Oh, all right," Oddleif grasped her hand. They went around the circle, hopped on the second beat, then turned on the third. After a couple of minutes, their breath came in gasps and they slowed to just a walk.

Nils teased them in Norwegian. "America must have put lead in your feet and took your breath away. I remember you dancing all night in Norway."

"You're lucky," Kjersti said half joking, half serious, "that two children and a drunk for a husband don't have me crawling on the ground yet."

Oskar staggered in from the street and tried to do a Danish dance to the melody. He tripped several times, then gave up and took a sip from his pocket flask.

Nils stopped playing. "Oskar, that will tangle your feet even more."

"Just practicing for the wedding, Nils."

Anna, who remained silent as she watched the proceedings, finally spoke. "My father promised to come and bring his violin. He plays Russian music, but it's not hard to dance to, you know polkas, waltzes. Did you invite Sigrid Dahl, Oskar?"

"Ja, she is coming with her parents. Some fellows from the stockyards will be here, too."

Nils nodded. "I talk to Arne from the mill. He come and maybe one or two man with him."

Kjersti noticed a trace of disappointment in Anna's eyes and looked away from the group. If Odd and Oskar invited their work and drinking buddies to Nils' wedding, the celebration would end up in a brawl—unless they could find some decent people to balance them out. *Decent* people, however, were nowhere to be found. She invited several ladies from church, but received polite refusals. Mrs. Fossheim pursed her lips and whispered in Kjersti's ear, 'You know, Nils is marrying that girl, and I really don't think it would be proper to attend. And considering that spirits will be flowing freely...'

Kjersti talked to Anna about inviting her friends and found that she had the same problem. Besides Anna's father, Emil Kruse and several union men, and a couple of girls from work, none of Anna's family, friends or neighbors planned to attend.

"Not even Fanny will come," Anna told her the day before. "She said, 'You know, you're marrying that Norwegian, and I don't think it would be proper to attend.'"

Kjersti and Anna laughed together when they discovered that the refusals sounded so much alike. Jews or Norwegians, they were still people, and were not so different as they wanted to think they were. *I hope Nils and Anna won't be too disappointed,* Kjersti worried.

She turned back toward her family, spotted Oskar pass his flask to Odd, then wagged her finger at them. "Just go easy on the whiskey, and tell your buddies to do the same."

Nils and Anna stopped at Moyshe's shop on Wednesday of the following week to pick up the rest of Anna's things, which consisted of a box of books, odds and ends, and some winter clothes.

"I'll be there Saturday evening," Moyshe said, "like I promised, and I'll bring my violin. I think I know of something that will make a good present for a Russian girl and a Norwegian man." His brown eyes twinkled as he handed Nils the box.

"Please, Mr. Katz," the younger man replied as he tucked the box under his arm, "you do not have to buy us anything. A present for me, if you can teach me some of your Russian tunes. I show you Norwegian ones."

Moyshe handed Anna an armload of clothing. "It's a deal. I will trade you a tune or two. See you on Saturday."

Anna put on several layers of winter clothing and carried the rest. "Good-bye, Papa."

A few minutes later, Anna nodded to her father from behind the clothing and she and Nils headed north on Snelling. Nils glanced down at her and noticed the beads of perspiration on her brow. "Anna, you are very hot? Here I take them for you."

She tossed him a grateful smile, but followed it with a shake of her head. "You've got your hands full and it's easier to wear them than to carry them all."

"You ask me if you are tired." Nils paused, then added after a moment's hesitation. "Your father, he is a good man."

"Yes, Papa has always treated everyone with respect and kindness. I wanted the man that I married to be like him. I know that I found myself one, like you—" Anna stopped in mid-sentence. Chaim Rabinowitz and Leon Weissberg were less than a block away and headed straight toward them.

She hid her face behind the bundle of clothes and veered from the sidewalk onto the street. *Would Nils remember? Would they tell him about her and Mama's money?*

"Nils, those two fellows, they used to tease me. Let's cross the street."

"No, I tell them not to do that anymore. What they say to you, they first say to me. I am not too sick to protect you."

"Absolutely not." The blood drained from her face at the mere thought that Nils might confront the two men. "I forbid you getting into a fight for my sake. You know what the doctor said about your head. Just ignore them and say nothing, please."

Leon did a double take. "Hey, isn't that the redhead and the Norskie? Look, he's recovered from the beating, walking by her side with an armful of stuff."

Chaim's eyes narrowed as he gazed at the two figures. "What the hell, Leon. I thought both her and her Mama paid us to finish this fellow off."

"I guess one of them changed her mind. He broke my tooth, the bastard. You wanna try again?"

"Nah, not worth it. I only fight for money. What do I care about your tooth? Gives you more room to spit."

"Shut up. I don't think he remembers anything. We got his head pretty bad, but I'm sure the girl does. I wonder if he can even, you know..." Leon tittered under his breath.

"That's her problem. If he does remember, well..." He headed for the street. "Let's cross to the opposite side. Who knows? They might get the police involved." Chaim and Leon walked casually as they crossed the street.

* * *

Anna returned to the sidewalk beside Nils. "Hmm, I guess they did not want to meet up with us. Maybe they were scared of the big Norwegian who is with me."

Nils did not answer. He turned around to look at the pair as they increased their pace and headed toward an alley between the houses. His brow knitted in concentration as he and Anna continued down the sidewalk.

There is something familiar about them. I have seen them before, but where? That short one, with the scruffy face. At one time it was very close to mine. I have a clear picture of swinging my fist at it. The man then spat out a bloody tooth... Nils' frown deepened as the two men turned and sprinted for the far end of the alley. *There were four of them. They did not speak Norwegian. I gave them money for whiskey and still they wanted to fight, but why?*

"Anna," he said as he grasped her arm. "These men, now I remember them. They help send me to hospital. There was two more. I do not know why they hate me or you."

A knot of fear squeezed her stomach and pushed bitter-tasting bile into her throat. *If the Weissberg and Rabinowitz triggered Nils' memory of the fight, will he remember what I said to him minutes before? Will he still marry me? I can't hide behind Nils' failed memory anymore. It's time to tell the truth, and all of it.*

She swallowed hard, set her bundle of clothes on the sidewalk and began. "Nils, I know everything that happened the week that you forgot, but I was afraid to upset you when you were sick. Now that you're better, I owe it to you to tell the truth.

"After you asked me to marry you, I went home very happy. Well, Mama started screaming and Papa tried to be reasonable. He advised me to think about our marriage for a couple weeks. So, that Thursday when you saw me, I told you that I needed two weeks to think about it. Your pastor did not want to marry us, my mother would disown me as her child and forbid my brothers and sister to see me. I was scared. I needed some time, but when I told you this, you were upset with me. You thought I was leaving you forever, but I had no doubt in my mind that, as soon as two weeks went by, I would say, 'Yes.' So we went home, both angry at each other."

Her heart pounded against her chest as Anna paused to take a deep breath, and then expel it in a quivering sigh. "The next evening, Grisha comes into my room and says that the Irish twins saw someone that looked like you being beat up. I asked for a description of the men. The boys told Grisha that these fellows all wore hats and kept them on as they were beating you up. I guess they had to keep one Jewish tradition and break the rest." She tried to smile, but her lips trembled. She shrugged instead. "I had a pretty good idea in my mind who these men were, and I went to the local tavern where they usually spent their time drinking. I had a plan. I asked them if they wanted to earn some money to beat up a Norwegian fellow I did not like. Of course, they were drunk and one of them said, 'First the mother, then the daughter. We already took care of him.' When they proceeded to describe what they did to you, I was crying inside, but I could not show it. So, I listened and gave them two dollars and told them not to repeat this to anyone. By the time I got home, it was late at night and I did not want to wake up you, Kjersti or Oddleif. I confronted my mother with what she had done and that's when she told me who my father was.

"The next morning I found a room, then ran to your house, and then to the hospital." Anna's eyes brimmed with tears. "Nils, I had nothing to do with these men beating you up. Please, please believe me. I just did not want to see them again, like today. I want to be your wife and I cannot wait the few days until we get married—that is, if you still want to after all this." Anna covered her face and sobbed into her hands, afraid to look at the man next to her.

Nils' memories of that Thursday night came back in a rush. In a way, he wished that they remained forgotten. *Anna's father is a wise man. He had his reasons for cautioning his daughter on the marriage. Besides, I was too burned from Kari to give Anna a little time, but since the first day she visited me in the hospital, she has given me so much love and care. God must have been watching over me, because it is a strange coincidence that the twins saw the beating and told Grisha, who in turn told Anna. But then, God's ways are hard to understand. Why is it that, to get the girl I wanted, I nearly had to lose my life?* Nils put the issue of Anna's mother and the thugs aside. *What can I do about it now? It will be best to simply forget it.*

Nils set his box on curb and pulled Anna down onto the grass next to the sidewalk. He held her tightly in his arms, then reached for the handkerchief in his pocket and wiped the tears from her face. "Anna, sweetheart, please do not cry. I love you, and I never think you ask these men to do it. Of course I marry you. I know what your father say and he's right. You have to think about marriage. I am sorry I was upset with you, but I am scared you go away like Kari Hagen. I am sorry you go and talk to them where they drink. They could do very bad things to you. We just forget about the men. They know they done wrong." He paused and smiled at her. "I feel better now. I have you, and I can play my *hardingfele*. I do not need more. Now I take care of you, so you never go by yourself."

"Oh Nils," Anna said, holding him close. "I needed to find out....I hated them and what they did to you, but if I went to the police, they would take Mama away, and....and she would go to prison and our family..." Anna struggled to speak through the tears. "Please... forgive me."

"I cannot forgive you because you do nothing wrong. I understand about your family. You save my life. Without you, I was so sick, I die."

Anna looked into the kind blue eyes and smiled. "I had more than a month to think about it, Nils. In my heart, the answer has always been yes, and not because I feel sorry that you were sick, but because I cannot imagine life without you, not being held by your strong arms, not hearing your *hardingfele*, never feeling your kisses again."

Nils stroked Anna's hair and kissed her forehead. "We have whole life to love each other. Life has both happy and sad part, like music. Now I hear what you tell me and I love you even more. Here, little cat eyes have too many tears." Nils gently took off Anna's glasses and wiped them with a handkerchief.

"Thank you." She sniffed as she looked up at him. "I suppose it's time to pick up my clothes and get going."

"Ja," he answered as they stood. "We have busy day before Saturday. But Sunday we have little holiday."

"Where?"

"Oh, I tell you not now. Later. You see then."

Anna wondered, as they started walking home, what kind of a day Nils planned for them. Perhaps they would take a train and get away from the city for a day. The heat was oppressive and too much had happened in the last month. They both needed a day of rest. There was one small matter of a gray and white cat to attend to, however, before the wedding.

That Friday, after work, Anna and Margit Sørensen stopped at the corner of Pinehurst and Cleveland. Anna held a wicker basket as she placed a handful of chicken strips in a small bowl, near the bushes. "Kitty, kitty, kitty," she called, hoping that the stray would come.

They waited for ten minutes and, when no cat appeared, Anna stared at the full bowl of chicken. "Sorry I took your time, Margit. It was stupid of me to think the cat would still be here, waiting for us. I saw it occasionally during the past month, but I was with Nils and too busy to feed it. Besides, I had nowhere to take it."

Margit shrugged her shoulders. "You didn't take my time. Like I really wanted to hurry home and see six bratty kids and do chores? Anna, why do you want a dirty stray cat when they sell kittens at the farmers' market?" Margit's face lit up with an idea. "Before I come to the wedding, I'll stop and get you the prettiest one. I like those orange, black and white ones. They call them calico cats, just like the fabric."

Anna shook her head. "This cat is special, Margit. When Nils and I used to meet at this street corner, the cat was always there. Nils liked it so much. Why, even when he was delirious with fever and dying, he asked Kjersti and me to take care of the little gray and white cat. I just thought it would make a good wedding present, but I should have caught it a lot earlier."

"Like you had time. We'll wait for a bit. Here. Maybe he understands Norwegian." Margit went by the bushes and called it.

"I might as well try the Russian." Anna described the chicken in succulent detail.

Several minutes later, either prodded by international pleading or the smell of the chicken, a gray ear peeked around the side of the building, followed by a gray and white head. Margit slowly pushed the bowl toward the cat and took a step back. The animal hesitated by the wall, looking around cautiously before it eyed the chicken hungrily. Soon the urge to eat won. The cat licked its lips with a pink tongue, then padded toward the bowl. The chicken was gone only an instant later.

"Anna, get the basket," Margit whispered. "I'm going to catch him."

"No, wait, he's friendly. Let him come to us, like he did before, and then we can put him in the basket."

The girls did not have long to wait. The stray walked up to them and meowed, as though asking if there was more. He did not resist as Anna picked him up and held him close. She could feel each rib on his thin frame.

"Now," she said through clenched teeth.

Margit opened the basket and the two girls tried to stuff the cat inside. The contented feline was immediately transformed into a monster with teeth and claws that attacked from every direction. The girls finally succeeded in getting it into the basket, but paid dearly with their skin.

As they turned, Anna and Margit noticed the group of Irish kids who gathered to watch. Anna hoped that no one owned the cat, considering the amount of trouble she and Margit just went through to catch it.

One of the children's mothers walked up to see what the commotion was about. A small boy tugged at the woman's sleeve. "Mommy, they got that gray and white cat in the basket."

"Oh? That mangy thing?" she replied. She turned to the two young women before her. "Get it out of here. All it does is twine between your legs and beg for food. Scrawny little puss. I have barely enough food for the kids, so I ain't going to squander any on the cat. Don't know where it came from, but we ain't gonna miss it." She glanced down at her children. "Paddy and Kathleen, get yourselves home now."

Margit and Anna watched the woman walk off with two little kids in tow, then Anna turned to her friend. "I guess we better be going ourselves, Margit. Listen to him." Growls and hisses, accompanied by the sound of fast and furious scratching, issued from the basket. "He's trying to scratch out an escape route."

Anna held onto the basket firmly and Margit tied it with twine just in case. The latter then surveyed her handiwork. "That's tight. Now he can't get out."

The girls ran to catch the streetcar and hoped that the conductor would not question the contents of the basket. If so, Anna knew that Margit could assume a pouty expression that would melt the hardest of hearts.

Margit and Anna left the streetcar several stops later, and walked the few blocks to a small brick house where the Sørensen's lived—mother, father and seven children. Mrs. Sørensen opened the door, her gaze shifting from the mewling basket to her daughter and, finally, resting on the young woman with her.

"Margit, why do you have a cat in a basket? Heavens! Look at both of your hands. They're all scratched up." She switched to English and faced Anna. "I am Kristin Sørensen. Please, come in. I will wash your scratches and put medicine on them."

Mrs. Sørensen led the girls to the kitchen sink and motioned for them to place the cat basket on the floor. Margit dried her hands with the towel and introduced Anna.

"Mother, this is Anna Katz from work. She is the one marrying the Norwegian fellow that I told you about, who was very sick and plays the *hardingfele*. He wanted this cat, so she's giving it to him for a wedding present. But it's dirty and we need to wash it. Tomorrow, when I go to their house for the wedding, I will bring it with me, but it has to stay here overnight. Can it?"

Margit's mother smiled at Anna. "I'm glad to meet you Miss Katz." She opened a drawer and pulled out a tin as she continued. "Congratulations on the wedding." She turned to Margit and applied salve to her scratches. "*Uff da*, Margit. What can I say? Wash the cat real good and keep it in your room. For God's sake," she added as the cat screeched its frustrations, "put on some gloves and take him out of the basket. He sounds miserable in there."

Margit ran to the hallway and returned with three pairs of thick gray woolen gloves. She handed two sets to Anna and her mother, then put the third pair on and untied the basket. The growling cat launched itself onto the kitchen table. Margit and Anna jumped for the table and grasped the cat before he could flee, while Mrs. Sørensen filled the sink with water. "All right," the older woman said, "Bring him here."

The cat screeched his indignation when Mrs. Sørensen picked him up by the scruff and Margit grabbed his legs. Anna grasped the soap and began to scrub the dirty fur. Her eyes widened as she continued to wash and rinse the fur. Areas she previously thought to be gray were now white. The six Sørensen children heard the commotion in the kitchen and crowded around the sink to watch a most curious bath. Margit wrapped the cat in a towel and it meowed piteously, but was too tired to fight the humans who had turned its feline life upside down during the past hour.

Little Hans Sørensen pointed to the half-gray, half white mustache. "Look, it has a funny face."

"Now that it is clean, it is a pretty cat." Mrs. Sørensen warmed up a little milk and put a saucer on the kitchen floor. The cat wriggled out of the towel, looking more like a drowned rat, and started lapping up the milk.

Anna headed toward the door. "Margit, I have to go back to my room and pack. Thank you for helping with the cat. You're all welcome to come tomorrow. There will be plenty of Norwegian food and the Pedersen's have a boy and a girl your children can play with."

Mrs. Sørensen wiped her hands on a towel. "Thank you. We will try. With seven children, I have a lot to do." Mrs. Sørensen pointed a finger at Margit. "But, someone has to mind that girl, so she will not get into trouble."

Anna laughed lightly as she opened the door. *"Ha det,"* Anna said her good-bye in Norwegian, closed the door and hurried to catch the streetcar.

Anna's mouth opened in a yawn, then she glanced at the clock. "Almost ten, and I still don't know what I'm going to wear for my wedding tomorrow!" She continued to pull dresses from the closet then, and with a shake of her head, folded and packed them in the basket. Her best dresses were made of wool and one of plush. *Not exactly appropriate for a humid day in July.* She had no spare time—or money—to buy a wedding dress.

She reached for a white summer dress with little lacy frills, slipped it off the hanger and, holding both shoulders, gave the dress a once over. *It will do, considering the ceremony and celebration will be in Oddleif and Kjersti's yard.* She folded the dress and tucked it inside the basket, then rifled through a small wooden box of hairpins and combs. That, too, she slipped into the basket. *I'll do my hair after Kjersti and I finish cooking. Hope I won't wilt under the heat and excitement of the day*, she thought as she added a vial of rosewater to the basket.

Anna glanced around the room one last time to make certain she had packed all of her possessions, then blew out the lamp and hopped into bed. She tried to sleep, but it would not come. The air was a motionless, excruciatingly hot blanket around her, which refused to allow her to breathe or get comfortable.

Anna smiled as Nils' face appeared in her mind, and her thoughts turned to their new life together. *I can't wait to spend the rest of my life with him. I must be the happiest girl in St. Paul.* Immediately, a ball of fear gnawed at her stomach and she began to toss and turn in the small, narrow bed. *What will happen our first night together?*

Girls from work, the few she considered friends among her married co-workers, told her that it hurt and often bled the first time. "But that's what men do and how babies come about," one young woman told her, "so you will just have to put up with it."

"It becomes less painful later," another assured her.

"One thing is certain about men," the eldest and longest married of the group piped up. "They always want to do it at the most inopportune times."

Anna stared at the sudden light that flickered through the darkness from the window. *Will my Nils be like these other men or the Cossack that had his way with Mama? She shook her head in fierce denial* "No. He is so considerate and polite," she added in his defense, then frowned as nearby thunder rumbled from outside. *But will he take me by force and do that every few days?*

Anna shut her eyes tightly to dispel the image. She tossed and turned as the thunderstorm started to rage outside. It was several hours later, after the tempest rolled through and cooled off the air, before she finally fell into a fitful sleep.

Chapter Twenty-One

Anna arose early the next morning, paid for her room, and took the streetcar to Cayuga Street. She and Kjersti prepared part of the wedding meal several nights before, but there were few things that would keep in the cellar during the summer's heat. The civil ceremony would be held at one that afternoon. As soon as Anna walked through the door, she deposited her possessions in the living room, then rolled up her sleeves and headed for the kitchen.

Kjersti cleaned the house the night before and had even borrowed extra plates, silverware, pots and pans from neighbors. Oddleif and Oskar did their part as well. They scrounged the neighborhood for tables and chairs.

Nils followed the sound of clanging pots and pans, then smiled at the two bustling women. "I can help if you need me," he offered.

"Too many cooks spoil the broth," Kjersti yelled through the steam, "and, besides, a man will just be underfoot in here. Just mind Henrik and Solveig, so they do not cause trouble or get into things."

Nils took the children for a short walk around the neighborhood. Several blocks down, a woman pruned her rose garden. *Anna would look so beautiful with a bouquet of roses.*

Nils walked up to the gray-haired lady. "Excuse me. I ask you. I get married today. I pay you for several rose flowers for my new wife."

The elderly woman turned toward the accented voice and smiled.

"Congratulations, young man." She cut off a half dozen cream roses from a bush. "There is no need to pay me. Just take them for your bride." She handed Nils the flowers, then cut another one for Solveig. "Little girl, you would look just lovely with a pretty red rose."

"You are very kind. Thank you." Nils bent down and whispered in Solveig's ear."

"Thank you." Solveig smiled and smelled the fragrant flower.

Nils took the children back home a short time later. He kept an eye on them as he garnished the bouquet with green fern leaves and wild flowers from the back yard.

Kjersti and Anna left the kitchen several hours later. The counters and tables sagged with dish after dish of mouthwatering food, both Russian and Norwegian. The food that would remain unharmed by the heat they covered with cloth, and the rest they transported to the cellar to cool. Kjersti found Nils outside with her children. She sent him to his room, while she and Anna took turns washing off at the water pump. The two women had just finished when Oddleif and Oskar came back from their half-day of work, sweaty and covered with grime. One warning glance from Kjersti was all it took for the two men to head for the water pump themselves.

Kjersti glanced at the grandfather clock as they returned to the kitchen. "Anna, you better get ready. That man from the courthouse will be coming in an hour. You know the groom cannot see the bride before the wedding, so I'll take your clothes into my room and help you with your hair."

"Funny," Anna said as she followed the older woman, "the Russian women had the same tradition. There's not much to see anyway, Kjersti. I don't have a wedding dress. Just something I bought for a hot summer day."

"That will work for today. After the kitchen this morning, I think I can survive the fires of hell. Grab your basket." Kjersti continued as she headed for the steps to the second floor. "I'll tell Nils to stay upstairs. Just go to my room and make yourself at home."

Kjersti knocked on Nils' door a minute later, then admonished him the moment he opened the portal. "Now, don't go into my room. You can't see the bride before the wedding."

Nils nodded in understanding and handed her the silver brooch. "This is for Anna. I would like her to wear it today." Nils waved his hand toward the roses that lay on his dresser. "An older lady on Westminster Street gave me a half-dozen roses, too. I told her I was getting married and I offered to pay, but she refused."

"Oh, they are beautiful. I can't wait to see Anna with them."

Nils opened his trunk and produced a small cloth bag, which he handed to Kjersti. "This is for you or Solveig, when she is old enough to wear them."

She looked into the bag, saw two smaller brooches, and handed it back. "No, Nils. I cannot take it. These were your mother's. Save them for your daughter or Anna."

"Kjersti, this is how I would like to say thank you for everything you have done for me. For Oddleif, I can fix the fence and work in the yard, but for you, I want to give this."

Sadness clouded Kjersti's eyes before she acknowledged the gift. "Thank you, Nils. I feel like you are saying goodbye or something. Surely you are not leaving right away?"

"No, we stay until I am healthy and back to working and, through the winter, save up a little money. Come spring, I really want to buy a small farm. I don't mind St. Paul, but all my life I work the land and, truly, I feel like a fish out of water in a big city."

"How does Anna feel about it?"

"She grew up in a little village in Russia, had a garden, animals. She says she wants to give it a try."

Kjersti stepped inside, shut the door behind her and lowered her voice. "Nils, I want to tell you something as a married woman. Tonight, just be careful with her. The first time, it hurts. She may bleed a little and be sore the next day. It will get better, trust me."

Nils cleared his throat and struggled to battle down the blush that crept up his neck. "Thank you for telling me."

Kjersti left him then, and headed downstairs to her own bedroom. She sighed, grateful that Anna had slipped on her dress and was in the process of pinning her hair.

"Here, let me help you." Kjersti set aside the small bag Nils gave her. She buttoned the back of Anna's summer dress, and then helped to style her hair in a becoming bun.

"I think you are done, except for one more thing." She reached into the pocket of her dress and pulled out the brooch. "This is Nils' wedding present to you. It was his mother's, and he wants you to wear it. We call it *sølje* in Norway."

Anna's eyes widened in surprise as she stared down at the ten shimmering gold and silver circles, set amid an ornate silver latticework background. "Kjersti, it's beautiful and so exquisitely made. You mean he is giving this to me?"

"Yes, now let me put it on." Kjersti pinned the brooch to the front of Anna's dress.

Anna gently touched the brooch with her fingertips, then felt heat brush her cheeks. *How can a little, scrawny cat match the beauty of Nils' gift?* "I have his gift coming with Margit Sørensen. You'll see in a little bit. The children will like it, too."

"I wonder what it could be, but don't tell me," Kjersti added the last quickly before she lowered her voice. "Anna, the first time it will hurt, but it will get better and you'll find out that you look forward to it. There is just something about two people coming together to be one. I can't explain, but you'll see."

Anna nodded as her cheeks blushed again, this time to a color near crimson. "That's what I heard, too."

A knock sounded on the bedroom door, followed by Oddleif's voice. "Kjersti, the Justice of the Peace is here. Is Anna ready?"

Kjersti opened the door. "Yes, here she is." Anna walked into the living room with a tremulous smile as Solveig, Oddleif, and Oskar gasped with heartfelt "Ooh's" and "Ahhh's!"

Kjersti turned to address a thin, balding man in a black robe, who stood near the front door. "You must be from the courthouse. Would you like some water? Oh, and, of course, you're welcome to stay for the food. We have plenty."

"Thank you, ma'am," he said as he reached to shake Kjersti's extended hand. "It's a hot one out there. Well, the bride is beautiful," he said as he glanced around the room, "but which one is the groom?"

"He's upstairs," Kjersti said. She marched toward the stairs. "Nils, it's time."

Nils grabbed the roses and rushed down the stairs. When he reached the living room, however, he stopped dead in his tracks. Anna was beautiful. The simple white dress with lace at the collar and cuffs fit her just right, and the *sølje* pinned to the material at the hollow of her throat completed the effect. It reflected gold and silver sparkles throughout the room. Her hair was done in a loose bun, with wispy red curls surrounding her face. Finally, his mouth broke into a grin as he took a step forward. *I could kiss her right now.*

Anna's heart did a little flip-flop. She could not believe how handsome Nils looked. He wore the same embroidered vest and shoes with silver buckles she had admired at the picnic, but this time he held a large bouquet of flowers in his hands. One stray strand of blond hair hung across his forehead, refusing to stay in place, as he handed her the bouquet.

"Here is flowers for a pretty girl."

"Thank you," she replied with a blush as she hugged them close. "They're beautiful." She paused to touch the pin. "And thank you for the Norwegian brooch. I have not forgotten your gift. It's coming, very soon."

Oddleif motioned them outside. "Come on, you two. You can sweet talk all you want after you're married. The fellow from the courthouse is steaming in his robe."

They all left the house for the front yard. A tightness gripped her chest as the Justice of the Peace read several State statutes and Bible passages pertaining to marriage, and then asked the couple to exchange rings. Oddleif stepped forward then, took the box with the rings from his pocket and gave them to the bride and groom.

Nils took Anna's delicate hand in his much larger one and slipped the silver band on her finger. He breathed a sigh of relief. *It fits.*

Anna's fingers trembled as she put the metal band on Nils bigger finger.

The Justice of the Peace smiled as he continued. "As entrusted by God, the State of Minnesota, Ramsey County, and the City of St. Paul, I pronounce Nils and Anna Bjørnsen man and wife." He smiled at the couple. "You may now kiss the bride."

"Ja, kiss her real good, Nils," Oskar added.

Nils glanced down at his new wife, and his heart swelled with so much tenderness and love that he wanted to lift her into his arms and...

He glanced at the Justice of the Peace, the children, and Oddleif, Kjersti and Oskar, and realized that one short kiss would have to do for the time being. He gently drew Anna to his chest, lifted her chin and his lips brushed hers.

Anna closed her eyes with a mixture of rapturous pleasure and heartfelt pain. She was Nils' wife now—and not a single member of her family had witnessed the union. She felt Nils' reluctance as he drew away, and her eyes misted when she met his gaze—a gaze so blue and full of love that she had no doubt she found the right man.

Kjersti and Oddleif witnessed the signing of the marriage certificate, then the wedding celebration began. Everyone rushed toward the Justice of the Peace, offering him an assortment of beer, *lutefisk,* blood sausage, dumplings, *kvas*, and a variety of cakes and pies. He frowned in bewilderment at the strange assortment of foreign food, gulped down a mug of beer and was on his way. Soon after, the guests started to arrive, bringing even more food with them. Nils spotted Emil Kruse and, immediately, he and Anna approached the man.

"Thank you, Emil, for the money for my days not at work. Next time man get hurt and cannot work, I give money."

"That's the whole point of a union, Nils," the other man smiled. "We all help each other."

Anna spotted Margit Sørensen coming up the walk. She carried a wicker basket. Anna excused herself and ran up to greet her friend. "Margit, I was worried about you."

"Anna, the devil himself is inside this basket." She grasped the lid and squeezed it shut again as it began to open. "I have no hands anymore. They are numb, like wooden clothespins. And the screeching…"

"Shh, I want this to be surprise."

"Some surprise," Margit muttered to herself as Anna walked up behind her husband and tapped him on the shoulder.

"Nils, we have to go inside with Margit. Your wedding gift is in the basket."

His brow wrinkled in a puzzled frown. *Why did Margit bring Anna's present with her?* The basket lurched suddenly, and Margit slapped at the lid, then whispered harshly to whatever was inside. Nils' brow wrinkled even further with his level of confusion. "Anna, what she have in there?"

"You'll see in a minute." They walked into the house, and Anna closed the door behind them. Margit untied the basket and opened the lid. An angry gray and white ball of fur jumped out of its prison and ran toward the closed front door, then whirled and bounded toward the bedroom. The cat stopped at yet another closed door, shook its head as though aware it could not escape, and slunk under the couch.

Anna bit her lip in apologetic indecision. "I am sorry, Nils. I guess your present ran away from you. I remembered that you and the cat were good friends at the street corner. Margit helped me catch it and wash it…"

Nils resounding laugh echoed in the room, and his broad smile allayed Anna's fear. "That's the best present for cat and me. He has home and food now. Thank you both that you bring him."

"He's a troll, Nils." Margit stretched out her scratched up hands. "He jumped out of the basket on the streetcar, and that's what I got for shoving him back in. I was lucky. The conductor just laughed at me."

Nils' smile faded immediately. "I am so sorry you went through so much trouble for me. I could have probably caught him myself, so you wouldn't get so scratched up. Go ask if Kjersti has something to soothe the skin," he told her in Norwegian. "We will see if he is such a troll."

Margit headed out the door as Anna followed Nils into the kitchen. He filled one bowl with milk and another with choice morsels of meats from the festivities, then returned to the living room. He slid the bowl partially under the couch, crouched down on his haunches and waited. The cat sniffed, but would not touch the food.

Nils glanced at Anna, then shook his head. "I think I take him to our room and leave food there. Here, many people, they open door and he run away."

"That's a smart idea. But what if he needs to go outside?" Anna asked.

Nils went back to the kitchen, found a box, and filled it with cold ashes from the stove. "He use this, we hope." Nils crawled behind the couch and pulled the cat out by his scruff. He kept a firm grip on him with one hand and stroked him softly with the other. The stray did not protest as Nils carried him upstairs. "We tell Solveig tomorrow. Little cat, he is scared. He need rest."

"Nils, Anna, come out," Kjersti called from the yard. "The photographer is here. Bring your *hardingfele,* too. I want him to take a picture of you with it."

The bride and groom rejoined their guests a moment later, and the photographer told Nils to stand on the front steps, positioned Anna on a chair next to her new husband, then ducked behind a black curtain to take several pictures.

Nils held the instrument and whispered to Anna. "I now have two best things I love. My wife and my *hardingfele.*"

The photographer gathered his equipment and, as Oskar led the guest toward the food, Kjersti stood beside the married couple and ingrained the images in her mind. "By the way, what was in that basket?" she asked.

Nils grasped Anna's hand and helped her rise, then turned to Kjersti. "Something that Solveig would very much like, but we'll wait until tomorrow to tell her."

"Well, what?"

"A little gray and white cat that Anna gave me."

Kjersti smiled and nodded, understanding immediately. "You talked about that cat in the hospital, Nils. We thought you were leaving us, and all you could rave about in your fever was that stray cat and how it wasn't going to be taken care of."

"Ja, well, now he has a home. We have to think of a name. Perhaps Solveig will help with that."

"Just keep him out of the kitchen," Kjersti admonished. "I don't want him getting into the milk."

"Don't worry. He's locked upstairs. In time, I'll let him out. I just don't want him to run away now, when he is afraid and does not trust us."

"He'll trust us for sure by tomorrow. His belly will be so full it will be dragging on the ground." Kjersti laughed as she walked off to serve the food.

Anna and Nils followed, then sat down at the head of a row of picnic tables as, one-by-one, the guests congratulated the newly married couple, then dug into the food. Big men from the mills and stockyards chomped noisily at their plates, wiped their mouths with their sleeves, and washed the food down with large mugs of beer. Toasts were raised in Norwegian, followed by a hearty *skål* and, sometimes, rather lewd laughter. Nils translated the best he could, except for the phrases he was too embarrassed to repeat. After particularly prolonged titters and Oskar slapping Nils on the back, Anna could stand it no longer.

Her brow furrowed in confusion. "Nils, what are they saying? It must be something funny. I know whenever Papa plays for a wedding, he comes back with tales of long and silly toasts."

Nils shrugged his shoulders. "Anna, they just talk because they have too much beer. It is about what man and woman do after they get married. I do not know words for it in English. Not good for girl to hear it. I fix it."

Nils stood up and rapped his fork on the table for attention. "My wife wants to know about all these toasts you have been doing, but she does not know Norwegian and I cannot translate this fast. Please, say them in English now, so she can understand you better."

Anna had never seen so many big men turn red as beets and pretend to clear their throats or spit. Oskar rescued the uncomfortable silence by raising a glass to the new couple's future children. The men clapped and helped themselves to more food. Kjersti brought out a tray of *fattigmann* fried cakes and whispered in Nils' ear.

"Take out your *hardingfele* and play for a bit. They might at least dance off the beer, instead of sitting and filling up their glasses."

"You are right," he agreed. "It's too early and, if they keep on drinking like they have been, you won't want to see your garden by this evening. I'll give them something to do besides sitting."

Nils ran upstairs to get the fiddle and checked in on the cat. It was hiding under the bed, paws tucked under, but the bowls of food and milk were almost empty.

"Sleep good, little cat," Nils told the ball of fur under the bed and rejoined the party.

He played for a good hour before taking a break. The men stretched their legs, dancing with their wives or sweethearts. Oskar and Sigrid Dahl hopped to a polka. Margit Sørensen was on the arm of Trygve Haraldson, from the mill. Kjersti and Oddleif did a couple of turns for old times sake, while Henrik and Solveig skipped around the dancers, absorbed in their own game.

Anna stayed by Nils' side, listening to the magical tunes that poured from the fiddle—and missing her father.

Tom Trivisani, a man from the union, stepped forward. "Can I have a dance with the beautiful bride, since the groom is playing?"

"Thank you," Anna smiled politely, "but I would really like to wait until I can dance with my husband." She softened her refusal by adding, "My father is coming later on. He will bring his violin, so Nils and I will have a chance to dance."

Tom walked off and, while Nils played, Anna graciously refused a score of other men who asked her to dance.

Nils stopped playing after an hour, took off his embroidered vest and unbuttoned his shirtsleeves. Anna stepped away and returned with a glass of cold water. "The heat is too much, even for the fiddler."

"Thank you, sweet heart." Nils gulped down the cool liquid. Anna sat beside him again, and they watched as their guests, exhausted from the heat and the dancing, congregated back at the smorgasbord to fill up on beer and watermelon.

He pointed at Solveig, who ran around in circles pretending that the music was still playing. Henrik toddled after his sister, imitating her every move. "Children, they never tired. Look at them. Solveig, come here," Nils called to the little girl. She rushed to his side. "Remember you wanted me to play you a tune at the wedding? I have one for you now. Did you want to dance by yourself, with your father, Uncle Oskar, or Henrik?"

"I want to dance with you, Uncle Nils, because you spin me around the best."

"If you dance with me, who will play the *hardingfele*?"

Solveig giggled and wrinkled her nose. "I don't know."

"Well, you have to pick someone besides me. Who will it be?"

"Uncle Oskar. He is the next best. I go get him." Solveig ran off to find Oskar in the throng of people by the table, while Nils translated the little girl's conversation for Anna.

"Did you actually make up a song just for her?"

"I do not know. In my head, I have many, many songs. Maybe I play before, maybe it is half one and half different."

Solveig returned, dragging a tipsy Oskar by the hand.

"Nils," he said in a weary voice, "I just danced with Sigrid for a whole hour. Give the man a rest."

"It should not be too long." Nils put the fiddle under his chin. "Just give the little one a couple of spins. She likes it. I promised Solveig her own tune today." He began to play. One minute it was a gay polka, the next a spirited Voss tune. Oskar turned and twirled and spun the little girl in every direction, then wiped the sweat off his forehead with a plea. "Have pity, please. Play something slower."

Nils obliged by picking a waltz. For each one of Oskar's steps, Solveig took at least four, so she did not notice the difference in tempo. As the music ended, Oskar bounced Solveig up in the air, expertly caught her and gave her one last spin. He set her down on her feet, and she finally fell on the ground, laughing, dizzy and exhausted.

"She will sleep good tonight. How about you, Nils?" Oskar winked and walked over to the keg for another mug of beer.

Kjersti yelled from inside the house. "Solveig, someone, open the door for me."

Anna walked up the few porch steps and yanked on the handle, then stood back as Kjersti came out with a tray bearing the largest and strangest cake Anna had ever seen. A big ring began at the bottom, and each successive stacked ring was smaller, giving the cake the appearance of a cone. She gasped her surprise, then covered her lips with her fingers as she counted twenty rings, measuring two feet from the bottom one to the top one. The top ring bore a wax paper banner with the words

> *Nils and Anna Bjørnsen*
> *Congratulations*
> *July 16, 1899.*

Oddleif raced forward and helped his wife carry the towering cake to a nearby table. Guests clapped, then voiced their approval with many 'ahhhs," while Nils grasped Anna's hand within his and led her down the steps toward the magnificent baked tower.

Anna leaned toward Kjersti. "When did you have the time to make this?"

"Thursday, while you were at work. This is *kransekake*, a special Norwegian wedding cake."

Nils gave her hand a gentle squeeze. "Now we break first ring and eat it. Then people eat more."

"But, Nils, it's so beautiful. I can't imagine destroying it just to eat it."

"Solveig can imagine eating it." Nils pointed at the little girl, who skipped around the table, then stood up on her tiptoes, trying to get a better glimpse of the *kransekake*. "So, we start first, and then she can have her favorite cake. Follow what I do."

"Oh——" Anna battled a smile "——all right."

Nils reached for the top ring, and Anna followed his example. Together, they broke it in half. He then broke a small piece from his half and gave it to Anna. She tasted a sweet almond paste with an unknown spice.

"I'll give you a piece of mine." Anna handed a piece to Nils, not sure how to proceed.

Her action brought an enthusiastic response from the guests. She must have done the right thing, she decided, because the guests clapped and wished them a sweet marriage, with three times the happy years together as there were rings on the cake.

"Now they eat." Nils motioned to the little girl. "Solveig, you come first." He gave the little girl a piece, then turned to Anna. "We next pass cake out to all our guests."

Nils waited until Solveig stepped away to whisper softly into Anna's ear. "Cake, it is very sweet, but not so sweet like my Anna."

"I am not sweet," she whispered back. "I feel like I just made a fool of myself."

"Same like I make at Russian wedding," Nils replied. An image came to mind immediately—one that made Anna smile. She saw Nils being handed a wine glass wrapped in cloth and simply staring at it, unaware that he had to put it on the ground and break it with his shoe, so that the guests could all shout *mazel tov. He would probably try to fix the glass, as he cannot stand to have broken things lying around.*

Anna giggled under her breath as she passed the pieces of cake to the guests. Nils looked at her quizzically, and arched his eyebrows.

"Oh, I just thought of a Jewish tradition. I just can't imagine you doing it."

"What?"

"Breaking a glass."

"That is Oskar's thing. He do it very good. Why they break glass?"

"It's just a little wine glass, broken for good luck and long life. Ask Papa when he comes. He can explain it better."

Anna's smile faded as her eyes scanned the crowd. *Where is Papa? It is already well past dusk, and Shabbos is over. Maybe something happened at home and Mama found out...*

Nils took out his fiddle and, while he entertained the guests, Anna talked to Margit and a couple of other girls from St. Paul Garments.

"Oskar," Trygve Haraldson nudged his friend and pointed toward the short, balding man with a black skullcap and violin case, who walked into the yard. "Looks like we got ourselves another fiddler."

"Ja," Oskar said, nodding his head. "That's Anna's father. He plays his violin for weddings and she tells me he is good."

"She don't look nothing like him."

"That's the truth." The two men went back to the keg.

Nils stopped playing when he noticed Moyshe walk up behind his daughter, where she still visited with Margit and the other girls.

Moyshe tapped Anna on the shoulder, and she turned.

"Papa!" She flung herself into his arms and the tears were instantaneous. "Oh, Papa, I was so afraid you were not going to come!"

"And would I miss the most important day in my daughter's life?" He pressed a kiss to her tear-streaked face, then turned to Nils as the younger man approached them. He reached out to shake his hand. "Congratulations, Nils. My Anna will make you a wonderful wife."

"That I know already," Nils replied. "Please," he grabbed a clean plate. "Have some food before you play. We have many things."

Anna rescued her father from the predicament. "Papa, I will point to everything that I made, so you know it's *kosher*."

"But what about the dishes?" Moyshe asked quietly.

"They are all Kjersti's, but as far as I know, she does not follow our Jewish law of separating milk dishes from the meat ones."

"Well, then get me a little whiskey." Moyshe pulled out a shot glass from his pocket and lowered his voice. "Mama knows nothing. As far as she is concerned, I am in Minneapolis."

He handed Nils a bulky package tied with twine. "I have something for both of you. Nothing fancy, but I'm sure you will use it."

"Thank you. You are very kind to both of us."

"Well, go ahead. Open it."

Nils cut the twine and unwrapped the box. It contained two pots, a frying pan, and a large metal object, which resembled a teakettle.

Anna knew instantly what the object was and embraced her father. "Papa, a *samovar*. Thank you. Where did you buy this? Surely not from the Sears catalog."

"Oh, let's just say I twisted the arm of one of my customers for a couple free shoe repairs. I am sorry it's not new, but it should do the job."

Nils wrinkled his brow in confusion over this strange tea kettle Anna called a *samovar*. "What is job of it?"

"It's for keeping the water hot for tea," Anna explained. "Every Russian home has one, and now a Norwegian one will, too! You can have your coffee hot anytime you want."

"Look inside the box. There's more," Moyshe urged with a twinkle in his eye.

Anna reached down and pulled out several small packages of black tea and a small wine glass wrapped in cloth. Her eyes teared as she handed it to Nils.

His eyes lit with recognition. "Oh! Anna tell me about breaking glass at Russian wedding. I do that, but we have little children with no shoes, so we be careful."

"Let me get warmed up on the violin and the whiskey. When the music gets going, then we'll do it."

Anna fetched her father a glass. Moyshe took several small sips, tuned up his fiddle and began a waltz. "The first dance," he said, loud enough for all to hear, "is for the newlyweds."

Anna and Nils linked hands and danced alone, while the guests stood at the sides, deferring the first dance to the newly married couple. The bride's lips curved into a smile as she expertly followed her husband's steps. "And to think I didn't even know how to dance a month ago."

Nils returned her smile. "You do very good with your feet. We try faster dance later."

The first waltz ended and the couple returned to Moyshe's side. The music continued. It was from a different country and another fiddler, who played tunes in a slightly minor key, but to the tipsy guests it did not matter as long as it was danceable. Nils tried to follow along on his *hardingfele*, but it was a challenge to keep up with Moyshe Katz. His hand ranged all over the fingerboard, producing notes Nils did not know existed before this evening.

A soulful gypsy ballad turned into a lively *klezmer* melody. Nils could see the rosin rising like smoke off the strings. The music got even faster, and the dancers spun like wound-up toys. Moyshe played one last chord and was greeted with a round of applause from the breathless dancers.

He used the opportunity to raise his drinking glass in a toast. "In Russia, when two people marry, we do two things very well—we drink a lot of whiskey, and then we break glass."

Oskar laughed. "There's a man after my own heart."

"So, I invite you to fill up your glasses as I give a toast to my daughter and my new son-in-law." The adults did not need a second invitation to drink and soon every available glass held beer or whiskey. Moyshe continued. "We say *lechaim*, which means to life."

"*Lechaim*," the guests repeated, then they drained their glasses. "And now, the groom will break the glass for good luck." Moyshe bent down and put glass before Nils' right foot.

Nils gave it a strong stomp, as he would when he began playing a dance tune. The glass shattered under his foot.

"*Mazel tov, mazel tov*," Anna and Moyshe wished the groom.

"*Mazel tov* is best of luck to the new couple," explained Moyshe, and thirty Lutheran Scandinavians shouted *mazel tov*—a sight that neither Moyshe nor Anna would ever forget.

Moyshe scooped up the broken pieces of glass and wrapped them in a handkerchief. "I'll take a break now. Why don't you play your fiddle for a bit?" he asked Nils.

The groom took over the music at that point, and now it was Moyshe's turn to follow Nils trills and twirls. He figured out part of a tune, tried to play it and, to his great surprise, the tune twisted into a variation slightly different than the one he memorized. It was almost like reading a simple story, and then filling in the details piece by piece.

When Nils started playing a waltz, Moyshe took his daughter for a few spins around the yard. "You did good, Anna. He is a nice fellow. Just don't forget your family and your heritage. Your children will be fine musicians. Look at their Papa and Grandpapa. Between the two of us, we'll make them the best fiddlers in St. Paul."

"Papa, I won't forget, I promise. I can't think of children just yet, but—" Anna's face clouded with sadness "—it would certainly be nice for them to have a Grandma."

"I'll try my best, but you know how she is." He paused for a moment and drew his daughter's head against his shoulder. "It is hard to imagine that, just a few years ago, you sat on my knee and I read you stories." He held her away from him again. "And now look at you. A bride." Moyshe beamed at his daughter.

"I remember that, looking at the book and trying to figure out the letters. As a little girl, I would have never dreamed that I would be in America and married to a Norwegian. If someone showed me my life, I would have told them they were crazy."

"Well, fate deals us all kinds of surprises. Your Nils, I have no doubt he will take care of you, and you of him." The waltz ended, and Anna and Moyshe joined Nils on the porch.

By midnight the guests were exhausted from the food, drink, and dancing. They bade farewell to the newlyweds and headed home. Kjersti and Sigrid Dahl began to put the food away, while Oskar and Oddleif sang bawdy songs with the fellows from work. The whiskey had finally taken hold.

Moyshe packed up his violin and prepared to leave. He took Anna and Nils' hands in his own and bowed his head. "God bless you and give you a long life together and many children."

Anna's eyes misted and she hugged her father in a tearful good-bye. "Thank you, Papa. Thank you for coming. You made it the best day ever."

"I would never miss my little girl's wedding." Moyshe blinked away the sudden moistness in his own eyes, then turned to his new son-in-law. "You take care of her, now, Nils."

"I will," he replied, once again shaking the older man's hand. "Thank you that you give me so good wife."

"I better be going now. It's late." He turned to pick up his fiddle, then headed for the street so his daughter would not see his tears.

"Good-bye, Papa. Send my greetings to Mama, Rivka, Max and Grisha," Anna called after him.

Moyshe made his way past the guests, then closed the gate and waved. Anna and Nils returned the gesture of farewell, then Nils took his wife's hand as Moyshe headed toward the streetcar stop.

Chapter Twenty-Two

Nils stood in the yard and shuffled his feet uncomfortably. *How do I ask her upstairs for our wedding night?* "Well, we have a good day. I am glad your father come." He turned to face her. "So, you want to see little cat upstairs?"

Anna's stomach churned with fear at what would transpire next. *That.* "I suppose we better. He could use a second helping of food."

The drunken men watched them head toward the house, and their pointing fingers, winks and ribald jokes needed no translation. Anna blushed to a color near scarlet.

Kjersti leaned on the porch railing and shook her head. "Don't pay any attention to them. Their heads are full of whiskey and beer."

"In Norway," Nils said as he glanced toward the neighbor's house, "I play for three nights, so they dance away whiskey. I think Mrs. Fossheim will not be happy if we have wedding celebration for so long. I hope they do not wake up Henrik." He faced Kjersti. "Goodnight."

"Goodnight." Anna gave her new cousin a hug. "And thank you for everything, especially the ring cake."

"You're welcome, both of you. The children are tired from today and they will sleep through anything, but I don't want *them*—" she nodded toward Oddleif and Oskar "—to disturb the neighbors. Goodnight."

Kjersti left them then, to stomp toward her husband and his drinking buddies.

Nils opened the front door, and Anna gasped when he lifted her into his strong arms and carried her over the threshold. *I might as well carry her all the way upstairs.*

Anna's heart pounded with every step that Nils took. *I am in his arms, I love him, but I am so scared of what is going to happen now.* "We have the same tradition in Russia," her voice came out in a croak. "Not sure what it's for. Good luck maybe. Or perhaps this tells the little house devil to stop his tricks, because the wife is the new boss and she won't put up with it."

Nils breathed heavily as he neared the top step, then crossed to the entrance to their room. "We have little man," he paused as he slowly released her, "called *nissen* in Norway. He take milk and butter and things you cannot find. But if house have cat, he keep *nissen* away."

"For good reason," Anna said with a tremulous smile, "so the puss can have the butter and cream all to himself."

"Ja, smart cat. We see what he do." Nils opened the door to the room and looked around, then turned his gaze to the bed. Sooty black paw prints tracked the crisp white bedspread—a gift from Kjersti and Oddleif. The culprit, a contented sleeping cat, rested on the pillows.

Anna covered her mouth, then laughed. "I think the *nissen's* cousin made himself at home here."

"I am sorry. I do not think when I bring ash box here."

"It's nothing. We can shake it out and I'll give it a good scrubbing next time I do the wash."

"I help you. I wash clothes for many years now." Nils walked toward the cat and stroked it under the chin. The cat stretched toward him with a contented purr and rubbed its muzzle against his hand.

Anna stepped into the room. "I think you've just made a friend although he probably hates me because of the basket." She let her gaze travel around Nils' room. *Our room, now.*

There was not much furniture: a metal frame double bed, a freshly varnished desk and chair, which Nils told her he made himself, a black immigrant chest and a rod for hanging clothes. Anna's box and basket sat next to the clothes rod. Maps of Norway and America hung on the walls. The desk held a Bible, several books in Norwegian, and an English grammar textbook. An old photo of the Bjørnsen family stood on the desk. She walked over and picked up the picture to take a closer look. Nils and an older man, whom Anna assumed was his father, held their fiddles. Nils looked about thirteen in the picture, and the same unruly strand of blond hair hung over his forehead even then.

"That's a nice picture of you," she commented.

"It is very old, maybe 1885. Now, my mother and father are no more and my brother and sister are very far."

"I have a photo of my family," she said as she set the frame down again, "but it's in a box, like everything else that I brought." *I wonder if we will ever have a photograph of all of us: Mama, Papa, Rivka, Grisha, Max, Nils, me, and our children. God willing, maybe Mama will change once she finds out she is a grandmother. No, probably not.* Anna sighed and moved to the maps tacked to the wall. "So, where is Voss in Norway?"

Nils joined her, then reached out and drew a circle with his finger around the middle part of the country. "In Norway, we have like you have states here. So, I come from *Hordaland*, and Voss is a little part of that. See it on the map?"

Anna took off her glasses and, leaning close, squinted at the map and its foreign words. "Yes."

"Our farm is maybe 20 kilometers from town name Voss, but people who live around there, we say we are from Voss. But now, no more farm, just our room in St. Paul."

"Nils, tomorrow I will spend some time unpacking and making the room cozy." She glanced around, then took several steps toward the window. She paused beside the bed and faced her new husband. "I think it needs a little of a woman's touch. I will buy some fabric and sew us some curtains. Would you like that?"

"You do not have to do work for me, only if you want curtains." His eyes twinkled as he smiled. "And not tomorrow, remember?"

"Oh, that's right, we're going to a place you won't tell me about. I guess the curtains can wait." Anna turned to the window, her back to Nils, and lowered her gaze to her hands. She knew what was expected of her, but she had never taken her clothes off in front of anyone except her mother and sister; she stood still, frozen in indecision.

Nils realized that he had to make the first move. *Otherwise we will spend the whole night standing by the bed, each hoping that the other will begin—the 'you go first, no you go first,' of the two Norwegians meeting on a narrow mountain path.* He moved to stand behind Anna and put his arms around her, then gently sat her on the bed. He began to softly stroke her hair and back.

Nils' touch sent tingles racing through Anna's body, and her skin shivered where his fingers caressed it. She drew in a breath and turned to her husband. His hands cupped her cheeks, and then his mouth found hers. She parted her lips and felt Nils' tongue brush her own. Unsure of how to respond, Anna simply drank in Nils' kiss and let her body become limp and warm, like jam simmering in a pot.

"*Jeg elsker deg, jeg elsker deg,*" Nils whispered in between kisses. Anna's lips were soft and yielding and he grew conscious of the tension building within him. He finished the kiss and held her tightly in his arms.

A thud broke their reverie. Apparently, the cat had had enough of the activities on the bed and jumped to the floor. He padded off with a haughty look over his shoulder, as if saying, 'How dare you disturb my rest with your goings on,' and then settled under the chair.

Nils smiled as he gazed into Anna's emerald eyes. "Now I have two cats, you and the little one."

"At least I don't leave dirty paw prints across the sheets," she replied, relaxing a bit as she teased him, "and I usually don't use my claws." The room grew warm, and Anna felt the stickiness of the hot summer night air on her skin. "It's so hot in here. I don't know how the cat can stand it in its fur coat."

"Well, he cannot take it off. But..." Nils gave Anna a playful wink.

I suppose the dress has to come off now. Anna winked back and tossed Nils a smile. "I will be a minute." She rose from the bed, moved to hide behind the clothes rod and dug through her basket for a suitable nightgown. She fumbled at the buttons of her dress and corset ties, ripped a few that she could not reach, and then changed into a chemise.

Nils removed everything but his trousers, then pulled the covers back on the bed. Anna emerged from behind the clothes rod in a white lacy undergarment. Her hair was still partially done up, but several loose strands had escaped the bun.

"I'm sorry. I look like an orange-haired monster."

"No, Anna," Nils said with a shake of his head. "Can I ask you? You take things from your hair. It is very beautiful, I want to see how long it is." He sat on the bed and watched as Anna pulled the pins and rat combs from her hair. The tresses cascaded down to her waist. He blew out the kerosene lamp on the table beside him and Anna's hair shimmered like burnished copper in the moonlight.

"It is so beautiful, like fire at night." His voice was soft and husky with desire. Nils rose, crossed to Anna, and pulled her tightly against him. He buried his face in her hair and breathed in deeply. The scent of rosewater surrounded her, like the soft summer fragrance of the wild rose bushes in Voss. He could feel every contour and curve of her body through the chemise and he yearned to make love to her.

He slipped his hands under the gown and Anna felt the tingles again, racing up and down her spine. She sighed with an unfamiliar sensation of expectation. She was now a married woman and only one thing remained to make their union complete. She snuggled close to Nils, longing to be passionate and intimate, but too embarrassed to run her fingers over his body. *Perhaps in time I will learn what makes him feel good.*

Suddenly Anna became conscious of a hardness pressing against her thigh. *Is that what happens to boys when they become men?*

Nils lifted Anna and carried her to the bed. He sat beside her while she drew the covers up to her chin, and then he shifted to remove his trousers. He slipped in beside Anna and lifted the chemise over her shoulders. At last they were touching skin to skin. Her breasts were small and supple, and the nipples hardened beneath his hands. He could no longer harness his desire and covered her body with kisses. His hands shook from the unleashed tension inside him.

"Anna, my dearest, we try? You tell me if you have pain."

A ball of fear replaced the pleasurable warmth pooling in her chest and stomach. She nodded and closed her eyes, then felt Nils gently spread her legs and lightly brushed the inside of her thighs with his fingers. She drew in a quick breath, savoring his touch, again conscious of an odd fullness inside her. She wrapped her arms around Nils' back, and then tensed when she felt something firm enter her. He mentioned pain, but she felt none.

Nils moved slowly, carefully into her moist folds. His body seared with an unbearable tension that demanded release, and he pressed deeper. After several thrusts, he felt something give inside her. He paused to look at Anna's face, and saw her eyes squeezed tightly closed. "I am sorry. I hurt you?"

Anna shook her head and gritted her teeth, determined to blot out the pain that ripped through the core of her being. The ache slowly subsided as he continued to move inside her and, gradually it was replaced by a tingling sensation that grew by leaps and bounds within her. *It's like what Kjersti said to me this afternoon about two people coming together to make one.*

Nils watched Anna's face closely. She opened her eyes and, seeing the wonder in them, he knew her pain was gone. He closed his own eyes and buried his face in her neck as he continued the slow, thrusting movements. Making love to Anna was the culmination of his thoughts and fantasies over the past few months. He had heard fellows describe the act in dirty terms, but sin was the farthest thing from his mind. God had made man and woman so that they could delight in one another, and this was certainly the most pleasure he had ever experienced. Anna felt soft and warm inside and, with every thrust, he climbed closer to the point where the mountain stream would break forth into a waterfall. *This is almost like making up my own hardingfele tune—only better.*

His breaths came in short gasps as he moved faster inside her. He grasped Anna's shoulders and kissed her face feverishly, wanting to taste and feel every part of her. Suddenly, every muscle in his body tightened. He strained to prolong the moment, then shuddered in a powerful release. "Anna, Anna, *jeg elsker deg*," he moaned softly. Spent, he rested his head on her breast and sighed his relief. *They tried to break me, but I proved them wrong, I have now loved Anna fully!*

Anna placed her hand on Nils' head and stroked his hair. *So, that's all there is? Girls waste hours talking about it, being scared of it, when all the fellow does is work himself up and make part of a baby. There is nothing to be scared of.*. She felt silly for being so afraid, but wondered about the unresolved heaviness in her stomach and groin.

Nils rolled to the side and kissed his wife lightly on the lips. "Thank you, my sweet Anna. Thank you. You have pain?"

"Just a little at first, but I know it will be better next time. I love you so much, Nils." Anna wrapped her arms around her husband.

"I love you, too. Now we sleep. We have long day tomorrow," he added as he pulled the covers over them.

"My eyes are still wide open." Anna forced them shut, but the events of the day kept her awake. "I am so tired I can't sleep."

"I feel same way, so I sing you Norwegian song, make you very tired." Nils stroked Anna's hair as he hummed a lullaby that his mother used to sing to him.

Anna listened to the melody and the foreign words. The tune reminded her of the ones Nils played on his fiddle. She heard a soft thump, then light paws padded on her back and stopped by her pillow. The cat walked itself around twice before finally settling down above their heads. It started to purr softly, and Anna slowly drifted off to sleep, snug in her husband's arms.

Nils stayed awake for a while. After being brought from the brink of death, he treasured every moment of life, and today he lived it to the fullest. He looked forward to many years of loving Anna.

Through the open window, he heard Oskar, Oddleif and their drinking buddies breaking bottles and singing. They stopped for a moment, then the sounds shifted to the banging of pots and pans outside of Nils' window. A baby's wail pierced the night air and Kjersti yelled from somewhere inside the house. "Shut up and let them sleep. Stupid drunk pigs, you woke up Henrik."

The men quieted down, but not before waking Anna. She opened her eyes and mumbled something incoherent.

"Sleep my little cat. It's just Odd and Oskar." Nils kissed her lightly on the forehead and tried to catch a few hours of sleep with his face buried in cat fur.

Chapter Twenty-Three

Bright morning sunshine poured into the attic room. Nils squinted and opened his eyes, then smiled down at the red haired girl nestled within the crook of his arm. *I am really married. It was not just a dream.* Nils tried not to make any sudden movements that would wake Anna. Her pink mouth was slightly open, and he had to restrain himself from kissing it. The cat lay curled up on Anna's pillow, its silver nose tucked into its paws. Nils reached over to pet it. He realized his mistake when it stretched and walked across Anna to be near the source of affection.

She opened her eyes and looked around. "Nils, why are your claws so sharp?" she said in a voice that was still drowsy with sleep.

"Cat walk on you. You sleep good?"

"Yes." She snuggled closer. "At least when I didn't have a mouthful of cat fur. Nils, are we really married? Yesterday was not a dream, was it?"

He smiled at how her words echoed his own thoughts. "No. It happen. I wake up today and think like you, but it is not a dream. It is true. Odd and Oskar will not remember many things, because they drink too much, but even with my sick head, I forget nothing." Nils put his arms around Anna and held her tightly against him. His body ached to make love again, but he wanted her to heal from last night.

"I won't forget a minute of it, and we have a whole life to make new memories." Anna rested her hand on Nils' chest and caressed the reddish-blond fuzz then traced her fingers over the rippling muscles in his arms. Not even the sickness could wipe out more than twenty years of hard work. *He deserves to feel as good as I did last night. I wonder if his skin tingles when I touch it.* She drew tiny circles on his fingertips and kissed them. "My sweetheart, your fingers make such beautiful music."

Anna was less reticent about her touch than last night and brushed her fingers lightly over Nils' stomach, then moved on to his thighs. She watched with a small smile as his mouth curved and his lids partially shuttered his eyes. *Do my fingers hold such power over a man?* She tentatively moved upward and felt his member harden beneath her fingers.

Nils drew in a breath. He had never been touched so sensually before. He moved against her hand, conscious of his need to be inside her again. *But what if she feels pain from last night? I don't want to hurt her.* He released his breath in a sigh. *Maybe tonight.*

Anna saw the momentary frown crease Nils' forehead and made a quick guess. "Nils, we can do it again. I'm telling you the truth. I feel no pain."

"Thank you," Nils murmured thickly before he hungrily sought her mouth and stroked her breasts, then moved on to her stomach and thighs.

Anna responded to the kiss, flicking her tongue against his, and then running it over his teeth. *There's the one with the broken corner!* Her mouth burned and the feeling of unresolved fullness returned.

Nils broke the kiss and guided himself inside her. He moved slowly and languorously, like a contented cat stretching in a sunbeam, prolonging the building tension within him.

Anna was soon caught up in the molten trance. Tingles of pleasure raced throughout her body with Nils' every thrust. She wrapped her legs around his, moving with him, faster and faster. *What is it that he touches inside me? It's not that I feel heavy any more. It's like I am a violin string about to break!* Anna arched her back and her breaths became quick gasps. Every muscle buzzed until she could no longer control it. Her legs quivered and her body twitched beneath him as the most exquisite feeling flooded her, radiating from the point of their joining to the tips of her fingers and toes.

"Nils, I love you," she moaned, but wanted to scream his name over and over.

Anna's release pressed Nils to finish his own. Driven on by the shudder of her body, he moved within her, the fire of her passion burning his member. He raised himself on his arms and withdrew for a moment, then took a deep breath and plunged into her. "A-Anna," he let out his breath and his seed as, once again, his body was suffused with indescribable pleasure.

Nils lay beside her. Slowly, his heavy breathing eased and Anna smiled. *Kjersti was right. It does get better every time.* She sat up in bed and looked down at her husband. "Nils, when you put a new string on your fiddle, you have to tune it up and be careful, because you can turn that peg a quarter turn too high and then, pop, it breaks. I know. I have seen Papa do that too many times."

Nils nodded. "Ja sure, I do that, too." His brow wrinkled a little. "But why you think about that now?"

Anna grinned and planted a quick kiss on his forehead. "Well, I was thinking, when we make love to each other, it reminds me of tuning a violin. You are tighter than an over wound string and then," she felt heat burn her cheeks, "then it feels so good that it breaks! Do you know what I mean?"

Nils' face lit up with understanding. "Yes! That is good way to think about it." He drew Anna into his arms. "My little cat, now every time I tune my *hardingfele*, I think of you."

Nils rose and stretched until the tips of his fingers touched the slanted attic ceiling. "Well, I promise you, we have a little holiday today."

"I think we've started it already," Anna tossed him a playful smile from the bed.

Nils returned her smile and put on his clothes. "We eat breakfast, and then take streetcar far away. I have map, but I do not know where is place. Long way from St. Paul

"It will be a surprise for me, too. I'll wash up and pack us a picnic lunch."

Anna threw on an old housedress and walked downstairs into the washroom. She would have to get used to not having a bathtub and make do with just a sink or the water pump outside. Three years ago, when Papa's business started doing well and they moved into the Pinehurst Avenue apartment, for the first time they had a tub with claw feet in the bathroom. Some days when Anna was exhausted after work, she liked to run the hot water and daydream in the tub. It was very frivolous, according to Mama, considering that in Russia they had no running water at all and had to haul heavy pails from the village well. Bath time was a complicated affair of heating the pail, pouring the water into an old zinc tub, and then using the wash water for all four children. *If I put up with that for the first fourteen years, not having a fancy tub will be a minor inconvenience.*

Anna washed up and walked into the kitchen. The smell of coffee wafted from the stove. Kjersti was already up cooking breakfast for Solveig and

Henrik. She pointed to the bedroom. Loud snoring could be heard emanating from inside.

"It will be noon when Odd gets up, and with a hangover."

"Where is Oskar?"

"Stretched out somewhere in the yard." Kjersti smiled coyly. "So... did you sleep well last night?"

"Yes, no trouble at all." Anna did not want to elaborate and switched the subject. "I just can't thank you enough for making all the food and taking care of all the guests."

"Anna, thank yourself. You made at least half of it. I did not mind most of the guests, except the ones who were too heavy on the whiskey, my husband being one. They were up late last night, woke up Henrik, and I am lucky if I got a couple of hours of sleep." Kjersti rubbed her tired eyes.

Anna heard the creaking of the stairs and saw Nils enter the kitchen, holding two bowls in his hands. He bent down and whispered into Solveig's ear.

The little girl's eyes widened and she jumped off her chair. "A cat? We have a real cat? Can I pet him? Does he want some milk?"

"You can feed him," Nils replied, "but be very careful and don't let him out of our room. He is still scared and may run away if he finds an open door." He filled up the bowls with milk and bits of meat, and then took the little girl upstairs.

While he and Solveig played with the cat, Anna packed a picnic lunch of wedding leftovers in a basket and helped Kjersti with breakfast. When they finished, Kjersti poured a large cup of coffee from a black iron coffee pot on the stove.

"Norwegian men like their coffee," she said. "I have a pot going early in the morning before they leave for work. Today they will need two pots to kill the morning after headache."

"It's like the Russians and their tea." Anna pointed to the *samovar*. "That big metal thing in the corner there, it's to boil water. Every Russian home has one. You can use it for the coffee. The water stays hot for a couple of hours."

Kjersti walked over to the *samovar*, lifted the cover, and looked inside. "That's twice as big as my coffee pot. I'll have to give it a try."

Solveig came skipping down the stairs, followed by Nils.

"Mother, it's gray and white and it purrs when I pet it and did you know that it took a piece of chicken right out of my hand and it drinks milk like this." The little girl bent over her glass of milk and pretended to lap it up. Henrik copied his sister, spilling his cup on the kitchen table.

"*Uff da*" Kjersti exhaled with exasperation in her voice, then grabbed a rag to wipe up the mess. "Solveig, the cat uses its tongue because it can't hold a cup with its paws. Now, sit down and drink your milk like a young lady, and don't give your brother any ideas. He is a monkey and copies everything you do, but not as well."

"So, what are you going to name it?" Nils asked Solveig.

"I don't know. Little gray cat. Is he a boy or a girl cat?"

Nils wrinkled his brow for a moment. "Boy cat."

"Then we can call him Oskar or Nils."

"And if your mother calls the cat, and me or Uncle Oskar come instead, that won't be good. Pick a name that no one here has."

"Me and Henrik will think of one when you and Anna come back from your picnic. I am glad you had a big wedding and mother made the best *kransekake* and you played a song just for me."

"You ask me anytime, I'll play a song for you." Nils patted the little girl on the head, then sat at the table and translated the conversation for Anna.

"I think I am picking up a little Norwegian here and there," she replied. "The lunch is in the basket, and Kjersti was kind enough to show me how to make coffee, which she says is the water of life for every Norwegian."

"Ja, it is in the morning."

"And whiskey in the evening!" Kjersti added.

Nils gulped down the large mug of coffee, then took a piece of paper out of his pocket. "Anna, we go now. We have to catch streetcar in St. Paul near library and Capitol and it go one time in one hour." He spoke to Kjersti in Norwegian. "Thank you for breakfast. I hope you sleep during the day. Oskar and Odd owe you to take care of the children for a couple of hours, considering they kept you up half the night."

"I'll see how they are when they wake up. They will be whining about their headaches and hangovers and say they are in no shape to mind the children. I will just go to bed early today." Kjersti switched to English. "You have a wonderful time. See you later."

Nils and Anna rose and headed for the front door. "Goodbye, Kjersti, Henrik, Solveig." Anna waved and the baby raised his chubby hand to wave back. "Bye-bye, Henrik."

They caught a streetcar to downtown St. Paul, and then transferred to the White Bear Lake line. Anna knew now where Nils planned for them to spend the day. The lake had an amusement park, rowboat rentals, a beach, and was a place where young people went to have a good time. Couples jammed the streetcar as it made its way through St. Paul. Girls barely twenty with fancy hats, gloves, and parasols sat on the wooden benches next to dapper men with top hats and canes. Anna glanced at her clothes. The pale peach blouse and brown skirt were not quite up to the latest fashions and her straw hat was hopelessly out of date. *I'm not Fanny,* she told herself silently. *I don't have time for hats, but I got myself something much better than a fancy hat, and he won't go out of style every year!* She gazed lovingly at the man beside her.

"Nils, I have never been to White Bear Lake. I've just heard about it. They have all kinds of amusement rides, not somewhere my Mama would let me or my sister go."

"I read about it in Norwegian paper and think perhaps you like to see it." The streetcar left the city limits, and Nils eyes held longing as he looked at the grazing cows and the lush fields of corn that passed by outside the window. A foppishly dressed fellow standing next to Nils smirked. "You never seen a cow before or what? Keep staring out the window and someone will take the pretty girl away from you."

The dandy had barely spoken before Nils grabbed him by the shoulders. "I marry her yesterday and you do not look at her and make trouble."

Shocked, the man took several steps back. "Damn Norskies, can't even take a joke. No one is going to take the little lady from ya."

Anna rose from the bench and placed herself squarely between the two men, her green eyes flashing with anger. "I wouldn't allow myself be taken by anyone, so you both go back to your seats and stop this at once."

Nils sat down and, when Anna returned to the bench beside him, took her hand in his. "Anna, you are angry with me, it is true?"

"No, Nils. I just don't want you to get into another fight. I love you too much to see you hurt. What does that man know about you looking out the window? He's never left his homeland or lost a farm like you have."

"Ja, well, I try and save money for a little farm. You take breath here and it is more clean than in big city. I know if I was sick in Voss, I never go to hospital. I stay home and feel better soon."

Anna shook her head. "I don't even remember any more what clean air is. I am so used to the factories and the soot." She saw the outlines of the Ferris wheel and the roller coaster. "It looks like we're almost to the park."

The streetcar stopped a half-mile later and disgorged its passengers onto a cornucopia of rides, food booths, street vendors, and a crowd of people determined to try out everything that the park offered. An out of tune hurdy-gurdy turned by a monkey and a scraggly old man welcomed them into the Wildwood Amusement Park. "For only a penny, this little monkey will play you a song," wheezed the old man as people passed him by. Further down, women with heavy rouge on their faces, wrapped in a multitude of colorful scarves, told fortunes with cards.

"We don't need them, considering all that happened in the last month," Anna whispered under her breath and hurried Nils past the gypsies. She was a little superstitious and was not going to chance her life being read to her. This park reminded her of the town fair her father took her to, but bigger. *There were gypsies—old toothless women who clucked over the little redheaded girl and whispered something to Papa. He shrugged his shoulders and pulled me away from them. When I asked why he did this, he would not tell me. I wonder if they knew that I was not his.*

"I remember a place like this in Russia, but not so big. Did you have something like it in Norway?"

"Ja, but very little. We go to town every year and they have this, so we play *hardingfele*, make a little money, and then we can buy things for us."

"Wasn't there always something that you wanted in a booth, but never had enough money to buy? So, you hoped it would be there next year? I remember there were these porcelain dolls with real blonde hair and eyes that opened and closed." Anna closed her eyes for a moment, savoring the memory. "Oh, how I wanted one, but of course they were too expensive. I ended up buying a pound of candy for the younger children and a roll of calico for Mama."

"I know what you say. Thing for house come first and if there is little money, children can have it. I remember I want a knife for wood, then books about Indians in America, my own *hardingfele*, but one thing I still want to buy."

"What?"

"I do not know how you say in English." His brow creased in concentration. "Man sit on two wheels, do not need a horse, but he can go fast."

"A bicycle?" Anna exclaimed.

"Yes, almost the same in Norwegian. I go to work with it, so I save money and no streetcar. I can make basket, so I bring food home for you."

"Or I ride it myself to the store. There are even bicycles for two people, so we can take a trip together."

"Where you see it? In your Sears catalog? You tell me I can buy everything from it."

Anna gave his hand a squeeze. "Almost everything, but not quite. No *hardingfeles, samovars, sølje, kransekake, kvas*, or Nils."

He laughed and pointed at the ride before them. "So, you want to try this? What you call it? Ferris carousel?"

Anna looked up at the tiny seats on top and hesitated. "What if it breaks and we'll be stuck up there?"

"I hold you. Mountains in Norway are more higher than this."

"Well, all right. I'll try it. If I told Grisha that I was at the park and was too scared to ride the Ferris wheel, he would say I am a yellowbelly. He'd never let me live that down."

Nils paid the attendant, who then ushered them into a metal seat and locked the bar.

"See, Anna," Nils said in a reassuring voice. "That is so you do not fall."

The seat advanced upwards to let others on at the bottom, and Anna was not afraid—at first. They were only a man's height or so off the ground, but as their seat revolved toward the top, she clung closer to Nils and stole fearful glances down at the ground. People became small specks going about their business, while she hung at tree top level. It made her dizzy just to think she was that high.

"Anna, you feel better when you do not look below you." Nils held onto her tightly.

At last the ride started and, if being high and still unsettled Anna, the movement of the Ferris wheel completely unnerved her. The ground and trees whirled about her in a blur and she screamed, certain that, at any moment, she would hurtle toward the ground and her death. "Nils! Nils!" She turned and grabbed his shoulders. "Stop this thing! Please, let me down! Nils, I'm falling! Help!"

Nils saw an hysterical, mortified girl—one whose nails dug sharply into his shoulders. Her eyes were no longer green, but fully dilated and black, like a cat stuck on the topmost branch of a tree. The attendant noticed Anna's state and, as the seat came down, said something to Nils that he could not understand. *Perhaps the man cannot stop the ride in the middle, so it is up to me to calm her down.* He wrapped both of his arms around her and brought one of her hands over her face.

"Anna, close your eyes. You not see ground and trees. I hold you. Do not feel so scared. Now you sleep in bed with little gray and white cat. I sit and play my *hardingfele* for you."

Anna scrunched up her face and closed her eyes, trying to imagine a blissful domestic scene, but could not. "Don't make things up. You can talk about cats and fiddles all you want, but I know I am up here and I hate it." Her voice quivered and Nils saw tears rolling down her cheeks.

"You feel better with eyes closed?"

"A little, but I don't dare open them."

"So, I tell you what I see. Many green fields, and a man with a horse, one brown cow, and one black and white. Two big houses on lake, many boats on water and people swim. Now we are not so high and two boys fight over toy, man kiss a girl under a tree. I do this over a tree." Nils unclenched one of Anna's hands from her face and gently kissed her. Her skin tasted salty from the tears.

"Nils, if I open one eye just a little bit, it won't be so bad, will it?"

"You try. See boats on lake?"

"I think so. Where's the tree that the fellow's kissing the girl under?'

"No more, he go away." The Ferris wheel stopped and their seat slowly moved down until they could disembark. Anna was less nervous and looked about her, assured of protection in Nils' arms.

The attendant let them out. "You had quite a fright up there, little lady."

"Well, I have never been that high in my life. But I think next time, I won't be so afraid."

The man grinned. "Go on, I'll let you in for nothing now if you don't scream."

"No thanks," she replied as she rushed out of the chair, "not quite this soon. Perhaps next year."

"I'll be here and I'll watch for you two, so don't welsh on the deal."

Nils and Anna walked hand-in-hand toward the lake. Several people swam in the lake and even more sat on blankets and chairs on the sandy beach.

"Anna, what you think if we take boat and have picnic on lake?"

"Do they rent them here? But if it's too expensive, we can just eat here."

"Do not worry about money today. I check map and there is forest not too far over lake. Not many people." Nils pointed in the direction of a small tree-covered cape in the distance. "You know how to swim?"

"No. I'm afraid if I don't touch the bottom, I will sink."

"Doctor say I cannot swim this year, but next year I teach you. It is not very hard. You have to trust water and not be scared of it."

Anna rolled her eyes. "Oh, like trusting that the Ferris wheel won't break and throw me in the air? I think I have had enough fright for today."

Nils went to the booth and paid for the boat. A pimply-faced boy of about fifteen showed him an old wooden sloop moored along the pier.

Anna eyed the boat apprehensively as they approached it. "Nils, are you sure it's not going to sink? It looks so old."

"No, it's fine for this lake, but not to go from Norway to America. Here, I take you."

Nils helped her into the boat, untied the rope, and the vessel slid away from the mooring. The oars made a creaking sound as Nils swung them around. More than a year passed since he was last on the water and he regretted not having a fishing pole, but it felt good using his muscles again.

"So Anna, you like this better than Ferris wheel?"

"Much more so. The lake is so calm. It's almost like we're gliding across a mirror, and I don't feel seasick at all, not like on that ship."

"You feel sick because water go up and down, but it is no trouble for big ship, just for people. See, it is nice place here for lunch." Nils pointed to a sandy cove with tall pine trees. He made good time rowing the bay and soon Anna busied herself, unpacking the basket on the beach. After lunch, they took a walk along the the shore.

Nils breathed in the pine tar—a smell that reminded him of home. They found a bush of wild raspberries and feasted on the juicy sweet fruit.

"Well," Anna said, "we finally made it out of the city to eat berries, now we just have to find the mushrooms!" She glanced at the ground, but did not see any.

"In Norway they come in August and September, so we go then." Nils grasped her hand in his and they walked back to the beach.

Anna removed her stockings and delighted in the feel of sand and water on her feet. "Oh, Nils, this is so much better than the city."

"I know. It is good for your spirit to see lake and trees. All that work, streetcars, factories—they kill it. This place, it is good to play *hardingfele* and kiss my sweetheart."

Nils drew her to him and his tongue brushed the inside of her mouth and across her teeth. Anna felt her mouth tingle and she licked his lips, lightly scratching her tongue on his mustache.

He took a deep breath and, reluctantly, drew away. "Anna, I stop now or people take boat just to see what we do here."

Anna put her hand to her forehead and squinted across the lake at the beach. She could not make out what people were doing, but still, it would not be proper to do anything in public, even if she was married. "You're right."

"I like it here, but I think we go back. Very hot now and soon rain and lights come."

Anna looked up at the sky. It was no longer blue, but a hazy light gray, portending a late afternoon thunderstorm. She certainly did not want to be caught in the rain while in the boat.

They made it across the lake and stopped for ice cream at one of the booths. Anna watched multitudes of people throw away money on food, rides, and trinkets. *What is going through their minds?*

"Look at them, Nils. Well, for that matter, look at us. Here we all are, not a care in the world, filling ourselves with food and seeking a thrill on a ride. What if someone were to get all these people's attention and tell them about what happens in factories, the orphans on the streets, the immigrant tenements?" She clenched Nils' hand and made a fist with her other hand as her voice rose. "Would they listen and do something about it?"

Nils released her tight grip and lightly stroked the inside of her hand with his thumb. "I do not know, Anna. Maybe they work in factory six days and now they come here and they want to forget it, like we do today."

"Perhaps," she replied, "but it sure seems like most of them are not from the working class. At least not from the way they're dressed."

"The rich are more difficult because they know it is wrong, but do nothing. But I do not think it is good to talk to people on holiday. Maybe better to give them paper on street."

"The committee was thinking about a newspaper. I'll mention it at the next meeting. And, if they agree, I would be the first one to stand on a street corner to hand them out." A soft smile curved her lips. "It's going to be odd to be introduced as Anna Bjørnsen now."

"I come with you. I want to thank everyone for money. I only thank Emil Kruse at wedding."

The first fat drops of rain and the distant rumble of thunder assaulted Nils and Anna as they headed out of the park. They boarded the streetcar just in time. The storm hit with a vengeance and, for a while, nothing could be seen through the sheets of driving rain. The streetcar stopped to wait out the storm and Anna squeezed closer to Nils with each crash of thunder.

"My little cat," he said in a soothing voice, "it go over soon. It is the trolls. They are mad at us, so they make big noise and rain."

"I thought trolls lived only in Norway and, besides, why are they angry?" Anna asked.

"In Norway, we know more about them, but trolls live in whole world. They mad at me, because I marry a beautiful girl that the troll king want for his son. He take girls below ground and promise them money and nice dress, and all they have to do is marry this troll prince. But he is not like man. Has big ears and tail, and hair on toes and fingers. Sometime, if troll king like a girl, he come up from the ground, sit on rock and play his *hardingfele*. It makes girl sleep, and then he take her under ground with him. Some girls come back and teach fiddler the tune that the troll king play for them. I know two or three. I play for you."

The corners of Anna's mouth turned up in a mischievous smirk. "Now Nils, are you sure that you are not the troll king himself?"

"Anna, you think I am so ugly?" Nils' voice rose a notch as he feigned indignation.

"No, of course not, but you do play the *hardingfele* and it puts me in a kind of trance." Anna whispered into Nils' ear. "I just have to check on the tail and the hairy toes."

Nils chuckled. *For Anna, I will be the troll king or whatever else she wants me to be.*

The rain let up and the streetcar glided on the rails toward St. Paul. Nils felt the weight of Anna's head against his shoulder and knew she slept. He woke her when it came time to transfer to the northbound line. She was groggy, so Nils held her tightly around the waist as they crossed the slick cobblestone street and boarded the second streetcar.

"Sweetheart," Nils said as they again sat beside each other, "soon we come home, and then you sleep."

"But I have to make curtains, do the wash, and cook dinner."

He shook his head. "No work today. That you do tomorrow. We have many food from wedding. You go to bed and I bring big plate for you and little plate for cat."

"You do not have to do that for me. I am full from lunch and the ice cream, but I am sure the cat will lick up everything you give him." With that, Anna closed her eyes and napped until their stop.

The Pedersen's and Oskar were just about to sit down to supper and Kjersti put two more plates out for the newlyweds. Nils ate and, speaking Norwegian, told them about their day. Anna, still tired from the outing, picked at her food.

Oddleif put his arm around Kjersti's shoulder when Nils finished. "So, would you go up in that Ferris thing, if we took a trip there?"

A corner of Kjersti's mouth rose before she answered her husband. "Only if you and Oskar promised to stay off the whiskey for good."

Solveig stared at her father, then her mother, and finally Nils. "I want to go on it, then I can touch the clouds and see the birds. Can you take me next time, Uncle Nils?"

"You have to get a little bigger, Solveig," he answered.

"How much bigger?"

"Oh, maybe this high." Nils held his hand a foot above Solveig's head.

The little girl struck out her lower lip and pouted. "I'm always too little. I wish I was all grown up right now!"

"No you don't." Kjersti ruffled Solveig's hair. "Who does the cooking, the washing, the mending, the cleaning and the scrubbing?"

"You do, mother."

"Well, if you decide that you are grown up, you'll have to do all of it yourself and I'm going to play in the yard and swing as high as I can. So, tonight you can clear off the table, wash the dishes, put the food away, sweep the kitchen, empty the ashes, do the laundry, change Henrik..." She paused and hid a smile as the little girl's eyes grew wide, then she continued. "And make the bread for tomorrow, darn Uncle Oskar's socks, fix a tear in father's shirt, and when it's dark and late, then you can go to bed."

"I think I'll stay little for a while." Solveig slunk away from the table before any of the domestic responsibilities could be heaped on her.

"Silly girl," Kjersti chuckled as she closed the front door after her daughter. "In a few years she'll long for the days she could spend doing nothing."

"Well," Nils said, "I spent a whole month doing nothing, so tomorrow I go from a lazy fiddle player to a sweaty flour covered mill rat."

Kjersti stared at him, then shook her head. "If you call fixing just about everything around the house and tending to the garden lazy, Nils, Lord have mercy on Odd and Oskar, who hardly lift a finger except to pull the bottle nearer to them."

Oddleif stood. "Just for that comment, my dear wife," he said, "I will show you how helpful I can be." He started clearing off the table.

Nils rose as well. "Thank you for dinner, Kjersti. I am sure Odd will do a good job of cleaning up. Anna is tired from our trip, so I'll take a little food for the cat and we go upstairs." Nils put some chicken on a small plate and filled a saucer with milk. "Goodnight."

"Kjersti, thank you. I'll help you with everything tomorrow, I promise. I can barely put one foot in front of the other." Anna rubbed her eyes and, rising, rested her head on Nils' shoulder.

"Don't worry about it. You had a long two days. Get a good night's sleep." Kjersti waved to Nils and Anna as they walked up the stairs, then returned to her husband. "Oddleif, I should scold you more often. It might improve your disposition."

"If I could get money for scrubbing the floor, believe me, I would do it, but no, the man has to go out and break his back working." Oddleif put the last of the dirty dishes in the sink and hurried to the front door. "Oskar, I will see you outside. Get me a beer from the cellar. I want to forget that tomorrow is Monday."

"Odd, you drink enough, you won't care what day it is. They're all the same." Oskar went down to the basement for the beer.

Anna trudged into the room and collapsed on the bed. The wedding and today's outing wore her out completely. Through half closed eyes, she watched Nils place the dishes on the floor, call the cat, and then she heard the rhythmic lapping of milk. Nils took out the *hardingfele*, tuned it up and began to play.

The flowing and shimmering melodies transported Anna into a dream world. She was one with the music, running through a flowering meadow, hopping on the second beat like Nils taught her. When she approached the dark pine forest, an ugly little old man with a tail beckoned to her. "You must be the troll king," she heard herself say to the dwarf.

"Ja," he replied, "and I play fiddle tune for my sweetheart to sleep." *Funny, the troll has Nils' accent.*

She felt herself being lifted up from the meadow and held tenderly by strong arms. Anna's eyelids fluttered open as Nils cradled her in his arms and softly kissed her face. She looked into his blue eyes and liquid warmth spread from her heart to the tips of her fingers and toes. She felt blissfully happy and loved.

Nils stared down at his wife and, for the first time in years, knew he had finally come home. *That little cat, curled up into a gray and white ball next to the fiddle case, and I are not so different. We have traveled and endured hardships, yearning for a loving touch and a warm hearth. Anna has given us that and so much more.*

Nils covered them with a blanket and wrapped his arms around his wife. "Anna, I never think when I come to America, I find a girl because I lose my way in St. Paul. Odd's old map change my life, and I am so happy for that."

Anna smiled and stroked Nils' hair. "I ought to thank Fanny for not showing up at the union meeting. If she had decided to come on time, I wouldn't have waited on that street corner." She released a contented sigh and snuggled closer to her husband. "I can't imagine my life without you. Your *hardingfele* tunes are always in my head, and I want to dance with you for as long as I live."

"Remember, we hop up on two."

Anna offered a sleepy, contented smile. "Before I met you, I had never hopped on one or two or three, but I certainly will now. Just hold my hand and don't take me up very high."

"I will always hold your hand, my little cat."

Nils and Anna fell asleep in each other's arms. The cat snuggled between them, a witness to the love two people can share with each other—and a little gray and white stray.